PRINCESS OF DAWN

MEGAN GILBERT

PRINCESS OF DAWN
First published in Australia in 2023
by Crafted Press, an imprint by Megan Gilbert

Cover design by David Gardias: bestselling-covers.com

ISBN (Paperback): 978-0-6458553-0-2
ISBN (eBook): 978-0-6458553-1-9

Megan Gilbert
megangilbert.co

A NOTE TO READERS

Please be aware of the following content before reading *Princess of Dawn*:

Anxiety and panic attacks
Battles and hand-to-hand combat
Blood
Death, including that of family members
Misogyny
Murder

To enhance your reading of *Princess of Dawn*, why not listen to the official Spotify playlist? Visit megangilbert.co, or scan the QR code below, to find the playlist and listening guide.

To every woman that has ever been told she isn't enough.
You are more than enough. Don't let a broken system stop you from wearing your
crown; use your crown to fix the system.

THE STARLIGHT
MOUNTAINS

THE VALE

THE ENDLESS
SEA

THE MIDLANDS

WHARF
TOWN

SILKSHELL

BEAR JAWS
VALLEY

THE SOUTHERN
SHADOW

ELDERGUARD

THE ISLE OF
CRYSTAL

THE KINGDOM OF
CRYSTERRA

I

Princess Galdinia wasn't ready to be queen.

For ninety-three days, she journeyed to the Crystal Temple to pray for her father, to ask the Gods to bring him back to good health. She needed him to recover because she couldn't fathom wearing her mother's crown yet.

Day after day, Galdinia knelt at the altar, seeking healing for her father's illness. But in those three months, his condition had only worsened. His sudden decline came after he was caught in a vicious late summer storm on his way back from a tour of the villages in the Midlands Province. She thought the king would be back hunting at sunrise and addressing his court within the week, but weeks turned into months, and he still hadn't left his bed.

Although it broke her heart to watch her only living parent struggle to breathe, struggle to live, all Galdinia could focus on was what would happen if he didn't make it. While no one formally said anything to her, whenever she'd visit her father's bedside, members of the Crysterra Syndicate would give her sideways glances as she cried, already questioning how fit the young nineteen-year-old princess was to sit on the throne. No one even dared mention the gift that she lacked.

Galdinia watched as her father went from sneezing uncontrollably to hardly being able to inhale a full breath. Her father—the King of Crysterra, the ruler they needed—was dying, and there wasn't anything she could do about it.

The Gods, on the other hand, could.

Each morning, Galdinia travelled to the Isle of Crystal, where she was greeted by the high priestess, Saena, at the doors of the Crystal Temple. Saena would often use her gift to create small balls of Peacelight to surround Galdinia as she knelt at the altar. The priestesses were all Light Lenders, a gift bestowed on them by the Gods when they made their sacrament, regardless of their previous position within society. They could all draw on and manipulate various sources of light, be it candlelight, a raging fire, or that of the sun's rays. The high priestess, however, could conjure light from her own hands. Aside from those with royal blood, her gift was the most powerful. She used it most mornings to try to calm the princess' nerves with its warming glow. Aside from her father's bedside, the temple was one of the few places that Galdinia allowed herself to shed a tear as she came to terms with her father's inevitable demise and so she became quite fond of the Peacelight that encircled her daily.

Once settled at the altar, Galdinia began her prayers to the three Gods. She asked the God of Wisdom for knowledge in understanding how she might support her father in this time, seeking new herbal recipes that could bring about an improvement in his health and stamina. Next, she prayed to the God of Love, asking for his eternal affection to be shown through the healing of her father. Finally, she turned to the God of Guidance, where she would ask, upon her arrival back to the city, to be escorted to the castle in the hopes that she would meet someone who may be able to cure her father's ailments and pain.

To her dismay, Galdinia would arrive back at the castle after her prayer without meeting someone helpful, without learning a new medicine, or without finding her father healed by the end of the day. And yet every morning, she would rise before the sun had fully shown itself and bow at the altar of the Crystal Temple, praying all the same.

The only other request Galdinia would make on a regular basis was an appeal to be ordained with her own gift.

As princess, she had a high likelihood of obtaining a very powerful gift of one of the elements as either a Wind Wielder, Water Weaver, or Fire Flourisher. Her father had been a Wind Wielder and her mother a Water Weaver, so it was probable that she would eventually be given one of these gifts. Most citizens of nobility were bestowed one of the three gifts from the Gods, but those of royal blood were among the most powerful. While the gifts were a mark of the Gods' blessing, they also provided practical assistance in everyday life and, ultimately, in battle to protect the lands they had been given. She had spent many hours trying to control the water below the docks, trying to make the fire on her nightly candle move, trying to cast a breeze through the castle hallways, but she never found her power. When she was eleven, after seeing her father use his gift to calm an oncoming storm with just a single word, Galdinia tried to physically stop a great wind with her hands. She stood on the castle terrace, which looked out across Elder-guard, the capital of Crysterra, her hands outstretched, but the wind continued to shudder through her long golden hair, mocking her.

Despite her discouragement, her father assured her that her gift would come. It was promised by the Gods that true rulers of Crysterra would be bestowed with a strengthening of their power beyond that of any other honourable position of power or nobility in the kingdom.

It was also law, however, that one could not ascend to the throne without evidence of their gift.

Year after year, Galdinia questioned this supposed promise. What if she never received her gift? What if this was a sign of her weakness or her inability to serve the Gods as Queen of Crysterra? Almost all children of nobility in the capital had received their gifts by the age of ten and yet here she was, in her final teen years without a gift.

As a dull ache started to form in her chest, Galdinia turned her attention back to her prayers. She was there for her father, not her own selfish requests.

As she concluded her prayers to the God of Guidance, soft footsteps echoed around the quiet temple, approaching the princess. Galdinia opened her eyes, turning to face the high priestess, who looked down at the princess with careful eyes. High Priestess Saena was wearing a flowing white dress that was adorned with beads and pearls. She also donned a headdress of tiny luminescent crystals, which twisted through her braided white hair and draped over her deep brown shoulders. Saena looked particularly angelic today as she eclipsed the rising sun that glinted through the crystal walls of the temple.

"Good morning, Your Highness," Saena said, her head slightly downcast. Saena's face was cast in shadow and Galdinia found it hard to make out her expression.

"Good morning, High Priestess," Galdinia replied, standing to her feet, her knees rejoicing at the release. Galdinia leant down to straighten out the skirt of her dress that had bunched up around her generous hips and thighs.

"Princess, I have just been sent word from the castle about King Bartemus... about your father."

Galdinia's head snapped up. She could see now that Saena's face was grave and she looked down at a small piece of parchment in her hands.

"No, no, it can't have happened yet," Galdinia said, feeling a deep pressure rising in her chest. "The bells haven't tolled yet."

"I'm sorry, Your Highness." Saena's voice was soft, barely a whisper. "I think you need to return to the castle quickly."

Galdinia didn't need her to read the note to know what it said.

The king was dying.

Tearing herself from the altar, she hurtled down the aisle of the temple. She could feel the priestesses' eyes on her as she ran through their sacred building. All sense of her surroundings evaporated as she stumbled down the front steps and across the square to the dock. She was only a fifteen minute sail from Elderguard, fifteen precious minutes that she didn't have to waste.

"Back to the castle, now!" Galdinia ordered the soldiers onboard the royal sailing boat, her voice getting caught in her throat as her tears threatened to break. She forced herself to keep them under control. She was the princess and she didn't need her soldiers seeing her in such a state, even if she was losing her last surviving parent.

Galdinia watched with urgency as the soldiers unfurled the main sail and guided the vessel back to the capital. Although there seemed to be a Wind Wielder on board using his gift to propel the ship forward, it wasn't fast enough for the princess. She stared down at the water, wishing more than ever to be given her gift. If she were a Water

Weaver, she would be able to help push the boat by orchestrating the movement of the waves, getting her home to her father faster. But no matter how long and hard she gazed into the waves, she could not control them.

Fifteen minutes later, they were rounding on the eastern docks. Desperately, Galdinia tried to will the boat to reach land faster, but it very carefully came to a halt at the wharf. At the obvious eagerness in the princess' eyes, the soldiers made haste to set up the gangway, which she pounded down the moment it was secure. Instead of running to the capital's streets and main square, Galdinia turned north to the rock face on which the castle was built. There was a tunnel carved into the rock that led from the castle's library to the outside world and only three people officially knew of its whereabouts: Galdinia, her father and Governor Ryden. Having exited the castle by this route that morning, Galdinia had a key to both the gate to the tunnel and the trapdoor in the library's floor on her person.

As she weaved between the rocks and found the entrance of the cavernous tunnel, now out of sight of the soldiers, Galdinia could feel her tears spiking at the edges of her eyes. She was desperate to reach her father in time. She had to see him again before it was too late. The pressure in her chest was rising as her heart thudded in panic. She made quick work of the lock on the gate and climbed the ladder to the trapdoor, letting herself into her favourite room of the castle: the library.

She didn't have time to pause and catch her breath. Instead, she rushed through the warm room, the fireplace ablaze, casting a warm glow over the thousands of books that lined the walls. She ran down the hallway to the entrance hall, swept up the stairs and along the corridor to her father's rooms. Galdinia was so close, she could see the guards at the end of the hallway who watched her father's door. She clumsily wiped the tears from her eyes and the sweat from her lip as she tried to compose herself. She was the princess and she needed to act as such. Galdinia sucked in a deep, shaking breath as she walked with haste down the hallway, trying to stand tall.

The guards bowed at her approach and as she came to stand before them, a sound she had been dreading rang through the castle. The first chime from the castle's bell tower sounded. Galdinia's breath caught in her throat, and she froze. Again, the bell tolled, rattling through the princess' chest and buzzing in her ears.

These were not tolls to declare the time of day. No, these bells announced the death of the reigning monarch to the capital's citizens. Each toll represented the years he lived: fifty-two tolls for fifty-two years. Galdinia had feared the moment she would hear the bells ring. And now she was too late to say goodbye.

One of the guards opened her father's door and she stepped inside, her mind still. The room smelled of sickness and despair. It was bleak and dark, making his opulent room feel like a dusty corner in an abandoned cottage. Another metallic bell tolled, which echoed into quiet as the door closed with a click behind her. The silence between each shattering clang ripped through Galdinia, almost as pervasive as the metallic shockwaves themselves.

The moment the door was closed, now alone, Galdinia allowed the tears to start falling as the knot in her chest tightened. She slowly walked to her father's bedside and gazed upon his lifeless body through blurred vision as she sobbed. He looked so at peace, as though he had merely fallen asleep mid-conversation.

In the previous month, his olive skin had become so sallow, almost translucent, so much so that the veins on his once strong hands protruded like small rivers reaching up his arms. His eyes, now shut, had become heavy, accentuated by the dark pools of colour beneath. His lips were cracked and pale, now but a mere line across his face. Although he was a shadow of the man he had once been, Galdinia did not see him as anything other than her loving father.

With a heaving sigh, Galdinia fell to her knees at his bedside, grasping his still warm hand and weeping into his sleeve. She willed her life to be transferred into his, if only to give him just another day —another hour—breathing and telling her how much he loved her. To tell her that everything would be okay.

One thing Galdinia had always been sure of was her father's love for her and in his last moments, in his last breath, she knew that she was in his thoughts. His weighty and enduring love for her hung in the air and she wanted to sit there in that place until her own final exhale. She wanted to make a home on the ground beside his bed, reliving the many sunrises they shared when she accompanied him on his weekly hunt. She wanted to pretend that she was still a child, wrapped in her father's arms by the crackling fire in the midst of winter, reading books in the castle library. She wished so painfully hard that she could hear his honey-sweet voice say just one more time, "I love you, my princess. My Dinny."

Galdinia crouched by her father's body, swept away in tears, a heaving chest and a broken heart.

After two hours of grieving, Ryden Calcutter, the governor of Elderguard, came into the room silently. He was her father's most trusted advisor and had become somewhat of an uncle to the princess. He crouched by Galdinia and placed a gentle hand on her shoulder.

"Princess." His low and soft voice broke the silence she had been weeping into. "I'm sorry, but we need to move him."

Galdinia peered at the grey-haired man, his ageing brown eyes full of pity. The light of a nearby candle reflected off the silver hairs that ran along the dark umber skin of his jawline.

All logic and reason told Galdinia that she had to leave her father's side; she knew they would have to prepare his body for the funeral and she would need to leave the room, but her heart ached at the thought. She let out a strained cry as she clutched on to her father's hand, which had become clammy beneath her own. As she peered at their clasped hands, she noticed how lifeless he had become; their skin tones once matched, but his was now greying by the minute, while hers remained a light olive.

"I didn't get to say goodbye," she sobbed, her shoulders shuddering.

"You have now," Ryden said, patting Galdinia's back. "He knew how much he meant to you."

"But I should have been here," Galdinia cried. "I should have been here when it happened. I couldn't get back fast enough."

"Princess, you've been here every day for the last three months," Ryden said, his voice soothing. "There's nothing else you could have done."

"I just wish… I wish…" Galdinia's voice trailed off as she cried, imagining her father passing away on his own, his only child failing to be by his side. No amount of comfort would help her forgive herself for this.

"Let's go, Princess," Ryden said, his grip on her shoulder becoming firmer as he placed his other hand on hers, trying to coerce her from the king's bedside.

Galdinia sobbed as she let go of her father's hand and was pulled to her feet by the governor. Now, from above, she could see how much he had changed in the hours after his death. He was merely the shell of her father. The princess turned and cried into Ryden's shoulder, letting her emotions overcome her for a few more moments, her tears now stained and cracked on her cheeks.

Ryden led her to the door and here she paused. She took a deep breath and wiped the tears from her face and tucked her golden hair behind her ears, attempting to make herself look presentable again. While she wasn't ready for the title yet, she was the heir to the throne, and she was next in line to become queen. Queens were strong and brave. So she held her head high and followed Ryden from her father's room, feigning courage, leaving her father's body behind her.

2

THE CLACKING SOUND OF HIGH HEELS AGAINST MARBLE FLOORS ECHOED throughout the manor that sat atop the headland of the Shadowed Coast. The sound reverberated across the entrance hall, up the stairs and down the main corridor as the rushed breaths that accompanied the footsteps ascended to the second floor.

The halls were dark, despite the candles that hung along the manor walls. Although there were more attendants than necessary in Lord Draven and Lady Edana's home, it had never felt more lifeless.

The clacking in the halls came to a halt at the mahogany doors of the drawing room. A curt knock announced the maid and Lady Edana's voice commanded her to enter.

"My lord, my lady," the maid said breathlessly, bowing to her masters. "I have a letter from Elderguard."

Beside the heaving fire, Lord Draven leant against the mantle, creating small balls of flame between his fingers, which he periodically threw into the hearth. His dark brows furrowed as he glared into the flames, watching the fiery spheres drown in the fire. The disturbed blaze cast a flickering light over the lord's face.

At the large table in the centre of the room sat Lady Edana. Locks of her dark brown hair had fallen from her usually pristine bun; she was too distracted to notice her hair's disobedience. Her piercing amber eyes were fixated on the glass of wine in her hand, watching the liquid tilt from side to side. Lady Edana was not moving the glass goblet with her hand; instead, her gaze caused its movement.

The room was thick with tension and the maid felt like she just interrupted an uneasy conversation.

"Bring it here," Lady Edana commanded lazily, reaching out her hand for the crimson envelope in the maid's fair fingers. It wasn't until the envelope was in her grasp that she noticed the seal on the back. The golden seal depicted an owl with outstretched wings perched on the back of a roaring lion. It was the royal crest, the Elderwin crest.

Lady Edana sat up straighter in her chair, abandoning her goblet, her interest now on the envelope. Her wine slowly came to a standstill as it steadied in the wake of her attention.

"Go." She dismissed the maid with a much more intentional wave of her hand, not taking her eyes off the envelope. "Draven."

The maid shut the door behind her as Draven glanced at his wife, his mind still lost in the argument they were in the middle of when the maid interrupted.

Edana pulled back the wax seal and unfolded the letter within, her eyes hungry for its contents.

Dearest Lord and Lady Elderwin,

We regret to inform you that at dawn today, King Bartemus Wylliam Elderwin of Crysterra, Wielder of Wind, first of his name, sadly passed away in his sleep. We request your presence at his funeral, the day after next, to be held at the Crystal Temple at noon.

We send you both well wishes of health and happiness in this uncertain time.

May the Gods bless you,

The Syndicate of Crysterra

"Draven." Edana repeated her husband's name as she read the letter again, her eyes scrambling across the page.

"Edana." Draven sighed, running a hand across his forehead, trying to soothe his sharpening headache. "I don't know how we're going to secure the support of the Midlands, but I don't imagine my brother's pending death will be of aid."

"Draven," Edana cut in, turning to look at her husband as she repeated his name yet again. She thrust the letter in his direction and he approached with curiosity, taking the parchment from his wife.

His eyes ran over the words and as he finished reading, a dark and dangerous smile flew over his lips. He looked much like his brother— olive skin, dark hair and eyes—but his features were far harsher. As the years of animosity wore on him, his face became somehow sharper.

"My Gods," Draven whispered, looking up at his wife. "He's gone."

At the news of his brother's death, Draven had the air of a child who just won a race in which he had cheated.

"He's actually gone." Edana's tone mirrored her husband's and she stood to her feet and wrapped her arms around Draven. Their argument about military strategy was but a fleeting memory. Draven embraced his wife and practically lifted her off her feet. The fire in the hearth behind him surged at his words, moving in tandem with his thrill.

"Finally, darling, finally!" Draven leant back to look at his wife, brushing a curtain of loose hair from her face, his hand arriving on her porcelain cheek. "This kingdom will finally be ours."

Edana didn't know what to say. For once, she was lost for words. She buried her face into Draven's shoulder and exhaled in relief.

"My wretched brother is actually gone," Draven continued to croon, his arms tight around Edana. "I will finally be king."

Edana peered up at Draven, his face oozing with pride, his eyebrows harsh with determination. Her king.

"And you will be queen," he continued, his words cutting through the air like steel. "My brother spent so many years in conflict with other cities after our parents fought for that throne. Now we can finally rule this kingdom as it should be."

"King Draven," Lady Edana said, practically salivating as she spoke. "Your parents would be so proud of you."

Draven sat on these words for a moment, his heart racing with pure adrenaline, the likes of which he hadn't felt since his parents passed and they were to announce the new king. Draven assumed he would be crowned due to his brother's obvious inept ability to rule. Bartemus may have been older than Draven, but he was by far the more immature and frivolous brother. He spent his days swept up in alcohol, women and parties, unable to keep track of the day, let alone the political goings-on of the kingdom. To this day, it still baffled Draven that his parents' will announced that his grotesque older brother would be crowned as king instead of him. So much so that he spent the next twenty-five years loathing him.

But now they were both getting what they deserved: Draven, the throne and Bartemus, the grave.

"What will we do about Galdinia?" Edana asked, pulling Draven from his tunnel vision of the past.

"She doesn't have her gift yet and she can't become queen without it," Draven responded, letting go of his wife and moving to pour himself another goblet of wine; this glass was one of celebration. "The kingdom can't go without a ruler and I am next in line before a king's powerless and juvenile daughter. I suspect we can make our way into the Syndicate as interim rulers and change the laws before she even gets a whiff of her gift."

Edana mulled this over, unsure about her husband's confidence, yet unwilling to believe otherwise.

"After his funeral, they will crown me king," Draven said, taking a sip of wine. "The Syndicate will rule for the Week of Mourning, but ultimately, I'll be crowned."

He looked intently at his wife, waiting for her face to change from a look of unease to that of confidence.

"In other words, my love…" Draven turned back to the fire before glancing over his shoulder. "You'd better start gathering your things; we'll be moving to Elderguard next week."

3

Across the Kingdom of Crysterra, far beyond the Midlands and through the Wetlands, a jet-black raven flew like smoke on the wind. It soared towards the sun as it slipped below the horizon, the light now but a glow, giving way to the half-moon that dominated the cloudless sky above.

The raven pushed against a breeze that picked up across the Western Sea. It started to slowly dive lower as it neared its destination beyond The Edges.

～

"Your Highness, you must eat." General Reynard pushed the food towards his ruler, staring her down across the table. "We need a queen that is healthy and strong, not another weak leader."

The self-professed next Queen of Crysterra, Valah Pyrin, had been sitting at her illustrious dining table for what felt like many moons. Two days prior, she started to refuse to eat, her anticipation and lack of patience getting the best of her.

For weeks, the king's health had been the topic of conversation across the kingdom. She knew she had to start planning her family's reentry onto the throne long before the announcement of his death.

Of course she, along with everyone else in the country, thought it would be a quick exit for the king, due to his health deteriorating so quickly. But three months had passed and she still sat in frustration and impatience.

Her parents fought for the throne in the Great Confrontation forty years earlier, trying to defend the lands that their family had cultivated and ruled for hundreds of years. King Bartemus' treacherous father struck her parents from their rightful place and Valah was sent into exile.

She had been biding her time since and knew this was the moment to strike.

But alas, the king was dying, slowly. Obviously, the king didn't want to give up and accept defeat so easily. Valah thought that if she sacrificed her food to the Gods, they would speed up the process for her. And so, two days earlier, she refused to touch her morning eggs, declining to even look at them. Yesterday her dinner ended up on the floor, swept off the dining table by a frustrated yet famished hand. She specifically told her cook not to prepare her anything. It was to be sacrificed to the Gods. She would fast until the king took his last breath.

"Please, Valah," Reynard pleaded with his queen. "You're not doing yourself—or your kingdom—any favours by refusing to eat."

Valah leant forward in her chair. The flickering candle that sat between them cast a dim light across her face, emphasising the dark pools of colour beneath her eyes and her already sunken cheeks. Her face was losing some of its colour, but it wasn't clear if this was from a lack of food or her heightened stress.

"I am showing my respect and reverence for the Gods." Valah's eyes bore into Reynard's, but he didn't back down. "My sacrifice will bring us a victory."

Reynard stared at Valah, wondering how much longer he'd have to try to convince the future queen to eat. He held her gaze across the table for a few more moments before breaking eye contact and getting to his feet.

"At this rate, you're going to waste away before the king does." Reynard sighed as he poured himself another drink from the carafe that sat between them.

"Thank you, Reynard," Valah said with an air of contempt, moving her attention to the map of the kingdom set before her. "How are things looking in The Edges?"

"Captain Kelting said they're all very tired and overworked," Reynard responded, glad for the change of subject. "I imagine with their support, the rest of the Midlands will fall in line."

With her fingers, Valah traced the mountain range known as The Edges. It sat between the Midlands and the Wetlands, acting as a natural barrier between the two provinces. Her finger trailed the markings as if she were one of the Gods creating the lands.

"Will you travel to the Midlands at all this week?" Reynard asked before quickly adding, "If you survive the night, that is?"

"When Kelting is back, yes, that's the plan." Valah chose to ignore Reynard's snarky comment and moved on. "I'm hoping we will get there before the king's death though. The townsfolk of the Midlands will be far more impressionable with the prospect of a dying king as opposed to the possibility of multiple candidates pining for the throne. I imagine the king's brother will be seeking the crown the moment he is buried in his tomb."

"That snake would do anything for the crown," Reynard spat before taking another sip of his drink. "I want nothing more than to see him in the ground beside his brother."

Valah smiled at her advisor's passion, moving her fingers across the map, outlining the borders, looking over the kingdom as though it were already hers. Her eyes landed on Elderguard in the southeast and she rested her hand there for a moment. In the coastal city of her birth, then known as Pyringuard, her parents had been ripped from their thrones long before their reign should have come to an end. She was only five years of age when the Elderwins killed her parents, but she remembered the night distinctly. She had been in the castle library with her nurse, reading books in the evening before going to bed. Valah had begged to read another.

"Alright," her nurse finally said. "Just one more, then it's off to bed."

Before her nurse could reach for the book, the door to the library came crashing down. Valah had screamed as her nurse tried to protect her from the oncoming soldiers that barrelled into the room, pushing over furniture and brandishing swords the same size as the small princess. One of the onyx-armoured soldiers took their sword and buried it into the nurse's belly, her shrieks ripping through Valah in a wave of anguish and fear. Valah could not understand what was happening or who these soldiers were, but she was petrified.

In her terror, tears streaming down her face, Valah managed to pick up a small breeze coming through the doorway and sent it cascading through the room. Despite her small stature, her over-whelming emotions spurred her Wind Wielder powers on. She managed to expand the breeze into a gale, allowing it to surge through the library, knocking down soldiers and sending them flying into nearby bookcases and walls. Valah watched as the wind did her bidding for her, protecting her from the monsters that had infiltrated her home. Once each soldier in the room was unconscious, or worse, she sat back against the wall, her young body unable to cope with the overexertion of power.

Valah awoke hours later in a boat travelling through the Southern Shadow towards the west. She was alone and terrified in the dark as memories of armed soldiers, blood and gale force winds invaded her mind. Valah cried out in the depths of the hull, the chains around her wrists and ankles clattering as she tried to move from the firm bed she had been lying on.

The Elderwins had decided to spare young Valah's life. They knew she was not corrupt like her parents and they didn't want to harm the girl, they merely wanted to send her to the furthest point on the map. The next evening, young Bartemus Elderwin slept in Valah's bed in the castle. Valah, however, slept in the basement cellar of a tavern in the heart of the Wetlands—her new home—parentless and heartbroken.

"It will be mine again," Valah said, her words sharp. "I'll die before another Elderwin sits on my parents' throne."

Valah had been preparing her return to the capital for decades. Growing up as an exiled princess in the Wetlands wasn't easy and she had to learn to make her own way. She soon lost her childlike sense of wonder and had to learn gall and ruthlessness in order to survive. Here, four decades later, she had made a name for herself, gathered armies and established her authority as future queen among her allies.

As she gazed down at the crudely drawn capital, Valah's thoughts were interrupted by the shrill caw of a bird. A silky feathered raven fluttered through one of the nearby windows and landed on the table in front of Valah and Reynard. Reynard reached out to protect the carafe of liquor, worried for its safety in the path of the flapping bird. There was a small roll of parchment tied to the raven's ankle.

Valah pulled the parchment free and unrolled it, reading the short yet weighty note enclosed within. Reynard could see the Elderwin crest stamped on the back of the letter as his queen read.

Without a moment's hesitation, Valah pulled the plate of food towards her, plucked a grape off its vine and popped it into her mouth. A vicious smile spread across Reynard's face.

"Delicious," Valah crooned, reaching for a second grape.

FIRST DAY OF MOURNING

4

THE DAY AFTER GALDINIA'S FATHER'S DEATH WAS ONE OF AN
unbalanced mix of condolences and the whirlwind of planning a royal
funeral.

Although she was too young to remember her mother's funeral in
significant detail—she was only six years old when Queen Anae passed
—Galdinia was told that it was one of opulence and the city's reverence for the late queen was showcased in their final farewell to her.
Guests were welcomed into the Crystal Temple by a choir of one
hundred priestesses singing hymns before being seated in the pews,
which were surrounded by plumes of flowers, their scent carrying
across the grand hall. At the end of the funeral, the Syndicate released
thirty-three white doves in her honour, one for every year that she
lived. They were an echo of the bells that tolled the day prior when
she passed away, or so Galdinia's father had described. Queen Anae
had died tragically young, but she had been unwell for many years, her
health slowly deteriorating.

In the weeks leading up to her father's passing, Galdinia assumed
that his funeral would be of similar regard. She was spared the pain of
having to actually plan his funeral as the Syndicate had insisted that
they make all of the arrangements. In truth, they had been planning

the funeral for weeks in anticipation of the king's decline. All they had to do was set their plan in motion.

Galdinia did not wish to see anyone the day after her father's passing. She barely ate, each meal going stale at her door, where she left it untouched. She was restless in her sleep and spent many hours weeping in memory of her father. She curled herself into a ball in her bed, staring out her windows that looked over the western side of Elderguard. She pulled her throw up to her chest, cocooning herself in the soft fabric, searching for any kind of comfort she could find. Every time her heart settled, she was reminded that her father was no longer with her and the tears started to flood once again.

Galdinia gazed through the palatial window that looked down upon the kingdom. *Her* kingdom. Although it didn't really feel like hers and she wasn't sure when it would.

The clouds soon covered the rising sun as the people below also rose. Galdinia wondered how many of the nobles gifted with Wielder abilities were powerful enough to move the clouds over the sunshine. Perhaps it was the Gods' doing. Or maybe the clouds were simply moving on their own accord.

When her mother passed away, the king had drawn the entire country and its surrounding seas into darkness by covering the sky in a thick blanket of cloud. He had cried out on the castle terrace, his emotions alone moving the clouds over every inch of sky. It was as though he were a Light Lender and had forced the sun itself into darkness. Even the high priestess was impressed by his display of power. There was no record of a Wind Wielder being able to do this in centuries.

As she glimpsed the clouds, Galdinia wondered at what point her father's gift had been vanquished from his body. Had he relinquished control when he got ill? Or did he merely no longer have the strength to manage his abilities? She questioned if he had begged the Gods, as she did, for his health.

As the clouds moved to cover most of the sky above Elderguard, Galdinia's attendant, Brigitte, knocked on her door several times to check on the princess, but Galdinia refused to see her. There were only two people she was interested in seeing and they were both otherwise, and unfortunately, preoccupied.

Neryda Fleur was from one of the families of highest nobility in all of Crysterra, so she and Galdinia had spent a lot of time together as children. Her parents had enrolled her in school with Galdinia and a very small group of other noble children, which was hosted in the castle's library. Both Galdinia and Neryda's parents quickly learned how much of a handful they had served themselves by placing the two children in close quarters with one another. The girls grew up side-by-side, acting as makeshift siblings, causing trouble around the castle and its gardens, resulting in many looks of contempt from pompous visitors and attendants alike.

As children, they would skip hand-in-hand around the city, causing many citizens to laugh and clap in delight as they danced in the square, Neryda using her Water Weaver gift to send small bursts of fountain water over them as they twirled and twisted. They put on performances for onlookers and the guards that had been sent to follow them, although the girls weren't aware of their protective shadows at the time. Both Galdinia's and Neryda's parents became tired of trying to follow their every movement, so the king sent a trusted group of guards to trail the girls in their escapades around the city.

As they grew older, the friends spent less time on the streets of the capital and more time in the castle. Most weekends, the two would sprawl out in front of one of the library's many fireplaces with spreads of decadent cakes, silky smooth chocolate and sickly sweets. Here, they talked for hours about all manner of topics from their plans after they finished their studies, to the boys they fancied, to dreams of travelling beyond the Endless Sea. They had been by each other's side through every phase of life in their short nineteen years—every high and every low.

In the week before the king's death, Neryda had left on a fortnight long trip that she had been dreading all year. She went with her parents to nearby towns and cities along the east coast to meet with potential suitors. Both girls knew they would have to meet with suitors soon, given that they were soon to leave their teenage years behind. Neryda was closer to twenty by a few months, so her parents had insisted that they meet with respectable prospects before their options were exhausted. The thought of being married soon after turning twenty made Galdinia's stomach churn, even if she knew it was the way for many women of nobility, especially royalty.

Before leaving for her feared pilgrimage, Neryda had spent many days with her friend, consoling and distracting her from her father's declining health. Despite their daughter being vehemently against the trip, Neryda's parents pulled her from her friend's side to meet eleven suitors who all vied for her affection. Neryda had to be physically removed from Galdinia's rooms in order to leave the week prior and Galdinia would have done anything to have her back in this moment. She knew a message had been sent to her the previous day, but she wasn't sure if it would get to Neryda in time for her to make it home for the funeral. She willed with every fibre of her being that the winds would carry the sailing boat along the coast to her best friend with haste. She prayed for her father's Wielder ability to be upon her.

The other person Galdinia so desperately wanted to see was somewhere across the country being trained in combat, almost as far away from her as possible. He was likely being fitted in his soldier's armour, learning to shield against oncoming attacks, or scrubbing the filthy washroom of the soldier's training barracks.

Galdinia's chest tightened as she thought of Drystan Allard. The pressure surmounted and travelled up her throat, forcing an achingly quiet cry from her lips. She tried to suppress the threatening sobs. She already had her father to mourn and didn't need another reason to wish for her bed to swallow her whole.

Not today. She could not think about *him* today.

The next day, an hour before midday, Galdinia finally hauled herself from her bed. She allowed Brigitte to enter the room and she sat quietly as her attendant bathed, dressed and prepared her for the day. Ordinarily, Galdinia was more than capable of selecting her own clothing and washing herself, but today the task felt insurmountable.

The princess stood in the middle of her dressing room as Brigitte worked at arranging her pristine hair of golden waves. Although her attendant had tried to cover the dark circles beneath her eyes with makeup, Galdinia could still make them out when she inspected her face in the mirror. She looked down at her outfit: a sheer black dress with a long slip underneath, which clung to the ample curves of her hips and thighs. The sheer outer layer boasted billowing sleeves that covered the many freckles on her shoulders from days spent in the sun as a child. This layer of floating fabric trailed two feet behind her, forming a modest train. The headpiece Brigitte was securing was a golden headband that resembled the sun's rays. From this hung her black veil, which fell gracefully in front of her. With this final accessory in place, Brigitte stood back from the princess, guiding her towards the full-length mirror in the corner.

"You look beautiful, Your Highness," Brigitte said quietly, her rosy-cheeked face peering at Galdinia in the reflection of the mirror.

Galdinia liked having a younger attendant. At sixteen, she was still young enough that she would listen to Galdinia when she would give orders in protest against her father or Ryden. Now, she supposed Brigitte would be the one to communicate Galdinia's orders with others.

"Thank you, Brigitte," Galdinia said with a sigh, looking at herself one final time. "I think it's time to go."

Twenty minutes later, Galdinia and Brigitte stepped down from the royal ship on which they travelled from the capital to the Isle of Crystal with the Captain of the Royal Guard, Ilyon Trunder, and forty of his best men. Despite those around her, Galdinia felt utterly alone. She had sought out her friend that morning, asking Brigitte if she had received any word from Neryda or her parents, but she had not.

The trip across the Shadowed Sea was reasonably easy, as Ilyon, a Water Weaver, was able to propel the vessel forward smoothly. Although a noble himself, his gifts were heightened when he was sworn in as Captain of the Royal Guard. Galdinia's father had explained that if a man or woman in a significant position of power was seen as worthy by the Gods, they would soon see their gifts intensify in power.

"And if not?" she had asked her father.

"Well, it wouldn't be long until they'd lose their job permanently." The kings' words had felt heavy. "They would keep their gift, but they wouldn't be deemed adequate enough to hold such a position."

Galdinia had wondered how their worth was determined prior to being given their place of honour, but she was more concerned with her own lack of powers to ask him, afraid what his answer might be.

The captain held out his armoured arm for Galdinia as she took her final step from the gangway and onto the island, his dark eyes lowered to her own. Normally his expression reflected what one would expect from a soldier: firm and stolid. But not today; his narrow eyes were full of mourning and melancholy.

Galdinia turned from Ilyon and looked upon the Crystal Temple for the first time since her last visit on the day of her father's passing. It seemed that every citizen of Elderguard had arrived to pay their respects, crowding the bay in various boats, ships and barges, each person donning black attire, their faces downcast. Before her stood another two rows of guards, flanking either side of the wharf and up the path to the door of the temple. They too wore armour of black metal, but their heads were held high, looking straight ahead at their brothers, always vigilant, always attentive.

Galdinia could barely see the grass that so starkly contrasted with the crystal of the temple as every person of nobility she had ever met, along with at least five hundred more, was standing around the edges of the pathway behind the guards. They all wore the appropriate attire for the morning. They were a sea of black.

Galdinia began to walk along the pathway with her head held high, Brigitte trailing behind her. As she walked, every eye followed her and then, all at once, they bowed.

Galdinia faltered for a moment, missing a step. Never before had people bowed like this to her. She had always been with her father when people in the streets would bow at the waist or fall to their knees and she knew it was for him. When she was alone on the streets and not hiding beneath a heavy cloak, she would often see people downcast their eyes or lower their heads. This was different though. They weren't doing it out of necessity or obligation.

No. They were doing it out of respect, for her father, their king, and for her, the grieving princess.

Galdinia felt something like trepidation land in her chest, but she held her shoulders high and continued to walk, wishing the path to the temple doors wasn't so long.

Ahead of her at the end of the pathway, beside the doors of the temple, stood the most magnificent arrangement of flowers. Galdinia could only assume the flowers were lilies that had been dyed jet-black, their trumpet-like petals facing the heavens. Hundreds of flowers had been arranged around the doors, following the curve of the grand entrance. As she stepped upon the threshold of the temple, the crystalline doors swung open in front of her and she felt as though she were walking into an entirely different building to the one she prayed in two days earlier. On the mezzanine level stood an orchestra of singers, the choir's voices echoing through the hall as they sung a low, melancholic melody. The song reverberated in Galdinia's chest and she tried to ignore the tight feeling that sat there.

Through the aisles walked priestesses clad in their usual dresses of white and swinging plumes of incense throughout the temple. The incense enveloped Galdinia in the scent of burning cedarwood and moss, the aroma both warm and comforting, inviting the princess into a safe place. The vessels that the priestesses held from chains were lit from within, each one glowing with the gift of the priestess that handled it. They looked like flickering beacons among the black decorations of the funeral.

Galdinia turned from the spectacle of the priestesses and looked down the aisle. And then she saw it.

Ahead of her, upon the altar, sat her father's coffin. It was raised on a platform, its marble outside surrounded by collections of unnaturally inky native flowers cascading down the stairs and onto the altar's floor. Even from the back of the room, Galdinia could see her father's hands, a crescent of greyed, withering skin peeking over the edge of the coffin as they lay on his stomach. She glanced at the top of the casket where the tips of his profile emerged. She inhaled the comforting scent surrounding her and stepped forward into the aisle.

"Your Highness." The high priestess bent at her middle before the princess as they met on the altar of the temple. "I'm sorry for your loss."

"Thank you," Galdinia practically whispered.

"We will bring such honour to your father today," Saena said, straightening up, her shimmering gown moving in waves around her waist.

As per tradition, the priestesses were the only attendees who would wear white, in line with their everyday dress. The white of Saena's dress and her stark white hair contrasted with her rich brown skin. Her braided hair was arranged like a crown atop her head and strings of jewels and shining stars twisted in a perfect pattern around her head. She looked radiant.

"His grandeur will be reflected in the ceremony," Saena remarked, smiling softly at the princess.

Galdinia wondered how that might be possible, but she thanked the high priestess again. She took her seat in the front row, trying to divert her gaze from her father's body, now mere metres from where she sat.

The first group to enter the temple after Galdinia was the Syndicate, led by Governor Ryden, who greeted the princess sadly before sitting beside her. The rest of the Syndicate, including Captain Ilyon, filed in around them. Behind them, people started to enter the temple, moving quietly down the aisle to their seats. One such person seemed to make a commotion as a muttering began to work its way down the pews. Galdinia turned back to the doors of the temple, peering through her veil. She saw two soldiers barring someone from entering. The guests around them stared back at the person in horror. Galdinia saw a flash of curly deep russet hair and instantly ordered Brigitte to tell the guards to let her best friend into the temple.

After a brief exchange, Galdinia's best friend, Neryda, shuffled down the aisle, all eyes on her. As she came to the altar, the two girls looked at each other for a moment. Despite her pained expression, Neryda always looked playful and childlike thanks to the array of freckles that dotted her golden-brown skin. As Neryda's eyebrows knotted, Galdinia's attempted strength shattered before her friend. Neryda pulled her into a hug of utter warmth and desperation, allowing her sobbing friend to cling to her just like she did when they were children.

"Oh, Gal," Neryda cooed. "I'm so sorry I wasn't here when it happened. I wish I had been here with you."

"I'm so glad you're back." Galdinia sniffed, burying her veiled face into Neryda's shoulder, hiding her tears from onlookers.

"And I'm not going anywhere," Neryda promised, holding her best

27

friend tighter in her pain. "I tried to move our boat as fast as I could. I'm sorry I couldn't get here any quicker."

"You're here now," Galdinia said between deep inhales of breath. "That's all that matters."

~

At the back of the temple, a slender woman in a long black dress entered through the main doors, the light from the east casting her long, willowy shadow down the centre aisle. Valah Pyrin crossed the threshold and the attention of many in the temple was drawn to the woman. No one expected her to be here; many in the temple assumed she would have been barred from the occasion and they awaited a guard to drag her away.

However, Valah strode freely down the aisle, Reynard close behind her. Hundreds of pairs of eyes followed her as she found a seat in a near-full pew halfway down the temple. Some people looked upon her with disgust, while others stared in disbelief, truly unsure if they could believe their eyes. Valah took a seat by an older noble couple who refused to look at the woman. They instead slid further down the pew away from her. Valah was delighted. She was glad that even now, she could draw the attention of the capital to herself and away from an Elderwin.

The whispers in the room, while hushed, didn't hide the distinct phrasing of her name as she was shot glances of disdain and hatred. What she hated more was that they presumably believed she hadn't been invited. Of course, she had wondered herself why the Syndicate had called her to attend the funeral of her mortal enemy, but she happily obliged.

Despite the quiet words of anger that bounced around the pews, Valah sat perfectly poised and her ruby-red lips curled into a conceited smile.

~

"I cannot believe she is here," Edana hissed to her husband as they walked down the aisle of the temple, gazing at Valah. "Who does she think she is?"

"Darling," Draven mumbled, holding his wife close as they walked into his brother's funeral, "I think half the people on this island are thinking the same thing about us."

As they stepped past the front row of pews, Draven halted for a moment, his eyes landing upon his brother's corpse on the altar. Draven felt a strange mixture of disbelief and victory.

He felt a tug on his arm and turned to the front pew, where his wife pulled his attention to their niece. Draven had not seen Galdinia since the late queen's funeral, almost thirteen years prior, so he shouldn't have been so surprised how much she'd grown. And what was more, she was almost the spitting image of her mother. Although Galdinia's face was veiled by a thin layer of black mesh, he could see the red circles that traced her eyes. He assumed that her elegant attire and deep grief hid what was left of her childlike appearance. One thing he had always noticed about Galdinia was the way her eyes seemed so much larger than most, as though she was in constant awe of the world around her. Today, however, she looked nothing but deflated.

"Hello, Galdinia," Draven said, bowing his head slightly toward her. "I'm sorry for your loss."

Galdinia didn't bother to stand. "And I'm sorry for yours, Lord and Lady Elderwin."

Despite their strained relationship and Draven's obvious disdain for his brother's family, he was still taken aback by Galdinia's lack of gravitas towards them.

"We are glad we could be here today to bid my brother farewell," Draven said, peering back at the king's body for a moment.

"I'm sure you are," Galdinia responded, momentarily holding her breath before adding, "And I'm sure my father would be glad that you're here."

"There is a seat here for you, Lord and Lady Elderwin." A small priestess interrupted the tense exchange, motioning towards the pew behind Galdinia, her friend and the Syndicate.

A look of contempt flashed in Edana's eyes. The notion of sitting anywhere other than the front row made her breath catch in her throat. Despite this, she shuffled into the seat with her husband, neither of them oblivious to the gesture.

The ceremony lasted for just over one hour and the bulk of the service was made up by the singing of the king's favourite hymns, eulogies made by his closest friends and allies and a blessing from the high priestess herself. The final presentation was from Galdinia. After the high priestess's introduction, Galdinia rose to her feet and stood at the podium by her father's coffin. She glanced down at his body and realised this would be the last time she would gaze upon his face. Although his body would be kept in the temple for the next seven days for others to pay their respects, his casket would be closed after the funeral and not opened again. She soaked in the moment for a few seconds before turning to address the full temple, everyone's eyes looking at her expectantly.

Although no one spoke, she started to imagine all the things that her guests were thinking.

Ah, the powerless princess…

She isn't even going to be queen. Why allow her to speak now?

If this is what we have to endure for the next five decades…

She tried to push the imaginary thoughts from her mind as she started to speak, drawing her shoulders back and standing tall.

"To you, King Bartemus was your ruler, your ally, or your friend." Her eyes didn't leave the parchment in her hands for fear of looking upon the faces of judgement. "But to me, he was my father and closest confidant.

"From the age of six, when we lost my mother, I only understood family to be one thing: my father. To me, he wasn't the king of the most beautiful land or a war hero who fought for our freedom. No, he was my best friend. He taught me how to play chess, he taught me to read, he tucked me into bed at night and kissed my bruises better when I hurt myself. He was my protector and my source of the kindest love I've ever known.

"Today we honour this man who was so many things to so many people. And I honour him as my father and friend. And I will continue to honour him until I too take my last dying breath. I will carry his flag and lead this country into the future he promised it."

Galdinia glanced up and saw some faces were now craned to stare more intently at the princess, eyes narrowed in judgement and lips tight. Although many smiled at her faith, others appeared wary of her claims for the throne.

"I will continue his legacy so he will never be forgotten." Galdinia looked down upon her father once again before taking a deep breath and looking across the hall at all of her father's guests, trying to ignore the expressions of doubt that lingered there. "I will be all you called me to be from a child, Father."

Galdinia read the final line of her eulogy in her mind: *I will be the queen you always wanted me to be.*

Would she, though? She did not yet have her gift and she feared that the Gods did not consider her to be the next queen. She felt like a fraud, as though every silent judgement in the room—whether real or imagined—was bearing down on her.

"I *hope* to be the queen you always wanted me to be."

Galdinia sucked in a deep breath as her eyes surveyed the faces of all in attendance. Despite her voice quaking with anxiety as she spoke the altered line, the entire temple bowed their heads in reverence. Every face lowered, except for four that stared back at Galdinia in utter detest.

Galdinia caught the eye of the woman halfway back in the temple, her eyes harsh and her lips pursed. While she hadn't met Valah Pyrin before, she was certain that this was her. Galdinia clenched her fists on the podium as she looked at the woman, a pain in her chest surfacing as she tried to steady her breath.

What is she doing here?

5

"He would be so proud of the way you spoke today."

Galdinia and Neryda stood arm in arm in the courtyard outside the temple, watching the ceremonial doves be released into the sky. Galdinia watched them fly into the tufts of shifting clouds above, disappearing in between wisps of white and the glare of the sun. She had pushed back her veil after the ceremony and now she blinked against the light that bore down on them, the grey clouds having parted at the end of the service.

"I can't believe he's actually gone," Galdinia said breathily, her voice getting lost between the horns that played to signal the end of the funeral and the beginning of the Week of Mourning.

When a royal passed in Crysterra, the capital observed one week of remembrance. While this ceased all usual work and for some was seen as a welcome holiday, it was also a week full of various ceremonies and services at the temple, which all citizens of Elderguard were welcome to attend in order to pay their respects. The most luxurious event, the Royal Feast, was held in the castle's ballroom on the fourth day for guests of nobility. At the end of the week was the Commemoration Banquet, where the entire city would come together to eat, dance and celebrate the life of the passed ruler. On the seventh day, the coronation of the incoming heir would take place.

Galdinia wasn't sure, however, how the Week of Mourning would end.

She was the rightful heir to the throne, but she did not have her gift. Even as the king's daughter, the Gods hadn't yet ordained her themselves and their blessing was of the utmost importance. Without her gift, she couldn't rule. It had not occurred for many centuries, but in these circumstances, the Syndicate would take control of the country and rule on the heir's behalf until their powers showed themselves. Galdinia's particular circumstance was also complicated due to another factor: her uncle, Draven. He had his own legitimate claim to the throne, as he was of royal blood and had his gift. Galdinia was sure that Valah Pyrin believed she could also take the throne.

As an immediate family member of the late king, Draven could become an interim ruler and rule until Galdinia received her gift. Galdinia knew that this was, of course, what her uncle and aunt would want. Draven wanted to become interim king because he would do everything in his power to overrule her pending coronation.

Her father had once warned Galdinia, almost as casually as though they were discussing the weather, that this might happen. Two years earlier, he had returned from a trip to the Shadowed Coast where, as he put it, he was, "tending to some unruly citizens." Galdinia asked if it had anything to do with her aunt and uncle, two people that she hadn't seen since she was a small child.

Her father had simply told her that his brother and sister-in-law were unlikely to speak to him before he was on his deathbed. He had laughed at this at the time. What a sad reality that had become. He went on to explain the tense foundation of his and his brother's relationship, explaining that given the right circumstances, Lord Elderwin would do anything in his power to take the throne, especially if Galdinia remained giftless. At the time, Galdinia was sure that her father wouldn't pass before she was ordained by the Gods, so they quickly moved on from the conversation and turned to the box of sweets he had brought back for her from his trip. Now she wished she had pressed for more information.

Despite the presence of her tyrannical uncle, Galdinia was more concerned with the power that still evaded her. She wouldn't be surprised if the secluded community from Lund in the far north

Starlight Mountains had even heard of how inadequate she was. Galdinia had been told that her mother hadn't truly stepped into her abilities until soon before her coronation; she had hoped that she would have a similar experience.

"Shall we get a drink, Gal?" Neryda asked, pulling her friend back to the present as the final dove disappeared into the clouds. The citizens of Elderguard were still on their boats in the cove, now chatting amongst themselves, starting to pull anchor and sail back to the mainland.

Galdinia nodded and the girls made their way towards the ship that was once again flanked by the Royal Guard. As they went to step onto the gangway, a warm yet breathless voice pulled Galdinia's attention.

"Gal."

Galdinia turned to see the only other person she wanted to see that day. Although her heartbeat quickened at the sight of him, the ache in her chest instantly dulled.

Drystan stood on the pathway behind her. The front pieces of his otherwise neatly tamed mop of chestnut brown hair fell in his eyes as he came to a halt before his friends. The sunlight radiated off his onyx armour, somehow making him glow more brilliantly than he already did in Galdinia's eyes. His soldier's helmet was tucked under one arm and the other rested at his hip on the hilt of his sheathed sword. At the sight of his kind eyes and gentle smile, Galdinia could feel the warmth of summer, hear the buzz of fireflies and smell the scent of the roses in the castle gardens where they would so often steal away together.

"Drystan." Galdinia's heart practically shattered as she said his name. She questioned if she should hug him. Ordinarily, she would have flung her arms around him and he would have pulled her in tight as she buried her face in his neck. But now he stood before her as a soldier of the Royal Guard and she was the princess at her father's funeral. She needed to remain professional.

Similar to Neryda, Drystan had grown up by Galdinia's side. They met when she was seven, Drystan eight, outside the local bakery in the capital's square. Galdinia and Neryda had wanted cinnamon scrolls for breakfast after their sleepover in the castle, so they bounded to the bakery. It was run by one of the few commoners that Galdinia knew of who had a gift: Raff the Fire Flourisher. As they drooled over the sugary baked goods, a sweet-faced brunette boy insisted that they order first even though he had obviously been waiting longer. Neryda didn't need to be told twice to order, but Galdinia smiled at the young commoner sheepishly, her cheeks reddening. When he heard what they were ordering, Drystan proclaimed that cinnamon scrolls were his favourite treat from Raff's too. On this basis alone, the girls invited Drystan to join them to sit by the fountain in the square to eat their morning indulgence. From that day, the friendship between them only blossomed.

Drystan followed the girls around the capital, often made to act as lookout when they were enacting one of Neryda's plans, or he would be sent to collect sweets from the castle kitchens when they became peckish after classes. He willingly obliged, making quick friends with Galdinia and Neryda.

Soon the three of them became inseparable.

After practically begging her father to let Drystan join their classes, the king obliged and Drystan started lessons with Galdinia and Neryda two weeks after meeting. He would go horse riding with them through the valley and, by request of the children, their families were made to celebrate most holidays together. There was a bond between them so strong that even now, as they stood in front of each other without contact for three months, the overwhelming sense of comfort and familiarity that Galdinia felt was palpable. Time and distance were inconsequential.

A long moment of silence suspended between them before Neryda interrupted. "Hi, Drys," she said quickly, breaking the tension.

"Hi, Ner," he said, looking to his friend with a sincere smile before turning back to Galdinia. "I'm so sorry about your father. I wanted to come and see you as soon as I heard, but I was stationed beyond the city walls before his passing and I had to practically beg my platoon officer to let me come back for the funeral. Your speech was perfect. He would have loved it."

The words tumbled from his mouth as though he didn't have enough time to say them all. He looked like he was going to take a step towards her but instead shifted his weight from one leg to another. Galdinia was conscious of the eyes of those around them that were watching, the keen ears of the nobles and other guards that were observing their interaction. Had they been in the privacy of her home, she would have been able to have a normal conversation with her friend about what had transpired over the last three months. The three of them would have sprawled out on the library floor in front of a raging fire and Drystan and Neryda would have done anything to make Galdinia laugh to distract her. Instead, she spoke to him as only a princess should.

"Thank you, Drystan." Uttering his name brought with it another stabbing pain to her heart. "I'm really glad you could be here."

"Me too," he said quietly, keeping his eyes on Galdinia, those deep wells of chocolate brown glistening in the sunlight. His usually lightly tanned skin was now a richer olive; Galdinia assumed that he had spent many hours in the sun during his training.

"Neryda and I are going to go back to the castle for a cider. Would you like to join us?" She already knew his answer before she asked.

"I would love to"—*here it comes*—"but I'm on duty for the first evening of the Week of Mourning. My condition for being able to return early was that I'd be scheduled on for the week. I'm patrolling the square though, so I won't be far away."

"Another time," Galdinia said, trying to mask how deflated she felt.

They looked at each other for a long moment. All she wanted to do was take him by the hand and bring him onboard with her, where they could laugh at his bad humour and she and Neryda could listen to his stories of the last few months. But she couldn't. Things between them had changed so drastically and so suddenly. She was the princess and he was training to become an officer in the Royal Guard. Their paths could never be as intertwined as they once were. Galdinia would have to settle for friends... no, worse than that: she was Drystan's ruler.

"See you soon, Drys," Neryda said as she coaxed Galdinia up the gangway, hoping to guide her best friend away from the inevitable heartache.

"Bye, Neryda... Gal." Drystan waved briefly from the edge of the wharf. Galdinia attempted to give him a half-smile.

"It's for the best," Neryda said, pulling Galdinia close, wrapping an arm around her as they stood by the edge of the ship, looking back down at Drystan still on shore. Neryda had dried Galdinia's tears after Drystan left for training and the princess didn't imagine that her best friend wanted to watch that heartache again.

And although she knew Neryda's words were true, she couldn't help but notice that the two most important men in her life had been ripped from her grasp within months of each other. Galdinia and Drystan's blossoming relationship had only just found its feet when he was drafted into the military, sending him hundreds of kilometres from her. And yet, despite the time and distance, Galdinia's love for him had not subsided and seeing him only reminded her of how much she cared for him.

As the ship left the port, she didn't take her eyes off Drystan until she could no longer distinguish which tiny speck he was on the Isle of Crystal.

On the journey back to Elderguard, Galdinia was reminded of the moment her feelings towards Drystan shifted. In the winter after her eighteenth birthday, the three friends had been in the castle library, taking cover from the whipping wind and piercing cold. They had lit the fireplace and cocooned themselves in blankets and throws in the heart of the castle, laying out a myriad of snacks on the ground in front of them, along with a steaming pot of tea.

Galdinia and Neryda had finished with their classes for the day and had intended on completing their homework together with Drystan, who had completed his studies the summer earlier. This plan, however, quickly dissolved into laughter and distraction.

Drystan, who had been lying on his back, threw a grape high into the air and caught it in his mouth with a short pop. The moment Neryda realised she couldn't do this herself, their schoolwork was abandoned and Drystan got to work teaching her how to catch grapes mid-air.

"You've got to throw it high enough that it will follow its trajectory but not too high that you lose it," Drystan explained, standing beside Neryda, holding a grape between his fingers. "And try to throw it as straight as possible, otherwise you'll be running in every direction following it."

"I had gathered that much, thanks, Drys." Neryda rolled her eyes, taking a grape from the spread on the floor.

Galdinia smiled up at her friends from the ground in front of the fire. Neryda and Drystan always had a sibling-like relationship. He tried to keep her out of as much trouble as he could, while she gave him a hard time—and a rude gesture—every time he did. Galdinia found a simple comfort in watching their exchanges.

"You're going to get mad at me when you can't do it on the first try, so forgive me for preemptively protecting myself," Drystan retorted, his eyes flashing to Galdinia's, alight with childish confidence.

"Let's get on with it," Neryda said with a frown, mirroring Drystan's stance as he held the grape out in front of him.

"Don't take your eyes off the grape, throw it straight, keep your knees bent and—" Drystan tossed the grape in the air, sending it three feet above him. He threw his head back as the grape slowed before falling straight down into his open mouth. He grinned, pleased with himself, as he chewed his target.

"Right," Neryda said, far too seriously for the activity they were practising. "Eyes on the grape, throw it straight, knees bent."

Neryda hurled her grape in the air and it flew far too wide, bouncing off a nearby shelf. Galdinia stifled a laugh, which was silenced by narrowed eyes from Neryda.

"Try again," Drystan said, bending down to pluck a handful of grapes from the bowl in front of the princess, his eyes meeting hers again. "Here."

Drystan handed Neryda one of the grapes and she took it, a look of determination set into her brow. Neryda watched the grape carefully as she threw it in the air. She stepped backwards, then left and right, trying to centre herself beneath it. It landed a few feet from where she originally stood.

"Close!" Drystan said.

Always the optimist, Galdinia thought as she watched Neryda take another grape from Drystan before he offered them to her. This time she stood with her feet further apart, ready to make a sudden move if needed. She threw the grape again, watching it closely as she shifted her weight from side to side.

"Yes, yes!" Drystan said, keeping his eyes on the fruit as well.

The grape started to fall through the air and Neryda was directly beneath it. Instead of landing in her mouth, however, it bounced off her forehead with a dull pop and settled on the floor beside them.

Galdinia and Drystan couldn't help but laugh at the frustration Neryda displayed over such a simple object.

"It's harder than it looks!" Neryda protested, frowning at them both.

In response, Drystan threw two grapes in the air and shifted from left to right to easily catch them one after the other. Again, Neryda rolled her eyes and shoved him in the shoulder. Galdinia grinned at the two of them.

"I'm getting more tea before I have to watch your insufferable gloating anymore," Neryda said dramatically, bending to pick up the now empty teapot before turning to leave the library.

Drystan walked around the room to pick up the discarded grapes, chuckling as he did.

"She was close," he said with a shrug, collecting one that had rolled down a nearby alcove. "She gave up too quickly."

"You know how stubborn she is," Galdinia, who was lying on her stomach and cradling her cup of tea in her hands, returned. "She wouldn't give you the satisfaction of watching her fail yet again."

"It was pretty funny, though, wasn't it?" Drystan said with a wink, coming to sit in front of Galdinia again. The flickering fire cast a warm glow over his features, its reflection dancing in his pupils.

"I'm not willing to put my life at risk in admitting that." Galdinia smiled, taking a sip from her cup.

"That would be a grisly death," Drystan agreed, moving so he was lying on his side, using his elbow to prop himself up. "I wouldn't wish that upon my greatest enemy."

"You don't have any enemies," Galdinia said with a disbelieving frown. Drystan was the kindest person she knew and he had never once crossed anyone.

"Not true!" Drystan said matter-of-factly. "Do you remember Elian Walric?"

Galdinia did in fact remember Elian. He was a local Elderguard boy who was around their age. He had a group of noble friends who had all been given their gift at a young age, which they made sure was known among the citizens of Elderguard. They were often found making torrents in the square fountain or slamming windows and doors shut with the power of three boys. They were the kind of children that needed early lessons in gift etiquette. They were always polite enough to Galdinia, given her title, but she knew they gave Drystan a hard time after they learned that he didn't have a gift and didn't come from nobility.

"Ah, yes, Elian," Galdinia replied with a knowing nod.

"He loved to ridicule me any chance he got," Drystan explained, popping another grape in his mouth. "We grew up on the same street, so I had to see him regularly, and he would often rub his Weaver gift in my face. I'm not sure I've told you this before, but when I was about eight, he pushed me into the fountain and used his powers to almost drown me."

Galdinia's mouth had fallen open in shock as she imagined a young Drystan being hurt by this insolent child. Drystan had mentioned that Elian hadn't been kind to him as a child, but he had never told her this story.

"He only stopped because a guard came over. I remember being pulled from the water, coughing uncontrollably. Elian and his group were already on the other side of the square by the time I could see straight again. The guard asked where I lived and started walking me that way, but I insisted on avoiding our street out of fear of seeing Elian. I ran straight to Raff's bakery instead. He dried me off with his gift pretty quickly." Drystan's face lit up as he recalled the memory. "That was the day I met you two, actually."

"Really?" Galdinia asked, remembering the smell of fresh cinnamon scrolls and the warm sun on her face.

"Yep," Drystan said with a coy smile, tossing another grape in his mouth. "I decided to hang around Raff's for safety until I could get home without being attacked. That's when you and Neryda showed up. Elian never really bothered me after you and I became friends."

"So you were using us for protection?" Galdinia raised a brow at him.

"Well, not intentionally." Drystan smirked in response. "But Elian wouldn't come near me when I was with the princess. A win-win, really."

Galdinia screwed up her face as he mentioned her title, taking a sip of her tea. Galdinia had put a strict ban on the use of her title by her best friends, insisting that her position in society wouldn't come between them.

"So, there you go. I do have one enemy, but he hasn't troubled me in years. I have you to thank for that." Drystan's eyes were sincere as he smiled at Galdinia in the light of the fire. "You kept me safe."

Drystan had always been her friend, her confidant. While Neryda was up for any adventure and always wanted to try new things, whenever Drystan was with her, Galdinia felt safe. He kept the girls out of too much trouble and after a few years in his company, the king decided they didn't need to be as heavily guarded inside the walls of the capital. Galdinia hadn't realised that she and Neryda had been such a safe place for Drystan as well. Hearing him say that made a bright fluttering rise up in her stomach.

She looked at him again in the light of the fire and something shifted. His kind eyes locked with hers and they gazed at each other for what felt like minutes.

"I'm sorry he was so awful to you," Galdinia said gently, nursing her tea on the ground, her hands within reach of Drystan's. He had been rolling a grape between his fingers, his eyes still glued to hers.

"I guess if he hadn't, we wouldn't be here today."

"Always the optimist." This time Galdinia spoke her thoughts aloud.

Drystan didn't reply. He merely smiled at her words, not taking his eyes from his friend.

"Alright, Drys!" Neryda's voice rang from the door of the library, bursting the quiet moment. "Let's give this grape thing another go."

Drystan smirked as Neryda placed a fresh pot of tea between them, taking another few grapes from the bowl. "Are you sure? I'd hate to bruise your ego."

"I will not allow you to best me at this extremely simple skill," Neryda said brashly, standing with her feet firmly spaced apart, ready to try again. Finally, Drystan pulled his gaze from Galdinia and stood beside their fiery friend, her auburn hair made all the richer in the light of the fire.

"Let's go then, Ner," Drystan returned, still holding a grape between his fingers.

Galdinia watched as Neryda tried to catch a grape in her mouth seven more times before she finally landed one. The three of them erupted into cheers and laughter as she did a victory lap around the oak table in the centre of the room. By way of celebration, Drystan caught a grape mid-air with his eyes closed, sending Neryda into a fit.

Galdinia giggled as she watched Neryda pelt Drystan with grapes. Drystan shielded himself with a nearby book and he caught Galdinia's eye and winked at her, sending a fresh wave of butterflies through her stomach, making her toes wiggle and her cheeks flush.

Any illusion that Drystan was just her friend popped that evening.

When they arrived back at the castle in the royal carriage after the funeral, Galdinia had barely stepped over the marble threshold before she was intercepted by Governor Ryden, who appeared to have been waiting for her arrival.

Ryden had been the governor of Elderguard for more than a decade and had served the Elderwin family since her father took the throne. Ryden was promoted to governor soon after her father's crowning and led the Syndicate, making decisions on behalf of the king when he was absent. Should Galdinia not be able to take the throne in seven days, this man would keep watch over the kingdom for her until she could. He was a kind yet assertive man. He had become family to her and she thought that perhaps this was who her uncle could have become had he not allowed anger and jealousy to seethe in his heart.

"Princess Galdinia," Ryden said with a modest bow. "What a lovely ceremony that was. Truly such an honour to your father."

"Thank you," Galdinia said, handing her now removed headdress and veil to Brigitte as they stepped into the entrance hall, Ryden still by her side. "Have you taken on the responsibilities of a welcoming committee, Governor?"

"Unfortunately, no, I haven't, Your Highness," Ryden said without an ounce of humour on his face, directing her away from Neryda and the nearby attendants. "Your presence is requested immediately in the drawing room."

"Whatever for?" Galdinia asked, perplexed, still yearning to share a cold cider with her friend.

"The reading of your father's will, Your Highness," Ryden said hesitantly. "As per your father's instructions, it is imperative that we read it today."

6

THE WALK FROM THE ENTRANCE HALL TO THE DRAWING ROOM FELT longer than usual. Galdinia managed to convince Neryda that she could handle the meeting on her own, without divulging the nature of it. She sent her friend to help herself to a drink from the kitchens and she promised she'd meet her in her rooms later.

Somehow the Syndicate had managed to swiftly regroup after the funeral, making their way to the castle and setting up a meeting without Galdinia's knowing. She made the mental note that this was something that she wouldn't allow upon becoming queen: all goings-on within the castle would be granted by her.

If, she reminded herself. *If I become queen.*

"Princess, please take a seat." Ryden sat at the head of the table and indicated to a seat beside him for Galdinia. Around the table sat a handful of Syndicate members, including the high priestess and Captain Ilyon.

Along the oval table also sat two people she'd hoped she wouldn't have to speak to again today: her uncle Draven and aunt Edana. They looked up at her smugly, the expressions of faux mourners failing to cover up their joy in this moment. While they had the common sense to wear black to her father's funeral, Galdinia fixated on the extrava-gant and glistening necklace around Edana's neck. Embedded in a heavy chain of white gold and nestled between her collarbones sat three jewels: amber, amethyst and the most magnificent starlight crystal she had ever seen. A jewel such as that could have only been mined in the Starlight Mountains in the north of Crysterra, a region that was fiercely protected by the inhabitants of Lund, the only known established civilisation in the mountains. How Edana secured the stone was a mystery. Galdinia didn't think her aunt and uncle did anything accidentally and she assumed they were making a statement by wearing such a lavish item to her father's funeral and will reading.

Looking away from them, Galdinia made the conscious choice to walk down the opposite end and sit at the other head of the table, directly down from Ryden. He momentarily raised his eyebrows at her.

As she surveyed the table, Galdinia didn't think that all these people had been corralled together at the end of the funeral. No, they were given express warning of the meeting, which Galdinia had been left in the dark about. She could feel her heart thundering in her chest as it tightened, a sensation she was becoming all too familiar with.

"That was a lovely speech you gave today," Draven remarked from three seats away, still trying to cover up his lack of empathy with some kind of false sincerity. "My brother would be so proud of you."

"Thank you," Galdinia responded, allowing her voice to be nothing but honey. "I'm sure he would have been so glad that you were both able to come. We know how busy your schedule is."

Galdinia was well aware of the Elderwin's lack of substantial power in their province. Her father had specifically chosen a small yet important territory for them to rule over. The Shadowed Coast was a curved stretch of land that bordered the Southern Shadow and was the home to most of the country's seafood distributers and merchants. They had the most ports and, therefore, most of the country's ships. Given the relative peace in the south, the military ships that moored there hadn't set sail for battle in many years. While Draven and Edana thought this to be a symbol of power, they were merely glorified over-seers of a sadly unpopular delicacy.

The doors of the drawing room swung open before Draven could reply.

"I'm sorry I'm late."

The Elderwin's and Galdinia's eyes widened in shock at the sight of Valah Pyrin standing in the doorway. Beside her stood a tall, muscular man with a dark, close-cut beard, wearing a full suit of fighting leathers. He stood close by the door, keeping his eyes fixed on Valah as she sauntered to the table, taking the final empty seat. Galdinia assumed he was her guard or advisor, perhaps both. He kept a hand on the sword at his waist as he watched them all carefully.

"What are you doing here?" Edana spat, her voice laced with venom.

"I was invited by the Syndicate." Valah nodded towards Ryden at the end of the table, the smile on her face far from removed. "The king has left me something in his will."

Galdinia was fuming. How could her father have included this wretched woman in his will? Her father only ever spoke about how treacherous and deceitful she was, describing her as someone who revelled in the pain of others, just like her parents. And he left her something in his will? Galdinia was incredulous.

"Yes, Valah has been summoned just the same as you have," Ryden said, nodding in agreement, although Galdinia noticed that he didn't appear too happy about it. "And now that she is here, we can begin."

Valah couldn't help but smile at these words; the anger and disgust that oozed from the princess, lord and lady gave her nothing but pure satisfaction.

"I ask High Priestess Saena to please read the final rights before we access the will." Ryden motioned towards Saena, her dazzling white gown of the funeral swapped for a white lace dress, something simpler but just as beautiful. The headdress that sat upon her crown of white braids fell down by her temples, a collection of pearls reflecting the light of the candles in the chandelier above their heads.

"King Bartemus Wylliam Elderwin of Crysterra, Wielder of wind, first of his name, summoned you all here today, wishing to bestow on you the rights, riches and remedies that he has held near and dear. He wished that there would be nothing in this room but peace as we read the will of the king. I ask that the God of Guidance would surround this table and guide our emotions and decision-making in these moments that we have together. Amen."

Galdinia felt her shoulders relax and her heart rest as the high priestess spoke. The woman's hands were glowing with Peacelight, which she sent in swathes across the table.

"Amen." The collective chorus of agreement hummed through the room and all eyes turned to Ryden.

"Princess, Ladies, Lords, Her Priestess, Captain and members of the Syndicate." Ryden nodded as he addressed everyone around the table, his eyes hovering over Valah for a moment longer than anyone else. "As the high priestess stated, the king asked for your presence because he has left something in his will for you. We do not know what these gifts may be, but we ask for your utmost respect in this matter. We shall not question the decision-making of our late king; as king, it was his right to leave his gifts as he saw fit. All that I read to you will be final."

Galdinia sat on these words, having not considered what her father would leave her. What if he suggested someone else was to be ruler? Could the king even do that? Did he think she was fit to be queen, even without her gift? The thought made Galdinia question herself and she felt torn between wanting to be good enough to be queen and knowing she couldn't take the throne just yet.

"I will now open the official will and rights of King Bartemus Wylliam Elderwin in the presence of these people." Governor Ryden ran his hands over the heavily bound book that sat on the table in front of him. Hanging from the opening of the book was a tarnished gold lock. From the chain around his neck, Ryden took a key and used it to unlock the fastening on the book, heaving it open with a thud.

Galdinia's eyes scanned the room. Draven and Edana could not take their eyes off the leather-bound book before them, anticipation glowing in their eyes. Valah sat poised, looking down her nose at the book, her long fingers stretched coolly over the armrests of her chair.

Galdinia brought her hands to her chest, unexpectedly nervous about the contents of those ancient pages. For centuries, kings and queens wrote their final requests in this book and now her father's dying wishes would be read aloud for all to hear. She tried to pluck more of the high priestess' Peacelight from the air around her, seeking refuge in its comfort.

Ryden began.

"I, King Bartemus Wylliam Elderwin, of sound mind and ill health, write this will in the anticipation of my demise. To Ilyon Trunder, Captain of the Royal Guard, I leave the order of Crysterra's army. This includes the Royal Guard, who so ably protect our capital's walls."

Captain Ilyon bowed his head and Galdinia noticed his shoulders relax momentarily before sitting up straight again. She assumed that this was all he could ask for.

"To High Priestess Saena of the Crystal Temple, I leave five percent of the royal coin, which she may spend in order to keep and maintain our beautiful place of worship."

Saena lowered her eyes for a moment, acknowledging the generous offering of the passed king.

"To the Syndicate and by extension the city of Elderguard, I leave five percent of the royal coin, in order to maintain the glory that is our great capital."

The Syndicate members nodded in acknowledgement. While the taxes of the capital were reasonably high, Galdinia had heard her father mention on multiple occasions how quickly the Syndicate could chew through gold. She imagined this amount of money would keep them busy for a time.

Ryden twisted in his seat to face Draven and Edana. They straightened in their chairs and Draven wrapped his hand around Edana's.

"To my brother, Lord Draven, and his wife, Lady Edana, I leave Elderwin Manor, where they are to rule as lord and lady over the Shadowed Coast and the southern ports."

Edana glanced at her husband and saw the vein pulsing in his neck.

"To Valah Pyrin—"

"That's all?" Draven interrupted, his voice even despite his trembling hands. "That's all my brother left us?"

"Yes, Lord Draven." Ryden nodded, turning back to the page, about to read Valah's inheritance.

"But we already have rule of the Shadowed Coast and we have lived at Elderwin Manor for years."

"It has always been the property of the crown, so I suppose the king wanted to ensure you were guaranteed the rightful lordship of the manor and province after his death." Although Ryden spoke graciously, he very obviously wanted to move on. The tension in the room became stiff and uncomfortable and Saena sent out another wave of Peacelight.

"Are you sure there isn't anything else he left us?" Edana joined her husband's aggressive tirade, breaking through the high priestess' gift. "Perhaps a throne or a castle? No?"

"Lady Edana," Ryden said, addressing Galdinia's aunt with an air of ease and patience, proving this wasn't the first will reading he'd had to manage. "The king has rightfully acknowledged your ruling of the province, which you have been doing for years. His final wishes were that you would continue to oversee the Shadowed Coast with the grace and wisdom that you have been doing for so long already. Now, I will continue the reading of the will."

Ryden stared the Elderwins down for a moment or two before he turned back to Valah. Galdinia watched the high priestess fix her soft eyes on Draven and Edana, the balls of Peacelight in the air above their heads shifting closer to them.

"To Valah Pyrin, a longtime friend of the crown who is well respected in the west, I leave the Pyrin family sceptre, which has been kept safe in the Crysterra Castle catacombs for far too many decades. It is time it is returned to the family that crafted it so thoughtfully."

Valah stiffened as an attendant walked towards her from across the room, her father's sceptre in his hands. As he presented the sceptre to Valah, the entire room went cold.

This sceptre was the last piece of the Pyrin Dynasty that survived the Great Confrontation; even the throne was melted down and reshaped to fit the liking of Galdinia's grandparents. Galdinia wondered if the last time Valah saw the sceptre was the last time she saw her parents still breathing in this very castle.

Galdinia could not imagine why her father would want to give it back to her, let alone name her as a friend in his will. Everyone in Crysterra knew that Valah was considered an enemy of the capital and Galdinia was still shocked that she was sitting just down the table from her.

Valah took the golden sceptre in her hands. The rubies and emeralds that lay encrusted in its orb glistened in the candlelight, their colours reflecting upon her face. She did not bow her head. She did not acknowledge anyone else; she simply held the heirloom in her slender fingers.

Galdinia felt a sting of pain in her stomach at the image of this woman and the sceptre. She almost feared it.

"Finally, to Princess Galdinia, my daughter." Galdinia's attention was brought back to the governor and the matter at hand. "There is no one in this world more beautiful, gracious, or humble than you. Your love for the people of this city is unmatched and it is this trait of yours that I saw shine in your mother also. For this reason, I leave you the remaining royal coin, run and ownership of Crysterra Castle and, finally"—Ryden took a breath before continuing—"I declare Galdinia my rightful heir to the throne and Queen of Crysterra."

Galdinia's breath caught in her throat and Ryden looked up from the will. Edana and Draven turned their stupefied faces towards their niece. Valah tore her eyes from her sceptre and stared at the nineteen-year-old princess.

"And that is the will of King Bartemus Wylliam Elderwin."

Ryden shut the book with a dusty thud.

7

"SHE CAN'T BE QUEEN. SHE'S FAR TOO YOUNG!" DRAVEN STOOD BY THE door arguing with Ryden, his frustration bubbling over and seeping towards the governor. The high priestess left soon after the will reading ended, as did her calming gift. Galdinia stood by the window on the opposite side of the room, watching the men carefully; she was just as surprised by the will reading as Draven, but she tried to keep her shock to herself until her enemies had left the room.

"As I said, Lord Draven," Ryden said, emphasising Draven's title so as to remind the man who he was and how he should have been conducting himself, "there won't be a coronation until the end of the Week of Mourning and until then the Syndicate will review the rights of the king and will govern until the seventh day. This isn't a new process, my lord. You are aware of that. No decision on the ruling of Crysterra beyond this week will be made until the seventh day."

"To hell with the rights of the king; he's dead!" Draven practically spat the words.

"He is still our king and we respect him as such."

Ryden stood taller than Draven and, thankfully, had been serving as part of the Syndicate since Draven was a young lord. Ryden was one of the most respected figures in the kingdom, mostly for his knowledge of and commitment to the country, but especially for his unwavering nerve in the face of hostility.

Galdinia turned from the men and looked down upon the main square of the capital, which didn't sit far from the castle's outer walls. From her vantage point, she could see the ink-black decorations already being set up for the First Night of Mourning as soldiers watched the attendants prepare the square. She wondered if Drystan was patrolling there somewhere. From the height at which she stood and with their glistening helmets, Galdinia couldn't even begin to distinguish between the soldiers.

"Are you admiring your kingdom, Your Highness?" Valah had silently approached Galdinia from behind before speaking, her voice hissing her final word. Galdinia looked sideways at the woman, refusing to turn to fully face her. Galdinia was, after all, named the future queen, so she thought she had better start behaving like it.

"I am, in fact," Galdinia lied, looking back out the window, beyond the castle walls and into the capital. "I'm thankful my father has left me with such an honourable role."

"Truly honourable," Valah replied. Galdinia could hear the frank sarcasm in her voice but tried not to let it concern her. "What an honour to take all of this over from your father."

Galdinia glanced back at Valah and then looked down her nose at the sceptre that was still clenched in her bony hands, the priceless gems and golden exterior dazzling in the sun. "And I'm sure you're thankful that my father was gracious enough to leave you with that."

"Gracious?" Valah scoffed, twisting the sceptre in her hands as she moved to stand by the opposite edge of the window, making it harder for Galdinia to avoid her scornful eyes. "This is a ridiculous attempt at a peace treaty, not a selfless gift."

"I'm sure my father only found it a short time ago. He probably thought it too precious to be delivered to you by an attendant. He would have loved to have given it to you himself, I'm positive." Galdinia was aware that her words were weak, but she stood tall regardless. Although she had never met Valah before, she lived up to every expectation she held of the woman.

"Oh yes, your ever thoughtful father only recently found the most valuable piece of history in his vault and left it on his deathbed for me to collect. Please!" Valah stepped closer to the princess, forcing her to meet the hostile woman's eyes. Up close, Valah's thin face looked even more rigid, her jawline and cheekbones creating slicing lines across her skin. "Your father, the abomination of a king that he was, couldn't wait to humiliate me any chance he got, and this was his final jab. He invited me to his will reading, promising riches, and left me with my own father's sceptre, the one he used to rightfully rule this kingdom."

Her words felt like ice, sending shards straight through Galdinia. She was taken aback by the brashness with which Valah spoke, unsure how to respond as all pretence and attempted confidence started falling away. She was also struck by how hypocritical Valah was being; according to the history books Galdinia studied, Valah's parents had been dictators who cared very little about their citizens. They raised taxes to support their extravagant lifestyle, sending even the most noble families into debt. By all accounts, they were self-serving tyrants and Galdinia didn't think Valah seemed all that dissimilar from them.

"Do not call my father an abomination," Galdinia said hotly, backed only by the ounce of confidence she had left.

"If you're willing to believe any of your father's lies, that is to your own detriment. But let me make one thing very clear." Valah took another step closer so that her lips almost brushed Galdinia's ear. "His final lie will not be upheld; you will not be queen. We will be at my coronation before yours."

With an awful, sickly smile, Valah pulled back from Galdinia and turned to the door, striding out of the room, sceptre in hand, her guard at her heels. Galdinia felt out of breath and positively blindsided. She looked around for help, but only her aunt, uncle and Ryden were still in the drawing room.

"We will be back at the end of the week and we expect an audience with the Syndicate upon our return," Draven practically growled at Ryden, his wife now perched at his side.

"We will send word when we have further information to share with you." Ryden was not budging. "Until then, good evening, Lord and Lady Elderwin."

Edana went to say something else, but her husband took her by the hand and they stormed out of the room, taking their cloud of anger with them.

Ryden turned to Galdinia and stood by her side at the window, looking upon the square where the black banners and flags with the Elderwin crest were being hoisted into the air.

"That could have gone worse," Ryden said with an air of relief.

Galdinia looked at him with narrow eyes. "Really? Valah practically threatened my life and my uncle is going to be banging on the castle door for a key by the end of the week."

"Well, it didn't end with a fork to the hand and the curtains up in flame." Galdinia looked at the governor in utter terror. "About eight years ago, we dealt with a particularly violent family of nobles in the north who thought they would be made lord and lady after the death of their parents. The will and your father's leadership said otherwise."

Ryden rubbed his left hand knowingly, his fingers brushing over four small scars that sat in a row on the back of his hand. Galdinia couldn't think on it for longer than a moment, her stomach already doing flips at the sight of the scars.

"Ryden, do you think I'll be queen at the end of this week?"

Of all the officials that Galdinia had come to know over the years, Ryden had always been her favourite, likely because he was her father's favourite too. He had always been loyal to the king, showing a great reverence and allegiance that was beyond anything the royal family had seen in decades. When the Elderwin family underwent multiple acts of treason during both King Bartemus' and his parents' rule, Ryden was always steadfast. Closer than a brother, the king would say. But given who the late king's blood sibling was, that wasn't too hard to achieve in a relationship. Ryden became the family's constant source of wisdom and guidance. After many years of serving the crown in the Syndicate, King Bartemus appointed him as governor the moment the position was made available.

"I think it's highly probable," Ryden replied, always careful with his words. "Your father named you queen in his will, which is unlike anything a passing ruler has done before. The heir is always assumed, yes, but he practically crowned you himself."

"But does that actually mean anything?" Galdinia asked.

"Honestly, I'm not sure that it does," Ryden replied simply. "The laws around ruling are clear: one must have their gift and be of royal blood. Though I have no problem with your aunt and uncle thinking the Syndicate will take your father's promise seriously."

"And what about my… limitation?" Galdinia asked, sidestepping the word "gift".

"Ah, that. Well, as far as we are concerned, if the heir is truly purposed to be ruler, then the Gods will bestow on them their powers in due course. As I'm sure you've been told, your mother's powers did not come until they were absolutely needed. While she was of noble blood, her gift didn't make itself known until moments before her coronation. Your parents' faith in the Gods was unmatched. Your father insisted on marrying your mother and had her coronation organised despite her gift. I'm still believing that yours will arrive in time too, Princess."

Ryden looked upon Galdinia with a mix of pride and pity, the kind of expression a parent might give their child when they lose a running race: they are proud that they tried but upset for them that they lost.

"Either way," Ryden went on, "I will meet with the Syndicate tonight and we will discuss what is to happen in the coming week."

"And there isn't another way for me to become queen?" Galdinia asked, almost surprised by her own growing desire for the throne. Being surrounded by her enemies seemed to have highlighted her desperation to keep the crown from their clutches.

"At this stage, I don't believe so." As Ryden spoke, he evaded the princess' eyes as though he may have more to share but wasn't willing to.

"And what about the others? Valah, Draven and Edana?" Galdinia asked, changing the subject.

"While they may each believe they have a claim to the throne, they can't actually take it before you have the chance to prove yourself."

"So I have to show my powers by the end of the week or—"

"Technically, if they really wanted to put up a fight for the throne, they could." Galdinia could tell that Ryden didn't want to say these words just as much as she didn't want to hear them. "There are grounds for them to be interim rulers until you receive your gift. But unless you renounce your title yourself, they cannot take it from you indefinitely."

"But what if I never obtain my gift?"

"An interim ruler can remain on the throne for decades. In order for that to happen, though, they have to go through the Syndicate, present their cases, and it is the Syndicate's job to assess their ability to rule in your place. It is a long and arduous process." Ryden looked tired as he spoke, his neatly cut, greying beard and weary eyes making him look older than he was. "While they would never officially become the king or queen, they could effectively rule as such with the Syndicate by their side."

"Unless something happens to me." Galdinia could feel the physical pressure of the situation on her chest again. Her hands became clammy at the thought of having to prove herself worthy to the Gods within seven days, while also fending for her own life.

"Don't even think on it!" Ryden said hastily, his eyes now full of determination. "You are well protected here, Your Highness. The Syndicate is resolute on seeing you take the crown, and, until we are given reason to act otherwise, we will watch over the kingdom on your behalf until your coronation."

"Thank you, Ryden. I truly am grateful for you."

Then, the governor did something Galdinia knew he shouldn't; he put his arm around the princess, allowing himself to give in to sentimentality before duty for one moment. They looked out at the capital side by side, the governor's arm pulling the princess in close. Aside from Neryda, he had quickly become the closest person to family she had left.

"I will always have your best interest in mind, Princess, whatever that may be."

8

GALDINIA ENTERED HER BEDROOM TO FIND HER BEST FRIEND SPRAWLED across her bed, goblet in hand, an array of books spread across the blanket.

"Why do you read so many books? Aren't you a princess? Don't you have more important things to do?"

"Well, when you're dealing with a sick parent, it's nice to escape reality." Galdinia shifted the books to the lamp stand by her bed beside a half-empty bottle of wine and an empty goblet. "I thought we were drinking cider tonight."

"Couldn't find any," Neryda said, rolling onto her back, careful not to spill the wine, very clearly affected by the drink. Galdinia imagined that Neryda was using her powers to keep her drink at bay; although her friend was a reasonably skilled Water Weaver, she didn't like the chances of her bedsheets going unscathed by the wine in her current state. "But Miss Giles gave me this. It's not the best I've ever had, but it does the trick!"

Galdinia gave her friend a disapproving look. Regardless, she poured herself half a glass and slowly sipped on the ruby-red liquid.

"So how was the meeting?" Neryda asked, leaning up against the silk pillows at the head of the bed.

"It was the reading of my father's will." Galdinia sighed, sitting next to Neryda, goblet resting on her legs. "I felt completely blindsided by the whole thing, to be honest."

"What did he leave you?" Neryda asked, some of the haziness from the alcohol clearing from her eyes as she came to realise the weight of the situation.

"The money, the castle and the throne." Neryda sputtered her mouthful of wine, sending flecks of red across Galdinia's sheets. "Neryda!"

"What? You're queen?"

"Not officially," Galdinia said, trying to wipe some of the wine from her bedding. "My aunt and uncle aren't happy about it. Neither is that Valah Pyrin woman. She practically threatened my life; she's desperate to be queen. But he did name me queen in his will."

"So it's complicated?"

"Very much so."

"And did they say anything about your gift?" Neryda was cautious with her words. The only time Neryda Fleur could be described as cautious was when she and Galdinia spoke about her lack of a gift.

"Governor Ryden said the ordination still stands," Galdinia explained, running a finger along the lip of her goblet. "If I am to be crowned by the end of the week, my gift will have to show itself."

The two girls leaned against the pile of pillows, both unsure what to say.

"More wine?" Neryda asked after a long pause, pulling the bottle from the lamp stand.

"Please."

The girls spent much of the afternoon drinking until the tense seriousness in the air faded into the darkness of twilight and their laughter replaced their earlier tears.

Once the sun's glow had completely sunk beneath the horizon, the noise from the square started to travel up to Galdinia's bedroom window. The voices of hundreds of Elderguard's citizens could be heard as they started to emerge from their homes, stepping out into the first evening of the Week of Mourning.

"We should go to the square!" Neryda stumbled her words in a flurry of excitement and intoxication.

"Oh, I don't want to go to another funeral today." The first night of the Week of Mourning brought with it a ceremony of remembrance in the square, a shorter funeral-like service for those of the wider public of the capital to attend to pay their respects. Galdinia had no interest in saying goodbye to her father again.

"No, no." Neryda shook her head with vigour. "I mean, let's go to the tavern! It'll be practically empty and we can get something better to drink than whatever this is." She swirled the final sip of wine that remained in her goblet.

"You know Lyndon won't give us more to drink. He'll be able to smell the wine from behind the bar."

"If there's any night that he won't refuse serving the princess more alcohol, it's tonight."

Galdinia considered this for a moment. While she didn't condone excessive drinking, she knew her father would understand one night of escape, one night of necessary freedom from the pain of the day. She'd been trying so hard to maintain her strict royal exterior and she was becoming exhausted by it.

"Let's go."

The two girls entered the square, carefully concealed under heavy cloaks, blending in with other citizens who wore their black dress robes. At the northern end of the square stood a temporary platform where the high priestess would share a similar eulogy as she did earlier in the day. The girls, arm in arm, skirted around the mass of people waiting quietly for the service to begin and made their way to the southeast end of the square. There, nestled in an alley off the main road, was their favourite tavern. Lyndon had owned the tavern since before they were born and as teenagers, they would often steal away from boring lessons or princess duties to enjoy a roast dinner or a non-alcoholic cider in its warm corners.

The two of them ducked into the tavern and were pleased to find it almost empty. Cast by the warm glow of the nearby candles were four guards who appeared to be on a break from their duties, while Lyndon stood behind the bar cleaning glasses.

"Evening ladies, what can I—" Lyndon's voice hitched in his throat as the candlelight fell across Galdinia's face. "Princess."

Much to her relief, Lyndon's sigh of her title didn't quite reach the guards across the tavern; she knew they would insist on escorting her home as soon as they saw her. It had taken the girls significant effort to escape the castle unseen already. This was something they were well-versed in, but doing so under the influence of red wine certainly added an element of challenge.

"Good evening, Lyndon," Neryda said quietly, approaching the bar with her friend, the hoods of their cloaks still shielding their faces. "Could we grab a couple of glasses of mulled wine? We need it after today."

Lyndon considered this, his eyes narrowing briefly on the two girls before him. After a moment he agreed and served them two mugs of steaming spiced wine.

The girls thanked Lyndon and promptly moved to the back corner of the tavern with their drinks, taking a seat in an alcove, Galdinia with her back to the guards and the door.

"Told you, easy!" Neryda smiled smugly as she took a swig from the glass. Galdinia drank too, the heat of the drink soothing her throat, chest and stomach, sending a welcome ripple of warmth across her skin, goosebumps appearing on her arms and neck. Though the drink was warmed by the fire of Lyndon's gift, the natural heat of the alcohol was something that Galdinia felt right down to her toes. She felt as though the muscles in her shoulders and neck had finally relaxed after a day of heightened unease.

"This is exactly what I needed after today." Galdinia spoke into her cup before looking up at her friend, who was distracted by something over Galdinia's shoulder. "Ner?"

"Hopefully this is exactly what you need too."

The clinking of metal approached from behind her and in a moment, the armoured body of a guard was standing by their table, looking directly down at Galdinia. With his helmet under his arm and sword at his hip, Drystan stood like a true soldier beside the girls, as though he was just another guard waiting to serve his princess.

"Evening, ladies," he chimed, the right side of his lips pulling up

into a half smile, significantly more upbeat than a few hours prior.
"Out for a nightcap?"

"Something like that." Neryda responded for them both; what
with the alcohol and being blindsided by Drystan twice in one day,
Galdinia felt she didn't have the right words to say.

"Would you mind if I joined you? I have a few minutes left until
my break is over."

"Of course, Drys," Neryda said, and he slid onto the bench beside
her before Neryda reached an arm around his shoulders and pulled
him into a hug. "We've really missed you."

While Galdinia was not surprised by Neryda's actions, she knew
the alcohol was making her more affectionate than usual.

"I've missed you too," Drystan said with a smile, returning Neryda's hug and looking back at Galdinia. "Both of you."

Neryda let go of him, and Drystan straightened up, now easily in
full view of Galdinia.

With his hair pulled into a knot at the back of his head and his
armour freshly polished for the night's festivities, Drystan looked just
as he did on his first day of training three months prior, right when
her father was getting sick. It was the same day that she was told by
her sickly father that she needed to start to consider potential suitors,
all of whom should be lords and certainly not a soldier that didn't
possess a gift.

Despite living in the capital, Drystan was not a lord and, therefore,
never a true prospect for the future queen. His being drafted into the
Royal Guard solidified this fact. Although she hadn't thought seriously
about taking a husband in her teenage years—not beyond her childhood fantasies of marrying Prince Charming from her fairy tale
books, that was—her heart broke the day Drystan stood before her
wearing his brand new armour. It was moments before he was to
travel to the Midlands to start his training, taking the only boy she had
ever truly cared for beyond her reach.

Despite the few months that had passed, Galdinia noticed that the
boy she had fallen in love with looked more like a man, forced to grow
up in a terrifyingly short amount of time. Galdinia wondered if he
had been in combat or had to, heaven forbid, kill someone. She
couldn't imagine this tender-hearted person being able to cause harm

to someone else, and yet here he sat, armour-clad and fashioning a sword that could slice her in half in a heartbeat.

"How were your ciders?" Drystan asked, looking from Neryda, then back to Galdinia, his eyes lingering on the princess for a few too many seconds.

"We didn't get to them." Neryda shrugged, taking another swig of mulled wine. "Gal had some important meeting about her father's will and I—ow!" Galdinia kicked her friend under the table, frustrated by her lack of confidence. "What? It's just Drystan."

"His will? Already?" Drystan asked, his voice achingly concerned about Galdinia, taking no mind of Neryda's response.

"Yes, unfortunately," Galdinia replied, shooting a few more daggers at her best friend. "It was fine, it was just... tense."

"Because she was made queen—"

"No, I wasn't," Galdinia said, choosing to cut in instead of kicking Neryda again. "Those were my father's wishes, but the Syndicate has to review it. My aunt and uncle aren't happy about it, as I'm sure you can imagine. Nor is that woman Valah. I'll be lucky to survive the week with my head, let alone my crown."

"I'm so sorry," Drystan said, and he went to reach for her hand but thought better of it and rested his hands on the table in front of him, inches away from Galdinia's. "That can't have been easy."

"Ryden made it easier. He's looking out for me."

"He's always been good to your family. He will keep your best interest in mind, I'm sure."

"I hope so," Galdinia said with another sip of her wine, looking at Drystan from above her cup. They sat in silence for a moment, interrupted only by a short snort from beside them. Neryda had leaned her head against the wall and was asleep, the hours of drinking finally catching up to her. Galdinia and Drystan shared a laugh, fully aware of their friend's inability to hold much alcohol before succumbing to its effects.

"How are you?" Galdinia asked, looking back to an amused Drystan, his boyish face peering through the new lines and shadow of facial hair.

He is still Drystan.

"I'm fine." His words were chirpy, but the way he pressed his lips together after speaking told Galdinia how untrue they were. He was protecting her.

"Drys, be honest with me." Galdinia's eyes pleaded with him, but he kept up his persistent smile. "I feel like I've done nothing but talk about my own life for the last three months. I need to hear about you. I need to know how you really are. I've missed you."

Drystan's smile faltered. "If I'm honest, I'm pretty exhausted." He let out a sigh. "I've been on patrol in Wharf Town, which is painfully dull, but new recruits have to do long hours in safe places. It helps build our stamina, or so I'm told. I've just come off a week straight of daily fourteen-hour patrols around the city."

"Sounds really thrilling."

"Trust me, it's not. Before our patrols began, we did a two-month training intensive in the Midlands. I learned how to fight, how to shoot an arrow, how to protect myself. All of that was tiring but rewarding. The patrols are mind-numbing."

Galdinia shuddered at the thought of Drystan in a sword fight. "It sounds like a lot of work."

"It's long hours and not a lot of sleep," Drystan said before releasing a long breath. "I wonder if I'll ever get a full night's rest again."

"I'm sorry it's been so tiring," Galdinia said, full of sincerity. "I'll add it to my list of policies to review."

"When you're queen, you can make changes as you see fit. I don't think the sleeping patterns of soldiers should be your priority though."

Galdinia shook her head, not out of disagreement, but rather out of disbelief. "I don't even know where I'd begin."

"At the start. One thing at a time," Drystan said, now reaching out to place his hand on hers. "You will be a magnificent queen."

His hand was rough, much rougher than it had been months earlier when they walked hand in hand by the lake in the castle gardens. They felt softer then. He had drawn her to the great willow tree beside the lake, its branches hiding them from the prying eyes of wandering guards, the fireflies dancing in the summer air aglow beneath the drooping leaves. They stood beneath the ancient tree, staring silently into each other's faces, their fingers twisting in each other's palms. Galdinia had wanted to remain there with him forever, soaking up every moment she had with him. Drystan finally broke their eye contact by leaning in and pressing his lips against hers. It was everything she wanted a first kiss to be. She felt safe and loved. She felt protected.

After their first kiss, the pair lived in a blissful bubble of young love for the following four weeks. Having finally professed their love for each other after years of friendship, Galdinia felt as though she was easing into her true self, being honest with who she was, all expectations of the crown aside.

One month after that first kiss, she was tearfully waving him goodbye at the castle gates as he left for his training after being drafted into the Royal Guard. Her greatest sense of security marched from the capital with one hundred other new recruits, and she returned to the castle and her sick father.

So much had happened so quickly. Yet here he was again, her Drystan.

"I'm terrified, Drys, absolutely petrified of being queen." Galdinia practically whispered the words, letting her hands melt into his. "I have to pretend to be brave in the face of a woman who wants my head and act as though I don't have any family left, all the while graciously accepting this mantle my father left for me. I know that I have to fight to keep the throne, it's the right thing to do, but I don't know if I'm good enough."

"Gal," Drystan cooed, his eyes drawing in to hers from across the table. "You were always meant to be queen."

"I know, but—"

"And you're not pretending to be brave," he said earnestly, a flicker of a smile crossing his lips as he held her gaze. "You are the bravest person I know. The last few months have flipped your entire life upside down, and yet here you are."

Galdinia could feel the warmth of tears begin to glisten in her eyes, the burning in her chest returning. Drystan squeezed her hands tighter.

"He's gone, Drys, he's really gone." The words fell from her lips, her voice thick with tears. Although Galdinia had spent weeks mourning her father as she watched his health decline so rapidly, now that the funeral was over, she felt a new wave of emotion hit her. She actually had to deal with the consequences of his death, many of which involved her. She snaked her other hand into Drystan's, and he held them both tightly, keeping her grounded with him.

"I'm sorry I couldn't be here for you when your father's sickness got worse, and I'm sorry that I left so suddenly when things were going really well for us." Drystan dropped his eyes to their hands when he said this, his voice full of regret. "I want to try to make that up to you. I'm back now and I want to be able to be here for you."

Galdinia sniffed, letting the tears slip down her cheeks and onto the table in front of her. Drystan freed one of his hands and reached out to brush his fingers across her face, drawing the tears from her skin.

"I've really missed you," Galdinia said, her voice just a whisper as she tried to control the tears. "Knowing you're here helps though... a lot."

"I'll be on duty at the castle before you know it," Drystan said, letting his fingers linger on her cheek before returning his hand to hers. Galdinia imagined what it would be like to have Drystan patrol the castle as one of her guards. She wasn't sure if she liked the prospect or not.

"I don't imagine that would be a productive shift," Galdinia said with another sniff, forcing herself to smirk.

"I'd struggle to stay on my post, that's for sure." Drystan returned the smile. Despite the changes he had experienced in the previous months, his face was still so warm and inviting. Galdinia was glad there was a table between them; all she wanted to do was find a comfortable spot beside him, nestle into his arms and rest. Her heart ached at the thought.

"Allard!" One of the guards from across the tavern called Drystan by his surname and he sat up straight again, releasing Galdinia's hands, drawing them both back to reality. "Time to get back on duty!"

"Coming!" he echoed back to his comrades with a short salute before turning back to Galdinia, remorse filling his eyes. "Gal, I'm sorry, I have to go. Will you be okay with her?"

"It's not the first time, and it won't be the last," Galdinia said, looking at the still unconscious Neryda, wiping away the few tears that had escaped onto her cheeks. Her heart tightened at the lack of warmth surrounding her hands as Drystan stood to his feet.

"I'll come visit when I can, okay?" He said this as more of a statement than a question, but she nodded anyway. After a cursory glance to his fellow soldiers, Drystan bent down as he stood beside Galdinia, pressing his lips to the top of her head, his hand brushing her arm as he did so. Galdinia closed her eyes at the feeling of his lips.

"I'll see you soon," he whispered into her hair before putting on his helmet and striding across the room.

Drystan followed his new life out the door, leaving his old one teary in the back of the tavern.

SECOND DAY OF MOURNING

9

AFTER HER ALL-TOO-BRIEF ENCOUNTER WITH DRYSTAN, GALDINIA dragged Neryda back up to the castle, attempting to hide them both below their heavy cloaks. She wasn't sure how successful she was at making an indiscreet path back home, especially after Neryda started to drunkenly sing an old fisherman's song when they were still walking up Main Court to the castle. Galdinia couldn't help but chuckle at her friend, glad to have a distraction from the emotions that the previous twenty-four hours had brought her.

The following morning, Galdinia awoke with a start. Neryda, who was sound asleep beside her in her bed, had turned over with great ferocity, her limp arm falling over Galdinia's middle, jerking the princess from her sleep. Although they had an abundance of guest rooms in the castle, Neryda much preferred to share Galdinia's room. And while the princess liked having her own space, Galdinia was glad to have her best friend so close, especially after her recent absence.

In the moments after she woke up, she was reminded of the pain of the previous day, the reality of her father's passing crashing into her. Galdinia tried for the next half an hour to corral her thoughts, but her mind could not be tamed and she found herself wide awake before the sun had fully risen. She could feel the pressures of the week ahead dawning, resting heavily on her chest, and she could no longer be alone in the silence with her thoughts.

Galdinia could make out the tangle of sheets and hair that was Neryda, her arm still slung over her stomach, Neryda's face buried in pillows. She silently slid herself from beneath her friend's arm and crossed to her dressing room. She took a few moments to brush and tie back her hair, fastening it at the nape of her neck with a decorative clip. Galdinia did not intend on donning her tiara today. Finally, she changed from her sleeping robes into an understated pale blue dress, shrugging on her heavy cloak and tucking loose strands of her golden hair beneath the hood. Galdinia didn't want to be recognised today.

Although she knew she could happily enjoy the sunrise from the privacy of the castle gardens, Galdinia felt she needed to leave the grounds, as though the dark cloud of her father's passing still hadn't shifted. She knew that if she wanted a moment of quiet in the coming days, this morning may be the only chance she would get.

Galdinia moved through the quiet castle quickly, pulling her hood up when she reached the entrance hall. Inside the main doors stood two guards. They were talking quietly to each other, one leaning against the sandstone wall, the other fiddling with the hilt of his sword. At the sound of her footsteps, they ceased their conversation and looked to the princess with narrowed eyes. It took them a moment to see who was approaching them in the shadowy, early morning light.

"Princess!" The one that had been leaning stood up straight, standing at attention. His companion mirrored his actions and Galdinia heard his sword slip back into its sheath.

"Good morning," she replied quietly, stopping a few feet before them both. "Would you open the doors?"

"I will organise an escort for you, Princess," the first guard said in a rush as the second soldier moved to pull open the right hand door.

"I don't think I'll be needing an escort," Galdinia said, starting to walk towards the opened door. The first soldier took a side step to stand in her path. The princess stopped.

"Apologies, Your Highness," he said tentatively, his eyes darting to her face. "Governor Ryden expressly informed us that you are to be escorted at all times outside of the castle grounds."

Galdinia looked at the soldier. The first glimpses of morning light were bouncing off the buildings beyond the castle gates behind him. She was so close.

"Is that right?" she asked with a sigh. Galdinia was used to having a Royal Guard escort; she'd had one since she was a child. She had hoped that by being up so early that she may be able to maintain some semblance of privacy.

"Yes, Princess." The guard nodded, standing firm.

Galdinia knew that if she wanted to leave the castle, she had no choice but to obey Ryden's wishes. Or she could use one of her and Neryda's favourite exits instead.

"You know what, never mind," Galdinia said curtly, a polite smile flickering over her lips, attempting to cover her impatience. "I think I'll just stay in this morning."

The princess turned from the soldiers and walked across the entrance hall to the hallway of the western wing. This led to only a few rooms: a washroom, a sitting room, and Galdinia's favourite room in the castle, the library.

Her father once told her about how her grandparents had sourced books from all over the kingdom to fill the shelves of their beloved library and it became Galdinia's favourite place to burrow away on quiet evenings. It sat at the end of the twisting hallway, tucked away in the heart of the castle. It wasn't easy to stumble across unless it was someone's intention to do so. Perhaps it was the seclusion that the library offered that Galdinia liked best.

Pushing open the door, she realised that aside from using it as a shortcut to her father's rooms two days earlier, she hadn't been to the library for weeks. Although she usually spent a lot of time there, particularly when Neryda was on various trips with her family, or when her father insisted she stay in the castle when the weather was unruly, she had been spending most of her time prior to her father's death by his side. She had brought piles of books up from this room to her own, picked out her favourites and read them with her father. Despite her lack of visitation, she still felt the comfort of this room the moment she stepped inside.

Running through the centre of the room hung a collection of wooden chandeliers carved to look like deer antlers. They were dotted with long, dripping candles, whose wax now covered much of the wood. Although the room wasn't as large as others in the castle, it was oddly shaped, with jutting out walls, alcoves and hidden corners throughout, making it feel much larger than it appeared from the door. Along each wall stood tall bookshelves, each filled to capacity with books. Some volumes were close to falling apart, while others were newer additions of Galdinia's. Through the middle of the room, right below the chandeliers, was a long oak table, its edges raw and organic in shape. It was flanked by chairs of a similar colour, some draped with furs and knitted blankets. In a wall opposite the table was a fire-place, its details ornate and intricate. Before it lay the tufted rug that Galdinia spent many days sprawled on with Neryda and Drystan, usually neglecting the schoolwork they had been given.

Moving through the library, Galdinia made her way to the back of the room, weaving between the stacks. In one of the far corners of the room lay the hatch that led to one of the few exits from the castle that wasn't patrolled by guards. Pulling the key from the chain around her neck, Galdinia bent down to open the door in the ground. Of course, Neryda and Drystan knew of its whereabouts as well, but Galdinia had chosen not to tell her father or the governor about that fact.

She quickly opened the hatch and climbed down the ladder below, shutting the door behind her. Once in the depths of the rock on which the castle was built, she followed the passageway to the caves beyond. The air was cool and damp and felt refreshing as the princess walked down the tunnel. When she made it to the gate, she unlocked it as she had a hundred times, stepped through, and secured the lock once again, then placed the key back on the chain around her neck.

Suddenly, she was free.

The streets of Elderguard were still quiet on the Second Day of Mourning; the evening before would have provided most of the city's citizens with a reason to roll out of bed late today. Most shop owners and tradespeople would take this week off work. However, some of the city's most beloved bakeries, grocers, fish markets and distilleries would remain open in order for people to buy the necessities for the various celebrations of the week. On the walk through the city streets, Galdinia could hear some shops starting to rouse in the early light, but otherwise, the usually bustling streets were strangely still. Despite there being fewer prying eyes than usual, Galdinia still pulled her cloak's hood close over her face and body, hoping to keep herself concealed from any wandering eyes. The autumn air was crisp enough that she didn't feel overdressed wearing her heavy cloak.

Weaving her way through the streets to the south, she manoeuvred around the dockyard and the fishermen that were arranging their nets for today's catch. Most of the fishers were either Wind Wielders or Water Weavers and would use their gifts to direct their boats and lure the fish to their nets. The docks held the boats of the fishermen, as well as the royal ship and royal sailing boat, which both held a permanent lodging at the docks. Beside the usual vessels, however, were a handful of other ships that Galdinia didn't recognise. She assumed they belonged to those who had visited from other towns for her father's funeral.

She walked in the opposite direction from the decorated ships where the maze of docks became less busy. She sat on an empty jetty away from the bustling docks, from which the fisherman would set sail soon. A few jetties over from her, a pair of children were playing, their laughter travelling across to her over the noise of the fishermen. She was careful to keep her face turned from the soldiers' barracks that sat beside the dockyard and ran along the southernmost tip of the capital. She didn't need a soldier recognising her and insisting upon escorting her back to the castle.

The crystalline blue water below her dangling feet shimmered in the early sun; flecks of green and yellow and pink caught on the dancing surface. She had always enjoyed the ocean, often spending time in the cove near the eastern docks, jumping from the jetties into the plunging depths beneath her. Galdinia, Neryda and Drystan had spent days upon days each summer in those waters. She wondered if they would ever get to do that again.

As she stared into the depths of the cove, she tried to imagine herself controlling the waves as they moved across the surface of the water. She had watched Neryda move most liquids with even the lowest water content without so much as a flick of her wrist. If Galdinia had any kind of connection with water like her mother, surely the ocean was a good place to start.

She tried to feel the rhythm of each wave, her eyes following the movement of the water as it surged in from the sea, moved beneath the jetty, and crashed into the seawall. Absentmindedly, she lifted her hand from her lap and brushed it through the air in time with each ripple and movement of the water below. Had someone who was oblivious to her lack of powers been watching her, they may very well have believed that she was causing the water to move herself.

At this thought, Galdinia dropped her hand, feeling utterly foolish. As though to insult her further, the water continued to move back and forth from the seawall, entirely independently. Galdinia wondered if she would ever get her gift. She'd been told for so many years by her father, Ryden and her friends that the Gods would bless her with her gift when the time was right, when she truly needed it most. Given it was already the Second Day of Mourning and her father had pronounced her as the next ruler, she thought today would be as good as any.

She was pulled from her thoughts of disappointment by the laughter of the children again, followed by a splash and the distinct sound of a water-filled cry. There was now only one child on the jetty and she was looking down into the water, which was rippling rapidly beneath her peering eyes.

"Jaron!" the girl called, kneeling down on the rough timber. Galdinia stood with a start. "He can't swim! Someone help!"

At this, the attention of many passersby turned to the child in her suddenly panic-stricken state as she looked frantically from the water to those on land. From the direction of one of the ornate ships strode a blonde man in a royal blue jacket, talking quietly with another well-dressed man with a full black beard. The first man was pulled from the conversation and looked to the commotion the girl was making just as Galdinia made a move from her own jetty. His eyes flashed a glance at Galdinia before he turned from his friend and hurtled down the docks to the crying child, Galdinia close behind.

"What happened?" the blonde man asked hastily, furiously unbuttoning his jacket as he spoke to the girl, her coiling black hair falling over her face where she wore an expression of sheer terror.

"It's my brother, Jaron, he got too close to the end and fell in," the girl said between fits of tears. "He can't swim and I can't see him anymore!"

The man didn't hesitate another moment; he threw his jacket to the deck and dove off the wooden planks, straight into the depths of the cove. Galdinia rushed forward, coming to kneel beside the upset girl.

"It's okay, he'll be okay," Galdinia said calmly, putting an arm around the girl as she heaved in heavy breaths.

"I was supposed to be looking after him," the girl cried, not taking her eyes from the surface of the water that the blonde man had just disappeared into, not realising who crouched beside her now. "Mother told me not to let him near the water's edge, but he wanted to see me twist the water. Then he got too close and—"

The girl began crying again and Galdinia pulled her into her side. The girl would have only been nine or ten years old, but her sobbing could now be heard across the docks. The faces of many nearby fishermen had turned to look over to where they sat. Galdinia tried to keep the hood of her cloak between her face and their eyes.

She kept her eyes on the water below, the shadows of fish dancing deep below them, tricking her eyes as she searched for the swimming bodies of Jaron and the blonde man. If only Galdinia were a Water Weaver, she could have easily plucked the boy from the water. She wouldn't have needed help and she could have saved him alone.

Now would be fantastic timing, Galdinia silently prayed, wishing more than ever for her gift.

Without warning, the surface of the water broke some five metres beyond the edge of the jetty, the face of the man appearing first, followed by Jaron, who lay limp in his arms.

"Jaron!" The girl's voice broke as she clasped her hands over her mouth, tears still flowing down her cheeks.

The man managed to keep Jaron's head above water as he quickly swam back to the dock. Galdinia rushed forward to take the small boy from his arms, laying him on the jetty in front of his sister. Jaron appeared to be only about six years old and he lay still on the ground before them as his rescuer pulled himself onto the dock, his shoulders heaving in breaths of air as he leaned on all fours over the small boy.

Jaron's sister rushed to his side, placing a hand on her brother's chest, her tears still staining her cheeks. The girl, suddenly calm and focused, closed her eyes and sucked in a deep breath. Moments later,

Jaron spluttered, water shooting from his mouth as his eyes flashed open. He sucked in a few deep breaths and looked up at his sister.

"Kaira." The small boy spoke hoarsely, his eyes squinting in the early sunlight. "Kaira, I swam!"

Kaira glared at her brother as a wide grin grew across his face, the tension in the air deflating.

"No, you did not!" Kaira said firmly, wiping the tears from her face. "You fell in, you had to be rescued, and then I pulled the water from your lungs!"

Jaron's grin faltered for a moment before he said, "But it was so fun!"

Kaira rolled her eyes and huffed. "Mother is going to have my head for this, you know?"

"So," the blonde man said, still trying to catch his breath as he leaned back on his heels, his hands braced on his thighs. "You're... okay... then?"

Jaron looked at the only other person who was soaking wet and realised the flurry of panic he had caused.

"Oh," he said quietly, lifting himself up into a seated position. "Yes, I think so."

The blonde man nodded, then turned his attention to Kaira, still taking deep breaths. "If you're a... Water Weaver... why didn't you... just use your powers?"

"I've never moved such a big body of water before," Kaira said, lifting her hands as though to prove it to him. "It's much harder than it looks. I've only had practice with smaller amounts of water, like what was in his tiny little lungs."

Kaira frowned down at her brother, who didn't seem to like being called "tiny" all that much.

"Hey, I'm not that small!" he whined in protest, crossing his arms over his chest.

"You are!" she countered, standing to her feet. "Thank you for rescuing my annoying little brother."

The blonde man nodded again and waved a hand in reply. Kaira then turned and strode down the jetty.

"Hey! I'm not annoying either!" Jaron squeaked, clamouring to his feet and chasing after his sister. He didn't give Galdinia or his rescuer another look as he squawked at his sister's side.

The children became lost in the tangle of fishermen who were now back to the busy work of loading up their boats, almost ready to set sail. Galdinia laughed in their wake and turned to the blonde man.

Without the flurry of Kaira's tears or the fear of a small child's demise, Galdinia looked at him with clearer eyes. She quickly realised that he didn't look much older than her, his bright eyes far more relaxed now that he wasn't trying to save someone's life.

"Thank you for doing that," Galdinia said quietly, getting to her feet.

"Oh, it's not a problem," the man said, trying to shake off as much water from his clothes as possible before standing up. "I felt like a swim today anyway, so it was good timing."

Galdinia chuckled before bending down to pick up his discarded jacket. "Here."

He took the jacket from her with a smile, now looking up to her face for the first time. His eyes lingered on her for a long moment, as if he was trying to place the face of someone he recognised. If he did recognise her, he didn't say anything; yet Galdinia still pulled her cloak's hood firmer over her hair.

As she looked at him, she noticed a tear in the knee of his trousers.

"It looks like your trousers are ripped," Galdinia said, pointing to his left leg.

"I think they were caught on an oyster shell," he replied, unperturbed.

"I'm sorry they're ruined. If you go to Moya Tailors on Eastern Avenue, I'll have them make you some replacements. They're the best in the city."

"Thank you." The man smiled, pushing up his wet sleeves and draping his jacket over his sodden forearm. Galdinia tried not to take notice of how see-through his shirt had become. "That really isn't necessary, though. I have more clothes on my ship."

"Please, I insist," Galdinia said, secretly glad she wasn't the one that had to jump in the water after the boy; she couldn't imagine how much attention she would have pulled when word of the princess diving into the bay started to spread. He had also saved the life of one of her citizens, even if said citizen had been less than grateful.

The man ran a hand through his dripping hair and let out another laugh. "Alright, then. Thank you. And who exactly should I say will be picking up my bill?"

"How about I take you there now?" Galdinia asked, hoping to repay him sooner than later.

"If you say so," the man replied with a compliant shrug. "I'm Bentley, by the way. Bentley Penrose."

"Neryda," Galdinia returned, taking his dripping, outstretched hand and shaking it briefly.

It wasn't the first time she used her best friend's name instead of her own. Thankfully, many of those who lived outside of the capital didn't actually know what the princess looked like, at least not in any recognisable detail. Although she had her father's smile and her mother's face shape, neither of these traits seemed to make her stand out, and she was often able to keep her identity a secret from those who lived outside the city's walls. It was those in the surrounding streets who would soon be woken by the rising sun that she was more concerned about.

"Nice to meet you, Neryda," Bentley replied, a small smile tugging at the corner of his mouth, creating a dimple in his rosy right cheek. He had the look of someone who was privy to a hilarious secret he couldn't wait to share. "I wish it had been under less dramatic circumstances, though."

"Yes, there's nothing quite like saving a child's life to start your day." Galdinia smiled, leading him back to dry ground and up a side alley between the barracks and the dockyard. "May I ask what you're doing in the capital?"

"Do I not look like a local?" he asked in imitation offence, spreading his arms wide, his hair, sleeves and trousers still dripping.

"Somehow, no, you don't," Galdinia said with a raise of her eyebrows, "but I've lived here my whole life and I can't say I recognise you. The ship also gave it away."

Bentley clicked his fingers in mock disappointment before smiling and looking down at his feet briefly. He seemed to hesitate answering her question and Galdinia watched as the droplets of seawater in his hair caught in the glistening morning light.

"I came in for the funeral yesterday," he said almost gravely, his smile disappearing. "I'm from The Edges and I came on behalf of my family."

"Oh," Galdinia said quietly, looking ahead of herself again as she led him around a corner. Her stomach started to tie itself in knots, wondering how he hadn't recognised her yet from her eulogy in the Crystal Temple. "That's good of you to come for such an occasion."

"Yes, we had hoped to make it onto the island, but by the time I arrived, there was only room left to anchor just off the shore." As Bentley spoke, Galdinia released a silent sigh of relief, her churning stomach settling for a moment. "Were you there too?"

"Yes, I was on the isle," Galdinia replied, glancing at the man quickly; he was watching her from the corner of his eye as they walked, attentive yet casual. "It was a lovely ceremony."

"From what I saw, it really was," he said solemnly, nodding in agreement. "And I must say, I was not expecting the celebration that followed. Who knew the capital was capable of such an unruly and disorderly event?"

Galdinia had heard of the parties that were thrown during Weeks of Mourning past, and she was not ignorant to the true nature of them. She knew that the festivities in honour of her mother included seemingly bottomless barrels of wine and much dancing that continued until sunrise. She did not become aware of this until many years after her mother's passing, of course. Although it may have seemed brazen to outsiders that the capital would celebrate the passing of their royalty in this way, Galdinia, and most of the city, knew this was a sure-fire way to kick the pain that came with death.

"Ah, yes." Galdinia nodded in return, her lips turning up into a knowing smirk. "Elderguard certainly does know how to throw a party."

"Oh no, a party is when a group of friends gather together with a cask of wine or two, a hearty meal and a few rounds of cards," Bentley began, his pseudo disbelief masking the hints of a smirk. "Last night is what could only be described as a drunken tirade of immodesty and reckless abandon."

"Yes, exactly what I said, a party." The pair laughed as they rounded another corner and made their way up Eastern Avenue. "I'm glad you were able to see Elderguard in all its glory."

"So am I." Bentley nodded, looking down at his feet again as they walked, that painfully brilliant smile pulling at the edges of his lips once again. "So what brought you to the docks so early today then, Neryda? Aside from the allure of rotting fish and drowning children."

"I work at a bakery on Main Court, near the square." The lie came easily to Galdinia as she described the location of Raff's bakery. "I was on the night shift preparing today's loaves, so I thought I'd spend some time by the water before going home to rest before tomorrow's early start."

"You don't look like you've been baking for hours," Bentley observed, looking to Galdinia's spotless cloak and the hints of a simple, yet refined dress beneath. "Most bakers I know are covered head to toe in flour."

Galdinia silently cursed herself, trying to find the words to piece together yet another lie.

"I don't love walking around town in my workwear, so I tend to wash it at the bakery. I just threw these on after I finished my shift." She spoke rapidly, her pace quickening, hoping to arrive at Madame Moya's shop before she had to weave another lie. "It's nice to feel more like myself, even if it's for a few minutes at sunrise."

Bentley didn't reply. He just nodded his head in quiet acknowledgement. Galdinia supposed that her final words weren't all that far from the truth.

As they approached the red awning of Moya Tailors, Galdinia slowed to a stop.

"Here we are," she said, turning to knock on the door, ignoring the *Closed* sign that hung in the window.

"You know, not all tradespeople are awake at the same time as bakers," Bentley queried with a raised eyebrow, throwing his jacket over his shoulder.

"Oh really?" Galdinia asked sarcastically, looking from Bentley back to the shopfront, peering into the window.

Bentley didn't reply to this. He just remained standing in the centre of the quiet road with a smirk plastered to his face.

Moments later, Galdinia pulled back from the window, a look of triumph on her face. The door swung open and the chimes of hanging doorbells clattered into the street.

"We don't open for—" The woman at the door paused mid-sentence as she settled her eyeglasses on her nose and focused on Galdinia's face. The woman's silver hair was pulled back in a neat bun and her eccentric sleeping robes fell elegantly from her tiny frame. Madame Moya had been stitching Galdinia's clothes her entire life, having worked for the royal family since her grandparents took the throne. Aside from a few pieces from outside the capital walls that Galdinia made sure not to wear when around Madame Moya, everything she owned had been sewn by the hands of this slight yet spirited elderly woman.

"Good morning, Madame Moya. I'm sorry to bother you so early," Galdinia said, keeping her body between Madame Moya and Bentley, her eyes narrowing on the woman, hoping to silently communicate more than she could with words. "My name is Neryda. I work for Raff over at the bakery."

Although she had to crane her neck to look up at the princess, arguably the most powerful person in the city, her expression was firm. Thankfully, however, she understood Galdinia's purpose and did not miss the inclusion of a name she was all too familiar with. On many occasions, Neryda had joined Galdinia in various fittings in the back room of Madame Moya's shop. While the elderly seamstress did not appreciate the way Neryda sprawled on her chaise or drank seemingly endless cups of tea, she never grew tired of the girl's excitement when she saw Galdinia in one of her creations.

"Ah, yes, Neryda." Madame Moya nodded slowly, her eyes still sceptical as she tried to make sense of the situation. "What can I do for you?"

"This is my new friend, Bentley," Galdinia said, stepping aside to present the sodden mess of a man that stood in the street before the old woman's shop. Bentley waved almost sheepishly. "As you can see, he is in dire need of an outfit change and I was hoping you may be able to be of assistance. Perhaps you could fit him in some of your pre-sewn dress trousers and shirts? There isn't anyone I'd trust in the whole city more than you."

Madame Moya's eyes had not left Galdinia's face. "You know, I am not supposed to open for another three hours."

"You know I wouldn't ask if it wasn't important," Galdinia urged, her eyes now pleading with the woman.

Madame Moya looked from Bentley to Galdinia and back again. Bentley now had an expression of apprehension on his face.

"It is barely six o'clock and you bring me a half-drowned puppy to turn into a stallion," Madame Moya said. After a beat, she threw her hands into the air and turned to stalk away, back into her shop. "Let's go, Pup!"

Bentley hesitated for a moment before moving quickly to Galdinia's side by the door, leaning close to her to whisper, "Did she just call me Pup?"

"Just do as she says and stand very still," Galdinia warned in hushed tones. "You'll be fine, I promise. She's a brilliant woman and tailor."

"But she called me—"

"Trust me, your masculinity doesn't matter, nor exist, for the next twenty minutes or so," Galdinia said, pushing the wet Bentley into the shop before calling out, "Thank you, Madame Moya! I will fix you up later today."

"You're leaving?" Bentley urged, turning back around to stare, dumbfounded, at Galdinia.

"Come on, Pup, you don't want to be walking around in wet rags all day!" Madame Moya's impatient voice rang out from somewhere behind racks of dresses and shelves of elegant material.

"I really must be going." Galdinia's words turned into a yawn. "Remember, the night shift? My bed is calling me. I promise you'll be safe with her."

Bentley looked into the depths of the shop, fear and trepidation painting his face.

"Should I survive the ordeal that awaits me beyond that display of corsets," Bentley said, turning back once more to Galdinia, "will I get to see you again?"

"Should you survive," Galdinia said, smiling as she started to close the door between her body and his, "you may very well see me at the festivities this evening."

Galdinia felt safe leaving him with one last lie; she knew that she didn't have any intention to be at that evening's party in the square and imagined he'd be long gone back to The Edges before she left the castle again. A part of her wouldn't have minded sharing a drink with him at the tavern, though.

"Little Pup!" Madame Moya's voice was clipped and impatient.

"You owe me a very big glass of wine," Bentley said, walking backwards into the shop.

"This is my favour to you, remember?" Galdinia asked with a smile.

"A very interesting favour." Bentley disappeared behind a shelf with one final flash of his teeth and dimple. Instantly, Galdinia could hear Madame Moya's instructing words.

"Now, let's dispose of this sad excuse of a jacket—how much did you pay for this? Whoever made it utterly swindled you. What are you waiting for? Out of those rags, Pup!"

Galdinia chuckled at the thought of Bentley undressing in front of the old woman. As she blushed, she closed the shop door with the clanging of the bells attached.

As she walked through the city streets back towards the castle, she tried to ignore the warm feeling that made itself known in her stomach. It was a feeling she hadn't experienced in a long time, and she wasn't quite sure how she felt about it.

IO

Galdinia took the long way back to the castle, relishing the quiet walk home that she knew would be hard to come by in the following days. While some citizens had stirred from their slumber, most kept to themselves, shielding their still drunken eyes from the glaring sun. Galdinia imagined that Neryda would be feeling the same way in a few hours when she finally awoke.

Upon arriving back at the castle through her secret passage, Galdinia felt a rumble deep in her stomach, prompting her to head towards the kitchens in the southern end of the building. She navigated her way through the stairwell made for the servants that curled between the walls of the castle. These provided more direct and less obstructed passage between the main corridors. Galdinia used these entrances, hallways and stairs frequently, finding it much faster to manoeuvre through the castle when she couldn't be stopped by someone or something that was vying for her attention.

The kitchens were the liveliest rooms of the castle at any given moment of the day. Here, the cooks and attendants would prepare and distribute food for the royal family, visitors and those working in the castle. There hadn't been many guests recently due to her father's ill-health, but in normal circumstances, the king would have visitors from neighbouring cities stay in their guest rooms, and the Syndicate would meet with the king a number of times a week in their own chambers in the eastern wing of the castle. Galdinia's father used to say that the Syndicate only met in the castle so they could be fed at least two meals a day by Miss Giles. Miss Giles ran the kitchens, and she had prepared most meals for Galdinia in her life and was a queen in her own right. Her kitchens were run as a tight ship, and she knew it.

When Galdinia entered the kitchens, Miss Giles was in the thick of the morning preparations, calling orders to sous chefs and handing plates to attendants. Galdinia took a seat in the corner at a small table by the fireplace. Galdinia was known to enjoy a meal or two a week at this table with Miss Giles; it often turned into a rushed snack between mealtimes, but Miss Giles never denied the company of the princess.

"Good morning, dear. I'm sorry I've not yet prepared your breakfast," Miss Giles said, not taking her eyes from the eggs frying in the pan before her. "Your Brigitte said you would not wake until at least nine o'clock."

"Please don't fuss, Miss Giles," Galdinia assured her, unhooking her cloak and settling into her seat. "I don't imagine anyone thought I'd be awake at this hour."

"Nevertheless, what would you like for breakfast, dear?" Miss Giles asked. She was one of the few people in the kingdom who regularly called Galdinia anything other than her full title.

"Eggs smell quite good," Galdinia said, craning her neck to look into the pan in front of Miss Giles from across the room. "And perhaps a spearmint and oak bark tea, if you have it."

"Certainly, dear," Miss Giles replied, plating the now cooked eggs, pairing them with a relish and a piece of toasted bread straight from the buttered pan beside her. After passing it to Galdinia, she moved to the boiling pot of water over the fire in the corner and scooped some into a cup. She then stirred in her concoction of tea from an amber jar. After delivering it to the princess, she turned back to her pan and cracked in two more eggs.

"I'm sorry, I've taken someone's breakfast," Galdinia said, looking down at the perfectly cooked breakfast before her.

"Not to worry, dear. We always have a constant stream of eggs cooking in here at this time," Miss Giles said with a smile, jiggling the pan. "You just happen to rank a little higher than the original recipient."

Galdinia smiled, then took a bite of her breakfast. Her body instantly warmed as the toast started soaking up the dregs of alcohol left in her stomach.

"Miss Giles, this relish is delightful. Is it new?"

"I bought it from Raff yesterday," Miss Giles responded, flipping the new eggs over in the pan. "He's been working on this recipe for some time, but I think he's finally perfected it. It's the late autumn tomatoes, I think, that really made this batch shine. He's a talented man, that Raff!"

"He certainly is," Galdinia said, taking another few mouthfuls of her breakfast. Miss Giles flipped the eggs one more time on her searing cast iron pan before turning them out onto a plate, garnishing them as she did Galdinia's. Galdinia then noticed an identical plate already dressed on the bench.

"Kayda!" Miss Giles called across the room to a group of maids clustered together near the sinks, washing the dishes. A small blonde girl, no more than fifteen years old, scurried from the gaggle of maids, wiping her hands on her apron as she approached Miss Giles. "Take these plates to the breakfast meeting; they should be the last two." Miss Giles handed the plates to the mouse-like girl and sent her off before quickly adding, "Raelle, accompany Kayda and keep your eyes on the plates too please; I don't need any more smashed crockery today."

Galdinia watched the girls go up the stairs she had come from earlier as she took another bite.

"There's a meeting this morning, Miss Giles?" Galdinia asked, watching the woman's back stiffen for a moment before she took the pan off the fire she had it resting on.

"The Syndicate is in a meeting." Her response was brief and she busied her hands with utensils.

"The Syndicate?" Galdinia questioned, her fork lingering in front of her lips. "What are they meeting about? And why wasn't I made aware?"

"I'm sorry, Your Highness, I don't know." Galdinia wasn't sure which question Miss Giles was directly responding to, but she noted that the woman had gone back to a formal greeting, something she only ever did in uncomfortable circumstances.

"Miss Giles," Galdinia pressed, her eyes boring into the back of the woman's head, focusing on her greying curls. "What is the Syndicate meeting about in my castle?"

Miss Giles lowered her hands to the edge of the bench before turning to Galdinia with a sigh. "I don't know what they're meeting about, but there were a few handsome young men arriving by carriage about twenty minutes ago, or so the maids who were collecting the eggs this morning told me. Caused them to drop three fresh eggs because they were too busy ogling them; I nearly had a fit!"

Galdinia frowned as she looked at Miss Giles, her response not quite sufficient.

"I promise, dear, that's all I know. Governor Ryden wanted enough plates of eggs ready this morning for a Syndicate gathering, plus another five, and it seems those were for the men who arrived this morning."

Galdinia looked from Miss Giles to the girls across the room, who were not-so-subtly listening to their conversation while washing and drying dishes. The princess' frown was still set into her brow.

"Thank you, Miss Giles," Galdinia said through gritted teeth as she took the final bite of her breakfast before standing and taking her cloak from the back of her chair. "A delicious breakfast, as always."

Galdinia walked from the room with a glorious sweep of her cloak, heading back up the narrow staircase she had come from, leaving Miss Giles apprehensive in her kitchens.

When she arrived at the top landing on the third level, she came face-to-face with Kayda and Raelle, their hands now empty. The two girls gasped and immediately bowed their heads, now blocking Galdinia's way.

"Thank you, girls, as you were," she said, marching past the maids before they had a chance to straighten their posture.

Galdinia strode down the hall towards the eastern wing, passing the top of the main staircase and walking beyond the drawing room. She paused a few feet from the entrance to the wing; from down the hall she could hear the echoing of chatter, clinking glasses and cutlery. Laughter and the sound of hearty voices emanated from the meeting room at the end of the hallway. Galdinia rushed down the remainder of the way, placed both hands on the doors that separated her from the secretive meeting and pushed them open.

The room was similar in style to that of the drawing room but on a larger scale. The oval table in the centre could house at least twenty individuals and currently appeared to be at capacity. At the head of the table was Ryden, leaning over his plate of breakfast, laughing with another greying man to his left. Around the table were a myriad of Syndicate members and scattered between them were young men who Galdinia did not recognise. She assumed that these were the guests that Miss Giles had referred to.

The doors struck their neighbouring walls with a thud, causing all conversation to cease and all eyes to turn to look at the princess. Some of the older Syndicate members had to awkwardly crane their necks to see Galdinia as she stood in the doorway assessing the room, her brows knitted in concern.

"Princess?" Ryden asked, his voice dripping with confusion and surprise; he pushed back his chair and quickly rose. "I wasn't expecting to see you this morning."

"Strange," Galdinia countered, "I could say the same for you."

Ryden hurried to the princess' side and stood between her and the others in the room.

"This is a surprise, Your Highness," Ryden said in a flurry. "May we speak outside?"

The governor motioned to the hallway. With a frown, Galdinia turned and moved back through the doorway with Ryden, the governor closing the heavy doors behind them.

"At what point did holding secret meetings in my home become part of our agreement that you would have my best interest in mind, Governor Ryden?" Galdinia placed emphasis on his title as she spoke, unease coating her voice.

"I can explain, Princess," he said almost sheepishly, holding his hands in front of him as though in defence. "Perhaps we could meet later this morning for a more formal meeting."

"I don't think so, Governor," Galdinia retaliated, crossing her arms over her chest. "Explain yourself. Now."

Ryden hesitated before addressing her command. "Before your

father passed away, he and I pondered the possibility of you taking the throne without your gift. As we discussed yesterday, it isn't strictly possible for one to be coronated without their gift, but there are ways around this, like becoming an interim ruler."

"I'm still not seeing the correlation between my ruling and my closest ally using my home for classified meetings." The princess was getting impatient.

"So," Ryden went on quickly, "he floated the idea of having someone by your side at the coronation in order to legitimise you as queen through their own gift."

"You mean like an advisor?" Galdinia questioned, eyebrows raised.

"Well..." The governor hesitated. "More like a husband."

Galdinia's eyes flashed darkly as her jaw dropped, her arms tightening and her hands balling into fists. She felt heat rising from her chest, up her neck and to her face. Surely, she misheard him.

"Excuse me?" she asked, her voice softer than it was before, barely a rasp but even more lethal.

"We think it would be best for you to take the throne with a king by your side. The Syndicate also agrees that with a husband you could be crowned queen, regardless of the status of your gift."

"You mean by the end of the Week of Mourning?" Galdinia gawked, finding her voice.

It was at this moment that she realised who the men were on the other side of the door, happily enjoying a breakfast with her city's officials.

"They're suitors!" Her voice bounced off the walls and shuddered down the empty halls, her fury unable to be contained. "You thought you'd just choose a husband for me to marry at the end of the week, say, 'Job well done!' and be done with it?"

"Princess, you must understand, we have already gone through multiple groups of candidates before today and we have narrowed it down to five wonderful suitors who we think you'll really like."

Galdinia took pause, her eyes boring into her governor's. "How long have you been going through this process?"

"About six weeks, give or take—"

"So while he was on his deathbed, my father was cherry-picking lords from across the kingdom?" Galdinia was overcome with disbelief, and she spoke frankly, not intimidated by Ryden's age nor his status.

"He wanted to make sure he left you with a suitable option," Ryden said, lowering his voice. "He couldn't bear the thought of leaving you on your own."

Galdinia was reeling now. "So for six weeks you've been looking for a man for me to marry without asking *me?*" Ryden went to speak, but Galdinia continued, the words rushing from her. "And you didn't think for a single moment that perhaps the future queen may wish to know about this?"

"Princess, I—"

"And what is the purpose of today's meeting then?" Galdinia asked, her words hot. "Were you hoping to make them battle for my affection? Or perhaps have the citizens of Elderguard vote on their favourite? One of them will be the king after all, and evidently, my opinion holds very little weight."

"Your Highness, that isn't the case at all," Ryden said, holding up his hands in defence. "What with the stress of your father's illness and your pending coronation, we didn't want to worry you with such matters."

"So you thought you'd just present them to me with one week to decide who I might like to spend the rest of my life with? Let's not even consider the fact that perhaps I don't want to get married at nineteen years of age." Galdinia scoffed. "Surely neither you nor my father thought it was truly in my best interest to keep this from me."

"Galdinia, I don't think—"

"Sorry I'm late!" A bright voice rang through the hallway, one of cheer and optimism. One that, unfortunately, Galdinia recognised. "I had a bit of an accident this morning that held me up."

Slowly, Galdinia turned and was faced with Bentley, who was adjusting his new cravat as he sauntered up the hallway. As he looked up from his hands, his face fell in confusion.

"You?" Galdinia asked, her eyes narrowing on the blonde boy who was now bone dry and in dress clothes reminiscent of the ones in Madame Moya's windows.

"Well, this is a nice surprise," Bentley said with a smile. "I wasn't expecting to see you until tonight, Neryda."

"Neryda?" Ryden asked regretfully, starting to catch on, while Bentley's eyes still swam with a hint of confusion. "You've met?"

"He's one of them?" Galdinia asked, turning back to Ryden, venom in her voice.

"Am I missing something?" Bentley asked, coming to stand beside Galdinia and Ryden.

"It seems that I am the one who has been denied any real information today," Galdinia said, pointing her frustration at Ryden.

"Princess—" Ryden began, taking a step towards Galdinia.

"Get them out of my home," Galdinia said quickly, taking a step back from the two men, Bentley's face shifting from confusion to realisation. "I want to see the Syndicate in my throne room in fifteen minutes."

"Princess, please wait," Ryden practically begged as Galdinia turned and walked back down the hallway towards her chambers.

"I want them gone," she said, her voice burning, "now!"

"Princess?" she heard Bentley say as she turned a corner and disappeared from sight.

II

GALDINIA HAD ALWAYS DREAMED THAT SHE WOULD BE QUEEN SOMEDAY. Of course, at the ripe old age of seven, she assumed this meant she could wear pretty ball gowns, go to parties, and ride a horse through town, where she would bestow gifts of flowers and cakes upon her loyal subjects. She wanted to be everything she assumed her mother was. As she grew older, however, she came to realise that being queen involved difficult decisions and arguments rather than sugary treats and roses. It was as though each year she learned something new about the title and slowly, the disillusionment grew.

When she was eleven, Galdinia had to experience the earth-shattering realisation that queens didn't stay in bed until midday, but were expected to be by their husband's side each morning to address the court. At fourteen, she learnt that queens often had to miss their meals for vital meetings with dignitaries. On her sixteenth birthday, her father had to leave for a battle across the country, and she was informed by an attendant that her mother often went with him, even once on the anniversary of their wedding. And now at nineteen, Galdinia was slapped in the face with the rude awakening that queens could have their husbands chosen for them. And what was worse: she may not be able to be queen without a king.

In a flurry of rage and frustration, Galdinia slammed the door to her chambers as she crossed the threshold. Neryda sat up in dazed confusion, her eyes still closed, her curls of russet hair curtaining her face haphazardly.

"What—what's happening?" Neryda croaked out, looking around wildly. Galdinia stomped into the room, throwing her cloak over a nearby armchair.

"Suitors!" Galdinia practically cried, resting her hands on her hips. "They have suitors for me!"

"Suitors?"

"Yes, five of them!" Galdinia went on, now starting to pace the length of the end of her bed.

"Who has five suitors?" Neryda asked, trying to push herself up against the headboard with her exhausted limbs.

"Me, apparently! Ryden organised five suitors to come to the castle for breakfast with the Syndicate this morning."

"I take it that you were not invited to this meal," Neryda said between yawns as she pushed a bundle of hair from her face.

"No, I wasn't. I found out about it from the maids in the kitchens!" Galdinia's fingers clenched around the fabric of the skirt of her dress as she paced. "So I went to see what all the fuss was about, thinking that surely—*surely*—Ryden hadn't gone behind my back like this. What a fool I was! There they all were, happily chatting with members of the Syndicate."

"Were any of them cute?" Neryda asked, pulling the blankets up to her waist and adjusting the strap of the nightgown she had taken from Galdinia's closet the evening before.

"Neryda!" Galdinia scolded her friend, pausing her steps to glare at her.

"Sorry," Neryda replied with a cheeky grin.

"I didn't even look at any of them. Well, except the one I met this morning. Oh, *that* was a fun surprise!" Galdinia's voice was dripping with sarcasm.

"Who did you meet this morning?"

"One of the suitors. I met him down at the docks," Galdinia explained, pacing again as she waved a hand in the air so as to diminish the moment. "He dove into the bay after a child who fell in, practically saving the young boy's life. I took him to Madame Moya to get new clothes because I felt I should, because I'm the princess, you know, duty and all that. Not that titles mean anything to anyone at the moment!"

"So he knew who you were?" Neryda queried.

"Well, no," Galdinia admitted, her hands finding their way back into the tangles of her skirt. "I used your name. I thought it would be simpler to avoid princess talk."

"So what did he do?" Neryda asked, raising her tired eyebrows.

"He didn't tell me who he was, not really," Galdinia said, beginning her tirade once again. "He gave me his name, and that was all. If he was chosen by Ryden and my father, then I imagine he's a lord."

"Your father?"

"Oh, that's the best part!" Galdinia said sardonically, coming to a halt, bracing her hands on the wooden end of the bed, staring at her friend. "My father set this up with Ryden weeks ago. They have been going through rounds of possible suitors and narrowed it down to these five, as if I'm some kind of farm animal being auctioned off at a market!"

"For what purpose?"

"They believe that having a promised and powerful betrothed by my side will give me a greater claim to the throne if, you know, my gift doesn't arrive in time."

"It's a little traditional, but I can see their concern." Galdinia's eyes narrowed on her friend and Neryda quickly explained herself. "Neither Ryden nor your father want to see anyone else on the throne, other than you. They especially don't want to see your uncle and aunt worm their way into being crowned, so they likely set this up as a precaution. Without your gift, there's not a lot the Syndicate can do. If they could find a loophole, like a gifted lord who could legitimise your coronation, then I can see their logic."

Galdinia stared at her friend in silence. Although Neryda often had a questionable influence on Galdinia's decision making when it came to sporadic and spontaneous social outings, she was by far the more pragmatic of the two. Galdinia rationalised the world with her emotions, while Neryda did so with her wits. Although the princess understood Neryda's reasoning, she was still angered by it.

"But why make this decision without me? I'm the one that's going to hypothetically marry one of these men!"

"Oh, and you seem so pleased about the prospect." Neryda chuckled. "They knew that this is how you would react; better to do it when you had no other option rather than when you could have just rejected the idea as preposterous. Not to mention your father's health—there's no way you would have left his bedside to meet with suitors. They know you well, my friend."

Galdinia let out a huff of air, frustrated that both her best friend, her departed father, and her most trusted advisor knew her so well.

"I'm not saying that what they did was right, but I can understand why they chose to do it like this." Neryda yawned, speaking as though they were deciding what they would eat for breakfast. "You're feeling this the most because someone else is trying to make a fairly hefty decision for you, so you should be mad. I would be. But I think they truly did have your best interest in mind."

"I still can't believe they were having the meeting in the first place, and in my home, of all places," Galdinia said softly, not willing to give up her annoyance just yet. "I was so mad. I ordered them out of the castle."

"That's one way to make a lasting impression on them."

"I said it to Ryden, not all of them," Galdinia amended. "And Bentley too, I suppose."

"Bentley?" Neryda asked.

"Fish boy, from this morning." Galdinia rolled her eyes. "And now I've asked for the Syndicate to meet me in the throne room."

Neryda didn't reply. She simply looked at her friend with wide eyes.

"I'm tired of having decisions made for me just because I haven't got my gift yet," Galdinia said, her voice finally finding an even tone. "I want a seat at the table—better yet, a throne. They need to know that."

"Good plan," Neryda said with an approving nod.

"And I need to meet them in about five minutes."

"Make me proud."

∼

Ceremonially, during the Week of Mourning, no court was to be held. It was considered uncouth to go about usual business when the capital was mourning the loss of one of their rulers. When the late queen passed, Bartemus refused to sit on the throne for two weeks; he had Ryden deal with any particularly pressing matters, but there was no way he would spend a moment doing his regular duties until he properly mourned his wife. After the Week of Mourning, he and Galdinia spent a week in the mountains together, playing in the snow, reading by the fire and shedding quiet tears by candlelight. There were guards stationed at the exit of their winter estate, but Galdinia didn't notice them. All she knew was that she and her father were away together, without her mother. She kept asking where her mother was and Bartemus resigned to trying to distract her each time she asked. Despite her mother's funeral and Ryden's attempts to rationalise the situation, her tiny heart was incapable of understanding that her mother was truly gone.

On day fourteen, the king decided to return to Elderguard, leaving behind his anguish and bereavement. The next day he was on the throne, crown on head, addressing his Syndicate as though he had been there all along.

Galdinia respected her father for this and was glad proper time was given to her mother's mourning, and she too intended on mourning her father appropriately.

But she also knew that she needed to mark her territory and take what was rightfully hers, regardless of how the Syndicate might interpret this impromptu meeting. Time was ticking and she needed to be the queen her father believed she was.

As the princess walked into the throne room, all eyes turned to her. Ahead of her, the Syndicate members stood in front of their chairs, which sat in two rows before the dais that held the throne. The room was longer than it was wide and the carpet that rolled out from the entrance to the throne was turquoise blue with gold trim. She walked between the two rows of chairs, not taking her eyes from the throne before her. It was equally delicate and commanding. The throne's back fanned out in a maze of solid gold vines and flowers, arching up to a point in the centre, haloing the one who sat in it. Galdinia had watched her father sit on this throne countless times and she herself had crept into this cavernous room as a child to sit on it and pretend she was a queen. She remembered feeling far too small for the seat then and she wondered how she might feel today as she attempted to command the room.

When she made it to the top of the dais, she felt a lump twist in her throat. She hadn't seen her father in his rightful place in over three months and she wondered how long her mind would be able to hold the memories of him as king. She forced the thought down with a deep breath and turned to face the Syndicate.

The princess sat and a buzz of adrenaline flurried through her chest as she came to the tangible realisation of where she was sitting and whom she sat before. She silently reeled with anticipation and terror.

"Syndicate members," Galdinia said with an air of authority she didn't think she had before sitting on this throne. "Please, be seated."

Each Syndicate member bowed their head briefly before taking their own seats. Galdinia noted that Ryden sat front and centre, just to the right of the aisle.

"I have requested your presence here today for an impromptu yet vital meeting." Galdinia spoke evenly, drawing her authority from the throne on which she sat. "I recognise that holding court during the Week of Mourning is unusual. However, it is critical that I speak with you all today."

"Your Majesty." Ryden stood and bowed his head as he addressed the princess, his tone far more formal than he had been in the hallway earlier.

"Yes, Governor?" Hesitantly, Galdinia allowed him to interrupt her.

"While we honour you and the position your father so graciously bestowed on you, we fear that this may not be the most respectful time to hold court. You are, undoubtedly, our future queen, but we do wish to honour your father in this sacred week."

Galdinia took pause.

She knew that there was truth to Ryden's words, and she could feel the child inside of her recoil as he spoke, as though she were being scolded at the dinner table for eating before giving thanks. Perhaps he was right. Perhaps this was a mistake.

Galdinia glanced across the hall to Neryda, who stood just inside the doors of the throne room, her eyes fixed on her friend. She raised her eyebrows, as though to say, *Don't forget who you are.*

Galdinia took a deep breath and turned back to face her Syndicate.

"I appreciate your candour, Governor, as well as your desire to pay respects to my late father." Galdinia allowed a soft smile to flitter over her lips; she didn't want her first rebuke to seem too harsh. "It seems, however, that in order to respect the king's wishes—the king that you have so diligently served for twenty years—you are going to need to respect my wishes, given that he did declare me as queen. I would also venture to say that despite this need for respect that you so duly hold, you were not afraid to interrupt my plans for the first evening of the Week of Mourning last night, right after my father's funeral, to read his will with traitors and enemies alike. Similarly, I don't believe it was particularly respectful to host meetings in search for a suitor I have no interest in marrying, in my home, without my knowledge. That being said, I think this is the most appropriate way to honour my father and his wishes."

"Yes, but—"

"I'm not finished, Governor."

Galdinia's face dropped and she looked down at the man who promised to take care of her after her father's death. Her eyes then scanned the other faces of the Syndicate as they looked on with a range of expressions: some were stunned, others looked proud, while some looked as though they were secretly enjoying the berating of the governor. Ryden sat as Galdinia started to speak again.

"I would not hesitate to say that in order to respect the king in this time, we need to do what he would want: we need to keep this throne out of the hands of his brother and Valah, who both pine after it. This isn't a secret to anyone, not even to our loyal subjects who roam the streets right now, hoping the rightful heir will take the throne at the end of the week." Galdinia crossed one leg over the other beneath the fabric of her dress that gathered at her feet. "That is why I propose that we begin plans now for my coronation on the final Day of Mourning, regardless of my marriage title."

Although she failed to mention her lack of powers, Galdinia knew that the entire room would fill in that blank for her. She charged on immediately.

"In preparation for my impending crowning, I have a number of stipulations I would like to make." Galdinia tried to maintain the authority in her voice as she went on. "Firstly, I wish to be part of all goings-on with regard to arrangements for my future, whether that be policy, national relations, the colour dress I am to wear to my coronation or"—her eyes crossed to Ryden—"the suitors that you wish me to consider. I am still the princess and I wish to be considered as such in all future conversations."

The Syndicate members looked at one another, heads nodding, accompanied by whispers of agreement.

"Go on, Princess," Ryden said, reaching a hand out for Galdinia to continue.

"I don't believe I require a suitor. For many years, my father ruled Crysterra alone, and while I understand that he was more experienced than me and also had his gift, I believe I have had a unique and meaningful introduction into the ruling of our great country. I am aware that my youth and lack of powers may be cause for concern, but I am also aware of how to distribute national taxes, communicate with the captain about military strategy and, as it seems, corral, organise and maintain court. Although these are certainly not the full extent of my royal duties, they are some of the more important ones. Thus, I do not see how marrying a noble husband at the age of nineteen would legitimise me further in my coronation. I will find a husband when I am ready."

Once again, the Syndicate looked to each other, whispers travelling between the members. Ryden's neighbour, Captain Ilyon, leaned in and said a few quiet words into his ear. This made Galdinia's fear rear itself once again; her fingers wriggled in her lap and she could feel the dull ache resurface in her chest.

"Do you have any other requests at this time, Your Highness?" Ryden asked dutifully from the front row.

"No, Governor," Galdinia said coolly, trying to steady her jittery body.

"Princess," Ryden addressed Galdinia as he stood to his feet again, inhaling deeply before speaking. "You know that I—*we*—want nothing more than for you to sit on that throne as the true Queen of Crysterra. As you said, I have served your parents for twenty years and my allegiance to your family is unwavering and will stay with me to my grave. However, my only concern is that we are not currently following the wishes of your father. He, more than anyone else, knows how strong and capable you are; if he didn't, I truly believe he wouldn't have declared you as queen in his will. But he did have his parameters—"

"Were these parameters in his will?" Galdinia questioned, her eyebrows raising to mirror her voice.

"They were not, Your Majesty. Your father confided in me personally, knowing that he could trust me, knowing that you would trust me." These words hurt Galdinia more than they should have. For a moment, she considered backing down, but she steadied her hands on the cool arms of the throne and pushed away her concerns. "You know that I think you are more than capable of taking the throne. But as the laws state, in order to become King or Queen of Crysterra, the heir in question must have their gift bestowed on them by the Gods. There is also the concern of your age.

"Our great kingdom has not seen a ruler younger than twenty in centuries. There are many decisions that have to be made as ruler—some terribly difficult decisions—and the Syndicate does not believe this should be placed on the shoulders of a child. While I know you are not a child—in fact, you haven't been for a long time—this is the Syndicate's concern. There are a number of edicts around young rulers, but just as I am loyal to you, I am also loyal to this country and its sacred laws." After a brief pause, he spoke again. "So I have a proposition for you that I believe will please both the future queen and the Syndicate."

Galdinia looked at Ryden with narrowed eyes, but she nodded briefly, inviting him to present his case.

"Come the Seventh Day of Mourning, we will have appropriately mourned the passing of the king; we will have the final service that morning and as per tradition, that evening will bring with it your coronation as our new queen. Between now and then, we will not hold court, nor gather privately without your consent; you have my word that you will be consulted before the Syndicate meets this week, should we need to."

Galdinia nodded, glad to have had her first request granted.

Ryden went on. "With regard to your coronation, the laws that the Syndicate holds about an heir without their gift state that the prince or princess in question may be 'contracted' to another of nobility who has been gifted with their power from the Gods. Now, to some this could mean marriage, or"—Galdinia could tell that the governor was choosing his words carefully—"this may mean an engagement. You could be deemed Queen of Crysterra whilst engaged to a noble with a gift, making your betrothed a prince. Upon your marriage, well, he of course would become king, and you would avoid becoming merely an interim ruler."

"I do not yet see how I am to be pleased by this plan. I think I made it abundantly clear that I don't wish to marry so young."

"My suggestion, Princess, is that you should take some time this week to get to know the suitors that we have chosen for you—rather, *suggested* for you—as you may very well be surprised by them. I would be shocked if a group of men who were selected by your father and myself did not include at least one viable prospect. All of them are age appropriate, come from noble families and, of course, have been given their gift. You have six more days of the Week of Mourning, which is full of celebrations, feasts, sermons and of course, the banquet on the Sixth Day, all of which can be used as time for you to not only pay your respects to your father, but also start your ruling duties."

"Like finding a husband?" Galdinia scoffed, leaning back into the throne.

"Well, if it means you will become queen, then yes. That is your duty to your country."

The governor's words hung heavy before her. She hadn't once considered that by agreeing to the Syndicate's plan she would be serving her country, just as a queen should. She hadn't thought that finding an eligible suitor would be the right thing to do as future queen. For if she didn't, she knew the Syndicate would not be able to break the laws, and the throne would quickly be challenged by her aunt and uncle, and also likely Valah, after the Week of Mourning.

Was it her duty to forgo her own happiness—and stubbornness—in order to properly serve her kingdom?

Galdinia sat up straight again and looked down at the governor. "So you're still suggesting that in the next six days I choose from your group of suitors a fiancé? A lifelong partner to rule with?"

"Yes. I know it seems rushed, but I only ask that you try. At this stage, it is our only option until your gift comes and I simply hope that you find one of them suitable enough to promise to marry in the future. You can be engaged for another year or even five years, if you'd like, and get married when you are ready. Of course we hope that the Gods will give you your gift before your coronation, but this is our safety net, as it were."

Galdinia could hear the earnest tone of his voice as he spoke. The Syndicate was desperate to have her crowned, that much was clear. But were they so desperate because they also had a legitimate fear that she wouldn't receive her gift this week? Perhaps this was the only way to guarantee becoming queen. If the Gods weren't willing to give her her gift, Galdinia would have to get the crown herself.

It took every fibre of the princess' being to utter a single word: "Okay."

The governor let out a silent sigh of relief and smiled up at Galdinia, his serious exterior cracking for a moment.

"I will meet with your chosen five tomorrow morning for brunch and I shall spend the rest of the week attempting to get to know these men. I don't promise that I will like any of them, but if this gives us a higher chance of rightfully taking the throne on the Seventh Day of Mourning, then I agree."

"Wonderful," Ryden said thankfully, and Galdinia moved to stand, but the governor's words kept her in her seat. "I have one final stipulation to address."

Galdinia eyed Ryden carefully before nodding for him to continue.

"In a perfect world, you would already have your gift and be able to wield it freely and with command." *Thank you for the reminder*, Galdinia thought, forcing herself to bite her tongue. "I pray each day that the Gods will bestow on you your gift in a timely fashion. Although we cannot speed up the time in which your spiritual ordination will occur, we are still able to prepare for it. I propose that while you spend time this week getting to know our suitors, you should also spend time each day with Captain Ilyon at the soldiers' barracks learning how to use and control your incoming power."

Galdinia was taken aback. She wasn't sure what she thought the governor was going to suggest when he started talking about her gift, but she hadn't imagined it to be training in preparation for powers she did not yet have.

"How exactly can I train to use something I do not yet possess?" Galdinia spoke her thoughts, looking from Ryden to Ilyon with questioning eyes.

"If I may, Your Majesty," the captain said as he stood from his seat across the aisle from Ryden. "I have trained countless soldiers in the art of battle, both with and without a gift. They are drafted and sent to me as children; in a matter of weeks they leave my training as men."

Galdinia couldn't help but think of Drystan as the captain spoke; she could feel his newly calloused hands in hers, his restless eyes staring back at her. She had experienced firsthand just how quickly someone could change once they donned their onyx armour and slicing sword.

"Preparing a soldier to use their powers, whether evident or not, is crucial. And, possibly more important, learning how to defend against said powers is invaluable."

"So you want to turn me into a soldier?" Galdinia asked incredulously. While she had experience with a bow and arrow after accompanying her father on numerous hunting trips, she had had little experience with any real danger.

"No," Ilyon said mildly. "I want to help you become a queen that will lead her soldiers."

The silence hung painfully once again as the princess considered her options. She supposed that her continual prayers had not yet been answered, so doing something practical to possibly help speed up the process sounded appealing. However, the thought of spending hours in the barracks did not sound particularly pleasant.

It is your duty.

"What time am I to be at the barracks?" Galdinia finally conceded.

"Feed yourself a large lunch and meet me there afterwards."

"Today?"

"Time is of the essence."

"Very well." Galdinia turned her attention back to the governor. "Ryden, please ask Miss Giles to prepare a brunch banquet on the terrace tomorrow morning for seven guests."

"Seven?" Ryden questioned, looking up at his future queen.

"You don't expect me to do this alone, do you, Governor? Of course Lady Neryda will be joining me in my search to find a husband." Galdinia's words were sharp; she didn't expect to find a husband in six days, but she thought she might as well allow her best friend to revel in the madness of it all with her.

Galdinia stood, and so did each member of the Syndicate, once again bowing their heads. The princess strode past them, up the centre aisle and to the door where Neryda stood, beaming.

"Court adjourned," Galdinia called over her shoulder before gliding from the room with her best friend at her side.

12

Upon arrival back in the west, Valah took her seat in the drawing room, placing her parents' sceptre carefully by her side. Even with Valah's powers as a Wind Wielder pushing their ship upstream through the Western Vein, it had been a long journey home after the funeral and will reading. However, she did not intend on wasting a minute in her preparations for the days ahead. At her request, Reynard and Captain Kelting took their respective seats at the table, along with Nova, Valah's own high priestess.

Reynard had always been wary of Nova, with her potions and long golden hair that was adorned with pearls, gemstones and feathers. She wore a similar garb to that of Saena, the high priestess of the capital, but she looked more rugged, tired even, as though the many years of living in the Wetlands had been wearing on her. Her once rosy skin was now dull and sunken. As a young priestess, she served in the capital, but after the fall of the Pyrins forty years prior, she fled the city, her allegiance to Valah's family outweighing her desire to live in opulence. When she finally located Valah in the Wetlands years after the Elderwins took the throne, she took it upon herself to serve the only remaining Pyrin, hoping to one day become high priestess of the capital, serving the rightful queen.

The woman was loyal to Valah, Reynard was sure of that, but he had the distinct feeling that she was working as a rudder to guide the future queen in a particular direction that did not always align with his own course. Whenever she was in the room, Reynard kept one hand on the hilt of his sword at his hip, aware of the exits closest to both him and Valah.

"We have six days." Valah placed her hands neatly on the table before her, not allowing her anger and frustration to bubble into more than a simmer. "We have six days to secure the throne before the Syndicate does all it can to make that brat queen."

While her face remained calm and the muscles in her jaw barely tightened, Valah nearly spat her final words. She could hardly believe she was having this conversation.

"I do hope that at least one of you has an idea we can actually use for our benefit." Valah looked around the room at her most trusted advisors. "I have no interest in becoming an interim ruler. I will be queen. How can we take the capital?"

"We did a lot of good work in the outskirts of The Hook this last week," Kelting began, breaking the painful silence. "While I didn't manage to infiltrate The Hook itself—we all know how secretive Lord and Lady Lidel are—I did make the mass of our army known to the Lidels' captain. We trained together in the early days and he has given me his word that he would sway the Lidels to our favour should we need them. Having the support of their army wouldn't hurt."

Valah did not acknowledge her captain's words. She merely looked to her high priestess next.

"Although I'm no longer accepted by the Crystal Temple, I know where their weak points are. There are plenty of snakes in that group of morally upstanding citizens." Nova spoke with malice, her hands clutching a tainted, three-pointed golden star that hung from a long chain of beads around her neck. This was the symbol of the Gods and she held it as though her very life depended on it.

"And you think these priestesses will help us?" Valah asked, giving the woman a sideways glance.

"Absolutely. There are a handful of them that want nothing more than for priestess Saena to be stripped of her high priesthood. They would happily take down the crown to do so. They just need a weak point. Although she has her loyal followers, there are always cracks." Her words slipped from between tight lips like a hiss.

Sensing the priestess had finished, Reynard took his cue to speak. "I suggest we make allies, and fast. Kelting has already secured much of The Edges, and it may not be too late to make amends with the Midlands." Reynard's eyes were hard and serious; Valah could sense his desperation.

While they hadn't explicitly spoken about it yet, Valah could tell that Reynard was worried. On their journey back to the west, he barely spoke a word to her as they sailed. Usually, he would be speaking with her about all kinds of strategy and future plans, but on this occasion, he spoke very little and avoided Valah's gaze. He spent most of his time on deck, staring across the country as they sailed.

"With the armies of The Edges, parts of the Midlands, and possibly The Hook, we would have a substantial force. Although it may not be enough to attack the capital alone, it would be a good start to build further allies."

"I have another idea for an ally." Valah spoke slowly and her three confidants looked on in anticipation. It wasn't a secret that Valah and the Pyrin empire were a difficult clan to assemble with, mostly due to Valah's own demeanour and lack of mutual trust. The thought of her trying to extend to another ally seemed near impossible. "Lord and Lady Elderwin."

All three of them spoke at once.

"Your Grace, Draven and Edana are snakes—"

"Please, we cannot align ourselves with them—"

"I don't think that's a good idea—"

"Enough." Valah's voice silenced them, and they looked on in concern, holding back further objection. "The Elderwins have been cooped up in their manor so as to keep an eye on the Shadowed Coast and its inhabitants, as though it isn't the most tiresome region in Crysterra. The king put them there strategically; he knew it would give them a sense of self-importance while also keeping them from dealing with any matters of true weight. However, the king's seemingly brilliant idea was short-lived. We now have two jaded family members who would do anything to take down the princess and her companions within the Syndicate, which we can use to our advantage. We can make a treaty with them to combine our armies to storm the capital, to lay siege together. We will, of course, take the throne but offer them the next best thing: governor and governess of the kingdom."

The room considered this for a moment.

"My Queen," Reynard said, treading lightly. "While I think the Elderwin army would be invaluable in our quest for the throne, I don't think placing our trust in the lord and lady is a particularly good idea. Draven would do anything to see you gone for good. If you turned your back for one moment—"

"You would be right there to protect me," Valah finished Reynard's sentence for him, looking at him down her slender nose. "I do not fear the Elderwins for their power or ill-advised decision making. I seek their army's numbers and will gladly do anything necessary to secure it."

Reynard chose his next words carefully. "Five years ago, in the Battle of the Midlands, I watched Draven turn on his own allies once he had what he wanted. He thought this would prove his loyalty to the crown, and yet his brother still kept him in the Shadowed Coast, where he continued to stew in his childish anger." Reynard could feel his own frustrations boiling beneath his skin; his concern was palpable.

"Again, I will be surrounded by a far stronger and more loyal army than his. I can anticipate his every move. Draven isn't nearly as clever as he thinks he is."

"My Queen, I don't think he is particularly clever either, but I do know that he will go to any length to sit on that throne. He will not agree to being governor while you rule, not unless he has already put poison in your wine or set a bounty on your head. He isn't to be trusted."

"And what makes you think I plan on trusting him, Reynard?" While her eyes remained narrowed on her advisor, her lips curved up in dangerous excitement. "Captain Kelting, fetch me a piece of parchment and a quill."

13

"She's practically a child!" Edana roared, sending another piece of breakable crockery—this time, a vase of flowers—crashing into the wall across the room, not too far from her husband's head.

"Darling, you must restrain yourself." Draven tried to calm his wife, but her frustration had risen past the point of boiling.

"No, darling," Edana mocked Draven's tone, "I think you need to understand the gravity of the situation!"

"I do understand how important it is, but I don't see the need to throw our tableware around the room!"

"She's a giftless child, Draven! And she thinks she can keep the crown from us!"

With her gift, Edana harnessed the wine in the carafe on the table in the centre of the room to send the breakable glass shattering into the wall above the fireplace. The pieces rained down upon the hearth like glittering stars.

"Of course we aren't going to let that happen," Draven said, taking slow, careful steps towards his wife.

"She doesn't even have her gift yet!" Edana continued in her anger, ignoring Draven's attempt to calm her. "And then Valah—oh, don't get me started on that wench! I saw the way she looked at us at the castle; she thinks she can take the throne from us! She isn't even of royal blood, not anymore!" Draven decided not to remind his wife that technically, she wasn't of royal blood either. "She can stay in the Wetlands where she belongs."

Edana found her next victim (a glass goblet on the table beside her), but before she could shower the room in shards of glass and its contents, Draven placed a hand on hers.

"Soon we won't have any dishes left for breakfast." Draven took Edana's hands in his and for a moment she strained against him, but her muscles softened, and she finally met his eyes.

"She's a child." She repeated her earlier words, this time in a whisper, so quiet in the wake of her thunderous rampage. "She hasn't got her gift, and she will be queen before you or I will ever get the chance to be crowned."

"And we are going to do everything in our power to make sure that doesn't happen," Draven crooned, pulling his wife into his arms. "Our army is nearly as large as the one in the capital. Yes, it's technically hers, but I've had our captain in the palm of my hand for years. He always detested my brother."

"So you just plan on attacking the capital? We'll lose at least half our army and then leave our backs open to be taken out by Valah and her soldiers."

She may show her anger in fits of rage, Draven thought, but his wife was a strategic and well-considered woman.

"Well, not exactly," Draven continued, leading his wife to the armchair by the fireplace, carefully handing her a glass of wine as they sat. "I have contacts in the east who I can probably swing to our side quite easily. And the Midlands, well, they can't stand the thought of Valah as queen. And they were big supporters of Bartemus, so I can just put on my best Elderwin smile and show them just how alike my brother I can be."

Edana looked at her husband, her eyes narrowing as she considered his words. "I suppose that with some more weight in our army, we may be able to take Elderguard." Her voice was even now. "But what if we infiltrated it from the inside, snaking our way into the Syndicate? If we can get that Governor Ryden Calcutter on our side, I'm sure we could make further headway there."

"And what do you suppose we say to him to get him to see us as prospective king and queen?" Draven was evidently unconvinced.

"He seemed as apprehensive as any of us at the will reading when Bartemus named Galdinia as queen!"

"I'm not sure about the governor," Draven said, shaking his head. "He's a loyalist to my brother."

"And your brother is no longer here. Sure, Galdinia may be his first choice, but if we can prove that she is unfit to rule, we may be temporarily crowned. And once there's a crown on my head, it will not be taken from me."

After a night of struggling to apprehend his thoughts between dreams of sieges upon Elderguard and his own blood spilling over the throne room tiles, Draven forced himself out of bed once the sun was well above the horizon, despite his own fatigue and exhaustion. He moved from his and his wife's chambers, along the main hall of the manor and down to the foyer. Beside the mahogany staircase that curved around the edge of the room and up to the galleries rested the largest piece of art in the manor. It took up much of the double height wall, where four sets of eyes looked down upon him.

There, within the intricate and ornate frame, sat his family—his parents, his brother and himself—staring at him from above.

The artwork was painted a number of decades prior, soon after his parents took power over Crysterra. They had commissioned a piece to be done for both of their children to hang inside the walls of their chambers and, eventually, their future homes; Bartemus' in the castle and Draven's in the family manor. His parents sat on their thrones, each of them adorned with their much-too-large crowns, the beauty of which the artist managed to capture. His father's stern eyes bore into Draven's as he gazed upon his long passed family. This was the first moment that he considered that he was the only one of the four left. This caused him to pause.

His eyes then moved to his mother, who sat to the king's left, her chestnut hair tied up neatly beneath the crown that she wore. She wore that crown on such few occasions, including their coronation and her sons' weddings. He more vividly remembered the tiara she wore every other day; it was dainty and delicate, an exquisite ornament of her power and grace. Draven recalled that the last person who wore his mother's crown was Queen Anae, the mother of his overambitious niece. He noticed quickly that his hands had balled up by his sides and his neck had stiffened. Anae never did like Draven and he knew it. Where his mother's crown was now, he couldn't be sure, but he knew he would make a point of placing it on his wife's head the moment he found it in the castle.

He then looked to his brother, who in this painting was simply just Prince Bartemus.

Oh, how the mighty have fallen.

Bartemus stood in front of his father, almost a mirror image of the king. His then teenage brother wore his hair the same as their father's and Draven remembered that Bartemus insisted on wearing the deep blood-red cloak that day, while his little brother could wear the blue one. He wanted to emulate their father in every way possible. At the time, Draven didn't think his brother could do any wrong and didn't question it. It wasn't until a decade later when their parents had passed away and Bartemus was crowned that he realised he had been second fiddle his entire life.

Finally, Draven looked upon his younger self. Having barely hit puberty and smiling like the child he was, Draven could hardly hold his gaze out of shame and embarrassment. He was so young, so naive to be standing in that spot, in the throne room of Crysterra Castle, where kings and queens had been slain time and time again. He was standing where his father took the lives of the Pyrins, and yet he was so blissfully unaware of the bloodshed.

Draven's eyes roamed across the painting, from parent to parent to sibling.

"Three gone," he whispered to himself. "Only one left for the throne."

Pulling his eyes from the painting, the lord made his way to the dining room. Draven sat at the head of the teakwood table that ran the length of the room and had hosted countless occasions. In the summer, the Elderwin dinner parties were among the most elaborate —and elusive—meals enjoyed by the nobles from across the southern border of the kingdom. At one time or another, this table had held thirty guests, each with a carefully designed table setting that often included multiple goblets, a floral arrangement and an ever-changing rotation of dishes. From the table, guests could look up to the flickering stars above them through the skylight above the table. Despite the many hours that their attendants spent cleaning this room after each and every party, the Elderwins would still occasionally find flecks of gold foil or rogue flower petals scattered on the ground beneath the table. Among their fellow lords and ladies of the south, the Elderwins were most known for the parties they held. Such events were conducive for keeping their allies close and could be used to masquerade political discussion with endless wine and midnight dancing.

Today, however, this room was a party for one.

"Good morning, my lord." Draven was greeted by his attendant, who poured him a glass of steaming tea and placed a plate of hot food before him. "This arrived by raven this morning."

Beside his breakfast his attendant placed a smoky grey envelope. It was adorned with his and his wife's names in calligraphed, stark white ink. He turned it over to find the ruby-red wax seal of the Pyrin family stamped on the back. It had not yet been cracked.

After a brief nod of thanks from Draven, the attendant promptly left the room.

Draven used his untouched butter knife to lift the seal from the paper. He removed the folded piece of parchment from within and noted that the handwriting inside used an unnecessary amount of flourishes.

Draven and Edana,

"Of course she didn't address us by our titles," Draven muttered to himself, already anticipating who had written the letter.

I will not lie to you; yesterday's will reading was an utter disappointment. Of course, I did not expect to be welcomed back to the capital with open arms, my throne awaiting me. I did, however, consider the pain and frustration that you both must have felt when the old king declared a powerless girl as the rightful queen of the kingdom.

This, in my humble opinion, will not do.

I don't need to tell you what a beautiful and powerful place Crysterra is. You both know that. I also don't need to tell you that our great country requires the strength and wisdom of a ruler who is actually worthy of sitting on that throne. Galdinia, however, does not possess such qualities.

This is why I write to you: to make a proposition.

There are many avenues into the capital, and I assume you have already considered a number of these: the Syndicate, the Crystal Temple, landing in Ryden and Galdinia's good graces. These, however, are of no interest to me. I believe the capital needs to be taken by force.

While it doesn't thrill me to think of you two seated on the throne, I can certainly rest easier knowing it will be taken care of in an adequate manner. And I would like to help you achieve that, with a few conditions.

As you know, the western army is strong and grows by the day. We have one of the largest populations in the kingdom and so our army is similarly proportioned. This is not an army made up of the children of entitled nobles and people with too much money to care what happens beyond the capital's walls. These are soldiers who have worked tooth and nail to try to overcome their own economic struggles and hardships (let's not forget King Bartemus' ruling last year that saw a rise in the taxes of those beyond the Midlands). My army is strong and ably led by Captain Kelting, who has three decades worth of experience in battle.

My proposition to you is that I will charge my army alongside yours in order to take the capital from the hands of Princess Galdinia and Governor Ryden. With those numbers, we will easily defeat the capital's defences and force them to surrender at the very least. You will, of course, take the throne. My advisor (General Reynard) and I will become governors of Crysterra, and we will rule alongside you until we lose our teeth and can no longer walk.

Should you agree to my terms, send a raven back before sunset today with your correspondence and we will begin our arrangements to take the capital on the final day of the Week of Mourning.

Take heed, though, fair Elderwins: should either of you cross me or attempt to take advantage of my offer for your gain alone, I will personally slice your heads from your necks and gladly take the throne myself.

I await your response.

Valah Pyrin, Queen of the West

Draven considered her words as well as those of his wife from the evening before.

Edana believed that the governor could be their key to the throne. If they showed some kind of remorse and convinced the man and his Syndicate that they were aligned with his brother, perhaps they could infiltrate the capital that way. It could be peaceful, and they could double their army by bringing the loyal soldiers of the south together with those of the capital. He and Edana could become interim rulers and after disposing of Galdinia, they could rule indefinitely.

On the other hand, Draven considered Valah's proposal. She was a spiteful woman, and he knew she wouldn't hesitate to remove the Elderwins the moment she could see her path to the throne. Trusting her would be a risk, but it could provide significant reward. Despite her threats, Draven knew that Valah had a powerful army and would be compliant in order to get into the castle. He could easily take care of her and her attendant once he had the royal scabbard in his grasp. While it was the bloodier option, it also seemed the fastest.

If they were to lay siege on the capital, he knew they couldn't leave it until the Seventh Day. After his threat of returning at the end of the week, the capital and their army would be waiting for their arrival on the last day if word got out that the princess still didn't have her gift. They would need some element of surprise, even if it was merely one day.

Without another moment of hesitation, Draven called for a piece of parchment and a quill and wrote his very brief response.

Valah,

Start making arrangements to travel south. We will leave Elderwin Manor, together with our armies, the morning of the Sixth Day of Mourning.

Lord Draven Elderwin, the rightful King of Crysterra

14

"Are you ready, Princess?"

Galdinia had felt apprehensive about training with her captain the moment Ryden declared it. She felt a completely different kind of unease, though, when she stood in Ilyon's training room in the soldiers' barracks on the edge of the city.

The barracks were set upon the southernmost tip of Elderguard and stretched along the edge of the city within the breakwater walls that separated the kingdom from the Shadowed Sea. Although the structure itself was ancient—grey stone archways, original wooden doors and peep-hole windows—the interior of the barracks was significantly more pleasant than she had imagined. The corridors were lined with hanging oil lanterns which lit the various paintings of kings, queens and captains past; the dining room held a number of long mahogany tables, each kept in good condition and repair; and the armouries and training rooms were organised and well-kept. Although Galdinia did not see the soldiers' sleeping quarters—nor did she want to—Ilyon assured her that they were also in very good working condition. She supposed that as future queen, these were things she should be concerned about.

On their way to the training room, they had walked through the courtyard at the centre of the complex. The courtyard was framed by the square-shaped building and, as Ilyon informed the princess, was where most large scale combat training took place. There were at least three hundred soldiers in their full armour and helmets following the orders of a commander as they sparred and blocked each other's blows. Galdinia was sure that Drystan could have been among them, but they passed quickly through this area and the matching suits of armour made it difficult to distinguish soldier from soldier.

Ilyon ushered the princess quickly down a flight of long winding stairs to the basement level and Galdinia noticed the frown at his brow as he also noted the soldiers who had lost their focus the moment the princess stepped into their vicinity. Below ground level, away from prying eyes, was where Ilyon had set up a private training room for them to try to harness whatever potential power may be flowing through Galdinia's veins.

The cavernous room was bathed in the warm glow of dozens of lanterns that dangled in the air, attached to ropes that disappeared into the depths of the dark ceiling somewhere above them. The walls were more jagged than the ones in the main building. Galdinia quickly realised that this room had been carved into the ground and the walls were made up of sedimentary rock. She was amazed by the vastness of the structure and couldn't imagine the amount of work that had to have gone into the creation of this room.

"Are you ready, Princess?"

Galdinia tore her eyes away from the walls and looked to Ilyon, who was standing in the centre of the room. Beside him were three pedestals, each with a different object on them. The first was a glass bowl that appeared to be filled with water. On the next pedestal was a lit lantern, its flame wobbling ever so slightly in its enclosure. The final object on the third pedestal was a midnight blue silk hand fan—on closer inspection its design resembled the night sky and was adorned with billowing clouds and silver stars. Galdinia looked at each of the items and then back to Ilyon.

"We're going to start with the three elements and see if any of them speak to you," Ilyon began, pacing along the length of the three pedestals as he spoke. "It's important to see if you have a particular bias to any of them, as this will often inform your future power."

The phrase "future power" placed yet another weight of expectation on Galdinia's shoulders as she considered the possibility of not being able to actually perform said powers.

"I can't say this is the first time I've tried to make a connection with the elements." It seemed obvious, but Galdinia felt she should explicitly tell the captain that she'd been trying to harness her gift for many years.

"I'm not surprised and frankly, I'm glad you've been trying. Regardless, I would still like to see if my tactics have any significant impact."

Galdinia nodded in response, her heart thudding in anticipation.

"We'll start by talking through each one and I'll try to glean some idea of which element we should be focusing on." He paused in front of Galdinia, his hands clasped behind his back and his dark eyes firmly fixed on hers. "Where did you spend most of your time as a child? Outside in the gardens, inside in the warmth, or swimming in the cove?"

Galdinia's brow furrowed as she pondered the relevancy of this question.

"Don't think about it too much. Just go with your gut answer," Ilyon pressed, maintaining his firm stance.

"Well, all three," Galdinia muttered, trying to think about where her time was most spent. "If I had to choose one, I suppose inside, in the library of the castle."

"Good." Ilyon nodded and moved on. "Do you have a favourite animal? It could be real or imagined. Anything from a mammal, to a centaur, to a fish."

"Certainly not a fish," Galdinia said, and Ilyon frowned; she was quickly realising that he only wanted her answer and not a justification for it. "Probably a phoenix."

Galdinia remembered a story that her father told her as a child about the mythology of the phoenix and she couldn't seem to wrap her mind around an animal that was able to bring itself back to life from its own ashes. She quickly became obsessed with the folklore and researched them for days and weeks to come, finding any and every book and story she could, some containing claims of their true existence. Strangely, she hadn't thought about them in a while.

"Interesting," Ilyon said with another nod. "Now close your eyes and consider the three elements: if you were surrounded by one right now, in this very room, which would you feel most comfortable in?"

Galdinia did as he asked and tried to imagine the elements, her mind jumping from one to another. She pictured herself in gale storm winds, enveloped by the whipping of sand and the uprooting of trees. She then imagined tongues of fire swirling through the air beside her, the heat of the flames burning everything in its path. Finally, she pictured the room full of water; she could imagine herself swimming through the liquid. In her imagination, this was the most peaceful of the three.

"Water."

"Okay," Ilyon said and she opened her eyes again. "You have demonstrated an interest in each, with a slight bias towards fire, which is where we will start today."

Galdinia wasn't entirely sure how he had come to that conclusion, but she trusted him regardless. Ilyon stood behind the centre pedestal and opened the top of the lantern to expose the flame to the air around it.

"The gift of the elements is arguably quite simple to tap into if you have the correct element at your disposal," Ilyon explained, presenting the flame with an open palm. "When someone with the gift comes in close proximity to their element, they are able to control and build upon it with relative ease. A drop of water, a light breeze or, in our case, a small flame can be contorted into something much greater."

By way of demonstration, Ilyon lifted his right hand towards the bowl of water and slowly moved his palm in an upward direction. As he did so, the water mirrored his movement. It didn't break its original form inside the bowl as it levitated into the air. Galdinia had seen Ilyon use his powers hundreds of times. As a child, she would watch him calm the seas or, better yet, create varying swells to propel the royal ship through the seas faster than was natural. Although she understood that would have taken a significant amount of control, she was almost more impressed by this current display of his gift as he kept the water in the shape of the bowl as it floated through the air above their heads, independent of its original shell. With a quick flick of his wrist, Ilyon sent the water back to the bowl, where it crashed with the force of a wave. Not a single drop fell outside of the bowl and in a second it was still once again.

Galdinia mouthed a silent "wow" as she turned to look back at Ilyon, who was stoic as ever.

"Of course, this takes practise. My connection with the water is one that has grown over many years and my command of it is thanks to my dedication to the gift—and to the Gods." Ilyon now looked down at the fire. "The act of brandishing any of the elements is reasonably similar, or so I'm told by Wind Wielders and Fire Flourishers. As a Water Weaver, I try to feel the water in my hands as I instruct it to move. I can feel the liquid rising and falling, growing and shrinking. It becomes an extension of the person brandishing it, like a sword in battle or a pen when writing."

Galdinia was glad for the second analogy, as she had very little experience with a sword.

"So where do we start?" Galdinia asked.

"We start by having you make a connection with the flame." Ilyon made it sound so simple. "Many people feel a connection to their given element before the Gods even bestow on them their gift, hence my line of questioning. I want you to look into the fire and see if you can feel it. You may feel it in your palms, on your face, in your gut, or even in your veins. I find staring into and concentrating on the element being a good place to start. You may wish to move a hand around it to help trigger the feeling."

Galdinia looked at him for a moment before realising that was her invitation to begin... feeling? She wasn't quite sure what she was meant to do or think exactly, but she hoped it would all make sense in the moments she began.

She stared at the flame as it flickered ever so slightly with the movement of her breath. It glowed as her eyes adjusted to staring at the bright light. She wondered how long she could stare at it like this without doing permanent damage to her sight.

Focus.

She strengthened her gaze, or at least she thought she did, by standing firmer on her feet, planting the soles of her impossibly flat leather slippers into the ground below. She tried to imagine the flame moving like the water did at Ilyon's command, willing it to leave its perch on the wick and hover in the air, disconnected from its source of oil below.

After she had been staring at the flame for what felt like minutes, Ilyon quietly interrupted. "Perhaps try with your hand, Princess."

Galdinia did as he instructed and reached her hand out towards the flame. She let it hover just in front of the pedestal at first, feeling the residual warmth against her palm. It was pleasant and seemed to warm most of her hand. She slowly moved her hand closer and the heat travelled up her arm, the temperature increasing significantly with each inch. This, however, did not feel any different to the way fire normally felt at this close proximity.

Galdinia continued to move her hand near and around the flame, trying to push, pull and coax the fire to move, but other than it shifting in the breeze that her hand created, it simply did not budge. After a few more minutes of feeling utterly ridiculous as she tried to command the flame to move, she dropped her hand and sighed, almost extinguishing the flame in doing so.

"Nothing," she said flatly.

"It can take time, Princess," Ilyon replied.

"Well, time is somewhat sensitive in this situation."

"Unfortunately, we cannot rush these things, Your Highness."

"Could we try a bigger flame? Surely if I had more to work with, my body may respond differently."

"It takes an extraordinary amount of energy to make even the smallest of elements bend at your will. A larger flame would only be more difficult. At first, I could control only the dripping of water from the ceiling after a storm; it took many years for me to be able to control the tides."

Galdinia sighed again, hanging her head in disappointment.

Don't give up.

"Okay, let me keep trying."

Two hours later, Galdinia stood in the middle of the training room, sweat dripping from her forehead as her hands swirled around the still unmoving flame. Her muscles ached and she had adopted a reasonably diabolical headache. Never before had she stared for so long at a single object; she knew she would be seeing the flame in her vision for days to come.

"I think it's time we end for today," Ilyon said, having not moved from his point of observation across from the pedestal. As Galdinia had moved around the flame and the room, trying to find the best vantage point, his feet had remained firmly planted, his arms crossed over his chest.

"No, I can keep trying," Galdinia said, betraying her weary body.

"We can pick this up again tomorrow with a different element, but I think you need to rest."

Reluctantly, yet also with gratitude, Galdinia lowered her arms and moved to sit on a bench that backed onto the side wall of the training room. Her ribs and back muscles cried out as she sat and leaned against the rock wall. She winced as she moved, practically melting into the cool stone.

"It can take a long time to find the gift within," Ilyon said as he moved towards her, standing by her side. She wondered if he ever sat and rested or if he slept standing up. She wouldn't be surprised if he did.

"Isn't it something the Gods give you?" Galdinia asked, wiping the sweat from her brow gingerly, the muscles in her forearm tensing.

"I think you'll find that it's a gift that we are all born with. It's just a matter of the Gods igniting the flame, as it were."

"But it hasn't manifested itself yet. I've never even had an inkling that there may be some kind of power within me."

"It can be hard to find, but we must have faith," Ilyon said, his tone softening ever so slightly. "If I'm honest with you, I think everyone has a glimpse of it, but some don't believe they can harness it, so they never do."

"But so few commoners are able to tap into it," Galdinia protested. "And even then, they usually come from nobility, even if by long and distant connections. There are very few recorded exceptions."

If she knew one thing like the back of her hand, it was the history of the country that she was set to lead. At least half of her studies growing up related to the history of Crysterra and she even studied the original records of gifted individuals, both those of nobility and commoners.

About four hundred years ago, after a brutal battle in the Midlands that made way for Pyrin rule, a small population fled to the Starlight Mountains and they eventually came to reside in Lund. Here they established their own society, protected by the natural barrier of the deep mountains and often harsh weather, glad to be separated from Crysterra's conflict at the time. Some brief records showed that the descendants of this population had Light Lender abilities. Given their reclusive nature, there wasn't a lot about the people of Lund in the official capital documents, so some scholars believed they were falsified. Galdinia, however, was intrigued by them.

"That's exactly why I believe that everybody is capable of being given a gift from the Gods. It isn't just about blood," Ilyon replied, his voice firm as ever.

Ilyon turned back to the pedestals to extinguish the flame and clean up the elements. As he did so, Galdinia stared at him, pondering his words and whether there was any truth to them. If a princess couldn't tap into her gift, then how was an average citizen to do so?

"Come back here to the barracks at the same time tomorrow. We will train each day in the lead up to the Seventh Day."

"Very well," Galdinia said as she stood; even her leg muscles rebuked any movement after standing in such a stiff and rigid manner for hours.

"We will train you until your gift can be harnessed, Princess," Ilyon said as he placed the elements and the pedestals to the side of the room. "I promise."

Galdinia made her way back through the barracks from the training room on her own, leaving Ilyon to, as Galdinia would describe them, his more important duties. She insisted that she didn't need an escort every moment of the day. She walked around the edges of the centre training yard this time; despite her title of princess, she felt hesitant about walking through a battalion of training soldiers as they charged at each other with swords and moved with quick and sudden movements.

As she edged her way around the yard and towards the entrance hall of the building, she heard the call of her name through the madness of the training area.

"Gal!"

Galdinia turned and saw Drystan jogging towards her, his sweep of brown hair now loosed from the knot it was in yesterday, bouncing with every springy step he took. He was dressed in his regular civilian attire, and his sword and shield weren't in sight. He far more resembled the boy she had said goodbye to months prior than the one she saw the previous day.

"Drys, hi," Galdinia said as she halted at the door to the entrance hall. For a moment she thought Drystan may hug her, but he stopped a few feet from her, and Galdinia was glad she didn't need to deal with the awkward stares that would ensue from those around them.

"What are you doing here?" he asked, crossing his arms over his chest. Now that she saw him without his armour, she could see how much his training had impacted his body; the muscles along his forearms and upper arms looked like they'd grown by at least half their size, and his hair was at least an inch longer, sitting just below his ear lobes. Perhaps he wasn't just as she had remembered him.

"I had a training session with Captain Ilyon," she replied, trying not to make it obvious where her eyes had been lingering. "You're not wearing your usual attire; you're not training today?"

"I just finished up," Drystan said with a grin. "Since I got the First Night of Mourning shift, I get tonight off."

"Any grand plans?"

"None at this stage." Drystan smiled again. "I'm pretty sure I'll be asleep by sunset, though."

"It must be so tiring, all the training that you're doing."

"I'm getting used to it." Drystan shrugged, trying to be nonchalant about it. "But after a twelve hour shift on duty and a day spent training, I'm pretty exhausted."

"Twelve hours?" Galdinia asked, gawking at him. "I'll have to talk to the Syndicate about that."

She tried to pretend as though she had any sway within the Syndicate, but she knew they wouldn't necessarily listen to her until she had her mother's crown on her head, despite her speech this morning. She also doubted they would agree to changing any rules for soldiers to simply help the boy she cared about so he could get a better sleep.

"That'd be great." Drystan laughed before they turned and began to walk together through the doors to the busy entrance hall. "So how was your training session with the captain? He can be such a tyrant."

"He was fine; I'm the one with the issues," Galdinia said with a sigh, avoiding Drystan's eyes as she spoke.

"I know that's not true."

"Well, my gift still hasn't shown itself, so I'm just patiently waiting to feel the burn of fire in my veins or the overwhelming need to change the direction of the winds." She let her hands fall to her sides in defeat. "He said we'll keep training this week in the lead up to the Seventh Day, but I'm afraid I won't be able to produce any power before then and honestly, that's a really terrifying thought."

Drystan stopped by Galdinia's side, took her hand, and pulled her into a nearby room off the entrance hall. It seemed to be a broom closet and was small and dingy by the standards of the rest of the barracks. Drystan shut the door behind them and turned back to Galdinia, his hand still wrapped around hers.

"Gal, you don't need to be afraid." He spoke softly now, tilting his head so they were closer to eye level. "You've been destined to be queen since you were born. I've known it since I met you. You're wise, kind, and gracious. I mean, just look at you now; you're talking to someone who had the audacity to leave for three months to train to become a soldier at the drop of a hat."

"Well, that wasn't your choice," Galdinia said quietly.

"Regardless," he said, shifting uncomfortably at her words, "you do not need your powers to be a great queen; you're already the best candidate for the job."

"That's all very well and good of you to say, Drys, but I'm not sure the Syndicate, let alone the country, see it like you do."

"What if the Gods have already ordained you, but your gifts just haven't come to fruition yet?"

Galdinia raised her brows at him, disbelieving. Galdinia hadn't considered this a possibility, because it wasn't necessarily something she had read about in the history books, yet it aligned with Ilyon's thoughts earlier on the topic.

"You really are such an optimist," Galdinia said, but her smile faltered. "Maybe I'm not supposed to be queen, and this is the Gods' way of telling me."

"You've got to trust the Gods and their timing, even when it's slow. You're supposed to be queen, I know it."

Galdinia smiled up at Drystan. His eyes were still so full of the innocence and blind trust that they had always carried. She took comfort in this small part of him that hadn't yet shifted in his training. She supposed his heart had remained very much the same as he spoke of his confidence in the girl that he had once loved. Or still loved? Galdinia's curiosity around this topic got the better of her.

"Drys," she said, looking down at their still interlocked fingers. "What are we? I know you were shipped off to your training without much notice and I was dealing with my father, but one day we were walking through the gardens at sunset, apparently very happy, then suddenly... we weren't. I don't want to pretend that what we had never existed."

Drystan hesitated as he looked down at Galdinia, his deep brown eyes shimmering in the light that reflected through the textured glass of the window behind her. "When I was conscripted, I knew the fantasy we had been living in had to come to an end. We were kids in a fairy tale and the reality of the real world struck me pretty hard. I won't lie: I had hoped to spend the rest of my life with you." Galdinia could hear a faint quiver in Drystan's voice. His words felt like a dagger to her heart. "But we know that a princess only has a future with someone of nobility, and I am just not that, especially when I became a soldier of the Royal Guard. We swear to a life of fidelity to the crown, so we can't be attached to anything or anyone that may be a detriment to that promise. For me, that was you."

Another stab wound to the heart.

"It's really hard, Gal, seeing you and not being able to be with you. I've tossed and turned at night, agonising over how I could have handled the situation better, but we both know that you need to be queen and I... well, I need to move on."

Galdinia wondered what he could have possibly done to make the situation better. At the end of the day, she knew he had been conscripted into the army, and that wasn't his fault.

"We were dealt a really awful hand, Drystan," Galdinia replied, her injured heart hammering in her chest; she was sure he'd feel her pulse in her hand. "We were given young love only to have it taken away just as it could become something more. You know I want to change the laws around soldiers being able to marry."

Drystan paused before replying. "But would you be doing that for yourself or for the good of the country?" Drystan asked, his brows furrowing. "While that law is the worst case scenario for me alone, I can see how it would benefit the army as a whole, and ultimately the kingdom."

"So you would rather us not be together?" Galdinia asked, pulling her hand from his. The number of punctures in her heart were piling up.

"Of course not," Drystan said, taking a step toward her. "Gal, I want nothing more than to be with you. All I'm saying is that when you're queen, you have to be able to make altruistic decisions that are better for the masses."

Galdinia knew he had the best of intentions saying these things and he didn't mean to hurt her with his words, but all she could hear in that moment was that she was being selfish in wanting to choose him.

"Thanks for the advice," she said coolly, crossing her arms over her chest. She knew she was being childish, but he was treating her like a child, so she felt she could behave like one. "I know all about making decisions for the greater good."

"Gal, please don't take it the wrong way. I'm bound by my word and you changing the laws wouldn't necessarily mean we can even be together anyway." Drystan spoke quickly, taking another step towards her so they were now inches from each other. He placed his hand under her chin and lifted her eyes to meet his. "Please don't ever think that I don't want to be with you."

Galdinia sighed at his words and closed her eyes, her head now resting safely on his hand. She had never felt so equally comfortable and unsettled in one moment before. She opened her eyes and looked up at Drystan, the beginnings of tears pooling in her eyes.

"Of course I feel the same way," Galdinia said with a defeated smile.

Drystan leaned down and pressed his lips on Galdinia's forehead. Despite knowing that she should have left this room minutes ago, she stood still, lingering in the presence of his comforting touch and warming scent. Drystan was her home, and no law or edict could deny that.

"I should go," she mumbled softly.

His lips drew back from her and his hand released her chin.

"Gal?" Drystan asked, apprehension hanging on his voice. "We can still be friends, can't we? I don't think I could survive without you in my life."

"Of course, Drys," Galdinia said with a smile. "Always."

Drystan released a small breath of relief, and she felt the air in the room relax. In that moment, she saw again the boy she fell in love with, the one who sat on the edge of the fountain with her, dangling his feet in the shimmering water as they shared treats, secrets, and laughter.

"Do you want to come and get a pint with me?" Drystan asked with a smile that made her heart ache and goosebumps appear on her arms.

"You know I'd like nothing more—"

"But?"

"I'm not sure the future queen should be drinking in the shadowy corners of the tavern anymore." Galdinia smirked, thinking back to the many evenings she, Drystan, and Neryda had hidden away in one of the back tables of the tavern, using their charm to get themselves whatever alcohol they could muster. "I'm also pretty drained from my session with Ilyon. I think I just need to rest. I have a big week ahead."

Galdinia made a point of not mentioning her plans the following morning.

"Of course." Drystan smiled, turning to open the door. The noise from the entrance hall came flooding into their private space and Galdinia suddenly felt very exposed to the outside world. "I'll see you on the Fourth Day at the feast."

"Will you?" Galdinia asked, pausing in the doorway to look at him.

"I'm on duty. I've pulled the night shift again," Drystan said, a small smile on his face. "I'm not sure where in the castle I'll be posted. All I know is that I'll be there."

The Royal Feast, held in the middle of the Week of Mourning, was one of the most anticipated events of the week. It would be an evening with decadent food, drinks and music, and the guest list would consist of the most powerful dignitaries from the capital and its surrounds. It was the one event of the week held in the castle and was hosted by the Syndicate and the princess.

This event made Galdinia feel apprehensive as she considered the many conversations she would need to have with her various guests in order to prove that she would make a worthy queen. Knowing that Drystan would be in the vicinity calmed some of her nerves.

"It'll be nice to know that there's a familiar face in the room somewhere." Galdinia smiled as she walked through the door, making her way out of the entrance hall.

"It's all the talk in the barracks," Drystan said with a smile as they made their way up Main Court, back into the city streets. "The soldiers have been exchanging their shifts between each other for extra bathroom and kitchen duties."

Galdinia's eyebrows rose. "They're doing each other's dirty work to get an *extra* night shift?" Galdinia couldn't believe the soldiers would want to be on any more evenings this week.

"They all want to get a glimpse of the Royal Feast," Drystan said with a shrug.

"I can tell you right now it won't be that exciting."

"I think it's something to do with the mystery of it all. They want to see what the nobility get up to when they're away from the prying eyes of commoners." Drystan said this with a laugh and Galdinia shook her head. "One of my bunk mates offered to cover a week of my bathroom duties to get my shift."

"And you turned that down?" Galdinia asked, her eyebrows knotting together.

"Honestly," Drystan said sheepishly, pushing his hands into his pockets as they walked, "I wanted to be able to see you." Galdinia felt a blush rise up in her cheeks. "And if Neryda's going with you, then I look forward to the mischief she will inevitably cause," Drystan added quickly.

"I can guarantee that she will be far more interesting to keep an eye on than me. I think most of my evening will include conversations with dignitaries and the Syndicate."

"Maybe we can sneak a drink in together at the end of the night."

Galdinia knew it was a bad idea to agree to it, but she nodded nonetheless.

As they reached the edge of the busy square, they stopped on the road and faced each other. Galdinia didn't know how to say goodbye to Drystan anymore. Three months ago, he would have given her a fleeting kiss on the cheek, wrapped her in his arms, or held her face in his hands before leaving her at the door to her rooms, the castle, or her secret passageway. If saying goodbye when they were in their bubble of love was difficult, saying goodbye now was almost impossible.

"So I'll see you in two days," Drystan said, his boyish smile still having as great an effect on Galdinia's heart as always.

"Two days," Galdinia replied, trying not to become too attached to Drystan again.

They looked at each other awkwardly for a moment, unsure how they should say goodbye. Drystan, far less concerned with onlookers than Galdinia, pulled her into a tight hug. Galdinia buried her face in his shoulder, letting herself linger in the security of his arms. She felt just as she always had when he hugged her, his oaky scent lingering, his strong arms holding her close.

After a few too many seconds, he let go of her, and they smiled at one another. Galdinia didn't know if she'd get to hug him again like that—did princesses with suitors hug other men? She didn't think so.

"Bye, Drys," she said softly.

"See you, Gal," he replied, and they turned from each other, going their separate ways, Drystan to the tavern and Galdinia up to the castle.

THIRD DAY OF MOURNING

15

THE MORNING AFTER TRAINING, DESPITE HER LONG SOAK IN THE TUB the night before, Galdinia's limbs cried out as she tried to move, causing her to groan in response. Neryda, who was already awake, raised her brows at her best friend as she squirmed uncomfortably.

"Who would have thought that staring at a flame for two hours would be more painful than the time we tried to scale the capital walls to get out of our lessons?"

Galdinia frowned at her friend in response as Neryda moved across from the dressing room to the window. Although she still insisted on sleeping by her best friend's side for the remainder of the week, Neryda had kindly made herself comfortable on the oversized chaise by the bay window, which was already perfectly made. She claimed that it was more comfortable than her own bed at home.

"Honestly, you sound like you've been lifting barrels or running in an incredibly competitive foot race," Neryda scoffed, pulling open the curtains, bringing a fresh pain to Galdinia's eyes as well as her limbs. "What on earth is wrong with you?"

"What is wrong with *you*?" Galdinia countered, barring her eyes from the glaring sun. "When did you become a morning person?"

"The minute you agreed to a brunch with five handsome gentle-men," Neryda crooned, waltzing across the room and coming to perch on the edge of Galdinia's bed. "For some reason, the thought of that really energised me this morning."

Galdinia could see that Neryda was fully dressed in a silky, pale green dress, and her usually billowing curls were held in place at the nape of her neck by an array of sparkling clips. She wasn't just ready for brunch; she was excited.

"You've got to be kidding me," Galdinia moaned, rolling over to avoid the sunlight and her friend's all-too-chipper demeanour. "I thought we were on the same page about suitors and arranged marriages."

"I may not have found my match on my most recent tour up the coast—granted, my choices were extremely dull and, quite frankly, lacking in any kind of substance—but that doesn't mean we need to squander your chances to enjoy the company of some fine noblemen this week."

Neryda had spent hours listening to Galdinia prattle on about (and cry over) Drystan over the last year or so. It reached the point where Neryda forced her friend to make a move so she could carry on with her own life once again and avoid hearing Galdinia's concerns about him as her potential match. Given Neryda had encouraged Galdinia in her escapades with Drystan, Galdinia wondered if she felt somewhat responsible for the sad outcome; Drystan was not of noble blood, so their relationship was arguably doomed, even though Galdinia secretly hoped for Drystan to be given a gift even more than herself. When Drystan was conscripted, Neryda watched Galdinia's heart shatter. Perhaps she felt like she had the chance to make up for Galdinia's pain.

"Let's go, Princess," Neryda said, pulling at Galdinia's arms, coaxing her from her cocoon of blankets.

Within thirty minutes, Galdinia looked like a new person; Neryda had tamed her hair under her tiara, she'd covered her dark circles with sufficient makeup, and she'd chosen the princess a subtly elegant off-white dress to wear. Neryda had commented that it clung to the princess in "all the right places", but Galdinia didn't feel that brought any extra comfort. Although her demeanour was still lacking any kind of excitement, Galdinia followed her friend down the hallways and stairs of the castle towards the terrace on the first floor.

"I think I'm having second thoughts," Galdinia mumbled, her arm looped in Neryda's. Her friend seemed to be dragging the princess more so than leading her through the castle. "This all seems like a terrible idea."

"Gal, we've been over this," Neryda said sternly, not relinquishing her grip. "Perhaps none of these men will be suitable, in which case you can attempt to deal with the Syndicate at the end of the week. Or you can spend a few hours eating Miss Giles' best food, sipping break-fast sparkling wine, and ogling at some handsome noble men."

"Hours?" Galdinia gaped at her friend. "Who said anything about hours?"

"I'm being optimistic," Neryda said dryly, turning the corner to the final hall before the terrace. "Anyway, I think this is better than the alternative, right?"

Galdinia knew that the alternative that Neryda referred to could mean relinquishing her crown, but she was also quickly reminded of Drystan and her conversation with him the previous day. Galdinia had decided not to tell her friend about that interaction; she thought that the sooner she could move on from Drystan the better, and perpetu-ating the hurt by gossiping with Neryda was not going to help.

"Fine," Galdinia conceded.

The girls came to a stop at the doors to the terrace, beside which stood a guard and an attendant. The guard pushed open the doors and the attendant stepped forward.

"Announcing," he said loudly, gaining the attention of those on the terrace, "Princess Galdinia of Crysterra and Lady Neryda."

The terrace ran along half the width of the southern end of the castle and provided a view of the capital below. The terrace was covered in vines and bundles of wisteria that wrapped themselves around the many columns, hanging lanterns, and bannisters. Her mother's roses were growing in large plant pots that were dotted around the edges of the terrace, and their scent filled the air. A large table in the centre of the terrace was adorned with pearly white crock-ery, ready to serve seven guests.

Amongst this spectacular scene were five young men wearing an array of colours, all looking at the princess expectantly. Some had obviously been mid-conversation, as they stood in pairs, except for one. Bentley was leaning against the bannister of the terrace alone, sparkling wine in hand. The dimple in his right cheek surfaced as a gentle smirk danced over his lips at the sight of the princess.

"Good morning, Your Highness." Galdinia's attention was pulled from the blonde man on the edge of the terrace to a sprightly young man with dark hair, deep bronze skin and an eager expression. His outstretched hand was there to escort the princess onto the terrace from the step above. His smile was all charm.

"Thank you," Galdinia said, forcing as much warmth into her voice as she could muster as she took his hand and stepped onto the marble tiles. "Good morning, um—"

"Kaedric Novus," the man said, his smile not faltering. "I'm the son of Lord and Lady Novus on the eastern coast. My parents have served the Elderwins for decades."

"Thank you for your service," Galdinia said with a smile, her feet now firmly planted on the terrace.

"The pleasure is ours," Kaedric replied, finally relinquishing the princess' hand but not moving from her side.

"Princess Galdinia, it is an honour to meet you." Another man stepped forward, his broad frame moving between her and Kaedric, his rosy cheeks standing out against his pale alabaster skin. "Lord Evarius Wrynn from the Wooded Province."

Galdinia looked up at the man before her, having to crane her neck to get a good look at him. His chest was broad, and he looked at her with confident eyes and a knowing smile. Somehow she immediately knew what she thought of him, and she couldn't say it was a positive first impression.

"A pleasure to meet you," Galdinia said with raised brows, Evarius looking particularly pleased with himself.

She was then quickly introduced to Dillian Othid, a lord's son from the north whose russet-coloured hair seemed to be immovable in their tightly wound curls. As she made her way to the table, she met the charming Kell Ly, who handed the princess the gift of a single red rose, which he claimed his mother grew especially for her in her own rose garden on their estate along the Shadowed Coast. He had bowed when he handed it to her, smiling up at Galdinia, his dark eyes peering between the straight black hair that curtained his face.

By the time Galdinia made it to her chair, she already felt over-whelmed. Across the table from her stood Lord Bentley, who had watched the exchanges from afar. He stepped forward, opening his mouth to speak.

"Brunch will now be served." The attendant at the door spoke loudly as he announced the arrival of their food. "Please be seated."

"Is that fish boy?" Neryda whispered into Galdinia's ear.

Galdinia eyed Bentley as she moved to the head of the table, taking her seat and offering Neryda the one to her right.

"That's the one," she replied quietly as they settled at the table.

Lord Evarius quickly sat to the princess' left, followed by Dillian beside him, Kaedric to Neryda's right, then Kell, and finally Bentley at the other end of the table. A magnificent display of flowers, foliage and candles was laid out before them, each place setting ready with gold cutlery and ornate plates. Before she could look up from the table, dishes of food were being placed before them, each one splayed with steaming eggs, fresh bread, an array of berries, and fresh pastries.

"This is magnificent," Evarius noted, looking down at his plate of food with larger eyes than he had when he saw the princess. "I hope they have plenty more coming."

"Thank you for a marvellous spread, Princess," Kaedric said from across the table, smiling wide.

"This was all my cook's doing," Galdinia replied as the final serving was placed in front of Bentley. "Miss Giles is the best there is."

"Sparkling wine, Princess?" An attendant had approached Galdinia with a green tinted bottle of sparkling wine, nodding towards her empty glass.

"Please," she said quietly yet almost desperately. Neryda caught Galdinia's eye and she chuckled to her already suffering best friend.

"A toast to the princess," Kaedric said with a chime on his glass once the bottle of wine had been sufficiently distributed around the table.

Every glass around the table rose into the air, and Galdinia gave Neryda another sideways glance.

"To our most gracious host—"

"Most gracious and most beautiful host," Evarius cut Kaedric off with a smug smile, causing the other man to stumble on his words. Galdinia had to force herself not to roll her eyes.

"Yes, our most gracious and beautiful host," Kaedric agreed, eyeing Evarius with disdain before continuing. "May she live a long life and reign for many years to come. To the princess!"

"To the princess!" The words echoed around the table, each of the men raising their glasses in Galdinia's direction. Neryda snorted as she sipped. Galdinia looked down the table to Bentley, who had a look of pure amusement on his face as he lifted his glass in the air, eyebrows raised and dimple on show. He nodded to Galdinia before taking a swig of the drink, his gaze not leaving her own.

The following forty minutes consisted of Galdinia attempting to eat her breakfast as each man provided her with seemingly impressive facts about their lives, their homes, and their goals for the future. Evarius quite gladly spoke over anyone mid-sentence if he thought his contribution was worthwhile. At one stage, he interrupted Neryda, which earned him a deathly stare and a face full of sparkling wine the next time he tried to take a sip. It appeared that the burly man had accidentally missed his mouth, but Galdinia watched her friend flick her fingers in the man's direction from under the table, sending the wine down his chin and onto his jacket. He dabbed at it awkwardly but took the heat of the flame from the lantern on the table to promptly dry himself. Neryda didn't look pleased as he quickly recovered.

Kaedric was pleasant enough, but his constant attempts to woo the princess by complimenting everything from the castle to the meal to the colour of her dress became tiring. Galdinia squirmed in her seat every time she tried to accept his flood of compliments. At one point, he even tried to impress her with his ability to carry the fallen petals from the centrepiece on a light breeze that blew across the terrace. While he was somewhat exhausting, his beautiful, sparkling smile made it a little more bearable.

Kell sat casually in his seat, stirring his drink with his mind as he engaged easily with the conversation at the table. Galdinia quickly realised that his charm very much extended to his sense of humour as well. Whenever possible, the man made light of a topic, proving himself fluent in sarcasm. He even managed to make the table laugh when they were discussing something as dull as the trade routes between the south and the east. If he weren't here to court the princess, Galdinia would have recommended he try his hand at pursuing Neryda.

Dillian did not say a lot. He seemed almost apprehensive to be at the table. Galdinia could understand the pressure that was likely placed on these men by their families, but she would have liked to have spoken to him more throughout the meal, even if just to have a break from Evarius' constant drawl in her left ear. Although he didn't make a show of his gift, Galdinia assumed him to be a Fire Flourisher as his eyes were fixed on the flames in the lantern when they danced under the pressure of Kaedric's breeze. His attention darted from person to person as they spoke, watching each one with his thoughtful green eyes.

The only person who said less than Dillian was Bentley. From his seat at the end of the table, he was able to observe with what appeared to be a sense of entertainment as Galdinia tried to juggle the four other men. He seemed somewhat more polished than he had the day prior, as though he was well-prepared for this moment and was watching it unfold as he had suspected. Galdinia supposed that he was more prepared for these interactions than she was, even if he had only met his companions briefly the previous morning. He surveyed the group, contributing to the conversation only when called upon, and given the nature of the gathering, the others weren't all that interested in pulling the princess' attention from themselves. Galdinia also noted that unlike the others, Bentley didn't make his gift obvious to her during the meal.

Once the plates were being cleared from the table by the attendants, Neryda had the men engrossed in a story about how she had used her powers once to feign sickness. While this particular story made Galdinia's stomach flip, she had heard it enough times that she could recite it herself, but certainly not with the vigour that Neryda told it. The princess excused herself with her empty glass of sparkling wine, moving to the bar cart across the terrace to refill it, hoping to avoid the climax of the story when Neryda went into her most foul detail.

"You're not a fan of stories about forced regurgitation?" Bentley's bright voice rang as he came to stand with Galdinia by the many bottles of wine, freshly squeezed juice and water.

"Strangely, no," Galdinia replied, turning from the man as she looked between the bottles, quickly realising none of them were open.

"Understandable," Bentley said, taking it upon himself to pick up one of the bottles. From the waist of his trousers, he pulled a small retractable knife that he ran along the bottleneck in one quick motion, sending the cork flying over the banister, landing somewhere below in the gardens. A small puff of foam gathered at the top before dripping down the bottle and over Bentley's hand. He tucked his knife away again before holding out his free hand for Galdinia's glass.

"Do you work as an attendant?" Galdinia asked, placing her glass in his outstretched hand. "I wouldn't know, given how little I actually know about you."

"Oh, is that right, Neryda?" Bentley asked, pointedly emphasising the false name she had given him the day before. He didn't take his eyes off the sparkling wine as he poured it.

"At no point yesterday when you were dripping wet and I was offering you a brand new set of clothes did you think to tell me you were in the city to meet *me*."

"And at no point yesterday when you insisted on replacing my clothing did you mention that you were the princess," Bentley countered, handing the glass back to Galdinia before filling up his own. "I don't make it a habit of telling girls that I meet on the street that I'm actually in town to meet somebody else. I'm also not the one that used a fake name."

"Ah, yes. 'Hello, stranger that just saved the life of one of my young citizens, thank you very much for that. Oh, I'm the princess, by the way.'" Galdinia's tone was mocking. "That does sound like a delightful conversation to have, doesn't it? Not that I owe you an explanation, but I didn't think I'd see you again, so a fake name just makes the whole process easier."

Galdinia took a sip from her glass. Bentley was still holding the bottle and the shadow of a dimple was settling in as he started to smile.

"I apologise for being misleading," Bentley said honourably. "Had I known you were the princess, I would have said something."

Galdinia sat on his words for a moment before answering. "Apology accepted."

Bentley looked expectantly at her, as though he waited for an apology also. After a pause, he turned to place the bottle back on the cart, admitting defeat.

"Let's start over," he said, reaching his hand out to Galdinia. "I am Lord Bentley Penrose of The Edges."

Galdinia's scrutinising eyes rested on him momentarily before she took his hand and shook it.

"I'm Princess Galdinia Elderwin of... right here." She smiled as she shook his hand. It was a firm handshake and she noted that his hand felt rougher than she had anticipated.

"Nice to meet you," he replied, a coy smile playing over his lips.

"And you."

"So, are you enjoying your brunch?" Bentley asked as they parted hands and both turned to look at the table, the four other men wrapped up in Neryda's gruesome tale.

"I've had better meals," Galdinia said before glancing at Bentley, who looked almost surprised by her candour. "I've also had worse. I hadn't anticipated meeting with five suitors this week, so you could say that I'm a little ill-prepared."

"And how are you liking your prospects?" Bentley nodded towards the men. "That Evarius is a real treat."

Galdinia couldn't help but smile.

"They're all very... pleasant." She quickly realised that Bentley was probably the last person she should be talking to about her thoughts on the other men on the terrace.

"How diplomatic of you."

"I'm practising."

"Very convincing."

Galdinia knew Bentley was teasing her and it took every fibre of her being not to glance up at him again to see what was no doubt a smug smile on his face. She kept her eyes ahead, watching as Neryda got to the most grisly part of her story.

"So will we get to see you again for more events this week?" Bentley asked just as the table of men burst into a fit of laughter.

"I'll be sure to send a message to your ship the moment I organise another thrilling meal like this one," Galdinia said as she took a step forward towards her seat before quickly turning to look at Bentley once again. "You'll be the first to know, Pup."

Galdinia raised her glass to the lord before moving back to the table. She knew she shouldn't hold the events of the previous day against him, but knowing that he was a suitor, and given the awkward encounters she had been subjected to because of someone else's decisions, she couldn't help but allow sarcasm to briefly take the reins. If the nickname embarrassed Bentley, he didn't show it; he looked after her expectantly, as though he was glad to have made some impression on the princess.

As she sat down again, the laughter at the table simmered as Neryda's story came to a close.

"It sounds like you and Neryda had quite an eventful childhood, Princess," Kell said from down the table, leaning back in his chair.

"Being friends with Neryda has that effect, yes," Galdinia said with a smile to her best friend. "I can't say I was complicit in her decision making when forcing herself to be sick though."

"So when Neryda was making herself ill to get out of her lessons, what were you doing, Princess?" Kaedric asked.

"I was likely in my lessons convincing our tutors that Neryda was, in fact, at home sick and not gallivanting beyond the city walls."

"You weren't one to break the rules?" Dillian queried.

"I certainly did from time to time with Ner, but it never looked good when the princess skipped lessons that were held in her own home."

"And what a home it is," Evarius said, his eyes roaming the sprawling outer walls of the castle. "I don't imagine you were ever bored living here."

"It has its moments."

"So when you weren't studying, what did you get up to around here?" Bentley asked the question as he finally came to sit back at the table, his eyes not leaving Galdinia's.

"We would visit the eastern docks, take the royal sailing boat out on the bay, or spend time in the castle library." Galdinia tried to think of activities that demonstrated her more responsible side; she didn't need five men of nobility to get the wrong idea about her.

"Sure, on slower days, maybe," Neryda interjected, raising her brows towards the princess. "We would spend hours at the tavern, go horse riding through the Bear Jaws Valley and tag along with her father on his hunting parties."

"You two are hunters?" Evarius asked, sitting up straighter in his chair.

"I wouldn't say hunters," Galdinia explained, taking another sip of her drink. "Neither of us are too interested in shooting birds out of the sky with arrows, but we did enjoy using apples as shooting practice."

"So you're archers?" Dillian chimed in.

"You could say that," Neryda said with a smirk. "Gal is definitely the better out of the two of us." Galdinia shot a glance at her best friend. "Last summer she struck an apple mid-air, right through the centre while on her horse. She almost split it down its core. I, on the other hand, can hardly hit an immovable tree trunk. It's embarrassing, really."

"That's impressive," Bentley said, pleasantly surprised. "It takes a lot of practise to miss a tree trunk."

The table laughed, and Neryda narrowed her eyes on the blonde lord.

"It's much harder than it looks," Neryda said pointedly. Bentley merely smirked at her.

"I'm an archer myself," Evarius said, turning his attention back to the princess; Galdinia could feel the silent groans of those around the table. "Perhaps we could go shooting together."

"Perhaps," Galdinia said, hoping not to commit to being part of a situation where this man would have a very sharp weapon in his hands.

"I've not had much practise with a bow and arrow," Kell said, swirling his drink. "On the coast, we mostly use harpoons. I'd love a lesson."

"Don't you use nets to catch fish?" Evarius challenged, saving Galdinia from having to turn down the archery lessons. "That doesn't sound particularly difficult."

"Nets are used for tuna and cod," Kell returned, eyeing off the big man across the table. "I like to use a harpoon for larger fish like marlin or sharks."

"You hunt sharks?" Kaedric asked.

"If they're in our bay and feasting on our catch, absolutely."

Galdinia looked at Neryda as the men argued. They were well-versed in communicating with their eyes and Galdinia knew that Neryda was just as unamused with the direction this conversation was heading in. As the men went back and forth about their weapons of choice, Galdinia's gaze landed on Bentley, who was decidedly keeping his mouth shut. He was watching the princess, however, smiling behind his glass. She wondered if he too was enjoying the display of testosterone.

"Well, gentlemen," Galdinia interjected, putting her glass down and placing a hand on Neryda's arm, "it has been a lovely morning, but we really must be off. I have a number of duties to attend to."

The men ceased their conversation, and Kaedric and Dillian made a move to stand.

"Please, don't get up, we can see ourselves out," Galdinia assured them, coaxing them back into their seats before any of them could start kissing her hand or insisting they walk her to her rooms.

"It has been a pleasure," Evarius said with a grin.

"I hope to see you again soon, Princess," Kaedric said earnestly.

"It was lovely to meet you all," Neryda said as she got to her feet.

"I can't wait to hear more stories." Kell smiled at Neryda, his eyes hopeful.

A quiet "thank you" was all Dillian could muster.

"I'm sure I'll see you soon, gentlemen," Galdinia replied before quickly adding, "I'm sure I'll see you at more of this week's planned events."

"We look forward to it," Bentley said, and Galdinia couldn't help but take note of his dimple that was very much on show.

The men nodded in agreement and the girls turned to leave. Before stepping through the door, Galdinia turned to look at Bentley once again, who raised his glass and a brow in her direction.

16

"This seems futile."

Galdinia was standing in the training room beneath the barracks. Captain Ilyon stood before her with the silk fan, waving it in her face.

After their brunch, Galdinia listened while Neryda spoke about each of the men, her friend providing her opinions, noting who she did and didn't care for. Galdinia allowed Neryda to talk quickly from the edge of her bed while she got herself ready for her training session. As Neryda listed every detail and thought she had had during the previous hour, Galdinia changed in her adjoining dressing room, deciding that she would wear something infinitely more comfortable than she had the day before for her training session. She changed into one of her riding outfits: tan trousers, a long-sleeved linen shirt that had an obscenely large bow at the collar, and, arguably most importantly, her comfortable riding boots. She was not going to stand on the rocky ground of the barracks' basement for hours without proper footwear.

And now she was standing in said room, the soles of her boots planted firmly on the cool ground, staring at the Captain of the Royal Guard as he sent wave after wave of air into her face.

"We mustn't give up, Princess," Ilyon insisted, sending another plume of air in her direction.

Galdinia had started with the fan in her own hand, trying to feel the breeze she artificially created, attempting to control the air that blew around her hands. Ilyon had said that being a Wind Wielder was one of the easier gifts to master because there was a constant supply of air at all times. It simply needed shifting in order for one to harness it. This did not make the princess feel any better about her predicament when three hours later, she was still unable to manipulate the breeze from the fan in any way.

She tried with her eyes closed, eyes open, using the fan, then using her hand, and finally blowing air with her mouth. This was when the captain took over to control the wind with the fan, insisting that she might find it easier if all she had to do was focus on the breeze itself.

As the chill of the underground room started to take its toll, Galdinia felt goosebumps travel up her arms with the push of each gust of wind. She found herself sniffing as she tried to focus on the air that hit her full force in the face. She could only imagine just how ridiculous she and the captain would look to an outsider.

"The air is making my nose run and my eyes are itchy and watering," Galdinia protested, lowering her hands to her side, her forearms screaming again.

Ilyon didn't reply. He merely placed the fan back on its podium in the centre of the room.

"So perhaps wind isn't my thing," Galdinia concluded, wiping her nose on the back of her sleeve. "We still have one more element to work with. Or, who knows, maybe I'm destined to be a priestess and I'll be a Light Lender."

"That is doubtful, Your Highness," Ilyon said honestly. "You're a princess. The Gods know that you are the rightful queen."

"I would really appreciate being told that by the Gods themselves," Galdinia said, glancing up at the dark abyss above that was the ceiling, as though speaking to the Gods. "Can we try with water now?"

"I think we should take it one element at a time," Ilyon said, standing before her with his arms crossed over his chest again. "I do, however, think there's something else we should be working on that may be more fruitful."

"Oh?" Galdinia asked, rubbing her eyes in an attempt to calm them.

"It's one thing to harness the elements, but it is another thing entirely to defend against them." Ilyon turned towards the stairs that led back up to the main barracks. "I'll just be a moment, Your Highness."

Minutes later, Ilyon returned to the chamber with three soldiers. They all bowed to the princess silently, their faces covered by their helmets, and their black armour stilted their movements slightly. The only parts of their skin she could see were their shadowed eyes that sat behind the slits in their helmets. Each of them moved behind the podiums, standing at attention. The soldier behind the fan was the tallest and leanest of the three, the one behind the lantern of fire was broader and about the same height as Ilyon, and the third, behind the bowl of water, was the shortest, barely as tall as Galdinia. Aside from their build, there weren't any recognisable differences between the soldiers.

"These are three of my best gifted soldiers," Ilyon explained, coming to stand at Galdinia's side as she observed the three men. "They each have a different gift and are extremely skilled in both combat and the use of their powers. Maybe our time today would be better spent on some defence training."

The captain had also brought down with him a large metal shield, which he held out for the princess to take. The shield was as long and wide as her torso and was far heavier than she anticipated, but she held it up firmly as she strapped it to her arm.

"Combat?" Galdinia asked, looking quizzically up at Ilyon.

"You won't actually be attacking anyone yourself," Ilyon explained. "But learning to defend yourself against the elements is imperative. I don't imagine you'll be going into battle any time soon, but it would be wise to prepare you nonetheless. We know how ruthless your enemies are."

Galdinia considered this, looking down at the shield on her arm. Although she wanted nothing more than to keep trying to tap into her gift, she much preferred the idea of doing something more achievable for a change.

"Alright," she finally agreed. "Let's get to work."

One by one, the soldiers followed Ilyon's instructions, taking control of their respective elements to send towards the princess. Ilyon had them send shards of water, plumes of wind, and balls of flame in her direction. They all had control of their elemental weapons, but Galdinia was still expected to dodge and protect herself against them.

She listened carefully to the captain's directions to shield herself from the elements; when he instructed her to roll across the ground, she did so, using the shield to her advantage to help break her fall.

He taught her to parry the flames, dodge the water, and push against the wind that came her way. Although she wished to have these powers herself, she was glad to be doing something in their sessions that felt productive. Ilyon also told Galdinia to watch the soldiers' hands and eyes as they manipulated and moved their elements. Some of them twitched their fingers, others stepped forward before they attacked; all of them were skilled enough to show almost no sign of using their powers when instructed to do so. The princess was both impressed and intimidated.

Once Galdinia's face was flushed and her shirt was stained with sweat, Ilyon finally called an end to their training session. Each of the soldiers stood in front of Galdinia, weapons now stowed away. They bowed before walking towards the stairs at the back of the room. As they started to climb, Galdinia wiped the sweat and dirt from her brow, and her breath caught in her throat as she watched one of the soldiers pull off their helmets.

The shortest of the soldiers, the Water Weaver, revealed a long ponytail of blonde hair and high cheek bones as she walked up the stairs, talking quietly with her companions. She glanced back at the princess momentarily before turning around the bend in the stairs and disappearing from sight.

"She's a woman?" Galdinia asked, her breath still coming out in puffs as she looked to Ilyon. "I didn't think women were allowed to be soldiers. I thought they were only able to work as armourers or healers in the army."

"Ah, so your father didn't make you privy to our Royal Guard program then?" A rare smirk flew over Ilyon's lips. "We opened the program up to female applicants about five years ago. It was the king's idea. He assumed that we must have strong and powerful women in our midst who would want to serve the crown. He wasn't wrong."

"But why is it a secret? He never told me about that when teaching me about my royal duties."

"I'll be honest with you, Your Highness," Ilyon said, choosing his words carefully. "The Syndicate doesn't even know. Your father, Ryden and I made an agreement to start accepting female applicants and, well, the results speak for themselves. We wanted to trial it for a few years before making it public knowledge. The women were personally invited to apply by the three of us and were sworn to secrecy."

"And the rest of the soldiers? This seems like far too big a secret to successfully manage."

"To start with, there aren't many female soldiers, and they are trained privately in the capital. The other soldiers are also sworn to secrecy as part of their oath and everyone outside the program believe them to be, as you said, armourers or healers." Ilyon seemed quite pleased with himself. "I'd say that if the princess wasn't aware of it, then no one else in the capital will be."

Galdinia was surprised that such a secret was so well hidden, but then she contemplated the other secrets her father and Ryden had kept from her. She landed on feeling impressed.

"I look forward to supporting your decision to open the program to women as well," Galdinia said finally, causing another uncharacteristic smile to appear on Ilyon's face. "It will be at the top of my list to establish when I am crowned."

"Thank you, Your Highness," Ilyon replied.

Galdinia wiped her sleeve over her brow once again as she looked at each of the elements before her in turn, none of them appearing to have been disturbed by the soldiers who had just been controlling them. They were so effortless in their use of their gifts, twisting and shaping the elements into whatever form they pleased. She could feel a touch of resentment bubble up within her as she compared herself to their abilities.

"You did well today, Princess," Ilyon remarked as he stood beside Galdinia, also observing the podiums. "Not many people find learning defence techniques an easy task, and you picked up on them quickly."

"I can shield myself against them, but I can't control them," she replied quietly, the hint of a spiteful tone underlying her words.

"It can take time. I can rest easy knowing that you can, at the very least, adequately detect the elements should you need to, and you're already showing a capacity of being able to defend yourself against them."

Galdinia didn't reply. She just breathed in deeply, trying to regain her breath.

"We can keep working on both harnessing your gift and combat defence," Ilyon said, nodding before turning to the princess. "You worked hard today, Your Highness. If you don't mind, though, I'd better get this room back in order."

"Of course," Galdinia said, collecting her cloak from the bench at the edge of the room. "What else do you use this space for? Other than those three, I've never seen other soldiers down here."

"Group combat," the captain said, his words clipped as he started to move the podiums away from the centre of the room. "It can tend to get a little loud, and we don't like to bother the neighbours, so it usually takes place down here."

"Group combat?" Galdinia asked, looking around the room again. There were no signs of attack on the walls or floor and no pieces of weaponry ready for use.

"It is mostly hand-to-hand combat, close range attacks, with and without their gifts," Ilyon explained, moving the final podium to the edge of the room. "I split my battalions up into groups of five, and they have to strategise to take down an opposing group. It's a good way to build morale while also teaching them about each others' strengths and weaknesses. If they aren't aware of their weakest member, they don't stand a chance defeating the opposition."

Galdinia nodded, intrigued. "I'd be interested in seeing how group combat works one day."

Although Galdinia didn't revel in violence, she was fascinated by the strategy of armies, particularly on a smaller scale. She would have enjoyed seeing that play out under the instruction of Captain Ilyon.

"It's not usual to have spectators, especially not young princesses." The word "young" still struck a chord with Galdinia, but she tried to ignore it. "I'm not sure how productive my soldiers would be knowing that their future ruler was watching them."

Galdinia appreciated that Ilyon still spoke about her as though he was sure she would take the throne at the end of the week.

"I suppose so," she agreed, walking with him to the winding stairs, trying to mirror his confidence in her. "Perhaps I will visit once I am their queen and they have no choice but to put on a good show."

"I'm sure we can arrange that." Ilyon smiled as he directed the princess back up the stairs to the floor above.

17

WHILE STILL SORE, GALDINIA WAS GLAD TO STEP INTO THE SUNSHINE of the afternoon as she walked out onto Main Court, trailed by two guards who were to escort her back to the castle. The city was well and truly alive in the afternoon sun; some citizens were sitting in the windows of the opened taverns, others were perusing the markets.

In the square, a Water Weaver was performing for a group of citizens. He was controlling a collection of orbs of water in a variety of sizes, using his mind to levitate the spheres above the heads of his onlookers. With a simple flick of his wrist, they all collided, sending a fountain of minuscule droplets cascading over the crowd. A chorus of delighted applause followed as he bowed. Galdinia could only hope that she would gain such a connection to an element.

As she cast her gaze over the square, Galdinia's eyes fell upon the illustrious fountain in the centre. Sitting on its edge, talking to the same man he had been yesterday, was someone she was becoming all too familiar with.

"Princess Galdinia!" Bentley waved from the fountain, quickly excusing himself from his friend and jogging over to the princess. As if the two guards were not already attention enough, Lord Bentley calling her name caused many eyes to turn and look in her direction. Some citizens smiled, others waved, some bowed their heads.

"Hello, Lord Bentley," Galdinia said, attempting a pleasant tone as he bounded toward her. "I wasn't expecting to see you this afternoon."

"I happened to be meeting with one of my attendants," he said breezily, motioning to the man who was still sitting at the fountain, watching the two of them. "Are you going back up to the castle?"

"I am."

"Would you like an escort?" he replied, looking to the guards and then adding, "Perhaps one that's a little livelier?"

Galdinia eyed him off for a moment, looking up into his smiling face, his dimple on display. She reminded herself that she didn't have a legitimate reason to dislike this man; his being here was part of a plan organised by her father and the governor. He hadn't intended on stepping into the hostile situation that it had become. Galdinia's gripe was with the law, not Bentley.

"Sure."

The princess continued to walk up Main Court and Bentley fell in step beside her.

"I actually have something to tell you," Bentley said matter-of-factly.

"Oh?" Galdinia asked, putting her hands behind her back as she walked.

"Yes. Well, actually, I suppose I have to thank you," he amended, twisting his body to face her as they walked. Now that they were alone, Galdinia noticed that Bentley was significantly more animated than he was that morning at brunch.

"Mmm?"

"I wasn't sure if it would be appropriate to bring it up in front of the other gentlemen this morning, given that we had already met and I wouldn't want them to get the wrong idea."

"That would be tragic, yes." Galdinia's easy sarcasm had found its way back to her as she spoke to him.

"You see, after our encounter yesterday morning, I'm not sure if you remember, but you left me with one of the most..." Bentley pondered his words before continuing, "terrifying women I have ever met."

Galdinia couldn't help but smile, allowing her guarded exterior to drop ever so slightly.

"And I don't say that lightly. I have had plenty of experience with the mothers of desperate young girls who would do anything for a lord's hand." Bentley's face was serious as he spoke. "You left me with a woman who chastised my clothes, berated my stylist for the way they had cut my hair, and did not stop frowning at me for twenty minutes."

Galdinia smiled as she looked at the path ahead of her. She could imagine Madame Moya doing all of those things and more. She only wished that she had stayed longer to experience it firsthand.

"By the time she had me in a pair of trousers and a shirt that fit my 'too long limbs'—her words, not mine—I had to force myself out of her dressing rooms, insisting that I didn't need a necktie or new shoes. Well, that got me into trouble, didn't it?" Bentley continued his speech with vigour. "'Who let you into the capital with those things on? These are not made of quality leather!' She then proceeded to force me to try on nine—*nine*—pairs of boots until she found ones that were just the right shade of brown."

The satisfaction that Galdinia felt as he told his story was overwhelming.

"She didn't even give me my old clothes back. I watched as she threw them into a furnace at the back of her shop. Why does she even have a furnace? She's a seamstress! My guess is to humiliate anyone that steps into her shop and thinks they have any idea about fashion." Bentley threw his arms into the air in disbelief.

"So what you're trying to say is thank you for the new outfit?"

Bentley let out a long breath and said, "You took the words right out of my mouth."

"I thought so," Galdinia said, looking back at him with a smile.

There was a moment of quiet between them before he spoke again.

"Given that I am now up to speed with the current fashion trends, thanks to Madame Moya, I've got to ask: where have you been that you are dressed like this this afternoon?"

Galdinia looked down at her attire, aware that it was quite different from anything one would expect a princess to wear. She wasn't sure how much she was willing to tell Bentley, but after already lying to him the day before, she thought she owed him some semblance of truth.

"I've been at the soldiers' barracks with the captain," Galdinia admitted, watching Bentley's face as his eyebrows rose in interest. "He's training me in preparation for… I've just been training with him recently."

Bentley nodded slowly as though he was pondering how much he could pry.

"Is he training you in combat? Getting ready to send you out with the troops?" Bentley's intrigue was palpable. "Or are you teaching him a thing or two about archery?"

"Not quite," Galdinia said, treading carefully. "I'm sure you've heard that I am the giftless princess already. The captain is trying to help coax out my powers, preparing me for when they arrive."

Again, Bentley nodded. "I had heard that, yes."

"It seems the entire kingdom knows," Galdinia said, defeated.

"I'm sure not the entire kingdom knows. I hear those in The Hook are quite disconnected from the world. I'm sure they don't even know there's a princess."

Galdinia appreciated his attempt to make light of the situation. The level of inadequacy she felt was still overwhelming, and she could feel the heat rising in her chest just at the mention of her missing gift.

"Thank you for brunch this morning," Bentley went on quickly. "Did you enjoy yourself?"

She knew that he was pressing for insight about her thoughts on the other suitors. "Like I said this morning, I hadn't planned on meeting with suitors this week, but I suppose it was a pleasant morning."

"You keep saying that word, *pleasant*," Bentley said, scrutinising Galdinia. "Is it in the princess' handbook to always be so delicate about things?"

"If there's a princess handbook, I'd like to see it," Galdinia said with a scoff.

"Come on, what did you really think?" After a beat, he said, "I'll go first. Kaedric came on a bit strong, but he's nice enough. Dillian is quiet, but thoughtful and respectful. Kell—where to begin? He has the dreamiest smile I've ever seen." Galdinia chuckled now. "While he's obviously a very physically strong man, I don't imagine you thought Evarius boasting about his archery skills was your cup of tea."

"And you know what I like, do you?"

"I think I'm starting to, yes." Bentley's remark was subtle, but Galdinia felt some weight behind his words. "And I would be surprised if brutish and egotistical was your type."

"Did I forget to mention that a lack of emotional intelligence and self-awareness are two of my favourite characteristics in a man?"

Bentley's lips curled at Galdinia's words.

"Then you have found your perfect match in Lord Evarius, Princess." Although he was joking, Galdinia admired his confidence; she was still wary of it, but she respected it nonetheless.

"I did notice, though, you were the only one not touting their gift this morning." Galdinia peered at him as they walked. "What element do you have control over, Lord Bentley?"

Bentley didn't respond. He merely stopped in the middle of the street, causing Galdinia and her guards to stop as well. He turned to the front of a nearby store that seemed to sell an array of celebration supplies from lanterns to fireworks to alcohol. Out the front was a display of lanterns that hung on hooks of varying heights. With one quick movement of his hand, Bentley drew out one of the flickering flames, sending it flying over the street towards them, proving himself to be a Fire Flourisher. He twisted it into various shapes: that of a bird, then a feather, and finally, a rose. He let it hover before the princess, where she stared into the gliding flame, mesmerised.

A moment later, Bentley called the flame back towards himself, over his shoulder, and into its lantern once again. He turned back to the princess, who looked at him, impressed.

"That was... charming."

"Thank you," he said with a smile, starting to walk beside the princess again. "It comes in useful on cold days, or when you have to quickly dry your hair after diving into the ocean after a drowning child."

Now Galdinia returned his grin as she looked up at him. "You were walking with me through town for at least five minutes! Why didn't you dry yourself?"

"There wasn't a single flame in sight!" Bentley complained. "It wasn't until I harnessed the warmth of Madame Moya's furnace that I was able to dry my hair. This whole Week of Mourning thing has really impeded on my access to fire; people aren't awake early enough for my liking."

At the mention of the week's purpose, Galdinia's face fell, and she looked straight ahead again, casting her eyes on the paved road. She realised quickly that she hadn't thought about her father all day, his memory being forgotten in the flurry of brunch and training. Here she was, walking through her father's streets with a man who was pining after her hand in marriage, and her crown, when she should have been mourning her father. Her heart dropped and she suddenly felt unwell. How could she have forgotten about him so quickly? She was so disappointed in herself.

"I'm sorry, Princess, are you okay?" Bentley asked hurriedly, keeping up with Galdinia's quickening pace.

"Yes, fine," she stammered, hoping to get back to the castle quicker.

"Did I say something—"

"It's fine."

Bentley didn't say another word as they walked up Main Court, turning onto Royal Row and up to the castle gates.

"Well, thank you for the walk." Bentley smiled as he stopped in front of the gates.

"Yes, thank you for accompanying me back home." Galdinia didn't know where to look.

"My pleasure." Bentley nodded. "Will I see you tomorrow evening at the feast?"

With the madness of everything that occurred in the previous twenty-four hours, Galdinia had forgotten about the Royal Feast that would be held in the castle ballroom the following night.

"Um, yes, you will." Galdinia nodded, finally looking up at Bentley. His blonde hair was pushed back from his face, and he stood tall over her, his height made even more obvious now that she was in her flat riding boots.

"Fantastic," he said. "See you tomorrow, Your Highness."

"Yes, see you tomorrow, Lord Bentley."

Galdinia turned from the blonde man and walked through the gates, up the path, and disappeared into the entrance hall, her heart far heavier than it had been five minutes prior.

FOURTH DAY OF MOURNING

18

On the morning of the Fourth Day of Mourning, Galdinia made her way silently down to the kitchens, hoping to find some quiet reprieve before what she imagined would be a rather taxing day. The Royal Feast was arguably the most extravagant event of the week. While the banquet on the Sixth Day would host all of Elderguard's citizens in the square, making it the event of highest attendance, the Royal Feast was hosted by the royal family and the Syndicate in the castle's ballroom, and only those of nobility were invited. This event was more than a nice dinner with some dignitaries; it was an elaborate feast that did not compromise on expense when it came to food, drinks, decoration, and entertainment. Of all the events of the Week of Mourning, this was the most coveted. Lords and ladies from across the kingdom would travel into the capital for this event, bypassing both the funeral and coronation in some cases, simply because this was an event not to be missed. If you were invited to the Royal Feast, you attended the Royal Feast at all costs.

Despite her request to be involved in all the Syndicate's plans moving forward, Galdinia had decided to relinquish the control of planning the feast to the governing body. Ryden had suggested that she should focus on her training and other duties—and she knew that by "other duties" he meant getting to know the suitors. By the Fourth

Day, she was glad not to have the responsibility of planning the distinguished event when her limbs ached and her head was swimming with all sorts of decisions. She didn't have the capacity to also select flower arrangements or dessert options.

As she walked to the kitchens through the servant's walkways, she was reminded of mornings before her father passed. Before leaving for the Isle of Crystal, she would often join Miss Giles for a cup of tea. It seemed that no matter what time of the morning she went to the kitchens, Miss Giles was already standing by the stove or chopping something at the bench. Galdinia wondered if she slept in the kitchens and not in her chambers in the attendants' quarters.

By the time Galdinia walked into the kitchens, she realised that this morning was very unlike those that she spent here just a week prior.

From above her pots on the burners, Miss Giles was barking orders at the attendants who moved around the room in what appeared to be a wild, bustling dance. Some were chopping vegetables, others were whisking liquid in large metal bowls, and some were shining dishes. It seemed that the preparations for this evening's event began early. Galdinia walked slowly over to the fire, pulling up a chair to warm herself by the hearth.

"Raelle!" Miss Giles called across the room, her hands fervently stirring something in the pots in front of her. "Fetch me two dozen eggs from the henhouse! And I don't want to find any cracked shells on the footpath later today."

Galdinia held her hands out towards the fire, warming them amidst the frosty chill of the morning. She watched the flames as they danced into the air, embers and smoke floating into the chimney above. The endless nature of the fire intrigued her, moving as one yet also somehow independently, whipping into nothing at its tips.

"Good morning, dear." Miss Giles' rough voice pulled Galdinia from her trance as the woman approached her. "I wasn't expecting to see you down here this morning. It's a bit of a zoo."

"I'm sorry, Miss Giles, I can get out of your hair."

"Don't be ridiculous," Miss Giles scoffed, placing a pot directly on the flames in the fireplace. "I was going to send your breakfast up to you shortly, so it's no trouble to prepare it now. Eggs?"

"That would be lovely."

Minutes later, the cook had personally prepared Galdinia her favourite breakfast and placed it on the table beside her. Miss Giles also brought with her a bowl of batter and began stirring it as she sat at the seat beside the princess. "How are you doing, love? I don't imagine the last few days have been easy."

Galdinia hesitated, picking up her fork and using it to push and prod her eggs. She had nothing to hide from Miss Giles; Galdinia already knew that the woman would be privy to everything that had transpired inside the castle over the last two days.

"I'm alright," Galdinia said with a sigh, not taking her eyes off her breakfast. "Honestly, I have been quite distracted, what with training with the captain and meeting with the suitors—I imagine you've heard all about that."

Galdinia inclined her chin in the direction of the maids on the other side of the room, who quickly got back to work after staring at the princess.

"Ah, yes, I have heard my little birdies chirping about that," Miss Giles admitted. "They're under strict instruction not to repeat anything they hear within the castle though."

"I know." Galdinia nodded, staring at her plate. "The capital already knows about my infirmity anyway."

"Infirmity? Princess, there is no such thing!" Miss Giles said with a frown, still madly stirring. "You are merely waiting for your body to catch up with the Gods' plans."

Galdinia gave Miss Giles a brief nod before taking her first bite of breakfast. She didn't know how much of this conversation she could take after yesterday's training session.

"Have you been able to take some time for yourself at least?"

"Not really," Galdinia replied between bites. "Yesterday, I somehow forgot about my father's passing. I had brunch with the suitors in the morning, and then I went to training, and it wasn't until a conversation later in the afternoon that I suddenly remembered why all of this was happening. It was as if I'd subconsciously thought I'd go back up to father's room to see him after training, tell him all about it and laugh with him at how sore my arms were. But then it all came crashing down at once, as though it caught up to me within a few seconds. How could I have forgotten that my father had passed away? It feels ludicrous to say now, but that was honestly how I felt."

Miss Giles stopped stirring and set her eyes intently on Galdinia's. "Your father's passing was not short, love, you must remember that. You've been preparing yourself for this for three months, whether you meant to or not. It's not surprising that you have found ways to distract yourself, sending you back to the days that had become your norm. It can be hard to grieve a loved one properly in the best of circumstances, and given everything your young self is dealing with, it's no wonder your subconscious is playing tricks on you."

Galdinia nodded slowly, once again pushing her food around the plate.

"It's okay to mourn him too," Miss Giles said quietly, leaning in close to the princess. "Distracting yourself will only get you so far. You will have to let go at some stage, and that's okay."

Galdinia could feel the tightening in her chest and the heat of tears filling her eyes. She did everything in her power not to let them fall, breathing deeply, trying to hold her emotion in place.

"I think I'm afraid that by saying goodbye, I'll lose him. Or worse, forget him." Her voice cracked on her last word. Miss Giles reached out her weathered hand and placed it on Galdinia's arm, instantly warming Galdinia more than the fires beside her.

"Don't let the grief fester, my dear," Miss Giles said, patting Galdinia's arm now. "I've had to mourn many people in my time, and I can tell you that saying goodbye is far better than forcing yourself to hold on. Your heart wasn't made to hold this kind of pain."

Galdinia smiled sadly at Miss Giles.

From across the room, Brigitte came rushing in the door, looking around the kitchens. She caught Galdinia's teary eyes, looked at her as if she was going to speak, then backed down.

Galdinia took a deep breath and steeled herself. She would mourn her father, but not today. For now, she needed to attend to her duties as princess.

"Brigitte? What is it?" Galdinia asked, wiping her eyes. Miss Giles released her hand from Galdinia's arm, stood up, and took her mixing bowl back with her to the stove.

"I'm sorry to interrupt, Your Highness," Brigitte said timidly, scurrying across the room towards Galdinia. "Governor Ryden has arrived, and he said he needs to speak with you imminently. He is waiting for you in the entrance hall."

"Thank you, Brigitte," Galdinia said, looking down at her half-eaten breakfast; she took one more bite and picked up her plate, walking towards Miss Giles at her station. "Thank you for… everything, Miss Giles."

The older woman took the plate from the princess, smiling at the girl that she had come to care for so much. "Enjoy today, dear." Miss Giles reached out a hand and wiped a stray tear from Galdinia's cheek with the back of her rough finger. "You're allowed to."

The entrance hall was bustling with movement; the castle staff were moving in and out of the ballroom, some carrying flowers and candelabras, and others, pieces of furniture. The usual guards were posted at the doors, keeping a watchful eye on every attendant that walked through the hall. It seemed to be a well-oiled machine, working fervently yet organised. At the centre of the room stood Ryden, a roll of parchment and a quill in his hand, pointing various people in different directions as they prepared the ballroom for the evening ahead.

"I think a little higher," the governor said as he watched two attendants teetering on ladders on either side of the ballroom doors, trying to attach a multi-coloured flower garland around its frame. "Oh, here, let me do it."

With an easy flick of his wrist, Ryden sent a gust of wind towards the garland, effortlessly lifting it higher around the doorframe. The attendants got to work, quickly securing it in place.

"You seem to have everything coming together nicely, Governor."

At the sound of her voice, Ryden turned to face Galdinia. "Thank you, Princess. I can't say that party planning is my forte, but the Syndicate has managed."

"I'm grateful I didn't have to do it myself," Galdinia replied, watching a pair of attendants emerge from the storage rooms behind the stairs with arms full of crockery, carefully rushing to the ballroom.

"Ah, yes, how have your other duties been coming along?"

Galdinia silently laughed to herself at the governor's consistent use of that phrase.

"Well, training with Ilyon has been exhausting and not particularly fruitful. Who knew staring at the elements, trying to make them move could be such a tiring activity?" Galdinia tried to hide her frustration by speaking about the experience lightly. "And my brunch with your selection of lords yesterday was... somehow more painful."

Ryden's head whipped around to look at the princess, his eyes pulling away from the commotion around them. "You don't like them?" Ryden asked, concern in his eyes.

"They're fine, I suppose." Galdinia shrugged, averting her eyes to look at the decorations being set up around the entrance hall. "On paper, they're all very impressive. They have good connections in their provinces, they come from powerful families, and they're all fairly pleasant."

There's that word again.

"So what's the issue?" Ryden asked, his eyes narrowing.

"As soon as you put five men in a room, all vying for the same woman, all authenticity is lost. I've never been subject to so many compliments, peacocking, and staring all at once."

"They were probably nervous."

"I'm sure they were, but if you haven't noticed, I don't really have time for nerves. The only mildly interesting one was Lord Bentley." Both Galdinia and the governor heard the rise in her voice at his name. She wasn't prepared for it and tried to continue speaking quickly. "But he practically ignored me for the entire meal, so I'm not sure what to make of that."

"Perhaps you could spend more time with them tonight at the feast," Ryden suggested, looking from the preparations to the princess and back again. "And there is something else I need to ask you."

"Yes, Brigitte did say you needed to speak with me," Galdinia noted, also watching the pair of attendants who were awkwardly trying to fix the oversized garland to the doorframe.

"As per your request at the beginning of the week, I promised to keep you informed in any goings-on around the castle and capital, and I have a request." Galdinia could hear the apprehension in Ryden's voice as he spoke; he was never nervous when speaking to the princess. Perhaps her speech two days earlier had an impact. "Tonight will be the grandest celebration that the capital has held since the downfall of the Pyrins in your grandparents' time. I believe tonight is shaping up to be an event that will surpass all others in both decadence and attendance."

Galdinia's eyes flicked to the governor; he wasn't watching her but instead staring ahead at the struggling attendants. She too turned her gaze back to them.

"Because of this, we have many lords and ladies travelling from across the kingdom to be here, most of them expected to arrive by noon. We are anticipating more ships than ever in the docks, which is becoming contentious with our fishers. I had hoped to clear some space in the docks by sending a number of our fishers' vessels out into the cove until further notice. I'm sure you can imagine their response to this. 'These visiting ships are taking up enough space to house all of our fishing boats,' the dockyard manager told me when I proposed my suggestion yesterday."

"Who do the visiting ships belong to?" Galdinia asked, and Ryden looked at her with a pointed expression.

"Your five new friends."

"Right, well, just send the suitors' ships out into the cove to make room; we can ferry them in on the royal sailing boat. Problem solved."

"Yes, this would be most logical, but given how often they will be in the capital for the next few days—what with the Royal Feast and the banquet, plus there's five of them who need to be attended to at any given moment—I see that creating more issues at the dock than the ships themselves."

"Ryden," Galdinia said firmly, crossing her arms over her chest, "what is it that you want, exactly?"

"Could we invite the five men to stay in the castle for the remainder of the week?"

Galdinia's eyes tightened on him. "What about the plethora of inns at our disposal?" Galdinia asked, frowning.

"They're all full, thanks to our visiting guests for this evening. I've enquired with them all." Ryden spoke quickly, trying to fill in the gaps before Galdinia could protest further. "They can stay in the Syndicate's chambers and will leave on the Seventh Day, unless of course one of them proves to be successful."

Galdinia hated that he made her sound like she was part of some transaction.

"I would give them strict instructions to remain in the Syndicate's chambers when in the castle. They would not be allowed to wander through the grounds or the building unless otherwise instructed by you personally. You would be given jurisdiction over their stay, and I will post two guards at the door of the wing at all times to ensure they don't bend any rules."

Galdinia let out a huff of hot air, shaking her head in frustrated disbelief.

On a practical level, she agreed with Ryden. Of course she should invite them to stay here. Of course she should be a gracious and kind ruler. Of course she should put the interests of others before herself. But knowing that they would be sleeping under one roof made her stomach flip. It was one thing to surprise her with suitors, and it was another thing entirely to have them stay in her home.

"Fine," Galdinia finally said, and she watched Ryden's shoulders relax. "But if they come anywhere near the Western Keep, I will personally remove them from the castle and have them sent back home."

"A fair request," Ryden said, nodding.

"Governor, that isn't a request; it is a promise."

"Absolutely," Ryden said in fervent agreement. "Maybe having them nearby would allow for you to get to know them more in less formal settings. Those nerves of theirs might just disappear."

Galdinia thought on the governor's words for a moment. If she was going to secure her throne by the end of the week, perhaps what she actually needed to do was test their nerve. They were candidates to become king, after all, and ensuring they all had a backbone might actually be worth her while.

"That's not a bad idea, Governor," Galdinia said with a smile, and Ryden looked at her, almost concerned. "Would you please have an attendant fetch my suitors and Captain Ilyon? Have them meet me at the Northern Gates on horseback in one hour. I have an idea for my training session this afternoon. Tell the captain we will require enough bows and arrows for seven."

Ryden's eyes were furrowed, sceptical. "You're not going to take them to the valley and shoot them, are you?"

"Don't give me ideas, Governor," Galdinia said with a smirk. "No, in fact, the suitors requested a short excursion yesterday, so perhaps this is my chance to kill two birds with one stone… metaphorically, of course."

Ryden mirrored Galdinia's expression. "I'd best go invite them now then. I will see you this evening for the feast, Princess, along with all five of our guests, alive and well." Ryden emphasised his final words, looking at the princess pointedly. It seemed as though the tables had turned, and Galdinia was glad to have an ounce of power back.

"See you this evening, Governor," Galdinia said with a smile, turning from Ryden to return to her rooms before calling over her shoulder. "And I promise, not a scratch!"

19

Back in her chambers, Galdinia found Neryda sitting in the bay window, enjoying a breakfast parfait from the kitchens.

"You were up early today," Neryda noted, watching her friend walk into the room.

"I was peckish, so I thought I'd go visit Miss Giles," Galdinia said quickly, kicking off her woven slippers and coming to sit opposite her friend on the window seat. "You seem to have yourself sorted."

"Yes, Brigitte came looking for you earlier, and I asked her to send for some breakfast. I think Miss Giles has outdone herself." Neryda took another mouthful of food, licking the spoon clean. "Did Brigitte find you?"

"She certainly did." Galdinia sighed, looking out the window. "Ryden wanted to speak with me about a small predicament."

"Good to see he's listening to your terms from the other day." Neryda nodded once, giving her friend a triumphant smile.

"He wanted to ask me if the suitors could stay in the castle for the remainder of the week."

Neryda stopped eating, her spoon halfway to her mouth, lips parted. "You're kidding?"

"I wish I was."

Neryda let out a hearty laugh.

"I'm glad you think this is funny," Galdinia said, attempting to stay composed, but she too broke into a chuckle at her friend's reaction.

"This is brilliant!" Neryda put the glass bowl and spoon down on a cushion beside her, too preoccupied with the conversation to continue eating. "They'll be right under our noses! We can actually see what they're like up close and personal."

"I don't really want them *that* close to me."

"I meant proximity, Galdinia. Don't be ridiculous." Neryda rolled her eyes and continued. "Yesterday they were all poised and trying to impress you. If they're staying here, they'll probably be more comfortable and actually behave like human beings. Would it be terrible if you could really get to know them?"

"Well, that was my thought process when I spoke with Ryden," Galdinia admitted. "And I have organised to go shooting with them this morning with Ilyon."

Neryda was stunned. "You mean to tell me that you have willingly planned to spend time with these men?"

"Yep."

"Wow, there really are Gods. It's a miracle!" Neryda said in jest, her eyes filled with delight. "You don't plan on shooting *them*, do you?"

"Why is that everyone's initial assumption?"

"Because by all accounts, you hated these men two days ago."

"I didn't even know them then," Galdinia retorted. "I hated the idea of them. But as I see it, if one of them could potentially be on his way to be king in three days, then I'd better give them a real chance. So why not take them shooting, get to know them, and do some training all at once?"

"It's actually a really good idea," Neryda conceded with a nod. "So when are we going?"

"Do you intend on being present for every interaction I have with these men?"

"Of course," Neryda said, surprised that Galdinia would question her attendance. "How are you to make an informed decision without me?"

"Codependence does make for a healthy friendship," Galdinia said sarcastically. "So what does my other half think of them so far?"

"They all have potential," Neryda said, crossing her legs and leaning back into the cushions behind her. "Evarius, while a bit of a self-concerned individual, certainly has enough experience as a lord, and as a lord's son, to be king. And I can't be sure, but I think he comes from an impressive family."

Galdinia chuckled. Everyone present at the brunch heard about Evarius' family and status more times than they could count.

"I'm unsure if Dillian has much more to open up about, but he did seem to be a kind soul. I'd like to see him after a few glasses of hard whiskey. I think he'd be the kind of person who is overly philosophical about everything, thinking more than doing."

"I'm not entirely sure that is what we need in a king."

Neryda nodded in agreement. "Kaedric was nice and my goodness, that smile! Sure, the constant barrage of accolades and praise started to wear on me, but he was trying his hardest. I wonder if he is the type to calm down when away from a room of accomplished bachelors. I can't imagine what he'll be like tonight at the feast."

Galdinia shuddered at the thought.

"Now, Kell," Neryda said with a smirk, her eyes becoming fierce. "He was a charmer. Good with his words, impressive control of his gift, and he brought you a rose from his mother's garden, so we know he's probably a family man."

"Please," Galdinia scoffed, practically laughing in her friend's face. "You had him in the palm of your hand when you were telling that story. He is far more interested in you than he is in me."

"Well, perhaps being under the same roof will help prove that hypothesis," Neryda said with a wicked grin, happily thinking of the boy who had made her laugh and shared the same gift as her. "Finally, Bentley."

Galdinia found her heart picking up speed as Neryda said his name. It was involuntary, and she wished her pulse wouldn't speak for her subconscious.

"Honestly, the way he just sat back and observed made him seem a bit too self-assured, like he was lording over us or something. We don't even know what his gift is." Galdinia wasn't expecting this assessment from Neryda, and she didn't know how to respond to it. "Sure, he's got great hair, and that dimple is to die for, but I don't think he's in this for the right reasons."

"Do you really think any of them are?" Galdinia asked with an arched brow. "They're all hoping to make their way onto the throne, not find love. I don't think that is exclusive to Bentley."

"I don't know, he just seems a bit too smug."

"You don't really know him," Galdinia said, averting her eyes.

"We don't really know any of them," Neryda said pointedly, "remember?"

Galdinia nodded, still not looking at her friend.

"Do you like him, Gal?"

Neryda's candour took Galdinia off guard. "What? No." Galdinia stumbled on her words, trying to concentrate. "I just think I may have judged him too soon after our first meeting and yesterday—"

"Yesterday?" Neryda's eyes narrowed on Galdinia.

"I ran into him yesterday after my training session and he walked me back to the castle," Galdinia explained.

"What happened?"

"Nothing *happened*," Galdinia assured her. "It was very brief. He berated me for leaving him alone with Madame Moya and he showed me his gift. He's a Fire Flourisher."

"He berated you?"

"It was all very lighthearted."

"Right."

The two girls looked at one another, eyeing each other off.

"So you don't fancy him then?" Neryda asked, breaking the silence.

"No… I don't know. I'm very confused about my feelings right now." Neryda's eyes told Galdinia to elaborate. "I saw Drystan two days ago, and we had this conversation about… us. He made it quite clear that we can only be friends despite our feelings. I decided after then that I would try to move on and given my current circumstance, I'm trying to learn how to keep an open mind about them, to an extent of course."

"Are there any other boys you've been seeing secretly? Anyone else I should know about?"

"No, of course not, Ner," Galdinia assured her friend with a shake of her head. "Between training, attempting to spend time with these suitors, and trying to mourn my father, I've been a bit preoccupied. I feel like I'm running on empty."

Neryda sat on her words before reaching out and placing a hand on Galdinia's knee. "I'm sorry that you and Drystan can't be together." Her voice was sincere and quiet. "You know how much I wanted that to work for you, and I'm sorry that it can't."

"Thanks, Ner," Galdinia replied, placing her hand over Neryda's.

"We'll try to make the most of today and this evening," Neryda suggested, squeezing her friend's knee. "Maybe Dillian is a spectacular dancer, or perhaps Kaedric's barrage of compliments will cease the moment you have a bow in your hand."

"Or, if we're really lucky, you might accidentally hit Evarius with an arrow," Galdinia said, trying to play along.

"That's the spirit!"

Galdinia forced a smile, aware of her friend's avoidance of Bentley's name, her heart no more untangled than it was before their conversation.

20

As Galdinia and Neryda rode to the capital's Northern Gates, the princess' stomach tied itself in knots. While she had second guessed herself multiple times in the previous hour, Galdinia finally settled on knowing that at this point, she didn't have anything to lose. However, this didn't stop her nerves from manifesting in her body as she and Neryda arrived at the meeting point.

The large wooden gates were open and guarded by soldiers both on the ground and in the watch tower high above the entrance. Perched atop horses and looking to the princess expectantly were the five suitors and her captain. Most of the young men seemed quite glad to see Galdinia, while others (namely Kaedric and Dillian) appeared less comfortable atop a horse. Galdinia tried to avoid Bentley's gaze, which she felt was fixed on her. After Neryda questioned her feelings about him, she had been debating with her heart since.

"Good morning, gentlemen," Galdinia said, trying to channel the kind of confidence that Neryda often held in high pressure circumstances. "Thank you for joining me at such short notice."

Each of the suitors bowed their heads in welcome. Galdinia caught Bentley looking at her from beneath his brows, his watchful eyes unwavering.

"Of course, Your Highness," Evarius replied, coaxing his horse to step forward towards the princess. "Thank you for inviting us to join you... on a hunt, perhaps?" Evarius nodded towards the bows and arrows that they each donned.

"Yes, what exactly did you have in mind for this morning, Princess?" Ilyon asked from the end of the line of men, raising his eyebrows at Galdinia.

"We were talking just yesterday about going shooting together," Galdinia started to explain, addressing the suitors, "and after our training session yesterday, Captain, I thought it wouldn't be a terrible idea to refine my archery skills. It has been a while."

"So, target practice?" Ilyon asked.

"Yes, I thought that could be useful," Galdinia said with a nod.

"And what exactly do you intend on targeting?" Ilyon's lip turned up ever so slightly at his question as he glanced from the men back to Galdinia.

Galdinia too looked across the men, drawing out the tension further. She knew she shouldn't enjoy it as much as she was, but their apprehensive expressions invited her to revel in the moment. She glanced at Neryda, whose wicked grin told the princess that she too was relishing every second of their assumed fears.

"Well, I have no interest in shooting animals," Galdinia went on, her face plastered with a smirk. "So I was thinking trees, trunks and branches. We can go to the Royal Wood beyond the capital walls."

Evarius, Kaedric and Dillian appeared to relax a little at the princess' confirmation. Bentley and Kell looked impressed by her line of explanation.

"A good plan," Ilyon said, bringing his horse to come stand beside the princess. "Shall we?"

Galdinia pressed her knees into her horse's side and loosened the reins, inviting him forward and through the gates. Neryda, her captain and the five men followed close behind.

"This is going to be fun," Neryda said slyly as she passed by Galdinia.

They followed the path off the Eastern Road that took them into the depths of the Royal Wood that skirted along the northeastern walls of the capital and stretched all the way to the Bear Jaws Valley. The forest quickly became densely packed as they entered its boundaries. However, at this time of day, the canopy was drenched in sunlight, creating a halo around the branches.

"It's a fine morning for a spot of archery, Your Highness." Evarius' booming voice sounded as he came to trot beside Galdinia. "How long has it been since your last soirée with a bow?"

"A few months ago now," Galdinia replied, thinking back to the last time she joined her father on a hunting trip. "It would have been in the summer."

"Did you catch any good game?" Evarius continued.

"Like I said, I'm not one to enjoy hunting animals. I did have a knack for finding wild berry bushes and acorns though."

"She had a knack for hitting them straight through with an arrow too," Neryda chimed in, eyeing Evarius.

"You can hit something as small as a berry?" Evarius asked, eyebrows raised. Galdinia couldn't discern if he was impressed or in disbelief.

"I did," Galdinia went on. "It took a lot of practice, but when you go on as many hunting trips as I, without actually hunting any animals, you get quite good at improvising."

"I myself go hunting once a week with my brothers," Evarius explained, sitting up a little taller, his shoulders back. "We have competitions to see who can bring home the largest animal. I once hauled back a deer twice my size. Our servants made its skins into eight pairs of riding boots and the stew we brewed from its carcass fed us for a week. It was a monster of a beast."

Galdinia scrunched up her nose and gave Neryda a sideways glance. Her friend pulled a face before saying, "I'm not sure the deer was the monster," in hushed tones.

"I beg your pardon, Lady Neryda?" Evarius was defensive, yet forcedly polite.

Galdinia gave Neryda a warning look.

"I just said that sounded quite impressive," Neryda said coolly. "It must take great skill to take down such a large animal. Quite impressive, indeed."

Evarius stared at Neryda with narrow eyes. "Thank you, Lady Neryda," Evarius said through gritted teeth.

Before the two could continue sparring, Kell sidled up beside Neryda and drew her attention away, while Galdinia steered her horse to trot beside Ilyon, who had pulled ahead of the group.

"Having fun?" Ilyon asked, keeping his eyes on the path ahead of them as they weaved through the surrounding greenery.

"We're off to a good start," Galdinia replied. "Neryda has already irritated Evarius and Kell is now cosying up next to her, so I imagine she's having a good time."

"And what about our princess?"

"I'll be glad to have my bow in my hand. It will be nice to train in something I'm actually skilled at for a change," Galdinia explained.

"Don't confuse a gift with skill," Ilyon stated. "Our gifts come from the Gods. We might be able to improve in our ability to use said gift, but it's not granted based on skill."

"Well, I look forward to doing something I am practised in, then," Galdinia amended, brushing her hand over her bow and sheath of arrows that hung from her saddle by her legs.

"Just don't hold back."

"What?" Galdinia asked, turning her eyes to Ilyon.

"Don't be afraid to give these lords a run for their money." Once again, the hint of a smirk tugged at Ilyon's lips. "It wouldn't hurt for a couple of them to see what they're signing up for."

Galdinia returned his smile. "You make it sound like they have reason to be afraid."

"Not afraid," Ilyon replied, "but they should be prepared. You're powerful in your own right."

Galdinia raised her eyebrows at Ilyon and confidently pushed her horse into a canter as they moved further along the path and into the depths of the wood. At the centre of the forest, they rode into a clearing that was dotted about with bushes, lone trees, and the rustlings of small animals. The clearing was lit from above by the morning sun and would provide the group with a good space to practise their archery.

Galdinia pulled at her horse's reins, drawing him back around to face the group as they entered the clearing. Ilyon trailed the princess closely; Neryda was laughing at something Kell had just said; Evarius still looked unimpressed by his interaction with Neryda; Kaedric looked around the space with wide eyes; and at the rear, Bentley and Dillian spoke jovially as they rode in, engrossed in a conversation.

"I think this will do," Galdinia announced, swinging a leg over her horse and sliding off her saddle. She loosed her bow and sheath of arrows from their buckle and slung the latter over her back, fastening it in place over her chest. She held the bow firmly in her left hand, a thrill of excitement racing up her arm as she anticipated firing her first arrow in many months. "I know we aren't all as well practised with a bow and arrow as some, so we can start with some simple training exercises using trees as targets."

Each of the men followed suit and dismounted from their horses. Evarius, Bentley and Dillian took their weapons from their horses most naturally; Evarius was quick to remove and nock his first arrow, keeping its tip pointed to the ground. Kaedric and Kell, on the other hand, appeared less comfortable with the weapons in their hands.

"Captain," Galdinia said from the front of the group, addressing Ilyon. "Perhaps you could run the men through some of the basics before we start shooting?"

"Certainly," Ilyon said, dismounting from his own horse and pulling his bow from its quiver on his back. "My first two rules when practising archery are as follows: don't point an arrow at someone unless you want to kill them, and don't walk in front of someone with a nocked arrow unless you want to die."

A ripple of laughter—both nervous and genuine—washed over the group of men.

"It's important that when holding your bow, your wrist should be straight, not curved," Ilyon explained, holding his bow out to the side by way of demonstration. "You will maintain far more control this way. And when placing your arrow," he went on, taking an arrow from his quiver and adjusting it in the bow, "rest it on your index finger, place the nock in the bowstring, pull it back, and—"

Ilyon drew his arm back without taking his eyes from the group of men. He released the arrow, and it flew through the air and struck the knot of a nearby tree trunk. All eyes followed the arrow, then travelled back to the captain as he lowered his arms.

"As beginners, you'll want to look straight down the sight of your bow in order to land a shot with any kind of accuracy," Ilyon said, pointing to the spot just above his bow's grip. "Princess, would you care to demonstrate?"

By way of response, Galdinia stepped forward, standing in line with Ilyon and the tree he just shot at. She pulled an arrow from her quiver and nocked it in place. Shutting one eye, Galdinia looked straight down the sight of her bow, along her arrow, and to her target. In one firm movement, she pulled the bowstring back before releasing the arrow, then watched it land directly beside Ilyon's in the knot. Galdinia was glad she was still a competent archer, at the very least.

The suitors smiled, Kaedric clapped and Kell let out a low whistle. Bentley nodded, seemingly pleased with Galdinia's display of talent.

"That's impressive, Your Highness," Kell said, crossing his arms over his chest.

"And she hasn't even warmed up yet," Ilyon added, looking at Galdinia with a sense of pride.

"Thank you, Kell," Galdinia said with a smile. Neryda, still atop her horse, winked at her friend.

"Gentlemen, let's line up here," Ilyon instructed, pointing to an invisible line through the centre of the clearing. "Pick any tree in front of you as your target and let's start practising." Before anyone moved, Ilyon quickly added, "And should you want to leave this forest still standing, do remember my first two rules."

After securing their horses to a nearby tree, the men formed a line and drew their arrows. They started to aim for the trees along the edge of the clearing and Ilyon moved along the line, giving them various instructions.

"Kell, lower your back elbow."

"Keep your arm straight, Kaedric."

"Evarius, you might find more success by keeping one eye shut."

Neryda had come down from her horse and was happily stationed between Kell and Dillian, giving the two men advice as they sent arrows flying across the clearing, some far more successfully than others. Dillian was surprisingly adept at archery and consistently hit the same tree trunk, arrow after arrow. Along the line, Ilyon stood behind Evarius and Kaedric. Evarius was, to no one's surprise, also a skilled archer; however, Ilyon was still able to critique his technique, which brought Galdinia an extra ounce of joy. Kaedric, on the other hand, was struggling to send his arrow more than five feet.

"You need to draw your bowstring back further," Ilyon explained, lifting Kaedric's back elbow and tapping his fingers that were wrapped around the green feathers of his arrow. "Don't let the pressure intimidate you; you won't break the bow. Pull back against the resistance, look through the sight, and let it fly."

Kaedric did as Ilyon instructed, and he managed to send the arrow to the base of the tree trunk he was aiming for.

"Much better," Ilyon said with a nod as Kaedric smiled proudly.

"It's hard when the tree is so far away," Kaedric replied, taking another arrow in his hand.

"Don't blame the target, Kaedric," Evarius said, shooting his own arrow directly into the trunk above Kaedric's.

As Galdinia walked to the end of the line, she watched silently as Bentley pulled another arrow from his quiver and nocked it into place. He drew back his left arm and sent the arrow into the trunk of the tree where five other arrows already sat in an almost perfect circle, their blue feathers shifting in the breeze.

"That's clever," Galdinia said, coming to stand beside him as he prepared his stance for another shot.

"Thank you, Princess," Bentley said, sending another arrow to the trunk to complete his circle.

"When did you learn how to shoot?" Galdinia asked.

"When I was about eight years old," Bentley explained, placing the tip of his bow on the ground in front of him, using it as an anchor as he stood up tall. "Archery is a necessary skill in The Edges and Midlands, what with all the turkeys, deer and squirrels that need to be captured for meals."

"Squirrel… yum," Galdinia said, hesitant.

"You've not had squirrel from The Edges?" he asked incredulously.

"I can't say I have."

"It's far less gamey than you might imagine," Bentley assured her. "We douse it in chilli flakes, rock salt, garlic and thyme, and slowly roast it for at least three hours."

"Three hours for a tiny squirrel?"

"Yep, that's the secret to getting such a tender piece of meat."

Galdinia looked at the lord with scrutinising eyes.

"Do you think I'm lying?" Bentley asked.

"I just don't imagine squirrel is particularly delectable," Galdinia retorted.

"You'll just have to come visit The Edges and have me make it for you." As he spoke, Bentley took out another arrow and placed it in his bow. As he did so, Galdinia swiftly nocked her own arrow and sent it across the clearing before Bentley could draw his arm back. The red-tipped arrow landed squarely in the centre of the circle.

"I suppose I will," she said with a smirk.

"Alright, gentlemen," Ilyon said, addressing the suitors. "Bows down, go collect your arrows."

Bentley smiled at Galdinia before turning with his companions to the edge of the clearing.

"Why don't we make this a little more interesting?" Neryda said as the men pulled the arrows from tree trunks and searched for them in the bushes and tall grass.

"What did you have in mind?" Galdinia asked as she and Ilyon turned to Neryda.

"How about we add some moving targets and a healthy dose of competition?" The smile that spread over Neryda's lips was mischievous.

"I don't think shooting the men is an option," Ilyon said, raising a brow at Neryda.

"While that would be fun," Neryda said, walking towards her horse, "I thought flying fruit might be more manageable." She patted a hessian sack that was strapped to her saddle and called out, "What do you say to some competition, boys?"

The men looked up from their positions in the firing range, most of the arrows now collected.

"I'm up for it," Kell said, moving back to the centre of the clearing.

"Let's see," Neryda said, tapping her fingertips on her chin. "Whoever hits the most apples mid-air wins. But if you fail to hit an apple, you're out."

Galdinia could tell that Neryda was enjoying this far too much.

"And what does the winner get?" Kaedric asked as Bentley, Evarius and Dillian arrived back with their arrows.

"How about the pleasure of escorting Princess Galdinia to the feast tonight?" Evarius suggested, his expression confident and suggestive.

"I don't think so." Galdinia frowned, shaking her head. She didn't need to feel like a prize yet again.

"Come on, Gal," Neryda said, her eyes wide.

"You could play too," Bentley suggested with a shrug. "If you win, you could choose who to go with, or nobody at all if you like."

Galdinia looked from Bentley to Neryda to Ilyon, then back to the men before her.

You have nothing to lose, she reminded herself.

"Alright, fine."

Neryda smirked and hauled the hessian bag from her saddle. Kell quickly rushed to her side and took the bag from her, the fabric of his shirt tightening around his muscular arms.

"Take your positions, gentlemen," Neryda said as Kell placed the bag at her feet behind the line from which the men would shoot. "I will take an apple, throw it in front of you, and—"

"Uh, Lady Neryda," Ilyon interjected, stepping forward. "Might I suggest you keep score? I'd be happy to throw the apples for you."

Galdinia stifled a laugh. Ilyon knew all too well about Neryda's ineptitude when it came to any kind of ball sports. She may have been a skilled Water Weaver, but as soon as an uncontrollable object was thrown into the mix, she was more than hopeless. Galdinia could see the apples flying into the backs of heads if she were to be in charge of them.

"Good idea, Captain." Neryda nodded, stepping aside for him to take charge of the targets. "We'll go one at a time. Kell, we'll start with you."

One by one, Ilyon threw an apple into the air before the men and each of them made contact with the flying object. Kell's arrow managed to stab the apple, while Dillian, Evarius and Bentley all shot their apples straight through the centre, sending their arrows flying with a new accessory. Although Kaedric's arrow barely skimmed the skin of his apple, Neryda allowed him to move on to the next round. Galdinia easily shot her apple, and they all watched it fly to the edge of the clearing.

In the next round, Ilyon threw the apples higher and harder. Unfortunately, Kaedric missed his target and kicked the grass at his feet. The other five archers made their mark.

"Lord Kaedric," Ilyon said as he took another cluster of apples from the sack, "how about we make this a little more challenging for our archers?"

Kaedric's face brightened instantly and with every toss of an apple, he used his gift to move the fruit in zigzags, twirling loops, and sudden dips and valleys. Galdinia watched him closely as he manipulated the air around Kell's next apple; he was too preoccupied with making the fruit dance to try to sabotage the shooter's attempt. Unfortunately for Kell, this didn't matter as he overshot the target and his arrow landed somewhere in a bush in the distance.

"Nice shot," Neryda said, smiling at Kell. He stepped back beside her and shrugged, not seeming too disappointed with his loss.

"Look alive, Dillian," the captain said, tossing another apple in the air. Kaedric sent this one skyrocketing before letting it fall through the sky straight towards the ground. Dillian's arrow flew quickly, hoping to catch the fruit on its descent, but it closely missed and stuck into a nearby tree. With a sad smile, he stepped back, conceding defeat.

Next, Ilyon threw apples for both Evarius and Bentley, who despite Kaedric's movements, hit their targets swiftly. Galdinia watched her apple coil through the air, but she too easily struck it with an arrow.

In the next round, Ilyon tossed three apples at once, allowing Kaedric to manipulate the movement of all three pieces of fruit. They swirled in a circle, and each were hit one after another.

Evarius, pleased with his work, leant on his bow and chuckled. "Come on, Kaedric, make it a little difficult for us."

Galdinia saw a shadow of irritation flash over Kaedric's expression.

"Can do," he said quietly, nodding at Ilyon to throw another apple in the air. This time, Kaedric pushed the wind out from where he stood, sending the apple flying beyond its starting position immediately. Evarius was hardly ready to shoot and awkwardly shot an arrow in the general direction of his target, but it lodged itself in the branches of a tree.

Galdinia couldn't help but smile. She caught Bentley's eye, and his expression matched her own.

"How was that?" Kaedric asked, obviously pleased with himself.

"I wasn't ready for that one," Evarius mumbled, frustrated.

"Don't blame the target." Kaedric's joy was palpable.

Two more apples were sent into the air and one after the other, Bentley and Galdinia made quick work of them. Another apple was thrown skyward for Lord Bentley, and Kaedric sent it across the clearing in sharp lines, pulling and pushing the wind with it. This didn't deter Bentley and he shot the fruit as it made a quick turn back towards them.

"Do you want to give up, Princess?" Bentley asked, turning to look expectantly to Galdinia.

For a moment, she was distracted by the dimple that appeared in his right cheek. Ilyon threw another apple in the air and Kaedric made similar movements with it. Galdinia aimed her arrow, following the movement as best she could before releasing it from her bowstring and piercing the apple through the centre.

"I don't think so," she replied, mirroring his cocky expression.

One after another, Ilyon threw apples into the air and Kaedric manipulated their movement. And one after another, Bentley and Galdinia hit the apples with their arrows until they each only had one arrow left in their quiver.

"This is a tight competition, indeed," Neryda said, standing back with her arms crossed, watching her friend with a smile. "Captain, let's throw one more apple; whoever hits it first is our winner."

Bentley and Galdinia stood facing each other as they took out their final arrows, nocking them into place and holding their bows towards the ground.

"Nervous, Princess?" Bentley asked, raising his bow to his face, ready to aim, watching her out of the corner of his eye.

"Not at all," Galdinia replied, preparing her own stance, tightening her fingers around her arrow.

"Here we go," Ilyon said, coming to stand between the two of them, throwing the single apple in the air.

Kaedric sent the fruit on a twisting path, and both Galdinia and Bentley moved their bows, trying to keep up with the apple's erratic movements. When she thought she anticipated its slowing movement, Galdinia held her gaze down the bow's sight and released her fingers on the arrow. Half a second later, Bentley sent his arrow through the air too, the blue feathers twirling behind Galdinia's red feathers. There was a *thunk* and the apple was struck, sending it across the clearing and into a nearby tree. The other arrow flew too far to the right and landed in another tree in the depths of the wood.

The arrow that struck the apple was donned with red feathers. Galdinia smiled as she turned back to the party of archers, all eyes on her arrow. All eyes except Bentley's; he was watching her.

"Congratulations, Princess," Bentley said, lowering his bow and reaching out a hand.

Galdinia looked at his arrow, then back to him. How had he missed by such a wide margin?

"Thank you, Lord Bentley," she replied, taking his outstretched hand and shaking it. His hand was rough in places and his grip was firm, but at his touch, a ripple of goosebumps danced up her arm beneath her sleeve.

The others clapped for the princess as they turned to face the two of them.

"Well done, Gal!" Neryda cheered, coming to stand by her friend, breaking Galdinia's eye contact and handshake with Bentley.

"Good work, Your Highness," Ilyon said, taking the princess' bow from her.

"I think it's only right that the runner-up clears the arrows," Neryda said, a grin spreading over her face.

"Fair enough." Bentley nodded dropping his bow on the ground. "You are a worthy competitor, Princess."

Galdinia eyed Bentley as he turned towards the edge of the clearing where most of their arrows and apples had landed.

"So who are you going to have escort you this evening, Princess?" Evarius asked, arms crossed over his chest, standing tall.

Galdinia looked back at the ground before her.

"I haven't decided yet," she replied. "Why don't you all prepare the horses to travel back to the capital? I'll help Lord Bentley with the arrows."

Neryda gave Galdinia a pointed look before the princess followed Bentley into the overgrowth and bushes.

"You don't need to help, Princess," Bentley insisted, bending to pick up a handful of skewered apples. "You won fair and square."

"Did I?" Galdinia asked, picking up an arrow.

"Excuse me, Your Highness?" Bentley asked, standing up straight, his face nothing but innocence.

"That last shot of yours went uncharacteristically wide," Galdinia said, brow arched.

"It was just a bad shot." Bentley shrugged. "I didn't anticipate Kaedric's movement."

"Is that right?" Galdinia asked as they trudged beyond the line of trees around the edge of the clearing and into the thick of the wood.

"Yep," Bentley said, pulling an arrow out of a nearby tree trunk. "You're just a better archer than I am."

Galdinia stopped in her tracks and stared at Bentley, her eyes narrow. "Are you telling me that you didn't want to win the chance to escort me to the feast?"

"Frankly, Princess, I don't see you as a prize to be won." Bentley turned to look at her briefly before spying another arrow in a thicket by Galdinia's feet. "After all, I'd much rather ask if you'd allow me to accompany you to the feast rather than being given that right by virtue of winning a competition."

He looked up at Galdinia from his kneeling position, his blonde hair rustling in the light breeze.

"And is that what you're doing now?" Galdinia asked, shifting her weight to one foot.

"Well, would you do me the honour?"

"Yes," Galdinia said lightly, before quickly adding, "as soon as you admit that you forfeited that last shot on purpose."

Bentley smiled up at Galdinia before getting to his feet and brushing the grass from his knee.

"Sorry, I can't do that, Princess," Bentley said with a shake of his head. "Like I said, you're a better shot than I am."

"You know, just about any man would be jumping at the opportunity to take me to the feast, regardless of competition, ego, or whatever it is that compels you to lie to your future queen."

Bentley took pause before a smile played over his lips. "Is it not enough that I simply want to escort you to the feast because I enjoy your company? Do I need to have an ulterior motive?"

"No one courts the princess without an ulterior motive."

"Maybe you just have to trust that my motives are pure," Bentley said, offering his arm to Galdinia.

"Given the current circumstance," Galdinia said, waving the arrows and apples in the air, "you'll have to forgive me for being suspicious."

"Forgiveness granted," Bentley said, his arm still waiting to be taken. "But I really would quite enjoy your company tonight."

"I'm sure you would," Galdinia replied, looping her free hand through the crook of his elbow as they stepped through the tall grass and back into the clearing.

The others were attending to their weapons and preparing to leave the wood. Neryda and Kell were talking while he fed her horse the leftover apples in the hessian sack. Kaedric and Dillion were talking to Ilyon about, as far as Galdinia guessed, their archery technique as he held a strong stance, pointing towards the placement of his feet. Evarius stood by his horse and his eyes were full of burning irritation as he watched Galdinia walk from the wood arm-in-arm with Lord Bentley.

"Ready to go, Princess?" Ilyon asked, turning from his students.

"I think so," Galdinia replied as they came to stand by their horses.

"Allow me, Princess," Bentley said, taking the arrows from her other hand as she slipped her arm out from under his. He made quick work of pulling the arrows from the apples and threw the speared ones to his fellow suitors. "I'm sure your steeds will appreciate a snack."

They each caught the apples and moved to feed their horses. The look of detestation that dripped over Evarius' face bore straight into Bentley. Bentley, however, looked nothing but satisfied.

Maybe he didn't win the archery competition, but Bentley had certainly won something today.

"Shall we go?" Neryda asked Galdinia, as she took Kell's offer to help her up onto her saddle. Galdinia knew that Neryda required no help mounting a horse.

"Let's." Galdinia nodded.

The men turned to their horses to strap their weapons down and then climbed onto their saddles. Before any of them could offer their help to Galdinia, she quickly jumped into her saddle and made haste to the path that led back through the wood.

21

GALDINIA STARED AT HERSELF IN THE MIRROR OF HER DRESSING ROOM. She ran her hands down the sleeves of her gown, not in order to smooth them, but out of nervous compulsion. The confidence she held hours earlier in the wood had worn off as she contemplated the evening ahead. Neryda tried to distract her with a long afternoon routine, including bathing, scrubbing her nails, pinning her hair, and trying on dresses from a selection that Madame Moya had made for the occasion. Finally, Neryda convinced Galdinia to wear the most illustrious of them all.

The ruby-red dress hugged Galdinia's frame, accentuating every curve of her figure. It clung to her arms, waist and the top of her thighs. From there, it fell loose around her feet, circling behind her in a subtle yet elegant train. The dress rested just atop her shoulders, leaving her collarbones bare, which was more revealing than her usual attire. Galdinia felt a strange mix of self-consciousness and elation. It was an exact replica of the dress her mother wore to the Royal Feast after the king's mother died. It was a celebration gown, a gown to remind everyone in the room who was in charge. Galdinia didn't know if she was worthy of wearing such a garment.

"Honestly, Gal, you look beautiful." Neryda sat behind her,

admiring her friend in the reflection of the mirror. "And stop fiddling with the sleeves. They're fine."

"Are you sure it's not too much for such a sophisticated evening?" Galdinia asked, turning to look at her back where the dress dipped low, hugging each curve along the way.

"Absolutely not," Neryda assured her, now standing by Galdinia's side in her own shimmering gold dress. "It is simply perfect. You look like a true ruler… almost."

Neryda walked to the glass cabinet on the opposite wall. Inside were the jewels left for Galdinia by her parents, including her royal tiara. Neryda opened the doors and considered the pieces of jewellery; she was a child in a sweet parlour.

Neryda stood once again by her friend and handed her two golden earrings studded with clear luminescent crystals. The next piece of jewellery was a complementary necklace, which Neryda hooked around Galdinia's smooth neck with ease. Galdinia continued to stare at herself, feeling the weight of the accessories she now bore.

"And finally…" Neryda trailed off, lifting Galdinia's tiara to her head. She secured it in her silky, golden hair, careful not to ruin the delicately pinned arrangement of curls at the nape of her neck. Galdinia's gaze rested on the tiara, its crystals glinting in the setting sun that trailed into the room. The jewels sent shards of rainbows across the walls as she moved her head slowly to inspect Neryda's final work.

"You're a princess, my friend—a queen!" Neryda beamed in the mirror.

Galdinia was used to wearing her tiara, but the jewels on her ears and neck were especially heavy. "This feels both strangely natural and beyond uncomfortable."

"It will just take some getting used to," Neryda assured her, gazing at her friend in the mirror. "You're the spitting image of your mother."

Galdinia inspected herself once more, her fingers now moving up to the tiara to touch the crystals. A portrait of King Bartemus and Queen Anae from the night she wore this dress hung in her father's drawing room. Since her mother's passing, Galdinia had spent hours staring at the painting. Neryda was right; she looked just like her mother this evening.

"Let's go before I change my mind and hide under my bed all evening."

The two left the dressing room and as she walked the halls with her best friend by her side, Galdinia could feel there had been a distinct shift in the atmosphere. While the previous months had left a heavy melancholy hanging in the air of the castle, she was now aware of a sense of hope and—dare she say it—joy. The sweet smell of honey and sparkling wine seeped through the ancient building, and the light tinkling of romantic string instruments echoed through the walls, inviting guests into the ballroom.

Aside from the small glimpses she had caught that morning, Galdinia had not yet seen the ballroom in its fully prepared state. The Syndicate had assured her that it would be up to standard and suitable for the future queen. Galdinia didn't think she voiced such a standard, but for a moment, she enjoyed the sensation of authority it gave her.

"If anything, tonight can be a moment for you to relax," Neryda coached Galdinia as they walked towards the grand staircase at the end of the hallway. "We can drink wine, eat too many sweets, and dance until we fall to our knees."

"I'm not sure it will be that kind of an evening, at least not for me. I'm going to be surrounded by nobles and dignitaries from across the kingdom."

"So chat to them over the entrée, but then put your feet up—figuratively, of course."

They rounded the corner to the top of the staircase and there, hands in his pockets, leaning against the balustrade, stood Lord Bentley. He wore a velvet suit of deep violet. The sparkling gold chain of his pocket watch rested beneath his pocket and a matching rose brooch was secured to his lapel. At the sound of the princess' arrival, he looked up and stood straight, arms behind his back, chest high.

Galdinia couldn't help but notice how handsome he looked.

"Your Majesty, Lady Neryda." Bentley bowed low, his arms remaining tucked behind him.

"Lord Bentley," Galdinia said with a start, attempting to regain her composure after the surprise of his presence. *Be like your mother*, she

189

thought to herself. *Gracious, like your mother.* "You're not here to take back your earlier request, are you?"

"Ah, well," he said gently, standing straight again, "I was just getting ready in our quarters—which are lovely, by the way, thank you —and I thought to myself, if I don't go meet the princess before she enters the ballroom, one of these other fools will first, and I simply couldn't have that."

"How thoughtful," Neryda said, the lick of a sardonic tone on her tongue.

"But maybe I might have liked one of them to escort me this evening," Galdinia said, ignoring Neryda, her eyes fixed on Bentley.

"Oh, is that right?" Bentley said, his tone bright. "Well, shall I go get Lord Evarius now, then? Or perhaps Kell?"

Neryda's eyes narrowed on Bentley, her lips twisting into a half-smile, half-grimace. Even she couldn't deny Bentley's good humour.

"Well, I suppose I could be escorted by the second-best archer in the castle," Galdinia said smugly with a wry smile. "If that is in fact who you are?"

"That's me," Bentley replied with a short shrug. "Not nearly as skilled as our future queen."

"Maybe you were having an off day."

"Maybe," he replied, smirking.

Galdinia glanced at Neryda, whose arms were crossed and eyes were rolling. For all the charming allure that she had been wrapped up in with Kell, Galdinia didn't think she had a leg to stand on in judging Galdinia's choice of escort.

"I have a gift for you also," Bentley said, taking a step towards the princess, his hand sliding into his inner suit jacket pocket to retrieve a small bundle of purple silk that matched his suit. "It is a mere token of my loyalty to you as both princess and queen, and I thought you may wish to wear it tonight. You might like to consider it your prize for winning this morning."

He unwrapped the silk and beneath it lay a golden hair clip. It wasn't much longer than Galdinia's smallest finger and upon it sat a golden rose which wrapped around the tongs, the delicate leaves intertwining with each other. She noted that it matched Bentley's brooch.

"May I?" he asked. Galdinia turned to allow him to pin it in place in her hair.

Neryda frowned at her friend, her disapproval still alive and well. The very edge of her lip, however, turned up at the sight of the lord placing the clip in Galdinia's hair.

"This is very kind of you," Galdinia said sincerely. Once the clip was in place, her fingers reached up to rest on the cold metal for a moment before turning to face the lord again.

"It's the least I could do for letting you win—I mean, for losing against you this morning—"

"So you admit it!"

"What? No, never!" Bentley's lips spread out in a grin, and he winked before raising his right arm to Galdinia. "Shall we?"

Galdinia peered at Bentley with scrutinising eyes for a moment before returning his grin and taking his arm. He directed them to the top of the staircase, which they descended together, landing in the lavishly decorated entrance hall. Galdinia found she was glad to have Bentley there, if only for the physical support that he provided as they walked down the grand staircase. His playful countenance also distracted her from the purpose of the evening, and she felt she was walking somewhat lighter as they rounded on the entrance of the ball-room. Bentley's steady arm and steadier demeanour had her walking tall and proud.

"I wasn't sure if Neryda would let you go for a second then," Bentley said quietly, leaning down to speak into Galdinia's ear.

"She's protective and not easily won over," Galdinia said between steadying breaths. "The fact that she relinquished me at all is a wonder."

The attendant at the door of the ballroom took note of their arrival and turned to the doors, pushing them open wide. He stepped onto the landing of the stairs beyond the doors and his voice boomed across the hall.

"Ladies and gentlemen!" His voice quieted the guests in the ball-room. "Introducing Princess Galdinia Elderwin and Lord Bentley Penrose."

Bentley gave a brief reassuring squeeze of Galdinia's hand, then they stepped forward.

Galdinia found herself lost for both words and breath as they stood on the landing of the ballroom's entrance. The grand room had been decorated to look like what could only be described as her wildest dreams. The chandeliers above them had been transformed into clouds with the use of wool, the glow of the contained candles lighting them from within. She didn't want to think about whose power was keeping the fibres from catching alight. Dotted around the room were freestanding stone fountains, each one spouting a different coloured drink, some opaque, others iridescent. Beside each fountain stood an attendant, all of whom seemed to be controlling the running of the drinks through the fountains—Water Weavers.

Through the centre of the room was the dining table which spanned almost the entire length of the room. It was set with golden cutlery, enough places for the one hundred guests in attendance. In the centre of the table were elaborate boards of cheeses, berries, and honeycomb, which were separated by candelabras whose bases were wrapped in freshly cut vines of ivy. The most exquisite features of the room, though, were the flowers. Through the centre of the table, beneath the board of delicacies, ran an intricate collection of wild-flowers, interspersed with leaves, feathers, and berries still attached to their vines. The arrangement ran to the end of the table and spilled onto the floor, across the room, and trailed along the edges of the walls, making the room feel like it was set in a secret garden. Beyond the smell from the kitchens, Galdinia was overwhelmed by the scent of the flowers, their aroma encircling her immediately.

It was a wonderland.

"Heavens," she exclaimed in an exhale, attempting to take in the scene before her.

Although the room was full of the kingdom's most important nobles, Galdinia could barely pay them any attention. The two walked across the landing and down the stairs into the room, Galdinia's dress brushing against the waves of flowers that puddled at her feet along the stairs. Galdinia turned to see Neryda's reaction but realised that she was not yet in the room.

"How incredible," Bentley said, echoing her sentiments and pulling her attention back to the sight before them.

Dotted around the room were Galdinia's four other suitors, and each of them wore varying expressions of frustration and disappointment as they saw who the princess had chosen to walk into the Royal Feast with. She suppressed a grin at their expressions.

"Welcome, Princess." Governor Ryden greeted Galdinia and Bentley at the bottom of the stairs, bowing to them both. "You look beautiful; the spitting image of your mother."

"Thank you," Galdinia said simply, trying to emulate the confidence she knew her mother would have possessed when she wore this same ensemble.

"And Lord Bentley, it is wonderful to have you."

"Thank you for your invitation," Bentley said, bowing in response.

"Speaking of invitations," Galdinia said, looking to her governor, who wore dress robes of black and silver. "Is there anyone I need to make a particular impression on this evening?"

Ryden surveyed the room while Bentley collected two glasses of a sparkling pink drink from the tray that a nearby attendant was distributing. He handed one to the princess, who took it gladly.

"Across the room is a couple in matching fuchsia." Galdinia cast her eyes on a man and woman who were in fact wearing matching outfits for the evening; they were talking quietly to themselves, eyes scanning the room. "That is Lord and Lady Gnox from the west. It would be good to make positive contact with them this evening. We can't have too many allies in the west."

Ryden continued to scan the room. His eyes landed on Evarius, who was speaking loudly to another pair of guests.

"That's Lord and Lady Wrynn from the Wooded Province."

"Evarius' parents?" Galdinia asked with a sigh.

"Yes, and they're quite powerful in the Midlands." Galdinia forced herself not to make a snarky remark about everything she'd already heard about his family. "In fact, most of your house guests' families are here this evening. Except for yours, Lord Bentley. We did not receive a reply from them in time."

"My sincerest apologies," Bentley said. "I don't imagine they would have done so on purpose. I know it has been a difficult start to the season in some regions in The Edges, but I can only imagine they did not receive the invitation."

"Well, my apologies to them if that is the case."

"I'll be sure to ask them when I write to them next."

"Please do," Ryden said, before turning his attention back to Galdinia. "I wouldn't be too preoccupied with establishing political relations tonight though, Princess. That is the Syndicate's and my job at events like these. You should try to enjoy the evening for what it is; enjoy a drink, have a dance, and mingle."

"There's dancing?" Bentley asked, looking down at the princess.

"There is, and thank goodness you are here to escort Galdinia," Ryden said with a devilish grin that Galdinia had not seen before.

"Why is that?" Bentley asked apprehensively.

"Because, had she come alone, she would have been dancing with me." Ryden smirked at the princess before catching the eye of someone over her shoulder. "Enjoy the evening, you two."

Ryden left the pair alone, and Bentley quickly turned to face the princess.

"So we have to dance this evening?" Lord Bentley asked, offering his arm to Galdinia once again as they started to move around the room.

"I'd forgotten about that, but yes," Galdinia admitted, taking yet another sip, the bubbles tickling her nose as they walked. "During the Week of Mourning after they secured the throne, my grandparents decided dancing would make the Royal Feast more festive. I suppose they were right, but I doubt that they considered the feasts of their own lineage."

"Princess Galdinia!"

The pair turned and were faced with a group of four guests who were clinking their glasses and laughing as she approached. The group varied in age and Galdinia vaguely recognised their faces. Beside them, almost on the outer, were the fuchsia-clad couple that Ryden had pointed out.

"Good evening," Galdinia replied politely, smiling at her guests.

"I don't expect you to remember us, dear," said an older woman across the group from her. "We are Lord and Lady Toulston from Silk-shell on the Shadowed Coast. We met when you were a small lass."

Lady Toulston had kind, hooded eyes, which wrinkled at the edges as she smiled. Her dark, curly hair, which was sprinkled with greys, rested over her shoulder. Her husband's hair, however, was all white, standing in stark contrast to his wife's.

"It is lovely to see you both again." Galdinia smiled.

"And this is the governor and governess of our city," the woman went on, gesturing to the other couple, who were at least two decades younger, "the Keystons."

"A pleasure," Galdinia replied, and her new acquaintances bowed.

"Princess Galdinia, we are Lord and Lady Gnox." The man in fuchsia introduced himself and his wife with a short bow each. Lord Gnox's wide set eyes were scrutinising beneath his dark bushy eyebrows. As she stood up straight again, Lady Gnox pushed a sweep of ashy blonde hair from her pale face, an unconvincing smile on her lips.

"It is a lovely evening," Lady Gnox commented as she scrutinised the room around her. "Thank you for inviting us to such a lavish event."

"You're most welcome," Galdinia said, hoping her apprehension didn't show on her face. "I'm sure my father would be glad you could make it. And all the way from the west; that is quite the journey."

"Well, of course. We have actively supported your father's crown for two decades," Lord Gnox replied. "Our support is reserved for capable and powerful monarchs."

Galdinia felt the tension around the group tighten as he spoke. Her heart rate sped up and she felt the ache in her chest rise. She suddenly became aware of every piece of fabric that clung to her body, but she tried to remain calm.

"Good thing Princess Galdinia is next in line then," Lady Toulston chimed in. Her husband's eyes narrowed on Lord Gnox.

Under his breath, Lord Gnox let out a brief, gruff laugh, still evading Galdinia's gaze. "You'll need a little more than your father's surname to keep your allies in the west, Princess," he said casually.

"And yet, all of these guests from across the kingdom still came to honour both her and her father," Bentley said before anyone else could respond, motioning towards the crowd around them.

Galdinia peered up at Bentley with gratitude in her eyes. The list of reasons why he made for a satisfactory escort was quickly growing.

"I suppose." Lord Gnox reluctantly nodded. "And who might you be?"

"Lord Bentley Penrose of The Edges," Bentley said, keeping one hand firmly gripped around his glass while the other was still being used as Galdinia's anchor point. She was glad he didn't offer his hand to shake.

"And your family has shown its support of Princess Galdinia?" Lord Gnox asked, brows raised, speaking as though she weren't right in front of him.

"I wouldn't be here otherwise," Bentley said, and Galdinia felt the muscles in his arm tighten. "And you will need to forgive me, but I am under strict instructions to make sure the princess addresses all attendees this evening. She's a popular woman."

"It was good to meet you," Galdinia said, smiling at her guests, some with more contempt than others. "Thank you for coming this evening."

"It is our pleasure, Princess," Lord Toulston replied as the four from the Shadowed Coast bowed.

Bentley drew Galdinia from the circle, and the eyes of the Gnox couple didn't leave Galdinia's face until they were back in the thick of guests.

"Thank you, thank you, thank you," Galdinia said breathlessly once they were well and truly away from the group.

"Just doing my escorting duties," Bentley replied, leading her between crowds of guests.

"I don't imagine saving me from scornful nobles was what you had in mind when you offered," Galdinia replied, waving politely at a couple as they walked by.

"I've got to take the good with the bad," Bentley said with a shrug. "Snide remarks now, but dancing later."

"I didn't think you sounded particularly happy about the prospect of dancing," Galdinia said, looking up at Bentley's sly smile.

"I was surprised, but who doesn't want to dance with the most beautiful woman in the room?"

Galdinia didn't know if he was merely trying to charm her or if she truly meant what he was saying, but she decided the compliment was welcome either way.

"Very smooth, Lord Bentley," Galdinia replied. Bentley's grin only grew.

"So tell me, Princess," Bentley said, leading her along the length of the dining table, inspecting the intricate arrangements and table settings. "What do we normally expect from an evening like this? I was under the impression that it would be a sombre affair, but the drinks, the dancing and the company have me thinking otherwise."

"Traditionally, yes, it was a sombre event. One hundred years ago, we would have been eating in near silence, saying prayers before each bite and sobbing between courses. My grandparents, however, hosted a Week of Mourning for the late Pyrins, and they didn't necessarily see the need for such solemnity. I think they wanted to uphold tradition, but they made some modifications."

"So they took the throne from the merciless Pyrins and paid their respects after decapitating them both by throwing a week-long party?"

"Well, yes." Galdinia wasn't used to hearing about her grandparents' upheaval of the throne in such simple terms, but she couldn't fault his accuracy.

"Then what exactly are we celebrating tonight?"

"When my grandparents passed, they each had a Week of Mourning, and my father retained their decision to make the Royal Feast a joyful event. He wanted them to be remembered for their greatness, and I imagine it looked similar to what we see here," Galdinia said, waving her hand in the direction of the table and decorations. "This week has its moments to grieve, but also its moments to celebrate."

"How thoughtful," Lord Bentley said as he looked across the ballroom, his eyes scanning its inhabitants. He then looked to Galdinia through the corners of his eyes. "And when will we be sharing this elusive dance?"

"You're rather presumptuous to think I'll be choosing you as my dance partner," Galdinia replied with a subtly wicked grin. "I may still dance with Governor Ryden, or worse…"

"Good evening, Princess." Across the table, Evarius approached, his parents in tow. He was wearing a long coat of rich mahogany, a pin set into his lapel with a small silver leaf attached to it. His parents were similarly dressed, their outfits coordinated. Evarius' father was just as tall as his son but broader still, while his mother was rosy cheeked and sweet-looking.

After a brief introduction from their son, Draec and Galea Wrynn bowed and curtseyed to the princess from across the table.

"Thank you for having us this evening," Galea said softly, her tone much unlike her son's.

"Yes, it is quite an impressive home you have here," Draec said, casting his eyes over the room. How like his son he was.

"You're most welcome," Galdinia replied. "And this is Lord Bentley Penrose from The Edges."

"Penrose," Draec said, his eyes narrowing on the lord. "I'm not sure that I've come across your family before. Where in The Edges are they?"

"We are to the north," Bentley said smoothly, maintaining his strength in front of this otherwise intimidating gentleman. "We are involved in a lot of the mining that takes place around the mountain range."

"Ah, of course," Draec replied with a nod. "We are in the Wooded Province of the Midlands, further east."

"And what a beautiful part of our country that is," Bentley replied.

Galdinia was impressed by how easily he maintained this conversation.

"You look beautiful this evening, Princess," Evarius said smoothly, his eyes fixed on Galdinia.

"Thank you, Evarius," she replied.

"Princess, Syndicate members, ladies, lords, and distinguished guests." The voice that interrupted their conversation came from the attendant at the other end of the table, drawing the attention of those in attendance. "The first course will be served imminently. Please take your seats."

Galdinia and Bentley bade the Wrynns farewell, much to Evarius' dismay; his eyes lingered on the princess as they moved down the table.

A smattering of attendants filed through the crowd from their posts by the ballroom walls, directing people to their seats. Galdinia was guided to a setting halfway up the table, and there was a spare space for Bentley to her right. She wondered if the Syndicate knew she would have an escort, or if they merely hoped she would.

Across from her sat Ryden and beside him, High Priestess Saena and Captain Ilyon. Galdinia gave the governor a knowing look as she nodded towards Bentley's place setting. The governor did not reveal how he organised that seating arrangement so quickly; he merely grinned at the princess smugly. As she tried to make herself comfortable among all the clinging material at her waist, Galdinia inspected the place to her left. Neryda's name was written upon the place card in golden script like her own, but she was nowhere to be seen.

Galdinia had forgotten about her best friend, and again she looked for her in the tangle of people finding their seats.

"Would you like another drink?" Bentley asked, thinking Galdinia may be searching for an attendant.

"No, I'm looking for Neryda," she said hastily, craning her neck to see around her guests.

"I'm sure she'll be along in a moment," Bentley reassured her.

The governor stood to his feet, tapping a spoon against the edge of his glass to incite the attention of those in the room as the music faded to a deep lull. As he did so, the lords and ladies along the table cast their gazes upon Galdinia and Bentley, already brewing with judgements of who the future queen might choose to spend her life with, intrigued by this lord from beyond the capital walls. The eyes of the other suitors, who were dotted along the table, also glanced at them, some full of annoyance, others with disappointment.

"Honoured guests of the throne," Ryden began, his voice echoing across the room, "it is my greatest pleasure, and that of the princess, to welcome you this evening to the Royal Feast. We recognise that although we meet under somewhat solemn pretences, we hope that this evening can be one of celebration as we pay our respects to the late King Bartemus. What a great man he was!"

"Hear, hear!" Voices of agreement filled the room.

"As we honour the past, we also look to the future." Ryden held his glass out to the princess, nodding in her direction. "It was King Bartemus himself who requested that this night be one of festivities and enjoyment in order to usher in the next ruler of our kingdom. So with that said, please raise your glasses to Princess Galdinia and a night of jovial celebration!"

"To Princess Galdinia!" The voices echoed across the room, and Galdinia felt her cheeks flush once again. The eyes of all those in the room turned to her, as did the glasses in their hands, and she momentarily glimpsed what her future could look like.

For a moment, she thought that perhaps she could do it, perhaps she would be queen.

Her guests sipped their sparkling wine and the quartet started up its cheerful melody once again, welcoming in the line of attendants that moved along the table with glistening gold plates of food. In unison, they placed their dishes in front of the guests and Galdinia's eyes widened at the sight. Before her was a plate of the kitchen's finest vegetables, laid out in concentric circles, oozing in a sweetly scented tomato glaze.

As Galdinia cut into the food and went to take her first bite, a rushing breeze passed her and suddenly someone was in the seat to her left: Neryda.

"Where have you been?" Galdinia asked, abandoning her cutlery.

"In the ballroom, just chatting to some of the nobles." Neryda was puffing as she spoke, clearly trying to catch her breath.

"No, you weren't." Galdinia frowned, twisting to face her friend. "I've been looking for you."

Neryda sat on this for a moment and then briskly said, "I had to run to the powder room to fix my hair. I wasn't happy with how it looked." Neryda turned to her plate and started cutting into her entrée.

Galdinia didn't believe her for a second. "Your hair looked perfectly fine. You said it yourself when you finished doing it."

"Well, after your knight in shining armour swept you away, I suddenly felt inferior without my own date, so I thought I'd just make myself a little more presentable." Neryda wouldn't meet Galdinia's eyes. While Galdinia knew that her friend may not have been too pleased about her decision to be escorted by Bentley, she still wasn't absolutely convinced that this was why she had been missing. She also noted that she hadn't seen Kell since they entered the ballroom, but

Neryda didn't look like she'd just come from a rendezvous with a handsome lord. Galdinia took pause before responding.

"I'm sorry that he suddenly stepped in like that. I shouldn't have left you to enter on your own," Galdinia said, her voice low, not taking her eyes from her friend, who still stared down at her plate. "Neryda."

"It's fine," Neryda replied, finally meeting Galdinia's gaze, the hint of a smile on her lips, her voice lowering considerably. "Just be careful with that one, okay? I don't want him getting any funny ideas."

Galdinia reached her hands out to hold Neryda's, bending her head in close. "I promise you, no funny business."

The girls smiled at each other before parting ways to attend to their entrées.

More than almost anything else in their relationship, Galdinia was thankful for their ability to forgive quickly and move on as though no harm was done. It still lingered heavy on the princess' heart, though, that perhaps her friend wasn't being absolutely honest about her whereabouts.

22

Decadent food, endless glasses of wine and swirling upbeat music was what continued to pull Galdinia through the evening. Whenever her glass was nearly empty, Bentley would call for another round from a nearby attendant, the bubbles filling her head and the sweet taste almost numbing her tongue. Both he and Neryda had managed to keep Galdinia from the clutches of numerous dignitaries for too long, pulling her from dull conversations or ones that may have resulted in questions about the princess' gift or upcoming coronation.

Before dinner was served, Lord Kaedric managed to draw Galdinia into his grasp with his beaming smile. He commented on the elaborate evening and made sure the princess knew that she was far more beautiful than the night itself. They were soon interrupted by Evarius and Dillian, who awkwardly joined them and began tugging Galdinia to and fro with compliments and praise. Kell seemed to keep his distance, but Galdinia did find him gazing at her best friend from time to time. She was glad when the main meal was announced and she could return to her seat and the protection of Neryda and Lord Bentley.

As the night continued, the atmosphere in the room became lighter and livelier; lords and ladies laughed with Syndicate members, visiting guests marvelled at the beauty of the ballroom, and even

Neryda softened towards Galdinia's date. Slowly, the princess watched her best friend's frown ease each time Bentley spoke. As the main course was being cleared for dessert, he asked Neryda about herself, particularly about her plans for the future now that their studies were complete. Neryda spoke of travelling beyond the capital walls, wanting to see every inch of the kingdom and beyond.

"You will have to come visit The Edges," Bentley said as he scooped up a handful of blueberries from the replenished boards at the centre of the table. "My family's estate is nestled along mountains and it's particularly beautiful in winter."

"Is that right?" Neryda asked, lazily swirling the sparkling wine in her glass with her mind.

"Imagine natural hot springs in the mountains surrounded by snowcapped trees."

"You know," Neryda remarked, taking another sip of bubbles, "maybe this guy isn't half bad."

Galdinia attributed the brashness and volume of Neryda's words to the amount of alcohol in her system.

"Pardon me?" Bentley asked, turning to face them both fully, Galdinia now stuck between her best friend and suitor, the two facing each other across her.

"Look, Lord Bentley," Neryda said with a slight lilt to her voice. "I'll be honest, I wasn't a fan of you at first. I thought you were just another suitor seeking power and a title. It's hard to believe that anyone vying for the hand of the future queen would be doing so for honourable reasons." Bentley raised his eyebrows at Neryda, a boyish smirk playing at his lips. "But you know, I think if you keep the sparkling wine flowing like you are tonight, surely you can't be all that terrible." Neryda smiled, raising her glass towards the lord.

"Well, thank you for your delightful assessment of me, Lady Neryda," Bentley said, leaning his glass across the princess to tap it against Neryda's. "Your approval is noted and greatly appreciated. I will be honest though"—he leaned across Galdinia further to speak quietly to her friend, placing his arm along the back of the princess' chair as he did so—"I don't have a single interest or reason for being here that is dishonourable. I really do quite fancy your friend here."

Galdinia flushed again, taken aback by Bentley's assured and confident words. Neryda moved back from Bentley, wide-eyed and suddenly bashful, her eyes landing on Galdinia.

"What a good line." Neryda smirked, leaning back in her chair for a moment before standing up in a sudden rush. "Well, I'm going to go chat to that handsome lord over there."

Galdinia noticed that there didn't appear to be anyone in particular she was pointing at. Her friend simply winked at her and walked away from the table in the vague direction of a group of mingling visitors. Galdinia turned to Bentley, who was still leaning in slightly towards her, keenly aware that his arm was still resting on the back of her chair.

"Well, I think she's finally warming to me," Bentley said, taking another sip of his wine.

"You knew she wasn't particularly fond of you?"

"Loyal, Neryda may be. Discreet, she most certainly is not."

Galdinia let out a laugh, placing her hand on his forearm that rested on the table in front of her.

"She really isn't," Galdinia agreed, her fingers grazing his wrist momentarily before returning to her own lap. "She's painfully honest though. Always has been."

"How long have you been friends?" Bentley asked, not moving from his position facing Galdinia. "Based on your stories at brunch yesterday, it sounds like a long time."

"I barely remember life without Neryda. We used to get up to all sorts of mischief, by her guidance, of course. I always just went along for the ride." Galdinia thought for a moment, fond images of their childhood dancing through her mind as she spoke. "When you spend time with Neryda, it's hard not to have fun. You just have to trust her seemingly wild ideas sometimes."

Bentley smiled at Galdinia, his eyes softly lit by the surrounding candlelight. Galdinia became aware of how close he was sitting to her, his fingers brushing against her shoulder every now and then, his eyes flicking across her face and to her lips while she spoke. "I can imagine the two of you caused your attendants grief as children."

"Oh, they could hardly keep up! We knew how to break into—or out of—any room in the castle."

"Thick as thieves, by the sounds of it."

"More like sisters." Galdinia caught Neryda's eye from across the room as she spoke to a group of lords, all of them wrapped in what she imagined would be the most exciting story any of them had ever heard. If Neryda was telling it, it was likely that it was.

Galdinia's gaze was then drawn in by movement near the door of the ballroom. A group of guards who had been stationed around the ballroom walked towards the door and were promptly replaced by another shift of soldiers. Most evening guard duties were rotated at the ninth hour, and she was surprised by how quickly the first half of the evening had gone as she watched the new group of soldiers march uniformly down the stairs towards their positions around the room. What an evening of entertainment they had ahead of them.

As she went to turn back to Bentley, Galdinia saw a familiar face among the crowd. Although it was half concealed by his helmet, there was no mistaking him.

Drystan.

His eyes found hers immediately, and he smiled, the warmth of his face radiating across the room to her. Until that moment, she had forgotten that he was on duty in the castle that evening.

Galdinia watched everything that followed at what felt like half speed.

Lord Bentley saw his date's face brighten, and so he turned to the entrance, his arm still resting across her shoulders. Drystan saw the lord's arm, how close he sat to the princess and how comfortable he looked—how comfortable *they* looked. All of the light rushed from Drystan's face. Before Galdinia could remove herself from Bentley's encircled arm, Drystan tore his eyes from the scene before him and walked back out of the ballroom.

"Excuse me, Lord Bentley. I'll return in a minute." Galdinia's words were rushed as she placed her glass on the table, pushing herself up and away from his outstretched arm. The princess moved quickly through the ballroom, smiling as she did so as not to alert the other guests. As she weaved through attendants and visitors, she could feel the effects of the alcohol that made her feet foolish.

Neryda noticed her friend's sudden movements, her eyes following her out of the room. Lord Bentley sat confused in her wake.

In the entrance hall, she was met by watchful guards and busy attendants, but Galdinia found no sign of Drystan, her eyes scouring the room. She approached one of the guards stationed near the ball-room doors. He bowed in her presence.

"Did you see a soldier come through here?" Galdinia asked, her words rushed.

"There are many guards, especially at changeover, Your Majesty." The guard was polite but wasn't giving her the answer she needed.

"I am looking for a young soldier. He just came from the ballroom. He was on guard patrol this evening." Galdinia could feel herself getting impatient. "Did he come past here, or did he go up into the castle?"

"Most of the guards who finished their patrol in the grounds are already in the ballroom, but one did just go down the western wing, perhaps to do a sweep."

Galdinia did not respond to the guard; she turned on her heels and walked down the wide hallway opposite the ballroom.

The hallway was quiet and still. Galdinia knew Drystan would struggle to leave his post at the castle, no matter what he was faced with inside. It didn't take her long to consider where he may retreat to: the library.

The princess walked as quickly as her binding dress would allow, passing only the faces of her ancestors whose portraits dotted the walls in ornate gilded frames, lit by the flickering candles in their sconces. When she made the last turn down the hallway, she saw the door of the library left open ajar, a weak light from within cutting through the hall. Galdinia approached and pushed the door open with gentle hands.

The room was lit by the crackling fireplace across the room. Although this was her safe space and she knew it well, she felt uneasy as her eyes rested on Drystan. He stood with his back to her, leaning against the edge of the table in the centre of the room, his helmet and sword resting beside his clenched hands. His back was rising and falling in great heaving breaths.

"Drys?"

Galdinia's voice caused his hand to twitch, but he didn't move from his position. She had never seen Drystan even remotely angry before and she didn't know how he might respond to her.

"Drystan," she said with a breath, taking a short step closer to him. "Drystan, please, talk to me."

Slowly, he stood up straight, releasing his hands from the table before him, but he didn't turn.

"Drystan," Galdinia barely whispered, her heart racing beneath her chest.

Drystan turned slowly to look at the princess, and to her surprise, he wasn't angry, wasn't enraged. He was crying. Silent tears crept down his face and his eyes were a blotchy red.

"I don't think I can do this." The words strained from his lips, and he was unable to meet her gaze. "I don't think I can watch you fall in love with someone else."

"But I'm not——"

"Gal, you don't have to lie," Drystan said, wiping his hands across his tear-stained cheeks.

"I'm not in love with him."

"It's fine."

"Don't say it's fine when it's obviously not."

"He's probably a wealthy lord," Drystan went on, disregarding her words and still not meeting her eyes, "primed and ready to become your king, exactly what you need."

"Drystan, he's a suitor," Galdinia tried to explain, stepping closer to him. "The Syndicate selected five nobles for me to consider. Without my gift, I can't take the throne on the Seventh Day. They've found a loophole that would allow me to be crowned queen regardless."

"You have to marry one of them?" Drystan asked, piecing together the situation.

"I have to be betrothed at the very least." Galdinia had not expected to have this conversation with Drystan tonight; she hadn't planned how she might broach the topic with him, but this certainly wasn't what she had imagined. "But I'm not in love with him, Drys."

"He looked quite comfortable with you."

"Well, I'm not in love with him," Galdinia repeated herself, her words firm, hoping if she said it enough, he would believe her. "I don't love him. I've known him for barely three days!"

"You will be queen in three more and you will have to commit to one of them in order to become so. I just can't watch it happen." He continued to avoid her gaze. "I thought I could do this. I thought I could pretend to be okay with this, but I can't be a guard in your city and watch you have dinner with them at a party—let alone marry one of them—and pretend that I don't want to put my fist through a wall."

"Perhaps I don't want any of these suitors." Galdinia took another step forward, slowly closing the gap between them, now mere feet away from her friend. Was he her friend? She wasn't sure what he was to her anymore.

Drystan finally looked at her, his eyes still glistening with tears. "We've talked about this, Gal." His voice was scratched with heartache.

"No, *you* talked about it," Galdinia said, stepping even closer to Drystan, now only a foot away. "Maybe I'll marry whoever I want to marry. Maybe I'll be a little selfish."

Galdinia could feel her frustration boiling beneath her skin, being reminded once again why she had to choose a suitor before her coronation and why it felt so unjust. When she was away from Drystan, she could think about duty, but the moment he was near her, she wanted nothing more than to choose him and leave the crown behind. Her moments of laughter with Bentley felt worlds away now that she was in Drystan's vicinity.

"I thought I could do it. The other day at the barracks, when it was just the two of us, I thought I could be brave and let you go. But actually seeing you with someone else..." Drystan trailed off, his eyes full of hurt. "I know it's selfish, but I can't see you with him... or anyone. I'll get a transfer out of the city, across the kingdom. I just can't—"

"And what about me?" Galdinia asked, desperation in her eyes. "I know so much has changed between us, but I can't live in a world without you. You can't run away from me."

Drystan, teary-eyed and heartbroken, reached out and placed his hand gently on Galdinia's cheek, his rough hands reminding Galdinia once again that he was no longer the boy she watched leave for training months ago. But his scent of musk and oak was still there, reminding her of a simpler time.

"Drys." Galdinia's eyes fluttered closed as she pressed her cheek into his palm. A moment later, though, his hand was gone. She opened her eyes and saw a pained look etched onto his face, his brows hard. "What is it?"

"That's from him, isn't it?" Drystan asked, looking beyond her eyes to her hair. He was looking at the clip Lord Bentley had given her.

"It's just a gift, a gesture," Galdinia assured him, but he took a step backwards and leaned against the table.

Before Drystan could respond, a voice echoed down the hallway.

"Princess?" It was Lord Bentley. "Princess, are you down here?"

"There he is now. I need to go, and you should get back to your dinner." Drystan went to pick up his sword and helmet, but Galdinia's hands fell on his. He looked back up at her and froze. The pain in his eyes and the grief in his voice hurt Galdinia more than she thought it would if he were angry at her.

"No, please just wait here," Galdinia pleaded. "I'll go deal with him and come back."

Galdinia stared at him, her hands on his, until he nodded curtly, taking back his hands and crossing them against his chest.

"Princess?" Bentley's voice echoed again.

"I'll be right back," Galdinia said as she backed out of the room, her eyes desperate and hopeful. "Please, don't go."

She shut the door behind her and made haste down the hallway. As she turned the corner, she came face to face with a concerned looking Bentley. His face broke into a smile.

"Princess! Where have you been?" he asked, walking towards her. "Are you okay?"

"I'm fine, Lord Bentley," Galdinia said breathlessly. She turned him around and walked back towards the entrance hall, moving quicker than was natural.

"I thought perhaps you'd been caught in an unsavoury conversation with a fawning noble." Bentley's humorous tone didn't penetrate Galdinia's focus on getting him far away from the library.

"Oh no, nothing like that," she said as they stepped into the entrance hall where attendants were still moving about. "I'm actually feeling a little off-kilter. I just went by the washroom to catch my breath. I have some medicine in my rooms that I'll quickly fetch."

"I can escort you to your chambers. I don't want you walking up there alone if you're unwell." The lord's genuine concern and willing-ness to help, while admirable, was the last thing Galdinia needed in that moment.

"I don't think that will look particularly innocent, Lord Bentley." Galdinia chuckled, feigning innocence herself. "The princess going back to her chambers with her escort after many glasses of alcohol? I'd hate to know what the kitchen maids would say."

Around them walked more helmet-donned guards. Galdinia couldn't help but worry that one of them was Drystan, finding an easy disguise among his brothers in order to flee from the castle.

"I suppose I have to continue this honourable front that I've so successfully maintained thus far," Bentley said with a wink, recalling his earlier conversation with Neryda. "But please send an attendant to me if you need anything."

"I will." Galdinia smiled, watching him walk back to the ballroom. "I'll return soon!"

The moment the lord was through the doors and out of sight, Galdinia turned on her heels and raced back down the hallway of the western wing, holding the gathered material at her thighs in her hands. She moved briskly and was breathless as she pushed through the door of the library once again, before closing it quickly behind her.

Drystan was still there, leaning against the table, looking down at his interlocked fingers. He lifted his eyes, looking at her from beneath his brows. Did he still have tears in his eyes? Galdinia's already racing heart thudded in her chest.

"You didn't leave," she said, her breath catching up to her.

"You came back," he replied softly yet almost desperately.

In a swift movement, Drystan stood up straight, walked towards Galdinia, and took her face in his hands, looking deep into her eyes for a moment before leaning down and pressing his lips against hers. The kiss was equally gentle and fervent, sending Galdinia's already breath-less body into a lightheaded rush of emotions. She held on to his torso to steady herself, leaning into his lips as he held her face in his palms. She could feel the remnants of his tears on her cheek as she leaned into him, drawing him closer to herself. She pressed against his armoured body, the cool of the metal sending a shiver down her spine.

She would have taken him covered head to toe in hot coals and still have wanted to kiss him. Her heart was infinitely tethered to this boy, whether fate wished it or not. They were bound together in the crucible of young love and first kisses, and Galdinia never wanted that to be broken or discarded.

Just as she went to kiss him again, Drystan pulled back his lips, leaning his forehead against hers, his eyes closed. They didn't speak for a long moment. They simply revelled in each other's presence, soaking up the mixture of electricity, safety, and contentment. Galdinia breathed in his scent, stronger now that she was so close to him. She felt comforted by the familiar smell and was transported back to midnight rendezvous and secret glances. She felt a sense of security she hadn't in a long time.

"I should go," Drystan said on a breath, pulling back from Galdinia and letting go of her face. Subconsciously, she tightened her grip on his sides, trying to hold him in place.

"What?" Galdinia asked, her voice still low in the quiet of the library.

"I need to go back to my post and you…" he hesitated, looking away from her eyes for a second. "You need to get back to the feast."

"Drystan, you can't leave now," Galdinia said. She could feel heat rising in her face, tears bubbling just under the surface.

"I have to. We both do." The Drystan of a few minutes prior who was shedding tears of loss at the prospect of Galdinia with another man was gone. He was replaced with Drystan the soldier. He had a job to do: to protect the crown, to protect Galdinia, but not to love her. "We both know this will not end the way we want it to. I was a fool to even consider the idea. My apologies, Princess."

He only ever called her Princess in public when he didn't want to startle others by calling her by her first name. He reserved calling her Princess for moments of separation and detachment, to preserve her name for when they could truly be themselves. Calling her Princess in private hurt just as much a sword to her heart. It cut off her tears completely and she could feel the heat of her skin rise, the all-too-familiar ache in her chest burning.

He turned from her and picked up his sword, placing it in its sheath. He then picked up his helmet and went to walk around Galdinia towards the door, but she stood firmly in his way.

"Drys, please don't go." Drystan stared at her. Although his words and actions were reminiscent of a guard, his eyes showed his heartbreak and reluctance. "Please, we can stay in here a while, just us."

"I have to go, and you need to go back to the feast." He repeated himself, avoiding her teary gaze and making his way around her to the door.

"Drystan Allard, you cannot leave after…" Galdinia struggled to form her words as she spoke into his back as he faced the door. "After that. Don't you dare leave me here in tears, the scent of your lips still on mine. You are far more a gentleman than that." She left the niceties behind and let her emotions speak for her.

He turned around to face her and she could see the anguish in his face once again. "What do you expect of me, Gal? Do you wish me to carry on watching you and your suitor fall in love with each other and just wait for these secret moments for us to steal away together in dark corners in order to be alone? Is it your plan for us to do this for the rest of our lives?" He stood his ground, his own frustration with the injustice of their situation bubbling. "I cannot relinquish my job any more than you can, so it is each other we will have to let go of. What more could you possibly ask of me?"

"I wish—" Galdinia began, her voice catching in her throat. "I wish you would not kiss me like that and then tell me it can never happen again."

"Like I said, I was a fool to do that. I apologise." He reached out his hand as though he was going to take hers but withdrew it quickly and placed it on his belt. He turned to leave and paused at the door, turning his head momentarily to give his final goodbye. "It won't happen again, Princess."

Galdinia felt her heart shudder in her chest as he uttered her title.

She didn't reply, she merely stared down the hall after him and watched him turn the corner without another glance back at the girl he loved.

23

After a few minutes and once she had regained some semblance of composure, Galdinia willed herself out of the library. She closed the door behind her with a thud and marched down the hallway back to the foyer. She suspected that Drystan would be on a post outside the castle, likely having switched with a friend for his ballroom shift, which they would have gladly taken. Regardless, she kept her eyes ahead as she walked into the ballroom, avoiding eye contact with anyone else. To her surprise, many of her guests were too engrossed in their conversations and free flowing drinks to take much notice of her. She managed to move down the steps with little recognition of her absence.

Upon her reentry into the ballroom, though, Galdinia was quickly faced with Neryda, who swept past her and pulled her towards a quiet corner of the room beside the stairs where no guests or attendants could pry.

"Where have you been?"

Although she had been gone for no longer than fifteen minutes, Galdinia knew she'd need to explain herself to her best friend.

"I felt ill and went to get some medicine," she said, avoiding Neryda's eye, looking over her shoulder for Bentley.

"Be honest, Gal," Neryda scolded, frowning. "I saw you go out after Drystan."

"Then why ask where I've been?" Galdinia questioned, looking back at her friend. "You weren't honest with me earlier about where you were."

Galdinia could feel her frustration resurfacing and, unfortunately for Neryda, she could no longer contain it.

"Well, I'm not the Princess of Crysterra who is at her Royal Feast, gallivanting through a castle with a boy who is not her suitor." Neryda's words hurt more than they should have, but she was right. Although Galdinia knew that, she didn't feel like being lectured.

"You weren't honest with me, so why should I be with you?" She knew it was wrong to let her anger about Drystan out on Neryda, but she couldn't help it. She felt overcome with emotion, her cheeks and chest still warm in the aftermath of being called Princess by the only person she wished wouldn't.

Neryda considered her words for a moment and decided to take the ever so slightly higher road. "As I was about to make my entrance into the ballroom, I saw Drystan in the entrance hall. I was out there trying to convince him to take a post outside the castle for the evening, or at least somewhere other than the ballroom. I told him that it wouldn't do him any good to see you at an event like this where you had to be the princess and he had to be a guard. When the change of guard rolled around, he obviously didn't listen to me. I didn't want to make a big deal of it earlier or worry you. I was trying to protect you."

"I don't need protecting." Galdinia went to walk away, but Neryda took her by the arm and turned her around.

"I was honest with you, so now you tell me: where have you been?"

"Just like you said, gallivanting around the castle with a boy who is not my suitor." Galdinia spoke flatly and then quickly added, "I kissed a boy who is not my suitor."

"Oh, Gal." Neryda dropped her tough exterior and wrapped her arms around her friend, pulling her close. Galdinia didn't need to say that it ended badly; her thorny exterior and accusatory words spoke for her.

"It's fine, I'm fine," Galdinia whispered, holding back the tears, promising herself that she wouldn't cry over Drystan again.

"We can go back to your rooms if you want to," Neryda suggested, holding her friend close. "I can tell Ryden and Bentley that you aren't well and need to lie down. Perhaps the alcohol didn't agree with you."

"No, it's fine," Galdinia repeated herself, pulling back from her friend. "If anything, I think I could use more wine."

Neryda wiped a tear from Galdinia's cheek and took her by the hand, walking with her back to the dining table just as dessert was being served. She took her seat beside Bentley, who turned from his conversation with a nearby lord at her arrival.

"You're back! How are you feeling?"

"Much better. Nothing that a little medicine and some fresh air can't solve." Despite the heat in her chest, Galdinia smiled at Bentley, tucking herself into the table and draping her fresh napkin onto her lap. Once again, Bentley placed his arm over the back of her chair. Earlier this felt casual and inviting. Now it made her feel claustrophobic.

"Well, you missed the riveting conversation I was having with this lord from the east," Bentley said quietly, leaning in close to Galdinia. "Did you know that the trade routes between the north and south now move fifteen percent faster than they did a decade ago?"

"I didn't," Galdinia said, trying to keep her tone lighthearted.

"Oh yes," Bentley said, mocking excitement dripping off his words. "You wouldn't believe how much I learnt in the last few minutes. It's truly fascinating."

Bentley let out a sigh, rolling his eyes as he leaned back in his chair. Galdinia tried to force a chuckle, still feeling the remnants of her conversation with Drystan.

Before Bentley could say anything else, the attendants started placing the plates of dessert before the guests. The dish was a sickly looking cake with ribbons of chocolate teetering on top. Galdinia wasn't sure how much of this she could stomach in her current state.

During dessert, Galdinia was pulled into conversation by Ryden, who checked in on how her evening was shaping up. She lied about her whereabouts to him as well, looking down at her dessert, occasionally taking a small bite. It was just as sweet as she had anticipated, and she relinquished her spoon after that mouthful alone.

As the final course drew to a close, Ryden stood again to make an announcement. This time, Bentley chimed his glass for the governor, drawing the attention of the guests.

"Ladies and gentlemen," Ryden said, his voice carrying across the hall. "Thank you for joining us for this most delicious meal this evening. It has been an honour to share this dinner with you as we remember our late King Bartemus." People bowed their heads out of respect and nodded in agreement. "It has been a marvellous night, but it isn't over yet! We will be moving to the dance floor, where the future queen, Princess Galdinia, will dance with her escort, Lord Bentley."

There were claps and exclamations of sheer delight coming from around the table as everyone looked to Galdinia and Bentley. The princess caught sight of Evarius, who glared down the table at the two of them, his arms firmly crossed over his chest.

She now wished she'd have taken Neryda up on her offer to go to bed early.

Ryden continued over the chatter, "Once their dance is finished, everyone will be taking to the floor for the rest of the evening!"

The music started to pick up again from the end of the ballroom, inviting Galdinia and Lord Bentley to the dance floor in front of them. Everyone at the table stood and they started to move towards the other end of the room. Lord Bentley held out his arm for Galdinia to take, which she did with a reluctant smile that she hoped he did not notice.

"Here we go, I suppose," Lord Bentley said with an air of excited apprehension.

"I suppose," Galdinia echoed, moving through the crowd with him to stand in the centre of the dance floor.

The quartet began a new song and the two started to move in unison, Bentley's left hand holding up her right, his right hand snaked around her lower back. She rested her hand on his shoulder and tried to keep herself steady as he twirled her in her snug gown. She wasn't sure if it was the three courses and the multiple glasses of sparkling wine, but her dress felt suddenly tighter. All she wanted to do was rip it off and hide beneath her bed. Instead, she moved around a dance floor with a perfectly lovely lord, in a skintight dress, the eyes of the most important people in the kingdom upon them both.

Galdinia felt her breath hitch in her throat, and she drew herself closer to Bentley, hoping it would steady her; the sparkling wine in her bloodstream was making her a little less coordinated than she would have liked. It seemed Bentley took her closeness as a sign that she was enjoying herself, and he smiled down at her, his dimple appearing and his light eyes hopeful. Her heart was so conflicted; at dinner she had felt almost giddy sitting with Bentley and knew somewhere deep down she was happy to have his arm draped around her, but she could still feel Drystan's lips on hers.

Feeling guilty, Galdinia averted her eyes from Bentley's and tried to focus on the decorated walls and hanging lanterns. She struggled not to notice the approving faces of their audience as they watched the future queen dance with such an upstanding lord, a man who any princess would feel lucky to be dancing with. Any princess except Galdinia, for she could not shake the image of Drystan from her mind.

As they danced, she wondered if her mother ever felt like this, if she felt coerced into marrying her father or if she did so willingly. Was she perhaps the Lord Bentley of their relationship? Queen Anae's gift may have arrived belated, but she came from a powerful and revered family. Had Galdinia's father had someone he'd have rather been with, a woman he had known for many years who perhaps did not fit the bill of what was right and proper for a monarch? Of course she would never know, but the thought plagued her as she danced.

When the song finally came to an end, Galdinia stepped back from Bentley and he bowed to her, to which she curtseyed and smiled respectfully. The rest of the guests then flooded the dance floor and the evening truly began. While Galdinia retreated to her seat with Neryda, Lord Bentley found himself persuaded into a dance with one of the older widowed ladies of the capital who looked like she was ready to make him her own suitor.

"Another glass?" Neryda asked, holding up a bottle of sparkling wine that had been left on the table by an attendant. Galdinia gladly held up her glass and Neryda filled it to the brim before filling her own. "To an unexpectedly emotional evening that we shall hopefully soon forget."

The friends clinked their glasses and drank.

Galdinia took long swigs of the drink until the entire glass was consumed. She'd felt herself falling into the stupor of the alcohol after the main course, but this drink certainly started to drag her down. Where earlier the sparkling wine made her feel excited and caused more giggles to pass through her lips than usual, it was now heightening every emotion she could feel coursing through her, calling attention to every ache and pain. Anger. Frustration. Disbelief. Heartbreak.

The alcohol worked fast, and she held her empty glass out to Neryda to fill once again, waiting for the drink to do its work in helping her forget this dreadful evening.

FIFTH DAY OF MOURNING

24

ALL GALDINIA COULD FEEL AS SHE SLOWLY AWOKE THE NEXT MORNING was a throbbing pain at her temples. The chirp of a bird from outside her bedroom window sounded like a shriek as she tried to piece together why she felt so ill. She squinted her eyes open and immediately shut them again, the slightest shaft of light burning her eyes. She rolled onto her back slowly, her stiff limbs crying out to her.

She was, for the first time in her short life, hungover.

As teenagers, Neryda and she often had an underage drink at the tavern or would sneak a glass of wine from time to time from the castle's cellars, but never before had she drunk *too* much. Galdinia would always keep it to two or three drinks maximum.

But not last night.

What was last night? Galdinia questioned, trying to think louder than the pounding in her head.

She rolled her head to the other side and peeked a look at her room: a crimson dress was slung over the armchair in the corner, a pair of shoes discarded lazily to the side. Beside the chair was an obviously empty wine bottle, left to be cleaned up by some poor attendant once Galdinia had vacated her rooms.

Galdinia remembered walking into her chambers at one, perhaps even two hours past midnight and trying with all her might to take off her dress. She remembered being indescribably uncomfortable, but she couldn't do it on her own. Someone took her dress off for her. Suddenly, she sat up in bed—which sent another round of shooting pain through her entire body—before quickly remembering the sweep of red hair that accompanied her fragmented memories.

"It's okay. We'll get you out of this, then you can go to bed."

She remembered Neryda trying to soothe her, but why?

Neryda had taken her dress and shoes off, replacing them with her softest nightgown. Galdinia remembered tears staining the front of her bedclothes.

Why was I so upset?

As she leaned back into the pillows, she felt something push into her scalp, causing more pain than it ought to have. She found the golden rose clip and she ran her fingers across it gently.

Bentley.

Galdinia could remember saying a very messy goodnight to the lord, wishing him well on his trip back home—but he wasn't leaving anytime soon. Why had she said that? Was she upset that she thought the lord was leaving?

She considered the rest of the evening, or at least the pieces she could pull from the various recesses of her mind. She drank sparkling wine with Neryda and Bentley, they danced together (numerous times), and she could vaguely remember trying to forget something. Had she fallen down mid-dance? This was likely, but she didn't think she'd cry over that either. Had she made a fool of herself in front of the lords and ladies? Or in front of Ryden? Perhaps she caused grief for an attendant or a guard—

Drystan.

The library, the hallway, Bentley's interruption, the kiss; it all came rushing back in a wave of heat and heartache. Every single moment. Every single tear. Every single glass of alcohol.

Galdinia was mortified.

Had she really begged Drystan to stay like that? She, the future queen? Had she really kissed him and then hoped he would do it again? Had she actually kissed someone that wasn't her suitor?

Galdinia was ashamed. She lost full control of herself and could only imagine the mockery she made of her family name. Her mother would have never done such a thing. She was such an upstanding example of how to be a queen. Galdinia was already failing, and she hadn't even been crowned yet.

She rolled over and buried herself in her pillows, hoping she'd sink into them until they swallowed her alive.

"Good morning, sunshine." Neryda's sing-song voice pierced Galdinia's ears as her best friend walked into the room. Galdinia groaned in response, and she heard Neryda place something heavy on her bedside table. "Get up and eat. You'll feel better."

Galdinia groaned again, pulling the pillows over her head so as to block out all of her senses. The edge of her mattress sunk in as Neryda sat behind her, placing a comforting hand on her back.

"Come on, you need to get up," Neryda cooed, her voice warming and kind. "You know you have training today and I don't think Trunder will be too pleased with you being late."

"Tell him I'm sick," Galdinia mumbled in response, her voice muffled by the pillows. "Tell him I'm too ill to train today and he'll just have to go on without me."

"One does not tell the Captain of the Royal Guard what to do, especially not one as handsome as he." Neryda's voice became distant and hazy as she spoke about a man who Galdinia had known since she was crawling.

"He's at least twenty years our senior, Neryda," Galdinia huffed, peeling her face from the pillows and twisting (with a great deal of pain) to look at her friend. "Please don't talk about Captain Ilyon like that."

"Oh, you're on first name basis with him, of course!" Neryda said gleefully, smiling down at the princess.

"You're impossible," Galdinia replied with a roll of her eyes, slowly lifting herself up to a seated position.

"It got you up, didn't it?" Neryda smirked, to which Galdinia shook her head. This was a mistake. She felt like her brains were clattering around inside her head, all sharp corners and heavy thuds. Given the amount she had drunk, she was surprised she had anything left to rattle. Neryda leaned over to the tray of food she brought

Galdinia and placed it on her lap. She picked up one of the freshly baked cinnamon scrolls for herself.

"What time is it?" Galdinia asked before taking a large bite of her own cinnamon scroll, followed by a long gulp of water.

"At least the tenth hour."

"I don't have long until training then." Galdinia sighed, trying to force down more of her breakfast. With only two full days until her planned coronation, she knew she couldn't waste today without training.

"I take it that your private lessons haven't been as successful as archery?"

Galdinia hadn't yet filled her friend in about her most recent training session. She had been so wildly disappointed by it that she had hoped to forget all about it.

"I haven't been able to conjure a single element, not one." Galdinia dropped the cinnamon scroll back onto the tray. "It's infuriating. I stare at a candle for hours and hours and nothing. I don't know what he's expecting to happen, but I'm told that I'll know once the Gods have bestowed upon me the gift. So far, though, no holy ordination."

"I'm sorry, I can only imagine how frustrating that is," Neryda said, screwing up her face as she tried to empathise with Galdinia. They didn't often talk about Neryda's gift in conjunction with Galdinia's lack thereof. It was as though they made a silent agreement one day, many years ago, not to talk about it. Neryda went about her life as a Water Weaver and that was just who she was. Galdinia was merely waiting to catch up.

"It's really, *really* exhausting." Galdinia sighed again, rubbing her fingers across her throbbing forehead. "I don't know what the purpose was of all those years of prayer if the Gods won't give me what I need when I actually need it."

"Perhaps you don't need it just yet," Neryda suggested, almost sheepish. It was unlike Neryda to be so abashed; it took Galdinia by surprise. Galdinia could tell that Neryda knew that this was the last thing Galdinia needed to hear, even though it might be true. The uncertainty of the timing of her gift still hung heavy on the princess' shoulders.

"I would say that now would be fantastic timing." Galdinia took another sip of water. "It's so tiring. And after last night, I can't imagine trying to produce even an ounce of power today."

"Last night was... interesting."

Galdinia scoffed. "That's a nice way to put it. I made an absolute fool out of myself in front of Drystan, the Syndicate, and Lord Bentley. I feel like such an idiot."

"While I can't speak for Drystan or the Syndicate, I don't imagine Bentley thinks too poorly of you."

Galdinia let out a harsh and sudden laugh, which sent another line of shooting pain across her head.

"No, really! He wouldn't leave your side last night, not for a minute. Whenever another suitor came near, he steered you away from them. Perhaps that was selfish on his part, but you didn't seem too pleased when you saw them approaching. He even insisted on escorting us both up here at the end of the night and made me promise him that I'd take care of you, as if I haven't been doing that for most of our lives."

A disbelieving look crossed her face. In truth, she hoped her expression masked the sudden butterflies that made an unwelcome appearance in her stomach at the mention of Bentley's obliging manner.

"You really don't think he was put off?" Galdinia asked.

"No, I think he was merely concerned for you. It was kind of endearing to watch," Neryda said with a chuckle, popping another piece of the baked good in her mouth. "I think he genuinely cares for you."

"What happened to, 'We know what these suitors are like, all they want is the title and the inheritance, and blah blah blah?'"

"I think he managed to change my mind last night," Neryda said with a shrug, ignoring Galdinia's mocking tone. "If that's all he wants, then he's doing a good job of hiding it. He even offered to carry you all the way up here after midnight, even between your erratic mood swings. One minute you were laughing, the next you were sobbing. It was quite an ordeal."

Galdinia frowned at her friend. "Thank you for that."

"You're welcome," Neryda said, smirking. "But truly, he seems quite honourable. At the very least, he may be worth getting to know a little more. And let's be honest, he's kind of your only real option at this stage anyway, so it wouldn't hurt."

Your only option.

The fact that Galdinia couldn't be with someone she had cared for for nearly her entire life felt like a fist to the gut. What was more terrifying, though, was the fact that she couldn't become queen on her own, without a promise of marriage. She again became furious thinking about the injustice of the whole system. She was aware that her lack of powers very much impacted the entire situation, but she could hardly believe that the Syndicate—and her country—thought she needed a ring on her finger in order to properly lead the kingdom. She felt like she had been beaten at a game in which she started ten steps behind everyone else. Why had she agreed to this arrangement?

"Yes, I suppose it couldn't hurt," Galdinia said, somewhat absent-mindedly. "But I don't want to see him today, nor do I think he will want to see me. I need to prepare my speech for the banquet tomorrow as well, so after training I'll come and lock myself in here for the remainder of the evening."

"I'll make myself scarce and stay at home tonight then," Neryda said, and at Galdinia's apologetic expression, quickly added, "It's about time I faced the music that is Mother and Father. I imagine they have another tour of the coast planned for me to meet other prospective husbands, so I ought to stop avoiding them. You could use a good sleep before the banquet tomorrow anyway."

"Thank you for being here," Galdinia said with a smile. "It means a lot having you so close."

"Where else would I be?" Neryda replied, standing to her feet. "Oh, and if you need company at your lesson, you know I'm more than happy to be there as well, for you of course."

"Neryda, you will not be coming to my training session to ogle at a man who is simply too old for you." Galdinia rolled her eyes again, taking another bite of her scroll.

"At least my persistence is getting you out of bed!" Neryda said with a smile. "See you tomorrow, Gal."

She planted a quick kiss on the top of Galdinia's hair, sending another wave of pain around her head.

"Yes, tomorrow," Galdinia said in squinted pain, waving to her friend as she practically skipped out of the room.

∼

"We have one final element, Princess. Are you ready?"

Ilyon stood before Galdinia, the podium of water between them. The room beneath the barracks was as cool and damp as ever. She wondered if Ilyon could harness the water that she could feel in the air and that dripped between the rocks in the walls. She imagined that he could, given his unnaturally strong gift.

"I think so," Galdinia responded as she peered down into the clear surface of the water. Her still aching head made her question any ability she might be able to harness today, but she had no option other than to try nonetheless.

The captain had moved it so easily and eloquently on the Second Day when he demonstrated his powers; she thought she could only dream of emulating such a movement. She felt a tightening in her chest as she considered the very real possibility that she may not be able to control this element and, therefore, what that may signify. She tried not to let the doubt that had crept into the room affect her, but she couldn't help but be weighed down by fear and trepidation.

"While we are surrounded by air, we ourselves have much water within us," Ilyon said, reaching out his hand, palm up, coaxing the water from its resting place. "Our bodies call to water, they crave it, because of what a necessity it is to our lives."

He curved the water into a sphere, moving it to hover in the air between them.

"I was seven years old when I first tapped into my gift. I had been on a long trail walk with my older brother in the heat of summer. We had been hiking all day up in the Starlight Mountains. We hadn't realised that we took a wrong turn and spent hours wandering the trails in and around the mountains. Our water supply had run out quickly, and six hours later, after praying many silent prayers, we finally found our way to a nearby village. My lips were dry, and my tongue yearned for the taste of water; my body longed for it.

"We stumbled into a nearby tavern and were quickly shooed away by the barkeeper, who thought we were two street children looking for a feed, but all we needed was something to drink. As he pushed us out the door, I could smell it: water. I blindly followed my nose around the back of the tavern, where four horses were tied up, patiently waiting for their riders who were multiple pints into their night. That's when I saw the trough of water set before them, glimmering in the moonlight.

"I ran to the trough and submerged my head, frightening the horses and my brother, who thought I had gone mad. I was desperate, and it was more than a thirst. It had become a hunger." Ilyon was now spinning the orb of water in the air, its glassy surface shimmering, its form remaining solid. "The next day, I awoke to the sound of a dripping outside my bedroom window, my body waking me to go touch it. Within a month, I could shift the direction of the rain. Within six months, I could make waves."

Galdinia watched Ilyon through the sphere of water, his fingers moving gently, his eyes fixed on her.

"This is why I believe it so important to feel a connection with the elements before trying to control them. It's as if one day you can't distinguish which is more important, and the next your body is screaming for you to find it. The Gods knew that I needed to find the water. They blessed me when I truly needed it, when I had no option other than to rely on them." He halted the movement of the water. "Put out your hand."

Galdinia mirrored Ilyon, placing her right hand out in front of her, palm up. Slowly, the ball of water moved towards her, stopping when it hovered over her hand. She could smell the fresh scent of the water as it rotated just below her nose. Not a drop fell from the orb; Ilyon had it completely under his control.

"Move your fingers. Try to feel the weight of the water without touching it," Ilyon instructed.

Galdinia did as he said, moving her fingers like he did, trying to draw some energy or sense of connection from the water. Soon, she focused her eyes only on the sphere, trying to imagine that she was the one keeping it afloat.

"I'm going to lower it into your hand," Ilyon said quietly, not wanting to break her focus. "I will keep it steady, but see if you can hold it."

The water slowly lowered into her palm, its cool touch sending a shiver up her arm and to her shoulder. She tried to imagine that was some kind of connection and not her body simply reacting to the temperature.

Despite its solid form, the water still felt like liquid in her hand, dampening her palm as it turned. She could feel Ilyon pulling the water back together with each rotation. She was aware of the subtle movements of the water, its scent, its glistening outer. She felt like she could wrap her fingers around it and hold it like a ball.

"Let it go," Galdinia said quietly. "I want to see if I can hold it."

Ilyon hesitated but lowered the sphere further into Galdinia's hand, its surface now covering her curved fingers as well. It sat there for a moment as Galdinia cradled it and revelled in the sensation of holding water. Then, the next moment, it lost its shape and crashed through her fingers, spilling onto the floor by her feet with a splash.

Galdinia stared at the small puddle on the ground, her hand still outstretched, now dripping. With a heavy sigh, she dropped her hand and looked up at the captain once again. While he still stood at attention, he had a glimmer of pity in his eyes. The ache in her chest grew. Galdinia had truly believed that this one may work.

"You should be proud of yourself for trying."

Galdinia did not respond to this. She wasn't sure how proud of herself she was. She felt more disappointed than anything else. Ilyon glanced at the princess, noting her solemn gaze. Quickly, he moved his hand in an upward direction and the water that had stained the floor lifted off the ground and flew back to the bowl, not a drop left behind. Galdinia looked down at her feet and it was as if the water was never there.

She eyed the bowl and used all manner of thoughts and wordless commands to try to make even the smallest of droplets ripple in the water. She prayed to the Gods, asking again for her gift to break open inside of her. She pleaded with them to let her move it. She practically screamed from within.

Nothing.

"Perhaps it's never going to happen."

A tear rolled down her face and she crouched to her knees,

exhausted and exasperated, her temples still throbbing. She put her head in her hands and bit back a scream.

She was done.

"Princess, we must keep trying," Ilyon said in his usual stoic tone.

"No," she said softly into her hands, too tired to stop the tears from breaking on to her cheeks.

"But it's imperative that—"

"No!" she shouted, pulling her hands from her face and bundling them in fists by her sides. For a moment, Galdinia swore she saw a flicker of fear cross Ilyon's face. "I am not going to be made a fool any longer. I will not stand here trying to conjure a power that does not exist."

"Perhaps some more time could be spent praying in the temple."

"And look at all the good that has done for me," Galdinia huffed, standing to her feet and moving to one of the benches by the edge of the room. "I've spent time every morning since my father fell into sickness praying for these powers to come, and I've spent every waking minute since his death believing that they will, yet here we are."

"We may not understand timing of the Gods, but we must trust it and keep believing," Ilyon said, coming to stand beside the princess.

"Oh, the precious and perfect timing of the Gods. Of course, how could I forget? The timing that assures me that my powers will come when they see fit. Today would be as good as any to bestow on me my gift!" Galdinia spoke in mock reverence, and then she tilted her head to stare at the ceiling and beyond to where the Gods may be looking down at her. "They aren't listening to me. They obviously don't want to give me my gift. I don't know why I bother."

Ilyon's lips pursed at Galdinia's scathing words.

"Careful, Princess; it is not wise to grieve the Gods," Ilyon said. Although she knew he was trying to protect her, Galdinia could not help but be angered by these words.

"Why shouldn't I? They have neglected me in the pain and frustration I have felt over the last few days—no, months!" Galdinia knew this wasn't Ilyon's fault, but she was prepared to make anyone or anything her target at this stage. "I've lost my father, and I've been told I'm not ready to be queen, not only by my enemies, but by my very own Syndicate! I'm being forced into a relationship that I don't even

229

want and have to make a decision in the next forty-eight hours whether I want to marry one of these lords. I can tell you right now, Captain, I am grieving far more than they are."

"I can't begin to imagine the pain you are feeling, Princess, but I can assure you that the Gods share in your pain."

"Then that sounds like all the more reason for them to fix this situation." Galdinia sighed, letting out a long and heated breath.

Ilyon came to sit beside Galdinia on the bench, still maintaining his space. "Perhaps the solution in this situation doesn't solely sit in gaining your gift."

Galdinia couldn't imagine anything else placating her at this point. "I am just so very tired, and I want this all to be over."

"I know you do," Ilyon replied, resting his elbows on his knees. "Frankly, so do I. Not for my sake, but for yours. Once you have your gift, I will still gladly train you, but I can see the pain you're in now and it feels cruel."

Galdinia didn't respond. She fidgeted with her fingers, her frustration still palpable.

"Let's cancel training until further notice." Galdinia frowned at Ilyon's words, turning to look at him in confusion. "It's not doing either of us any good right now, and you need to focus on two very big events over the coming days. I don't want you to be so worn out from training that you're not able to perform how you need to in those situations. We all need you to be well-rested and we know that these sessions are not helping. So let's call off training until after the Seventh Day, whatever the outcome."

Galdinia, who had become lost in her irritation, was overcome with a sudden sense of gratitude for this man. He had been thoughtlessly expected to not only train a princess in an art she did not possess the capabilities to actually execute, but also continue to lead the Royal Guard in such a politically tumultuous time. He had been patient with her through their training sessions. Galdinia imagined that he had found it just as frustrating and disappointing as she did; he was just far better at hiding it.

"Thank you," she simply said, reaching out to pull Ilyon into a hug. For the briefest of seconds, he reluctantly returned the gesture.

Galdinia knew this was probably the most uncomfortable he had felt in her presence.

"You're welcome, Princess. Now, go get yourself something to eat and prepare for tomorrow evening's banquet. It will require a lot of you."

Galdinia nodded and stood to her feet, wiping the tears that had escaped down her cheeks as she left the room.

25

THE NIGHT BEFORE THE COMMEMORATION BANQUET, SLEEP WAS proving impossible for Galdinia. Despite her love of festivities and delicious food, after the events of the Royal Feast, she didn't feel like going to another event. Although she knew there wouldn't be any libraries or secret kisses, she didn't particularly feel like celebrating. She felt defeated and much preferred the idea of hibernating in her chambers instead.

While the Royal Feast was the most lavish event of the week, the Commemoration Banquet had the highest attendance. All citizens of the capital were welcome to attend the final celebration of the passing ruler in a sprawling dinner in the city's main square. For one evening, the square would be filled with fifty long tables, each covered in meals prepared by the citizens. Each family would provide a plate of food: roast turkey, pumpkin and rosemary soup, freshly baked bread, and the most decadent cakes one could imagine. So as to keep the remaining royals and Syndicate from any harm of potentially contaminated food or unfriendly party-goers, Galdinia would be seated at a table with the Syndicate members on a raised dais at the north end of the square, facing all of the citizens, eating food prepared by Miss Giles' own hands alone. They would be surrounded by royal guards, and anyone who tried to approach their table would quickly be turned in the other direction.

Before their meal commenced, Galdinia, as the incoming ruler, would need to make a speech in honour of her father. This one, unlike the one she gave at his funeral, would be significantly more upbeat. She would encourage everyone to think of fond memories of the king and share a lighthearted story or two of her own. This was a time to commemorate his life and look to the future, the thought of which made the knotted feeling in her chest reappear.

If the Royal Feast and her fruitless lessons with Ilyon taught her anything, it was that she wasn't sure just how much of a ruler she felt like at this stage. She felt deflated and unprepared to address her citizens.

As such, her nerves, mixed with the overwhelming concern she felt for her future, had her staring at the piece of parchment on her writing desk in her chambers on the eve of the Sixth Day of Mourning. She had written a few sentences of welcome and generic jovial sentiment, but she couldn't get any further as she wrote by the light of the dripping candle by her side.

In an attempt to clear her head, Galdinia got to her feet, wrapped her cloak around herself, and made her way down the corridor. The castle was silent at this time of night as she walked down the western staircase and out to the gardens. Even at night, the castle gardens looked magical.

The gardens were her mother's pride and joy before she passed away. Queen Anae would spend hours tending to the rose bushes, trimming dead leaves, and watering each garden bed. Although the gardeners tried to take the work off the queen's hands, she insisted on maintaining it herself. After she passed, it was left unattended to for many years until Galdinia was old enough to start planting new seeds and working in the space herself. When she began her more serious studies at the age of thirteen, her father insisted that they hire gardeners to maintain the grounds when the princess did not have time. She reluctantly agreed and still tried to visit the sacred space regularly to check in on her flowers.

Galdinia meandered through the grounds in her all-too-restless state, admiring the recent work of the gardeners. Given her father's slow decline, she hadn't been able to spend much time here, so she was glad to see it had been kept to her liking. Within moments, she started to relax as the familiar scents of her flowers and the sounds of sleeping crickets and cascading water danced around her. After the madness of the previous week, she found herself quickly resting into the quiet moment alone.

Galdinia followed the path around the fountain, its white marble lit by the moonlight. At the centre of the fountain stood a lion on its hind legs, roaring silently into the evening air. Perched atop the lion's mane was an owl, its wings outstretched to their full span. The animals also appeared on the Elderwin crest and represented the family's most valued traits: bravery and wisdom. Galdinia tried not to focus on the statues for long as a sense of inadequacy fell upon her.

She moved through the centre of the grounds where the trellised archways guided her path. They were covered in vines and spotted with wisteria and jasmine, making the enclosure permeate with the sweetly fragrant scent of the flowers. She continued to walk through the lush gardens, making her way to the lake at the easternmost point of the castle grounds. Her bare feet revelled in the pillowy soft grass beside the lake, and she ran her fingers through the branches of the nearby willow tree, its delicate leaves tickling her palms and wrists. She sat down at the base of the tree, sinking her toes into the grass and resting her head against the tree's trunk. Across the lake were a family of fireflies that flitted over the water's edge, their lights blinking in the darkness. Merely months prior, she had been in this exact spot with Drystan, sharing their first kiss. The air was cooler now and the fireflies fewer, but she could transport herself back to that moment instantly.

Suddenly, the sound of footsteps broke through the calm of the garden and Galdinia shifted around the trunk, hoping to conceal herself from who she imagined was an incoming guard on his rounds. The footsteps, however, got closer. The last thing she wanted to do was explain herself to a guard who would insist on her going back to her rooms.

"Princess?" The soft voice carried across the edge of the lake, instantly giving Galdinia permission to move—and breathe—again.

"Lord Bentley," she said with relief, standing to move around the trunk to face her suitor. He was dressed in the least formal attire she had seen him in since they had met; he was wearing a black shirt with black trousers, his shirt unbuttoned to his mid-chest, the sleeves rolled to his elbows. His fair hair appeared to be wet and was tousled casually on his head.

"I thought it was you that I saw coming out of the castle," he said with a smile.

"I couldn't sleep and so decided to come get some fresh air," she said before tightening her cloak around her waist, suddenly very aware of her own appearance. "I suppose that's quite obvious though."

"Yes, I can't say I've seen many guards wandering the halls in their robes," Bentley said with a smirk before looking across the lake. "I had just returned my nightly wash basin to the kitchens when I saw you leave through the patio doors. It's a lovely evening, isn't it?"

"It really is," Galdinia agreed, gazing over the lake again herself. "Why are you out here then, Lord Bentley?"

"Please, Princess, call me Bentley," the lord replied. "I think we're well beyond pleasantries at this stage."

Galdinia wondered if he was referring to the previous evening. She chose not to ask.

"Then I insist that you call me Galdinia," she retorted, smiling at the young man. He looked ahead again, maintaining his most upright posture.

"I will do no such thing," he said with a cursory glance in her direction, his tone more formal than she had heard it all week.

"Then you will remain Lord Bentley, or would you prefer 'Pup?'" Galdinia asked with a smile, crossing her arms over her chest. "Now answer my question."

"Well," Bentley began, looking back at Galdinia, choosing to ignore the reminder of his new nickname, "it is so late, and I was concerned about you, particularly after last night's events. I may be imagining things, but I feel you may have been avoiding me, so I thought I'd come see if you were alright."

Galdinia looked to her feet and brushed her toes in the soft grass, wondering if what Neryda had said to her earlier that day about Bentley was worthy advice. She decided she would only find out if she tried.

"I apologise for last night," she said quickly, keeping her gaze away from Bentley. "I was acting like a child, and I did not treat you very well at all—I certainly wasn't behaving like a princess—and I'm sorry for that."

"There's no need to apologise, Princess," he said quickly as she watched his feet move towards her. She then looked up into his blue eyes full of sincerity. "This has been such a difficult week for you, and I imagine last night brought up a lot of emotions, not to mention you weren't feeling well. I'm sorry if you felt like you needed to behave a certain way because of me."

Galdinia could hardly believe that this lord was standing before her apologising for his dutiful behaviour in a situation where she drank too much, lied, cried, and kissed someone else. If he believed that she was upset because of her conduct the previous night, because of her father's death and her obvious lack of self-awareness, she wouldn't be the one to correct him.

"You never made me feel like that," Galdinia said, almost completely genuinely. "It's been a demanding week to say the least, so I appreciate your patience and tolerance of my questionable behaviour as I attempt to deal with it."

"If I weren't trying to impress the Syndicate and prove to them that I'm good enough to simply breathe the same air as you, then I would have had a few more glasses of wine myself." Bentley gave her a heartfelt smirk, his dimple being made prominent in the moonlight.

"I really did drink a lot, didn't I?" Galdinia asked tentatively, a smile spreading over her lips.

"Let's just say that I think they had to rummage through the cellars for more bottles after you asked for your seventh glass."

Galdinia buried her face in her hands and groaned. "What a fantastic impression I must be making on you," she mumbled into her palms, shaking her head in embarrassment.

"Honestly, it's refreshing." Galdinia looked up at him with a quizzical expression. "My parents have been searching for the 'right' match for me for the last three years. We have travelled across the kingdom and given my parents' wealth, they have particular standards by which they live. This has meant that the kinds of women I have had the pleasure of meeting mostly included the ones who are horri-

236

fied by the thought of getting their feet muddy, can't be seen without a personally made outfit on, and wouldn't even think of drinking more than one glass of wine with their dinner."

Galdinia felt a little self-conscious again as she realised that she had failed at maintaining all three of those attributes within the previous twenty-four hours. She reminded herself that the lord thought this was a good thing.

"They're usually very stuffy, provide little in the way of conversation, and send me into a lull," he continued, smiling at Galdinia as he spoke. "The only thing that saved me from a forced proposal to a girl in the Midlands about two months ago was the announcement that you may be in need of a suitor."

Galdinia internally seethed at the thought of Ryden and her father putting out the call to the provinces as they began looking for a worthy suitor for her. She knew she couldn't hold this anger forever, especially as she found herself becoming more and more enamoured by Bentley, but she still couldn't shake the sense of betrayal she felt.

"I'll be honest," he said carefully, looking back across the lake, "I only agreed to it in the hopes of avoiding marrying this other woman. I thought that perhaps I'd have a little extra time to convince my parents that I didn't need to be married at twenty. I didn't, however, expect to actually have a chance with the Princess of Crysterra, let alone be interested in her. You've surprised me in more ways than one."

Galdinia turned to face him, her eyes meeting his as he gazed at her, a smile playing on his lips.

"That's what all the suitors say," she said quickly, turning to lean against the trunk of the willow tree once again.

"I'm sure they do." Bentley smiled as he took a few slow strides in her direction. "It's true though. I assumed that I'd have to spend my life with someone I resented. Trust me, I hadn't planned on falling for someone my parents picked out for me. Really, they'll be so glad, which, I'll be honest, does irritate me."

Bentley let out a soft chuckle as he stopped a few feet from Galdinia.

"So you've fallen for me?" Galdinia asked, aware that she was standing in the shadows of her castle's garden in front of a very wealthy and very respected lord in her nightgown and cloak. She could only imagine just how proud Neryda would be.

"I'm in the process of it, yes." He inched forward another half step.

"And what exactly made you feel that way?" Galdinia asked, aware of his close proximity.

"Well, your winning personality, of course, your adventurous spirit, your skills in archery, and"—a wicked smile flickered across his face— "your apparent stomach of steel."

Galdinia let out a great sigh and laughed once again, hanging her head in mock shame.

"How long will you hold that against me?" she asked as he took another step closer, reaching his left hand up to rest against the tree trunk inches from the top of her head. Galdinia could see the muscles in his forearm tense as he held himself there.

"For as long as you bestow on me the honour to be in your company, Princess," Bentley said in an almost whisper, the scent of his cologne now drifting towards her. He smelled of citrus and pepper-mint; it was bright and light. It was... different.

"Then I must ask that you leave, immediately," she said sarcasti-cally, smiling up into his eyes that still managed to sparkle even in the dim reflections of the moonlight from the lake.

"I'm not entirely sure that's what you really want," Bentley retorted, quietly confident.

"And what makes you think that?"

"I think you would be utterly bored without my company," Bentley said, his face inching ever closer to hers. "And I have the sneaking suspicion that you may also be falling for me as well."

Galdinia held her breath as they gazed at each other for the briefest moment. Bentley slowly closed the gap between them, tenta-tive, as though waiting for Galdinia's reaction. In response, the princess met him halfway, drawing her lips to his. His lips were soft against her own and she leaned into them quickly. His lips, his scent, even his hands inches from her face on the trunk of the tree were so unfamiliar to her. This kiss was nothing like the one she shared with Drystan the previous evening. While that was full of unspoken words and heartache, this was exciting, light, and sparkling. It took everything within her to push Drystan from her mind and lean into Bentley's lips.

Bentley relinquished one of his hands from his balancing act and rested it on Galdinia's cheek. As they parted lips ever so briefly before meeting again, he traced his fingers down her jaw and along her bare neck, where he held her so gently. His fingers played along the length of her neck, occasionally brushing through her hair that rested over her shoulder. At his touch, Galdinia was able to mask the residual pain from the night before. She found herself getting lost in the ease and excitement of this moment; this was a man who fulfilled all of her requirements of a suitor, was approved by the Syndicate, and, most importantly, truly wanted her. There wasn't a policy or any legal guidelines keeping them apart and that assurance allowed the princess' heart to find some rest. Galdinia let herself to sink into the kiss, bringing her hands to his sides, drawing him closer to her.

After a minute of their lips revelling in each other's company, Bentley barely pulled back from Galdinia, his hand still on her neck and his eyes drifting open.

"I think I may be right, Galdinia," he said with a breath against her lips, addressing her by her first name for the first time. "I believe you have well and truly fallen for me."

By way of reply, Galdinia took hold of his jaw with both hands and pulled him in to kiss her once again.

SIXTH DAY OF MOURNING

26

At dawn of the Sixth Day of Mourning, after travelling along the Western Vein, a ship with black sails travelled into the waters of the Shadowed Coast. The ship anchored in the bay and sat in the shade of Elderwin Manor, which was perched upon a cliff on the edge of the coast. The gangway was hoisted to connect the ship with the docks, making a way for the inhabitants to come to shore. Fisherfolk who were preparing to set sail for their daily catch watched expectantly from their boats as a slender woman with red lips and ebony hair, who was flanked by four guards, stepped off the ship. It took the onlookers no time to recognise this woman as Valah Pyrin from the Wetlands. A chill ran over the crowds.

Valah made her way down the gangway, across the docks and back onto dry land. She was glad to be off the water, which they had been sailing on since midnight. She and Reynard spent much of their travel time discussing strategy as they prepared to work with two people that they didn't trust as far as they could throw them.

"Draven and Edana aren't interested in anything other than their own skin. You must remember that," Reynard warned Valah, standing close by her side as they walked to the carriage that the Elderwins had sent to retrieve them in. "They will do anything to get to the throne before you, including putting your head on a spike."

Valah didn't appreciate Reynard's almost condescending tone. She ignored him as a guard opened the carriage door, and she and her advisor stepped in, sitting opposite each other.

"They're a storm of strategy and anger," Reynard went on as the driver coaxed the horses into movement. "They have their strengths, and they will use them at all costs to see an end to you just as quickly as their niece."

Valah continued to stare down her nose at Reynard, her brow furrowed, head held high.

"You make it sound as though I've never come up against these two before," Valah said, now the one patronising him. "You mustn't forget whose family threw mine out of the capital and sent me to the other side of the kingdom."

"I know, but I think——"

"No, no," Valah said, silencing Reynard with her words. "I'm not interested in what you think anymore, Reynard. We have strategised and planned the next twenty-four hours down to the minute. By the end of it, there won't be any Elderwins left breathing, and I need you, my most trusted advisor, to stand with me on that. More so, I need you to believe in the plan, to believe in me. If you do not, then you can leave this carriage right now."

Valah's words cut through Reynard, but he understood her frustration. While they had been planning for the last week, they had truly been preparing for Valah's ascension to the throne for almost a decade. He couldn't let his fears impede on their plan now.

"My apologies, my lady," Reynard said with a rueful bow of his head.

The pair travelled in silence up the road to the cliff's edge where Elderwin Manor sat proudly, awaiting their arrival.

Lady Edana couldn't say she was too pleased having Valah Pyrin in her home, yet here she was, the woman who had been one of their greatest adversaries for years sitting mere feet away from her. In the sprawling sitting room of Elderwin Manor, Edana and Draven sat beside each other in two high-backed armchairs, the fireplace behind them blazing, cutting through the cold chill of the dawn air.

Opposite them in a deep armchair sat Valah, her slender legs crossed beneath the trailing black skirt of her dress. The fire cast a warm, flickering glow across her features, accentuating her harsh lines and sharp edges. Behind her stood Reynard, a hand permanently resting on the hilt of his sword at his hip. He stood casually, yet always at attention.

"Where is your captain?" Draven asked after the forced niceties of their introductions.

"Kelting is confirming some of our allies further north," Valah explained, her voice like velvet. "He has been securing the support of other armies quietly yet quite successfully."

"It sounds a little late to be confirming allies, doesn't it?" Draven asked, his hands clasped firmly on the intricate arm rests of the chair. "I thought you had already secured the numbers you promised."

"Unlike you, Lord Elderwin, I do not have the advantage of such a powerful surname," Valah said dryly, her eyes boring into Draven's. "My allies have been forged over years of proven trust and quiet partnership. You'll have to excuse my supporters for needing some final manoeuvring to ensure they are willing to take on the capital."

Edana knew that her husband would have been seething at Valah's patronising words. She herself wanted more than anything to send an ocean's worth of water at the woman, drowning her before her eyes. But she knew that she was integral to their plan.

"Assuming your captain is successful, what is our plan moving forward with your allies?" Edana asked, hoping to break through the tension and focus on the practicalities of the day ahead. "We have soldiers from the east that are ready to march at a moment's notice, as well as our southern army who can leave from port here."

In their brief correspondence earlier in the week, both the Elderwins and Valah had decided to discuss their plans for the Sixth Day in person. The concern of a letter being intercepted on its journey or a nosey attendant getting hold of their strategy was far too high.

"I have my army who will be arriving momentarily, plus our allies in The Edges and just further north," Valah explained. "I've instructed Captain Kelting to lead those armies by land through the Bear Jaws

Valley soon before sunset today. Unless he hears from me prior, of course."

"And what about those in The Hook?" Draven asked, pressing Valah further.

"Unfortunately, I was not able to secure their army," she said, a note of defeat in her voice. "It seems that Lord and Lady Lidel don't have any interest in supporting either side at this stage. They're quite happy living in ignorance in their quiet little corner of the kingdom."

"What is your proposal then, Valah?" Edana asked. "How do you see our siege on Elderguard playing out?"

"I suggest that your armies in the east meet my allies at the valley entrance, taking the capital from the north. Reynard and I will rendezvous with them there, leading the charge to the Northern Gates." Valah's tone was even as she shared the plans she and Reynard had been discussing for days on end. "Your armies here should board their ships and sail with mine, attacking from the south. We have been informed that the Royal Feast was in high attendance by the lords and ladies of the kingdom, at least those that allied with your brother. Assuming most of them will remain in the city until the Seventh Day, we have the luxury of demolishing a few other enemy's ships in the process. I suggest that you both lead our armies by sea."

Draven and Edana turned to face each other, silently communicating, before turning back to their enemy-turned-ally.

"Go on," Draven drawled.

"Once we have breached the capital's walls, I will make it my duty to find the princess," Valah started again, her eyes briefly flickering from Draven to Edana, watching their expressions closely. "Upon locating her, I will take care of her, then work my way down the line, first doing away with her governor, then the remaining Syndicate members. Anyone who doesn't wish to bow to me or the new reigning Elderwins will be executed. Reynard will be by my side at all times."

Reynard adjusted his footing, his fingers lightly tapping on his sword's handle.

"And how do you plan on finding Galdinia?" Edana asked, brows raised. "It's unlikely that she will be in the castle the moment they smell the attack, and the city is sprawling. They could put her on a boat and sail her out into the Endless Sea before we step foot in the capital."

"Let me worry about that," Valah crooned.

"Do you really expect us to trust you to do the job?" Draven asked, narrowing his eyes on Valah. "What if you save her life and pin the attack on us, giving yourself sway with the Syndicate?"

"Frankly, Elderwin, I don't trust that you wouldn't do the same thing to me," Valah said, adjusting herself in her seat. "If one of you really wants to be there, then by all means, please join me. I wasn't sure that you'd want to watch your niece have the oxygen sucked from her lungs, that's all."

Draven and Edana stared at Valah for a moment, her ruthlessness taking them both off guard.

"And how do you plan on communicating the whereabouts of the princess with us when the time comes?" Draven asked.

"I have my ways." Valah whispered the words, but Draven and Edana heard her voice as clear as if she were sitting right next to them. She had used her gift to carry her words on her breath, delivering them straight to their ears.

The Elderwins both felt uncomfortable at the violation of Valah's breeze touching their ears in such an intimate and intrusive way. Edana squirmed in her seat. Draven, however, caused the fire behind him to billow, the cracking and rumbling of the flames echoing behind them. If she could use scare tactics, then so could he.

Reynard took a step forward, coming to stand by Valah's side. She raised a casual hand at him, waving him down. Her advisor held his ground beside his queen.

"Say you reach the valley, and your allies don't show themselves, how do you plan on getting through the Northern Gates without them?" Edana asked, drawing Draven and Valah's attention back to the matter at hand.

"While I trust that they will arrive," Valah replied, her sharp eyes locking onto Edana's, "they aren't my only way into the capital."

"If you expect us to be allies, you should share any and all contingency plans with us," Draven said, his voice rumbling almost in a growl.

"A number of those plans include taking both your heads off, Elderwin, so you may just wish to trust me this time."

Edana could feel the fire grow ever so slightly warmer behind them as her husband's anger rippled across the room. She knew it would be difficult for them to build trust in such a short amount of time, especially given the contempt for Valah that burned deep within Draven. Edana knew that she needed to keep the conversation pragmatic; she could keep her husband focused if they kept discussing their strategy.

"If your plan is to travel by land, you will need to leave almost immediately," Edana said evenly, trying to ignore Valah's comments. "How can Lord Draven and I trust that your fleet will arrive once you leave and you won't leave us high and dry with our army alone?"

Valah didn't reply. She merely lifted her hand, sending a force of air around them and to the curtains by the large window along the southern wall. After a cursory glance towards each other, the Elderwins stood from their chairs and approached the window with trepidation. Edana glanced back at Valah, who had a proud grin on her face. Lady Elderwin pulled her gaze from the Wind Wielder and looked out the window, astonished.

Below them in the cove, reaching out at least one hundred metres into the sea, was a fleet of ships. Their inky black sails danced in the wind as they lay anchor.

"How's that for assurance, Lord and Lady Elderwin?" Valah's voice was velvety smooth from across the room. "Perhaps we can start trusting each other now."

27

Galdinia awoke on the Sixth Day of Mourning refreshed, with an air of joyful anticipation around her.

She lay sprawled out on her bed, the light of the mid-morning sun warming her face as it slithered between the curtains. No other morning this week had she so openly welcomed the sunshine. The most marvellous smile spread over her lips, causing her to twist and bury her face in her pillow. She was like a giddy child, the butterflies in her stomach doing laps as she thought about the night before.

After their tender moment by the lake, Bentley suggested a quiet walk around the gardens together. Although she had hoped to stay within the shadows of the tree with him for a little longer, enjoying the otherworldly experience of being with him, she knew the walk would help her on her quest for sleep, so she accepted his invitation. She looped her arm in the crook of his and the two of them walked around the gardens, speaking about nothing in particular, simply enjoying one another's company. This was not something the Galdinia of four days prior had anticipated enjoying and she quickly admitted to herself that Bentley, with his boyish sense of humour and dazzling smile, wasn't the horrendous person she assumed every suitor would be.

Once it was well and truly past midnight, Bentley walked her back to the castle, all the way to the door of her rooms.

"Goodnight, Galdinia," Bentley said as he looked down at her with a grin, accentuating every syllable of her first name.

"Goodnight, Bentley."

He leaned down and kissed her once again, just as sweetly as he had in the gardens. She let her lips linger for as long as he would allow before he broke away from her, running his fingers through her hair, then turning to go.

Galdinia could still feel his lips on hers the following morning as she curled up in her bed. All memory of her kiss with Drystan had faded and she felt she couldn't remember anything prior to the night before. If anything, she was mad with herself that she hadn't taken Bentley seriously until the previous evening. It seemed that he truly did care for her. The thought of this made her stomach flutter once again.

Before she could float away in her thoughts of the lord, there was a knock at her chamber door.

"Princess?" came Brigitte's voice as she cracked open the door.

"Yes, Brigitte?" Galdinia called, pulling herself up to a seated position and wrapping her blankets across herself.

"I'm sorry to pester you, Your Highness, but I was given this message to be delivered to you in haste." Brigitte scurried over to Galdinia, her arm outstretched, her hand holding a piece of parchment.

Apprehensively, Galdinia took it from her, quickly unfolding the note and reading it furiously. Brigitte turned to leave the princess.

"Brigitte, would you run me a bath and prepare my lilac dress?" Galdinia asked before her attendant had made it across the room.

Brigitte looked at the princess for a moment, knowing exactly what the lilac dress meant to her. It was her mother's and was a dress she hadn't worn since before her father's illness. It was a dress reserved for cheerful occasions and celebration.

"Of course, Your Highness," Brigitte said with a childlike grin before turning to run the princess a bath.

Galdinia looked down at the note once again and read every word four more times.

Dear Princess Galdinia,

I would be honoured to share a meal with you today, should you be awake and feel up to such an occasion. I have asked the cooks to prepare brunch on the terrace and I will meet you there whenever you are ready.

Yours,

Lord Bentley

"And Brigitte," Galdinia called, her eyes not leaving the parchment, "would you send word to Lord Bentley that I will be with him momentarily?"

∾

Galdinia swept through the castle with such ease and grace, still feeling the effects of a truly restful sleep. Her dress fell delicately by her sides as she walked. The bodice and inner skirt of the dress were a light lilac colour, covering her from her breastbone to her ankles. The outer layer of the dress was made of a much lighter, sheer material, which matched the base layer in colour. This draped over her body from the base of her neck to her wrists and all the way to the ground. Stitched all over this outer layer were small, fluffy flowers, each one attached to a vine that trailed over her body. Galdinia always felt heavenly in this creation of Madame Moya's, even more so now than ever.

As she reached the doors of the terrace, Galdinia took pause, taking a second to compose herself. She considered how different this moment was to the very similar one three days prior. On the Third Day, she felt uneasy, underprepared for and coerced into the meal she was about to step into. Now, she felt excited, practically dripping in anticipation. She was taken aback by her own enthusiasm and wondered how her heart had shifted so much in such a short amount of time. Was it the impending coronation that willed her into accepting Bentley? Were her lack of powers and the ever-ticking clock of the week making her see Bentley through rose coloured glasses? Or had she had her heart broken one too many times that she was ready for it to be healed by someone new? She couldn't be sure, but given she hadn't felt this light in weeks, she was positive that she needed to explore the option regardless. Finally she felt like she was making her own decisions, making her own path.

She nodded to the guard by the terrace entrance and he pushed open the doors. Galdinia stepped out onto the terrace and smiled at her surroundings.

In the southwest corner of the terrace, a table much smaller than the one from three days prior had been prepared for two, although she estimated that the amount of food piled on the table could feed at least a family of six. There were pastries, cooked eggs, cheeses, baked goods and berries. Filling the crystal goblets that sat at both place settings was a very handsomely dressed Lord Bentley. He was wearing a deep forest green jacket and trousers, with a matching waistcoat. He stood with one hand behind his back as he poured the water. At Galdinia's arrival, he stopped, smiling up at her, placing the carafe on the table.

"Good morning, Princess," he said with a smile from the other side of the table. He briefly checked his pocket watch before adding, "In fact, it's nearly afternoon."

"Didn't we already discuss how we ought to address each other?" Galdinia said slyly, taking a few meandering steps forward, ignoring his comment on her late rise. She heard the click of the terrace door being closed behind her. They were alone.

"Ah, yes, of course," he said, moving swiftly around the table to meet her, taking her hand in his and pressing his lips against her skin. "Galdinia."

Galdinia welcomed Bentley's bright citrus scent mixed with his ever-charming demeanour. She wasn't sure how she would get used to it.

"This looks like quite the spread, Bentley," she returned, moving towards one of the vacant chairs.

"I thought that after what may not have been your longest sleep, but before what may be a long day, you could use a good breakfast." The lord pulled out Galdinia's chair before sliding it underneath her as she sat. He then moved to take his seat beside her. Now that the food was right under her nose, Galdinia felt particularly famished and was able to truly gauge just how decadent the spread was. "In saying that, you certainly slept longer than me."

"I hope you weren't waiting long," Galdinia said, starting to serve herself with the food before them.

"It's no trouble," Bentley replied, watching her. "I share a wall with Evarius and he's a snorer, so I needed an excuse to leave my rooms once I woke up this morning. I even went to visit Miss Giles to enquire about breakfast. Heavens, I thought Neryda was protective of you." A smirk spread over Galdinia's lips. "You are surrounded by people who are hard to please."

"And yet you're still willing to try," Galdinia replied.

"Of course, Princess," he said, before catching himself and promptly adding, "Galdinia."

The sound of her name on his lips made her arms tingle with goosebumps.

While serving them both a helping of berries, Bentley went on. "I had realised, though, that other than a few short, fleeting conversations that were interrupted by alcohol, late nights, and a certain seamstress"—Galdinia laughed at his mention of Madame Moya once again—"we really ought to learn a little more about each other. Particularly if it's looking like we may spend more time together, hopefully minus the seamstress."

Galdinia was quickly reminded that the Syndicate would struggle to place a queen's crown on her head tomorrow evening if she hadn't agreed to her future marriage plans. She tried to push the thought from her mind and chose to respond to Bentley's request. "What do you want to know?"

"Is it too overwhelming to say everything?"

Galdinia smiled at Bentley's eagerness. "How much time do you have?"

"For you? All the time in the world."

Galdinia then proceeded to tell Bentley all about her short nineteen years, including her few hazy memories with her mother, her rambunctious childhood with Neryda (trying as hard as she could to exclude any stories about Drystan), and her devoted relationship with her father. She told him all about how she and Neryda would escape the castle through secret tunnels beneath the library or bypass the soldiers on guard at the main gates by shuffling their way through the hedges. They discussed his life in The Edges and what his upbringing was like. He told her it wasn't nearly as interesting—or lavish—as hers and insisted on moving the conversation topic back to her.

After two hours of conversation between bites of decadent food, Bentley went on to ask her what it was like growing up in Elderguard and, even more so, as a princess. She tried to explain how she didn't have anything else to compare it to and so it was the only life she could understand. Bentley was able to empathise as a lord with wealthy parents and an undeniable expectation placed on his shoulders.

Galdinia was glad to talk with him about this. Although Neryda had grown up with her and was nobility herself, she never truly understood how much pressure was placed on Galdinia, as she was not a lady expected to run a piece of the country one day. At least Bentley, who was the oldest child of three and had parents of a particularly high stature in The Edges, could share in some of the same struggles as Galdinia, just on a slightly different level.

"I suppose being born into a life like this is something some people will never understand," Bentley said, taking a sip of water from his goblet.

Galdinia couldn't help but think of Drystan and how he always struggled to understand Galdinia's experience as a princess. Although she knew this wasn't something she could hold against him, she still noticed such a stark difference between him and Bentley, having not ever had a conversation with someone her own age who could truly empathise with her situation.

"That's true, unfortunately."

"I'm glad to have found someone who understands though," Bentley said, gazing at Galdinia with a small, almost sad smile.

"Me too," she said, reaching out to place a hand over his. He took her fingers in his palm and held on to them firmly, reassuringly.

"I'm surprised you haven't got anyone else in your life that has had a similar experience," Bentley went on. "Being the princess, I thought you would have had an entourage of nobility."

Galdinia laughed. "I've tried to choose my friends wisely," she explained. "I was taught from a young age to be careful about who I let in. After the fallout with his brother, I think my father was always cautious about the friends I chose."

"Was it always just you and Neryda, then? Did anyone else manage to fit into that equation?"

Galdinia busied herself by taking another sip of water. She questioned whether she should tell Bentley about her first love or skip the topic entirely. She thought she may eventually have this conversation, so perhaps there was no better time than the present.

"We were also good friends with a local fisherman's son, Drystan." Saying his name stung, but Galdinia tried to ignore the tension she felt.

"Were?"

"We grew up together, but he was conscripted into the army a few months ago," Galdinia said, trying to sidestep certain details. "We haven't been as close since then."

"Surely distance and full-time service couldn't be that detrimental to years of friendship." Bentley paused as he studied the princess' expression, reading her quickly. "Ah, it was more than a friendship."

Galdinia nodded. She could feel sweat beading on the back of her neck and her pulse shuddered in her chest.

"He... he isn't nobility, nor does he have a gift, so it couldn't ever be anything serious anyway." Galdinia thought she may have been trying to convince herself just as much as Bentley that their relationship wasn't nearly as intense as it was in reality. "And now he's a soldier in training, so who knows where the captain will have him stationed in the country."

Galdinia could see that Bentley's usual buoyant air had diminished considerably as she spoke. She knew she should have avoided the topic of Drystan, and the look on Bentley's face was all the confirmation she needed to change the subject.

"It's all in the past now anyway," she said with a reassuring smile, squeezing Bentley's hand, the light in his eyes igniting once again. "I'm glad to be here with you now."

Bentley raised her hand to his lips and kissed it softly, his gaze not breaking her own. "As am I."

The two looked at each other for a long moment before he spoke again.

"Speaking of the captain," Bentley said, "how is your training faring? From the little interaction I've had with him, I don't imagine he would be the easiest to train with."

"It's been tiring, to say the least," Galdinia explained, lifting her eyes to Bentley's. "Working within the Gods' unknown timing in a very real seven-day period has been difficult. The Syndicate has their workarounds, which I'm sure you know all about, but I can't say this is exactly how I envisioned my ascension to the throne."

"I'm sorry," Bentley said quietly, looking at Galdinia with a genuine sense of concern. "What happens in the case that you don't obtain your powers? And you don't choose one of the workarounds?"

Galdinia knew he was referring to himself and she appreciated his lack of fear when it came to suggesting that she may not want to tether herself to him forever in a matter of hours. She imagined that a number of the other suitors would not be so gracious.

"The Syndicate would oversee the running of the country. Those of royal blood who display their powers are allowed to present themselves to the Syndicate for consideration in becoming king or queen though. This hasn't actually happened in hundreds of years, centuries before my family was on the throne."

"Yes, I forget that the Elderwins have only been crowned for two generations—well, nearly three." Bentley gave Galdinia's hand a light squeeze. "It was someone from the west on the throne prior to them, wasn't it?"

Galdinia's smile faded into a frown at the thought of Valah.

"Valah Pyrin," she almost spat. "Her parents practically led the country to starvation in order to maintain their wealthy lifestyle here in the capital. They tripled taxes within a five-year period and closed public access to the most rich and fertile lands in the country. They essentially privatised everything so they could ensure they received all the wealth necessary to live their terrifyingly lavish lives. Even the nobility was treated like animals during their reign."

"Thank goodness for your grandparents then."

"I don't believe it was an easy takeover, or so my father told me. He was a child at the time, as was Valah, but he had vivid memories of servants cleaning blood from the marble floors of the castle. I don't imagine the Pyrins would have gone down without a fight."

"So what happened to her?" Bentley asked.

"My grandparents recognised that she was simply a child, a reasonably innocent one at that," Galdinia began. "But they feared for her life living here in the capital. They knew there were far too many nobles that wanted her executed, just like her parents, so they sent her away to the Wetlands in the dead of night by boat."

"They sailed all the way to the west?" Bentley asked, shocked. Galdinia nodded.

"My grandparents thought it was the only way to help keep her alive. The night after their attack on the capital, they put her on a royal sailboat and sailed across the country to take her to the Wetlands. They had to get her far away from the capital where people wouldn't recognise her. No one outside of Elderguard had ever seen Valah, so her life was fairly safe in the Wetlands, where she lived a modest life among the people there. Little did they know, the child of their greatest enemy was walking among them."

"She still goes by Valah Pyrin though," Bentley considered, his forehead wrinkling. "Wouldn't they want her dead once they learned who she was?"

"I don't know a lot about those that are loyal to her now, but I believe it has something to do with rumours spread about my father over the last decade or so. My guess is that she has turned her parents' downfall into a sob story in order to gain power within that province."

Bentley looked thoughtfully at Galdinia before replying. "I've not heard the history of Valah Pyrin told like that before."

"Oh?"

"In The Edges, there are such varying versions of it floating around that I simply chose not to listen. In fact, there are a lot of stories that get told that I think I'm quickly realising are simply far from the truth."

"Such as?" Galdinia asked.

"Such as the Battle of the Midlands," Bentley went on, sitting up straighter in his seat. "Depending on who you ask, you'll hear one of three recounts: it was an honourable Elderwin victory, a tactical loss by the provinces, or it was a slaughter on both sides."

"I can say with confidence that my father was extremely affected by the outcome of that conflict," Galdinia said sadly, looking down at their hands. "It was what, ten years ago? I still remember how exhausted he was. He was worried he wasn't doing right by his people, but he knew he had to protect the innocent against people who only saw their own self-interest."

"People like Valah?" Bentley asked, his expression curious.

"Exactly."

Galdinia tried to put herself in her father's shoes, imagining how she would choose to deal with conflict within the people of her own kingdom, let alone facing someone like Valah.

"So she wants the throne too? Along with your aunt and uncle?"

"Unfortunately, yes." Galdinia sighed, leaning back in her seat, her hand still curled up inside Bentley's. "That's why it is imperative that my powers make themselves known before sunset tomorrow. My uncle has a relatively serious claim to the throne, especially as a Fire Flourisher. My aunt is also a Water Weaver, so they have a lot of power supporting their claim."

"And Valah is a Wind Wielder?"

"Yes, although I've never seen it myself."

"It's sad that you don't have a close relationship with your family," Bentley mused, speaking his thoughts out loud.

"I don't agree," Galdinia said flatly. "They have been unruly and troublesome since before I was born. Draven always thought he deserved the crown because my father wasn't the perfect image of morality in his early twenties. My uncle has been holding on to a decades long grudge against us. He chose not to maintain a relationship with his family first, so I can't say I miss them all that much. They've never wanted me to be queen."

Galdinia could feel her frustration bubbling beneath her skin and she noticed Bentley's sudden change in countenance.

"Well," Bentley began, smiling as he leaned forward in his seat towards Galdinia, pulling his chair closer to hers so that their knees were now touching, "I can think of someone who very much wants to see you crowned as queen."

He lifted her hand to his lips again, this time allowing them to linger a little longer. With his other hand, he caressed her forearm, his fingers getting lost in the billowing, sheer lilac fabric, the stitched flowers trailing between his fingers. Galdinia's mind was well and truly distracted from their conversation; she was now one hundred miles away with Bentley.

"Why, I think you may be trying to distract me, Pup," Galdinia said with a smirk.

"I'd never," he responded in a thick sarcastic tone, narrowing his eyes on her at the mention of his despised nickname.

His lips slowly moved along her upper arm and towards her collarbone, where he left a trail of three soft presses of his lips. His face then became buried in her neck as he travelled up towards her jaw. This was where he paused and pulled back to look at the princess, now centimetres from her face. Galdinia could feel the return of the butterflies, her arm feeling weightless in his hands, her head fluttering in elation.

"You really aren't what I expected," Bentley said, voice soft against her cheek. "I had prepared myself for an entirely different person, but I'm quickly realising that those stories aren't true either. You're so much more than I had anticipated." Galdinia felt her stomach twist as he spoke. "I need you to know, Galdinia, that you are my queen. No matter what the Syndicate, your enemies, or the rest of the country thinks, you deserve to be on that throne, with or without your gift."

"Thank you," Galdinia return gently, feeling equally ravished and valued.

"It would be an honour to stand by your side and help make that a reality for everyone else in the kingdom."

Galdinia, still revelling in the heaven that he had created on this terrace in a matter of seconds, stared back at Bentley.

"Are you asking me to marry you?" Galdinia asked, looking intently into his blue eyes.

He hesitated for a moment, his lip pulling up at the edge, his characteristically boyish dimple making itself known once again.

"Something like that," he said wistfully before sending his lips along the length of her jaw, leaving a tingling feeling in their wake.

She had known this man for barely five days, and she had to admit, he had been nothing but the perfect image of a suitor. He made her laugh before she even knew who he was, he didn't try to impress her around a table of other pining men, and he did all that he could to win over her watchful best friend. She admitted that she cared for him, quickly and deeply. But was she ready to commit herself to him? If the Gods didn't intend on giving her her gift, she would have to find a way to take the throne herself. Perhaps this was how she could take her destiny into her own hands.

"I, uh—"

"Princess." A voice came from the door of the terrace, bursting the bubble they had created. Bentley pulled back from her face, placing her hand on her armrest in a second. Galdinia looked beyond Bentley to Brigitte, who stood in the doorway, looking at her with apprehension and an ounce of fear, an expression that she seemed to hold often.

"Yes, Brigitte?"

"I'm so sorry to interrupt, Princess, Lord Bentley," Brigitte said quickly, and the lord responded with a brief wave of his hand, not bothering to turn around; Galdinia could only imagine how embarrassed he must have felt in that moment. "Governor Ryden wishes to see you in the drawing room... immediately."

Galdinia sighed and looked at Bentley, whose small smile was plastered on his face as he rested his hand along his jaw, his index finger at his temple.

"Thank you, Brigitte, I'll be along momentarily," Galdinia said without taking her eyes off Bentley. Her attendant took her leave and Galdinia was now the one to lean into him. "Can we finish this conversation later?"

"Of course," Bentley said, obviously a little disappointed they were cut short, "My Queen."

Galdinia closed the space between them and kissed him. Her lips had been aching to do that since he wished her goodnight the previous evening. She could feel his smile beneath her lips as he leant into the kiss, placing a hand around the nape of her neck, his thumb resting along her jaw.

"I could get used to this," she mumbled against his mouth, her teeth scraping along his bottom lip.

"And you should." Bentley kissed her again, more fiercely this time, his hand keeping them joined.

After a few long moments, Galdinia pulled back from him and

stood to her feet. She looked down at Bentley, his expression content. She let her hand sweep up his arm as she walked past him, leaving the handsome lord on the terrace.

28

GALDINIA LEFT THE TERRACE FEELING LIGHTER THAN SHE HAD IN DAYS. She was glad to have found a safe place with Bentley, no matter how much it took her by surprise. As she walked through the castle to the drawing room, she realised that this was what had been missing from her life since, if she was honest with herself, her father got sick: somewhere safe.

Her two best friends had been taken from her in a time that she really needed them, and her father hadn't been the same since the beginning of his illness, so she had missed having someone close by with whom she could discover herself. She was thankful for that, but she didn't think she necessarily wanted to tell Ryden just how thankful she was for the arranged meeting of her suitor. Galdinia wondered if the other four men were privy to her rendezvous with Bentley. She quickly decided that she didn't care if they knew; the goal with the suitors was to select one, and she thought she may have just done that.

In the early hours of the afternoon, the castle felt surprisingly still. Most of the attendants were in the square, arranging the tables for the evening's festivities. Anyone else would have been assisting Miss Giles in the kitchens as she prepared the castle's share of dinner.

Galdinia found that she was looking forward to the evening and planned to gladly join the inevitable festivities that would ensue at the end of the night: dancing in the square. It was tradition that at the end of dessert, everyone would clear the tables and, often haphazardly, push the furniture from the centre of the square and dance to the music of the chosen troubadour and his band of minstrels for the evening. She had hoped to rectify her performance from two nights earlier by dancing with Bentley once again, this time in a far more emotionally stable state.

Galdinia approached the drawing room door and let herself in, stepping into the warmth of the crackling fire and the mild scent of sandalwood. Galdinia realised then that she hadn't been in this room since the reading of her father's will five days prior. She cast her eyes over the window where Valah had berated her and where Ryden had later soothed her concerns. He stood there now, his back to the door. Galdinia joined him at the window and followed his eyes down to the square, where the dark banners and decorations of the previous days were being replaced by flags of bright colours and sparkling lanterns. It looked significantly livelier.

"It's going to be a good evening," Ryden said almost solemnly as he gazed at the preparations being made below.

"I do hope so," Galdinia agreed, watching as a group of ten people drew the longest tablecloth she had ever seen over one of the many tables in the centre of the square.

"This is one of the better parts of this week," Ryden observed. "With all the mourning, commemorations, and tears, it's nice to end with an evening of jovial celebration."

Galdinia simply nodded. Now that her mood had improved, she too was looking forward to the evening.

"So," Ryden said, finally pulling his eyes from the square, "have you had any more time to think about your possible future with Lord Bentley?"

Galdinia wondered if the governor had known about her meal with Bentley and had timed this conversation thusly. Galdinia didn't imagine Bentley had kept Ryden informed, but the coincidence felt too great for her not to notice.

"Well, as it so happens, he just asked for my hand." Galdinia smiled, folding her arms across her chest and leaning against the window pane. She was far too pleased with herself, and she didn't think this moment, if any, was the one to hide her true emotions.

"And what did you say to that?"

"Brigitte interrupted us with your retrieval of me," Galdinia said with a cocked brow in Ryden's direction. "I wasn't able to give him a response, so it is still pending, you could say."

A small smile broke out on Ryden's lips. "I'm very happy for you, Princess."

"I suppose I do have you to thank for that, in part," Galdinia admitted, looking down at her feet as she did so, still surprised by her actions in the last twenty-four hours that led her to this decision.

"I'm glad it worked out." With those words, his smile dipped, and he cast his eyes to the ground also. Galdinia heard the shift in his tone and looked up at him in mock concern.

"You can take the credit, Ryden. Really, it's fine. I'm sure the Syndicate will be very pleased." He didn't reply to this, and Galdinia could feel a sense of unease in the atmosphere. The curtains in the window billowed in a breeze that Galdinia thought had been controlled by the governor himself. What wasn't he saying? "Ryden?"

He hesitated for moment before he finally met her eye again. He then spoke, a hint of pain in his voice. "Princess, the Syndicate is still concerned about your ability to run the kingdom, with or without a suitor—or fiancé, as it may be." It took Galdinia a moment to register what he was saying. She dared not speak until she heard his further explanation. "They fear for your safety as such a young queen who is yet to come into her gift. They worry that you won't be able to completely lead the kingdom without your proper ordination."

Galdinia felt a heavy rock settle in her stomach. The airy atmosphere she had brought with her was being sucked out of the room on Ryden's words. She felt anger, sadness, disappointment, and spite all wage war somewhere near her sternum as she tried to process his words.

She closed her eyes and took in a deep breath before uttering the only word she could muster. "Why?"

Ryden looked unsure, perhaps even concerned, about how she may react to an explanation. "They worry that it would be an act against the Gods to swear you in before you receive your gift."

"Why is this suddenly an issue?" Galdinia asked, her brow creasing. "You do remember our conversation at the beginning of the week when we came to an agreement about the way to move forward, don't you?" Galdinia asked.

"Yes, of course—"

"And you remember," she powered on, ignoring him, "how the Syndicate said they would allow me to wear my mother's crown tomorrow if I took the option of a suitor—who you had specifically selected for me—quite seriously, no matter the situation with my powers?"

"Princess, this isn't a matter of—"

"And do you remember that my father, King Bartemus, named me as his heir at his death, without any stipulation of age, gift, or marital status?" Galdinia's face was heating, and she lowered her voice as she spoke through gritted teeth. "Do the words of my father—or your own words—mean anything anymore?"

Galdinia could feel her hands shaking as she balled them up into fists at her sides. She looked momentarily to the skies outside, their joyous blue mocking her in her fragile and suddenly angered state.

If any moment was a good moment to bestow on me my gift, this is it.

She could hear her inner voice spitting the words at the Gods. But nothing changed. The skies remained as quiet as they were. A lonely cloud floated unceremoniously across the city. The birds continued to glide down towards the docks and the sun maintained its crisp heat. Nothing changed.

Perhaps this was, in fact, a fight she had to win for herself.

"Princess, of course I remember the promises that we made." Ryden's voice mimicked the air of a puppy that was hiding in a corner after being berated by its mother. "And I don't want you to think that my word is any less true or honourable. The Syndicate has, however, had these concerns from the beginning, and we fear that we were too brash with the promises we made."

"And you didn't bother to talk to me about these fears until now?"

Ryden paused. "More recent events have solidified the fears of some Syndicate members."

"Recent events? What—" *The Royal Feast, of course.* "This is because of the other night, isn't it?"

"Some members believed it demonstrated a lack of preparation for the throne and highlighted that the Gods' timing should be trusted."

"I was mourning my deceased father," Galdinia said, her words heated.

"I understand that, as do a handful of other members," Ryden explained carefully, "but I must agree that it didn't reflect well on the crown."

"It didn't reflect well on the crown or on you?"

"Right now my interests and those of the crown are one and the same."

Galdinia looked at Ryden, her frustration palpable. "I understand, Governor; I'm a young princess who may, at times, show her age, but at what point did you think it was okay to break a promise you made under the protection of swearing to my father? You swore to protect me and my throne. He would be so disappointed by this."

Galdinia moved across the room, feeling the need to expel some of her frustration by pacing. She could feel the gripping tightness in her chest and her breaths became shorter.

"I wish there was something I could do, Princess, I really do," Ryden said softly.

"Isn't it ironic that the person who has the most amount of power in this room can't make this change?" Galdinia asked, pacing between the window and the table, her heart thundering in her chest. "Telling me you wish there was something you could do means very little when you are the only person with enough authority to actually do anything."

"I was outvoted." Ryden sighed. "The majority won. We still have to maintain some kind of democracy in this situation."

"Thank you for including me in that gathering," Galdinia said, her words scathing. "Breaking promises seems to be the theme of the day."

"I didn't think I'd be keeping my word about protecting you if I let you sit in a room with the Syndicate while they aired out their concerns about your ascension to the throne." Galdinia shot Ryden a deathly stare as he spoke, her expression incredulous. "As soon as your powers are bestowed on you, we plan to swear you in the very next day."

"And what's your plan in the meantime? Hand the crown over to Valah? Or perhaps crown Draven and Edana king and queen; they're married, which seems to be your preference."

"This doesn't have to do with that, Princess." He was trying to placate her now. "Ultimately, it's about the Gods."

"Do you really think their gift is the only signifier of a fit ruler? Last time I checked, there were thousands of people across the kingdom with powers. Does that mean any of them could take the throne before me?"

"Of course not. You know that the incoming king or queen must first be of royal blood—"

"Done."

"And they have to be ordained by the Gods. Princess, you know that the Syndicate will maintain authority until you are considered eligible to take the throne."

"And do you truly believe that Draven and Valah will stay quiet for Gods know how long until I have my gift? They will be knocking down your door the minute the Week of Mourning ends and there isn't a queen on that throne."

"We have already taken that into consideration, yes," Ryden said, nodding. "The Syndicate has put measures into place to ensure the city—and your crown—remain safe. As far as they're concerned, you're the future Queen of Crysterra. It's more a matter of timing. They will protect your throne against any potential threat, no matter who may challenge it."

Galdinia stopped pacing and breathed in a long, deep breath.

"If anything, this will allow us more time to prepare you to take control of the kingdom. We can teach you about the inner workings of the country, about trade, and how each province functions as part of the whole. Whether we have one week or—well, who knows how long —you will be far more prepared than any queen that came before you."

Galdinia pondered this for a moment. While she didn't hate the idea, she knew this meant she would still have to wait to actually be able to outwork the changes and implement the policies she hoped to improve. This might not be the most ideal situation, but it would help her prepare for, and also protect, her place on the throne.

Still frustrated, Galdinia asked, "Could we begin discussing changes in policy I may wish to make?"

"I think it would be fair for me to bring those to the Syndicate on your behalf, yes."

"Good. There are a number of changes I'd like to make in order to make this process much easier for my future children." Although she was still feeling spiteful, the sincerity beneath her words was unmistaken.

"We will certainly look into any problems, but the concern of the Gods and their ordination of the future king or queen will still stand."

"I was more concerned with a future heir's right to rule with a partner of their choosing."

"You know that was mostly your father's concern, Princess. And this process with the suitors only began by way of precaution."

"Yes, and so it is something I would like to see reviewed." Galdinia spoke firmly, maintaining the authority in her voice that she knew she deserved. "A queen should be able to marry whenever she wishes and whoever she wishes, be it nobility, soldier, peasant, or perhaps no one at all."

"I thought you were happy with your decision to be with Lord Bentley."

"I am," Galdinia said firmly, wondering if her answer would still be true if someone else had been an option. "But I think it's ridiculous that a queen—the leader of a kingdom—can't marry who she may want to, no matter their status."

"Ah," Ryden said. The puzzle pieces that were her words began falling into place in front of him. "You are referring to Drystan Allard. He may have proven not to be an option anyway." Ryden spoke coolly as he looked out the window, and Galdinia's eyes narrowed on him.

"What do you mean?"

"Nothing, it doesn't matter." Ryden shook his head, clearly exhausted from this conversation.

"Evidently it does." Galdinia spoke firmly. "I think you owe me the courtesy of honesty today, Governor."

Ryden sighed. "Your father wanted what was best for you. He

wanted to ensure that you would find the right person to rule this kingdom with you, particularly once he fell ill."

"I'm fully aware of your secret matchmaking sessions, yes."

"With that came eliminating the competition." Ryden spoke carefully now, his eyes still focused on the city below, unable to meet Galdinia's eyes. "Your father knew you and Allard were close, but he wanted you to be with someone of a suitable title. He wanted you to be equally yoked, as it were. So he made the decision to personally enlist Allard into the Royal Guard."

The ache in Galdinia's chest writhed and burned. Ryden finally met her gaze. Her jaw was set, and tears had begun to well in her eyes; he could see the pain and betrayal seething from them.

"That's not true," Galdinia whispered between tight lips. "His name was drawn, the same as everyone else's. There is no way my father did that."

"I'm sorry, Princess."

Galdinia felt as though her heart had been torn from her chest and laid out for all to see. She felt foolish, inferior, and embarrassed. As she simmered in her pain, she considered Ryden's earlier words.

"What did you mean that a change of policy around who an heir can marry may not have mattered? Drystan still ended up in the army, which is the issue that stood in the way."

Ryden hesitated, but he seemed to decide that now was not the time to lie to Galdinia. She knew she deserved the truth now more than ever.

"Although your father enlisted him, he only did so with Allard's consent." Galdinia's heart stopped. "Your father offered him a deal to relinquish his relationship with you so that you could marry someone of nobility and hopefully be crowned as queen after his death. Due to his fears around your gift, he was hoping to set you up for the best chances to be crowned by the end of the Week of Mourning."

Her heart was now well and truly destroyed—doused in oil, set alight, and discarded beyond repair. Tears welled in Galdinia's eyes as she stared at Ryden in disbelief.

"Your father proposed a very handsome sum of coin for the Allard family, allowing them to live quite comfortably for the remainder of their days if Allard himself agreed to no longer pursue you and to become a soldier. He thought this was the only way to ensure you would marry well; Allard couldn't be an option. Allard agreed and two days later, he left for training."

"He agreed to joining the army for money?"

"He agreed because the king ordered him to," Ryden said quietly. "The money was left on their accounts and couldn't be returned. Bartemus said it was Allard's decision, but you and I both know that no one could decline the king."

First the Syndicate, then her father, and now Drystan. Betrayal hung in the air like a dying stench. A heat was rising from Galdinia's chest, up her neck and to her face. A claustrophobic feeling was encroaching upon her, making her breathing shallow and sharp.

"I'm done." As she spoke, Galdinia's voice was low and dangerous, tears lining her eyes. "I am tired of other people—of men—making my decisions for me: whether I can become queen, who I will and won't marry, how I will present myself. I'm done."

Galdinia turned and strode from the room, too angry to cry or scream or stamp her feet. She needed to get out of this room; she felt restrained and stuck.

"Princess, please wait—"

She didn't hear the end of Ryden's sentence as she slammed the drawing room door behind her. She marched up the hall towards her chambers, her face now hot, sweat beading on her temple.

Once she was safely locked inside her rooms, Galdinia placed her hands on her hips and tried to catch her breath. She sucked in deep, shuddering breaths, and her vision became blurry with tears.

She had never felt so embarrassed. Not only did the Syndicate think she wasn't ready to be queen, even after playing along with their plans, one of her best friends and her father had lied to her. Drystan had chosen not to be with her and what was worse, he took money in exchange for his silence. She imagined her sickly father calling Drystan to his rooms and insisting that he break things off with Galdinia. This caused a fresh wave of panic to course through her body. All she could hear was her heartbeat in her ears, sending shock-waves through her head.

Still struggling to breathe, she tore off her dress and discarded it where she stood, needing more than anything to be free of the fabric.

In her dressing rooms, she found her training clothes freshly washed and pressed. She pulled on the tan-coloured trousers and white tunic easily, leaving the sleeves open and billowing at her wrists. She put on her old riding shoes and made for the door. She walked past her lilac dress which lay on the floor like a ghost of the person she was just half an hour prior. She wondered how she found herself here in this situation. She felt so ignorant; how could she have trusted all of these people and still come out the fool?

She tore her eyes from her dress and barrelled out of her rooms.

"Princess!"

She collided with a wall of a man and looked up to see Bentley staring down at her, concern written over his face. Galdinia could only imagine what he was thinking as he looked at her now dressed like a farmhand, eyes blotchy and makeup now smeared.

"I'm sorry, Bentley, I have to go," Galdinia said with a breath, trying to get around the man that commanded much of the hallway ahead of her.

"Where are you going? What happened?" He placed his hands on her shoulders, leaning slightly to bring his eyes in the way of her sight.

"I just need to go," she repeated herself, shrugging off his hands and once again pushing past him.

She felt guilty for her brashness; he had, after all, just asked for her hand in marriage. She paused halfway down the hallway to look back at him. He stood helplessly, his eyes watching longingly after her.

"I've just been given some unsavoury news and before you say anything"—Galdinia could see his mouth twitch at her words—"there isn't anything you can do for me right now. I need to go deal with this myself. I'm sorry. I will come find you later."

Galdinia did not give Bentley enough time to respond as she turned on her heel and marched for the castle doors.

29

The square had never looked so magnificent.

The bunting that hung along the length of the space zigzagged from lamp post to lamp post, each length of rope consisting of an array of flags in an assortment of colours. They beamed in the mid-afternoon sun that was slowly making its descent in the afternoon sky.

Beneath the bunting were the long tables, each set with a sage and silver tablecloth and spectacular centrepieces. Dried leaves and flowers, along with carefully placed candles and lanterns, were arranged down the centre of the tables and looked like something from a fairy tale. Each seat had a table setting of copper plates and cutlery. The minstrels were practising by the southern end of the square, preparing for an evening of festivities.

Galdinia, however, did not stop to revel in this magnificent sight.

She strode along the edge of the square, two hastening guards trailing her. She avoided contact with those working, her eyes set along Main Court that would take her to the southernmost point of the city.

Her heart was thudding in her chest, sending boiling blood throughout her body, heating her from within with a fury that she had never felt before. She was overcome with her emotions and did not know how she would ever start to calm them. As she stalked down the road, she came into contact with a number of citizens who smiled, waved, and congratulated the princess on her pending coronation that they didn't realise had just been nullified. She put on her best polite smile as she moved through the crowds, hoping her hastened posture would provide an excuse for her nonchalant responses.

Galdinia made it to the soldiers' barracks and bypassed the guards who opened the gates for her upon her arrival, not waiting to address them as they bowed for her. She entered the large building and moved through it with ease, having become familiar with its floor plan. She received a number of concerned looks from soldiers as she made her way through the lower floor and up the stairs to the higher level. They tried to simultaneously bow and move out of her way, her casual dress and the brisk pace at which she was moving startling many of them.

As she reached the threshold to Ilyon's quarters, she didn't bother knocking. She simply pushed open the door and walked in. The captain was sitting at his desk, pondering a roll of parchment that was spread out in front of him.

"Princess," he said quickly, standing to his feet.

"Ilyon, I need the royal sailing boat ready to set sail in five minutes."

"What—Princess, what's happening?"

"Please relinquish whatever duties you are currently undertaking to someone else and be ready to set sail in five minutes. I require you on board."

The captain appeared startled and utterly put off by the demand, but he briefly nodded and said, "Very well."

"Thank you," Galdinia said, turning to leave before stopping and asking the captain over her shoulder, "Where can I find Allard?"

"Drystan Allard?" Ilyon responded, Drystan's name still affecting Galdinia more than she would have liked to admit. "He'll be getting ready for his rounds in the square to begin, so I imagine in the armoury."

Galdinia nodded and continued ahead through the doorway, moving back down the stairs and towards the large room at the end of the main hallway. The armoury housed all manner of weapons: swords, daggers, spears, arrows, bows, and shields, as well as other less common weapons, such as an array of ball maces, heavy chains, and axes. One of the walls held items that would assist the gifted soldiers:

unlit torches, flint, different vessels for holding water, and a collection of metal, bamboo, and fabric fans.

Among all of these weapons, soldiers were finding their preferred tools and arming themselves. As they watched the princess burst through the doors, many of them froze in place or bowed. Some even dropped their weapons, and the room fell silent after a handful of metallic crashes. Never before had the princess been in this room. Her father would have never allowed it, and she doubted Ryden would feel differently.

She scanned the room, her eyes darting over the soldiers as they peered at her. Against the far wall, with a silver broadsword half sheathed in its black casing at his hip, stood Drystan. His surprise to see Galdinia was painted on the concerned expression on his face.

Galdinia stormed across the room, eyes blazing, pulse thudding in her ears. The other soldiers watched intently as they seemed to almost recoil against her anger, afraid they could be on the receiving end of it. She came to a halt two feet away from Drystan, her eyes burning into his.

"Galdinia, what's wrong?" he asked quietly, genuinely fearful for his own safety in a room full of weapons and a very distressed Galdinia. In his surprise of seeing her in such a state and in this context, he defaulted to addressing her by her first name. Galdinia tried not to hear it.

"Everybody, out." Galdinia spoke with the weight of all the blades in the room and in seconds, she and Drystan were the only ones remaining as the final soldier pulled the heavy door shut on his way into the hallway.

Drystan looked petrified.

"I just had a very interesting conversation with Governor Ryden," Galdinia began, holding her stance firm in front of Drystan. "And he told me about a conversation that my father had with you prior to his death."

Suddenly, Drystan understood. "Gal, I—"

"And he told me that you agreed to become a soldier, therefore forfeiting our relationship, in exchange for a lump of gold." Galdinia could feel her face getting warmer as her eyes began to fill with tears again. "I am trying really hard to work out why you would agree to such a thing, and I'm yet to come up with a reasonable explanation."

Drystan's expression was pained, and he didn't respond.

"Please tell me you didn't agree to that," Galdinia pleaded quietly, her voice becoming thick with tears. "Tell me that Ryden is wrong and misspoke."

Drystan lowered his head and spoke softly. "I'm so sorry, Gal."

Galdinia let the tears roll silently down her face as she accepted the truth of the situation. She wasn't sure where her heart was now—beyond burnt to a crisp—but she could decidedly no longer feel it. Every pain, every tear, every overwhelming moment she had spent agonising over the boy who stood in shame in front of her came flooding back at once. Her chest tightened, and her stomach churned; she thought for a moment that she may see the pastries and berries from her meal with Bentley once more. She turned from Drystan, her hands on her hips, her breath shaking. She walked nonsensically in front of him, moving, trying to keep her breathing even and her shaking hands still.

"Gal, I didn't want to agree to it, I really didn't want to," Drystan said, raising his head to watch her pace in front of him. "Your father didn't really give me another option."

"Yes, he did, that's exactly what he did," Galdinia said, watching him. "He gave you the option to stop loving me, and you took it."

"You know he wouldn't have let us be together anyway. He wanted you to be with a lord."

"And what about what I wanted?"

"You and I both know that's not how this works, Gal," Drystan said; his voice had a sharp edge to it. "Besides, he was sick, and I didn't want you to resent him."

Galdinia paused mid-step and stared at him. "So you did this for me?"

"That's not what I mean—"

"No, that is what you mean." Galdinia threw her hands in the air and let out a long, loud exhale.

"He had just become sick, and he knew he wasn't going to be around long, so he wanted to ensure that you ended up with someone that could stand by you as you became queen. If I had said no to him, he would have done everything in his power to stop us from being together, and I didn't want you to lose your father before he even passed away."

"Well, I'm losing him now anyway," Galdinia said, her anger palpable. "You didn't have to agree to it. You could have said no."

"He was the king, Galdinia. He was no longer your father in my eyes but the king." Drystan tried to explain himself, his voice pleading with her. "He gave me the money to try to persuade me. I didn't agree to it for the money though—I didn't even want the money. I did it out of respect for him and for you."

"And what about what I wanted?"

"You know that the Syndicate wouldn't allow you to be queen if you were to marry someone like me. I knew you wouldn't let go of me any other way. I couldn't take your opportunity to be queen away from you."

"Did you ever think for one second that perhaps I would have given up being queen to be with you?" Galdinia's words hung in the air for a moment, tearing through Drystan before she spoke again. "Perhaps I would rather be with you and live a quiet life in the countryside beyond the walls of this city than be queen and sit on that throne."

Drystan stared at her. "We've been over this," Drystan said, referring to their conversation in the broom closet down the hallway from where they now stood.

"No, you thought I ought to put my country first. You thought I ought to be selfless and noble. That wasn't a decision I wanted to be made for me."

"I'm sorry, Gal," Drystan said softly. "I didn't realise how much this—us—meant to you."

"Drystan, I've been in love with you for years! That's no secret to anyone—my father knew, for goodness sake," Galdinia said, her hands shaking once again. "Heavens, I've been praying that the Gods would give you a gift just as much as my own. I have never cared so deeply about someone." She paused before adding, "I've also never felt so betrayed."

Galdinia watched as her words sparked tears in Drystan's eyes. She could see the regret and pain painted over his face as he digested her words. He took a small step towards her, reaching out his hand towards her cheek.

"No." For the first time in her life, Galdinia stepped back from Drystan. "You don't get to do that, not now. You can't lie to me, then dangle yourself in front of me only to instantly turn me away and then expect me to come falling back into your arms the moment I learn the truth. It doesn't work like that, Drystan!"

"I don't expect anything from you. I'm just so sorry. Gal, please, can we—"

"No, you gave up the right to call me that when you turned your back on me two nights ago," Galdinia said, her breath hot. "In fact, you gave that up the moment you agreed to this ridiculous arrangement. I'm your princess, and that's all I'll ever be now."

Drystan chose not to speak. He stood silent, shrunken, his eyes full of regret.

"I can't do this anymore." Galdinia wiped her tears on the back of her hand. "The other night in the library, you said you'd request a transfer to another city. I think that would be for the best."

Drystan swallowed as he stared at Galdinia, pained.

"Goodbye, Drystan."

Galdinia backed away from him before turning and walking out the door. She passed all the soldiers who had been ordered out of the room at her word, all of whom bowed. She left the barracks and took a side alley to the docks. As requested, Ilyon was onboard the royal sailing ship, the sails dropped and billowing in the stirring wind. In the minutes that she had been inside the barracks, the sky had filled with clouds, and the deep rumbling of faraway thunder could be heard.

Galdinia walked up the gangway and looked out beyond the bow to the west.

"Where to, Princess?" Ilyon called out from the stern of the ship.

"The Crystal Temple, Captain."

30

On their brief journey to the Isle of Crystal, the clouds opened and sent sheets of rain upon the princess and her ship. Ilyon was using his gift to order the sea's water to push them towards the small island, focusing on moving quickly through the storm rather than protecting them from the now pouring rain. Upon arriving on the island, Galdinia clamoured up the steps of the Crystal Temple. Her tears were indistinguishable from the raindrops that poured down her face, her clothes now soaked through. Her body was aching as she heaved in strained breaths.

Galdinia reached the crystalline doors and pushed against them with all her weight. Although she lacked any real strength or power in her arms, the doors gave in to her body and opened easily, allowing the princess to enter the most sacred hall in the kingdom. Before her were the remnants of her father's funeral from the beginning of the week. Tradition said that the temple would remain open for mourners until the evening before the coronation. In weather like this, no one was going to pass through the bay—particularly not when the Commemoration Banquet was set to begin shortly in the town square. So as she stepped into the centre aisle of the temple, Galdinia trusted that she would be alone. She knew she was safe to let her emotional guard down here.

Inside the temple, the three-pointed star at the altar hung above the platform on which her father's coffin still sat, the lid now shut. Galdinia sucked in a breath. Although she hadn't expected any mourners, Galdinia also hadn't anticipated her father's corpse to still be in the room. The flowers around his coffin and along the altar were now dried and were set to be replaced the next day by the priestesses before her coronation at dusk. Despite knowing that her father's body would no longer be there the following day, and that her coronation was becoming less and less likely as the minutes ticked by, she couldn't help but imagine being overshadowed by the literal embodiment of her father by her side.

She knew she should have felt comforted by that thought, but she wasn't. Instead, the familiar sense of inadequacy sat heavy on her.

Galdinia wept as she made her way to the altar, her drenched hair clinging to the rounds of her cheeks. The muffled sound of the rain crashing onto the transparent ceiling above her echoed through the temple. She looked up as she walked, watching the storm hurtle towards her and then dispel over the peaked roof in sheets of rain.

When she made it to the altar, she once again lost any control of herself and fell to her knees, dropping her head to the ground, allowing the tears to flow. She finally let herself succumb to every thought and feeling that had plagued her all week.

"How am I supposed to be a queen?" she asked, her whisper not making it any further than her own lips. "You told me I could be queen and look what you left me with!" This time her voice was almost a growl. "You didn't trust that I could do it alone or make my own choices!" Her cries caught in her throat, but she continued to yell at the coffin before her. "First Mother was taken from me, then you! And you didn't even have the decency to tell me you had arranged so much of my life for me! How am I supposed to become a queen when I'm too worried about becoming a wife? Not to mention my lack of powers!" Galdinia turned her attention to the star, to the Gods. "I might as well go jump in the seas and let Valah and my uncle fight over the crown! You didn't let me have my mother, you took my father from me, and then, as if to make absolutely sure that I would live a life of ridicule and pain, you failed to give me my gift!"

Galdinia stood to her feet now, and any anguish she was feeling turned into a piping hot rage. She clenched her fists and walked towards the glistening star. The only thing between her and it was her father's coffin.

"The God of Love? At what point have you loved me? At what point have you comforted me? Oh, God of Wisdom! Please, help me to understand this treacherous life you have given me. And God of Guidance? I have never felt more lost! I hope you are enjoying yourselves watching me flounder!" Galdinia placed her hands on the coffin, the emotional pain still writhing through her body. "Even now, in my lowest point, will you answer my prayer? Will you at least hear my cry?"

Galdinia stood there, staring down the star as though locked in a tussle with an enemy. She wasn't going to back down. She was done with apathy and blind acceptance. She had spent too many years praying unheard requests, waiting for her gift to arrive, and waiting for a response. She was so tired. She placed her palms on the lid of the coffin, holding herself up.

"I've done all I can do in my own power to become queen, and yet here I am! I'm not accepted, I'm not blessed, I'm nothing—nothing!" With a quick and intense push, the coffin tumbled off the pedestal and landed with a crash on the other side, echoing throughout the temple. Galdinia's rage halted. She stared at the overturned coffin, unable to comprehend what she had just done. She let her anger get the best of her, and the crash of her father's coffin on the ground coaxed her back to reality. She rushed to the other side of the podium and stared.

On the ground sat her father's coffin, cracked open, its lid hardly holding on at the hinges. It was empty. She crouched beside the splintered wood and rested her hand on the cushion where her father's head should have been.

"Oh, Galdinia."

Galdinia whipped her head around. At the edge of the altar stood her father. He was wearing his royal robes, the ones she saw him wear thousands of times before, but these were white, not the ruby red that she was accustomed to. The edges of his body and flowing robes almost rippled as he stood looking down at his daughter from across the platform. Aside from looking transient and spectral in nature, Galdinia was most shocked by one detail: he did not wear his crown.

As she stared at him in disbelief, she tried to make sense of what she was seeing. Although her logic told her this couldn't possibly be her father, she couldn't deny her eyes.

"Father?" she whispered.

"My darling, Dinny." His voice was warm and rich, not like it had been a week earlier when he could barely speak or breathe. "I'm so sorry."

As she sat amongst the broken pieces of the coffin, drenched in rain and tears, these were not the words she had imagined her reincarnated father would say. "What?"

"I'm so sorry I left you with this responsibility," he said as he walked towards her, the air around him rippling in the shards of torchlight that reflected off the walls. "I'm sorry I didn't prepare you more before I left you. I thought I was doing you a service by keeping you out of the arrangements I had set. I didn't want to overwhelm you as you dealt with my sickness. It was selfish of me, and I should have been more thoughtful of how this may affect you once I was gone. I'm sorry."

He reached his hands down to his daughter, and Galdinia sceptically placed her palms in his. His hands didn't feel solid, but they were certainly there. It was as though there was a great force, like a gust of wind, keeping her hands suspended with his. He helped her to her feet.

"You're... dead, aren't you?" she asked, still in disbelief.

"All accounts say that I am, yes," her father said softly, graciously. "I have been gifted a few extra moments with my grieving daughter though. I'm sorry to have left you in such a state."

She wanted to tell him about all of her pain, about trying to become queen and the anguish she felt about her lack of powers, but her heart took control of her words.

"You sent Drystan away. You bargained with him to let me go." Galdinia could see a glimpse of regret shadow his face. "Father, I loved him. I've never felt so betrayed."

The king took a long moment before deciding to speak. "Early on in my sickness, I knew that I wasn't going to get any better. I started to panic. I knew that I needed to assure that you would be kept safe, and I thought the best way to do that was to find you a legitimate suitor."

"I understand that he isn't a lord, but what more could I need than someone who truly loved me for me?" Galdinia asked and then quickly added, "He could have still been graced with a gift if he was meant to be by my side."

"I will be the first to admit that perhaps I acted rashly on your behalf when I had that conversation with Drystan. I do not regret trying to protect my daughter, but it pains me to know that I had a hand in breaking your heart." His words were achingly soft. "I'm sorry, Dinny."

She wanted to be angry with him, to yell at him for being dishonest and trying to control her life. She wasn't sure if it was because of where they were or if she was just thankful to see her father again, but she felt an overwhelming sense of forgiveness wash over her. She didn't know how long she had before he would inevitably disappear, and she needed to talk with him about more pressing matters.

"I just feel so inadequate," Galdinia said, looking into the face of her phantom father. "I've tried all week to be the queen I know you want me to be—to be like Mother! I tried to find a husband, I tried to force my gift, I tried to be authoritative and confident. But I don't feel like a queen. I feel like a fraud."

"Dinny, that's not the queen I want you to be." The look of confusion on Galdinia's face was enough response for him to continue. "Your mother was a beautiful queen; she was strong yet kind, decisive yet humble. I was so lucky to rule with her for the years we had together. But this kingdom needs a different ruler, a new ruler. I didn't want you to become your mother. I wanted you to become the queen that you are called to be by the Gods."

Galdinia looked away from him, unable to look him in the eyes. Her hands remained suspended in his. "I'm still not good enough, though," she said with a sigh.

The late king cupped his hand under his daughter's chin, drawing her face to look back at him with the strange force that surrounded him. "Are you sure about that?"

Galdinia's brow furrowed as she scrutinised his words. "Yes, I am!" She took her hands from his and turned to face the three-pointed star behind her; the frustration was building in her again. "I have spent all week training to use a power I don't even have, and I spent the last three months praying for it to show itself. They let Mother go, they didn't answer my prayers asking for them to heal you, and I'm as good as dead if I don't show my gift before tomorrow evening. I'm obviously not their queen."

Her voice echoed in the temple, and her father spoke again when silence fell. "At what point did you decide you weren't good enough for the throne?"

Galdinia turned to look back at him. "I didn't decide anything!"

"Yes, you did. You've already disqualified yourself."

"But the law says—"

"The law says that the successive king or queen will be lifted up by the Gods and honoured in their power. *Their* power. Not the future queen's power, but the Gods' power." Galdinia felt her heart sink. "Oh, my beautiful daughter. You are so wise for your years, but you hold yourself to such high standards. How could you ever have enough power to be queen alone? It isn't your responsibility to become queen; it is the Gods' right to choose who will be the successor. It is in their power that we succeed, not in some human ability.

"As a young man, I spent many years flailing about with my gift, using it to obtain anything and everything I wanted. I had so much power yet wielded it with an unruly sense of pride. I was nowhere near fit to be the next king, but the Gods knew I would be. I didn't realise this until my parents were struck down. When I met your mother, she didn't yet have her gift, but she was so clearly called to be queen. To tell you the truth, I actually believe that I needed to become king so that she could be the true ruler of the kingdom; I had to be the gateway. You are the same, my daughter. You are the gracious and wise queen that this kingdom yearns for.

"While her gift arrived late also, she didn't need the power to be queen; she already was one. The powers simply confirmed it in the eyes of the Syndicate and her people." Her father spoke with such favour about her mother that Galdinia's eyes had filled with tears once again. "You may not have your powers now, but that doesn't mean you won't. That does not mean you aren't worthy of being queen. You are a ruler, Dinny, the greatest ruler this kingdom will ever see. With or without your powers. The Gods have destined it."

Galdinia did not respond. She merely wrapped her arms around her father and sobbed. She watched her tears fall to the ground at his feet. They didn't land on his sleeve; they fell straight through him and onto the stone below.

"They still haven't answered my prayers though. I'm not even sure if they've heard them." Galdinia kept her face buried in her father's shoulder, the strange sensation of the force encasing him trickling over her skin.

"You say that, but why can't everything that has led to this moment have been preparing you to become queen? Are you sure that they haven't been answering them in a way that is different from what you expected? Perhaps you just need to wait longer to hear their response."

Galdinia pondered this for a moment, her heart still fluttering in her chest. She considered the events of the week that brought her here, standing on the altar of the Crystal Temple with her deceased father, crying out to the Gods for an answer. If she had accepted Bentley's proposal and if the governor hadn't given her his bad news, would she be here now? If she had found comfort earlier in trying to be like her mother, perhaps she wouldn't be the ruler she was meant to be. Had her desperation called into being the very truth she needed to hear?

"It's time for you to become a queen." The king pulled back from his daughter and turned her around to face the star on the wall, his arm around her shoulders. "And it's time for me to go."

Galdinia pressed herself into her father's side, relishing the moment. She glanced up at his face and was again struck by the absence of his crown.

"Where's your crown? You were wearing it at your funeral."

The king smiled down at her momentarily before saying, "I'm no longer the ruler of Crysterra, Your Majesty."

Galdinia closed her eyes as she held on to her father's presence. Then she felt the force diminish and disappear, and she knew that he was gone.

Once again, the temple felt empty and cold. In that moment, she knew she had a choice to make: she could turn around and walk away, giving up on trying to hear from the Gods; or she could let her heart make one more venture, one more aching plea for guidance. Given the appearance of her father and his faith in her, she knew exactly what she had to do, and so she turned her eyes back to the star on the wall.

The silence of the temple rang in her ears, and she waited. She let her heart feel every request she had ever yearned for, every fear she'd ever asked to be taken from her and waited. She didn't know how long she stood there, feeling every prayer she had prayed run through her mind, but she didn't let herself move. She didn't let herself give in.

"Help me."

Although she was alone in the temple, she instantly felt the warmth and comfort that came with the light of a spring morning. The heat filled the hall, and while previously she may have looked around for some kind of answer for it, she knew exactly where it was coming from. She kept her eyes on the star on the wall and breathed deeply, letting the warmth envelop her from the outside in, wrapping around her limbs and over her fingers, right to her toes. She closed her eyes and was transported away.

31

THE PRINCESS WAS HOVERING ABOVE THE GROUND OF THE TEMPLE'S altar, the rainwater from her clothing trailing on the ground below her feet. Her hair had started to float around her, lifting off her shoulders and swirling slowly around her head. Every second that passed, a drop of water—both rain and tears—left her skin and her clothes. The princess, however, was not aware of this.

With her eyes closed, she had entered a sacred place, somewhere the Gods lingered, almost as if they themselves were hovering just above the kingdom's atmosphere, not quite on land but not quite in another realm. The warmth that Galdinia felt was accompanied by a similar light, one that had a glistening quality, and it shone all around her. Although she didn't know where she was, she felt at peace. She felt safe.

"*Galdinia, Princess of Crysterra,*" a voice called to her. She didn't think she was hearing the voice in her ears but instead could feel it reverberating throughout her entire being. "*We have heard your cries; we have heard your prayers. You are not forgotten.*"

Despite her body being elsewhere, Galdinia felt the tears trickling down her face.

"*You are a powerful queen in your own right; your lineage tells of your potential, and your heart speaks of your goodness. We have known since before your birth that you would be a great queen. We stamped you with that destiny before you knew of our existence."* The voice, while resounding, was gentle and loving. *"You tried to become a queen by your own merit and knowledge, but you failed to find comfort in this because you had forgotten the key ingredient of your queenship: us."*

Galdinia could feel every moment she had questioned herself and her ability as she tried to do what she believed to be the right thing in preparation to become queen. Not once had she considered the Gods' opinion in this matter over the previous week. Not once had she deliberately asked for their guidance; she had only asked for their power.

"You have tried in your own strength to be queen. Never did we expect you to do this alone."

Somehow, in this elusive and delicate space, Galdinia found her lips and managed to form words.

"But I felt so alone. I felt like I had been abandoned." She wasn't sure where her voice was coming from or even where her lips were in this mystic space, but the words rang true.

"You have been trusted with much, as you have shown many years of loyalty and fervour in the seemingly insignificant moments of your young life. We have been with you every second, even when you felt we weren't. Your father's demise was painful for many, including us. We cannot control the decisions or actions of people, but we can, and will, turn tragedy into prosperity. With his death, we were able to ready you to become queen. Without his passing, you would not be able to become queen in the timeliest manner that is to come to pass. Without that devastation, you would not be able to stand in victory. The foresight and knowledge of the Gods is a privilege we hold, yes, but it is something you must trust. It can be hard to understand why these things happen the way that they do until you look back on your years and are able to put the pieces together. You are not expected to know these things now, but we hope you can trust them."

Galdinia didn't respond to this. She merely allowed the warm glow of the light to bear down on her... her body? She knew her body was somewhere, but she didn't think it was with her now.

"You have been destined to rule Crysterra since before your birth and we know that your offspring will also rise up when the time is right. Despite your destiny, you've questioned the reason for your very existence. Yes, to be queen, but also to bring peace to this kingdom."

"Is the kingdom not at peace?"

"*Not quite how you may suspect it to be. There is conflict and tension in the far reaches of the kingdom, and pained citizens are bounded by this. Your father was a great king, but another ruler needs to bring the kingdom to order. A new generation. A new season. You, Princess, are the gateway to this new era.*"

"But what about my gift? Can I be queen without it?"

"*You believe that you don't have a gift because you can't control the waves or change the direction of the wind or build a raging fire from a meagre flame. Your powers go much deeper than that, young Princess.*" Galdinia pondered these words, her brow furrowing. "*This week you spoke with Captain Ilyon about the gift and how he believes that everyone has been given it, but not everyone has tapped into it. He was right.*"

Somewhere, Galdinia felt her breath catch.

"*All people have been bestowed upon them a gift of some description, and for some, they find it easily. They believe it to be there, and should the timing be true, they find it, trusting that we have given them something precious. Others, however, believe it to only run through noble bloodlines. This is not a truth set by the Gods; this is an idea that was fabricated centuries ago, and we have been working through our people to see this idea eradicated. All have access to the power, but not everyone believes it to be true or real for them. Many people have gone their entire lives believing this lie and they miss a beautiful opportunity. Unfortunately, there are also others who use it for their own advantage, using it to lord over our people with vanity and malice.*"

Galdinia thought of Valah and her aunt and uncle, but their faces were vanquished from her mind's eye as quickly as they appeared.

"*You have asked for your gift to be given to you. You have even tried willing it into being, but it is true that it will only appear when we see fit. This week was not for us to tease or hurt you, but rather to have you see that you first needed to trust us before you can see your gift realised. This trust is paramount for a future ruler.*"

"What does this mean for my gift?"

"*Your powers have been developing for many years, coming into their prime. They have been brewing beneath the surface. But now you have a choice to make.*" Galdinia could feel the muffled beating of her heart in her chest somewhere far away. "*You do not have to take the crown tomorrow. You can leave this place, get back on your boat, and tell the governor that you will abdicate the throne and give full power to him and the Syndicate. You could leave all responsibility and fear right here.*"

"Or?"

"Or you can choose to be queen, here and now. You will be given all the authority you've been waiting for, as well as the weight that comes with it. We know that you fear trusting us and you have wanted nothing more than to be a good queen. We will release you of all responsibility if that's what you choose, but do know, you are a queen already in the eyes of the Gods."

Galdinia thought on her decision. She could walk away from it all now. Had she not assumed after her conversation with Ryden that she would not be queen? She had felt so inadequate, but she wasn't sure that she still felt that way now. Her father himself had said that she was the destined queen and that he thought she could do it. The Gods, too, had said the same thing. Why was she struggling to decide?

She knew, though, that if she chose to relinquish the crown, she could live out a very specific dream she'd had since she was a young woman: growing old with Drystan. Despite everything she had just said to him and everything that had transpired between them, she could feel that a part of her heart was still tethered to him.

It was not lost on her that she had wished so much to relinquish her birthright and send herself into Drystan's arms. Would it be so bad to allow Ryden to oversee the kingdom with the Syndicate? Would it be so terrible if her uncle eventually sat on the throne? Would it be so bad to allow these things to happen, therefore allowing herself to be happy for the rest of her days? She was almost positive that there was nothing she wanted more. Almost.

"It is not an easy decision, we know that. It wasn't for any king or queen who has gone before you. We won't lie to you, Princess, there will be trials ahead. This will be difficult for you. But it will be much harder for you not to be queen, and we think you know that too."

Galdinia knew this to be the truth. She knew that she couldn't relinquish the throne and let someone else rule the kingdom. She knew that she couldn't live out her life knowing she could have changed this kingdom for the better. She couldn't live a comfortable life in a remote quiet town in Crysterra while also maintaining a clear conscience.

"If you can trust us, be assured that your happiness and duty will not always be in conflict. You can do what is right for both the greater good and yourself."

The words Drystan had said to her days prior about duty over self made themselves known once again.

She knew what must be done.

"I'm ready to become Queen of Crysterra." Her words echoed in this sacred space, reverberating through both her physical and ethereal chest. She felt the authority of her declaration shudder across her very being, the words ringing true.

"You already are, Your Majesty."

Galdinia's feet lowered to the ground and her eyes slowly opened. Her hair was no longer stuck to the sides of her face; it landed softly on her shoulders, now dry and flowing in her naturally billowing curls. Her tunic and trousers, which were once stained with rain, were now dry. She felt a strange sensation inside her chest... a buzzing. Before, there was pain, but now she felt like she had been lit from within with the light of the sun, her body emanating a strength she had never felt before.

The girl who had run from her city and almost refused to be queen was no longer present. She felt strong. She felt powerful.

She felt like a queen.

Galdinia took a step in her new self and could feel each part of the sole of her foot landing on the solid crystal floor. She had never experienced such a sensation. She felt as though she were drawing power from the crystal directly beneath her. She took each step down the aisle carefully, as though she was afraid of causing a stir with her authoritative footfalls. As she walked, she felt the heat of the torches on the walls like never before, as though she was suddenly aware of their strength and warmth. She could feel the heat in her palms, across her face and even in her veins.

As she stood before the great doors, she finally felt ready. She finally recognised the power that had been bubbling beneath the surface for so many years, but now she felt she finally had the body—and the perspective—to wield such power. Her fingers twitched at the thought of accessing this new strength.

Galdinia turned to face the nearest torch by the doors and looked into the quivering flame, her eyes alight with its heat. She raised a hand and beckoned the fire. Her heart shuddered as the flame left its perch on the torch and came to rest in her outstretched palm. It did not burn her, nor did it cause her any pain. It sat cupped in her hand as though she were holding an apple. She moved her fingers in succession, causing the ball of flame to ripple and twist at her command, curling around itself, ebbing and flowing. Hot tears welled in her eyes as she felt immediately comfortable with the flame.

I am a Fire Flourisher.

"You may take it with you," a soft voice called across the temple. At the foot of the altar stood High Priestess Saena, a knowing smile spread across her face. "You may find that you need it, Queen Galdinia."

Galdinia returned the high priestess' smile and turned back to the entrance of the temple. She knew that the moment she stepped out those doors she would be queen. She knew she had a country to lead and a kingdom to put back together.

Galdinia looked down at the flame that seemed to be attached to her palm. She silently commanded it to shrink, and it did, diminishing to the size of a grape. She clasped her hands over the fire and held her fist to her chest before looking up beyond the ceiling of the temple where the storm still beat down above her.

"Thank you," she whispered, finding solace in the warmth in her hand. Beyond that, she took courage knowing that it stood as a symbol of the Gods' faith in her.

She pulled one door open and stepped back out into the rain. But not a drop touched her.

From the deck of the royal sailing ship at the island's shore stood Ilyon, his hand outstretched to the princess, keeping her in a pocket of dry air by manoeuvring the droplets. The water continued to fall and even pool around her feet, but no rain landed on her. He looked at her with admiration and pride as he glimpsed the flickering flame in her hand. She wondered how long he had been watching the doors waiting for her to emerge.

From the corner of her eye, a flash of orange caught her eye. Over the water, to the north of the capital, she saw a red glow emerge through the dark, suddenly highlighting the silhouette of the castle.

"Ilyon," Galdinia called as she moved hastily towards the boat, quickly moving on board. "Captain, can you halt the rain?"

The captain looked at her from a moment and nodded, his face hard and determined.

He reached both hands above his head, his deep concentration setting into the lines on his face. He arched his arms from left to right with a great heave, and before a drop of water could fall on himself or the princess, he willed the storm to the south, sending the rain into the ocean. The light of the afternoon sun in the west flooded the isle and the surrounding sea.

Then she could hear it.

She could hear the enraged voices of soldiers travelling across the water to the island. She should hear the cries of frightened citizens.

Elderguard, her home, was under attack.

"Back to the capital, now!" she commanded.

Ilyon had already taken up his helm and used his power to tame the seas in their favour, pushing the boat back towards Elderguard.

Her heart shuddered at the thought of her enemies descending upon her home. She was now the queen, crown or no crown, and she had to protect Elderguard. Galdinia braced the flame tightly in her palm as she watched her city desperately, the smoke from the fire filling the sky above the buildings.

32

G ALDINIA'S SAILING BOAT ARRIVED AT THE DOCKS IN HALF THE TIME IT
would have naturally taken her. Ilyon pushed the vessel forward with a
force and velocity that came with the need to protect Elderguard, the
city he had been entrusted to guard. While his right hand continued to
propel the ship forward with a rumbling current at the stern, he
stretched out his left hand into the air above the bow to calm the
waves ahead, creating a pre-emptive gash in the water to allow the
ship to sail through with ease. Galdinia watched in amazement, letting
the gentle heat of the flame in her palm flicker. She hoped that her gift
could be half as powerful as Ilyon's one day.

When they arrived in the port, the captain managed to bring the
ship to an almost instant halt, calming the waters and steadying the
vessel. Galdinia ran across the deck of the ship to the gangway and
hurtled herself down to solid ground, her mind set on the noise that
was erupting from within the city.

She could hear the cries of her citizens as they ran for cover or, for
those arguably luckier, for their boats that were docked beside hers.
People ran in every direction, no one noticing that the princess was
beside them, the powers they had been hoping she would obtain now
at her very fingertips. Children cried in their parents' arms; people
hauled the supplies they could carry into their boats. Even some priest-

esses could be seen among the madness, lost and directionless. Soldiers raced along the edges of the high walls that bordered the city streets. They were in formation, swords at their sides. Galdinia's heart shuddered as she realised that the attack was upon them.

"Princess!" the captain called to Galdinia from the ship, one hand outstretched, pointing towards the cove. His voice was tired, betraying him as he used what little strength he had left to stand tall.

Galdinia clamoured up onto a crate beside the docked ship, craning her neck over the flurry of people and boats. Beyond the madness she could see what Ilyon was pointing towards.

A few kilometres out from the shore, coming from the direction of the Shadowed Coast, was a jet-black ship, its sails a velvet ebony. It was flanked by at least two dozen ships of a similar stature, and they were unmistakable. Valah's ships were making tracks towards the south of the capital.

They were attacking from both sides.

"I have to go find the governor and warn him," Galdinia called to the captain. "They're no more than fifteen minutes out, but we need to fortify the southern walls."

"I will organise the soldiers here and keep the skies clear; someone else is trying to fight against me to bring back the rain. I'm sure they want it for cover." The captain stared up into the sky and Galdinia could see the tension in his neck as he tried to hold off the downpour. "You should go!"

"Thank you, for everything," she said quickly before turning, jumping from her perch on the crate, and running towards the dockyard.

Galdinia hurtled forward, her power warming her from the inside. Her gift flowed through her like oxygen, as natural and necessary as a gulp of air after being submerged in water. She still held the flame in her hand, which she had shrunk to half its size. She could conceal it in her palm and its warmth felt reassuring on her skin.

The princess weaved between citizens as she made haste for the castle, trying to avoid being stopped by packs of families and rushing bodies. She took a shortcut down an alleyway which brought her out beside the tavern. She ran around the building and into the square, where she got her first unobstructed glimpse of the castle.

A billowing mass of smoke rose into the sky from behind her home, making it look like the castle itself was alight. Beneath the castle in the square sat the colourful remnants of the preparations for the banquet, all soaked in rain. She gasped as she tore across the square and into the last few streets that were between her and the castle.

Galdinia rounded the corner into the wide road that would normally be guarded by a handful of soldiers. Now, it was housing what looked like half of the royal army.

"Platoon B, we need more coverage on the gates," a commander called across a group of at least fifty men who stood in neatly packed rows.

"Sir, the Northern Gates are being attacked, but there are ships coming into the cove," a soldier at the front of the group responded, not breaking his stiff stance. "The messengers called for more posts to be filled along the docks where we can at least fend them off by way of cannons."

Galdinia watched the commander consider this for a moment as she made her way across the road towards the main gates of the castle.

"I will send Platoon C to the gates, then," he finally concluded. "The rest of you, get down to the docks and arm yourselves with airborne weapons. I don't want that slug of a man stepping foot in our city!"

Galdinia assumed he was talking about her uncle, and she realised very quickly that she hadn't yet considered him in this attack. She had seen Valah's ship incoming, but were Draven and Edana on the ship also? Who was attacking the gates if the Elderwins were on Valah's ship?

Galdinia didn't take another moment to process this information and instead tore off up the road to the castle gates, desperate to find Ryden; she knew he would be protecting the castle. She could only hope that Neryda was far from the violence with her family, who no doubt took their private vessel out into the reaches of the Endless Sea where they could wait out the attack. Although seen as cowardly by many of the commoners, families of nobility had always been instructed to flee an incoming attack in any way they saw fit. Galdinia knew her father had brought this statute into place before his death to protect the most gifted among them. Slowly she was realising just how much her father had been preparing for this moment.

"Let me through," Galdinia instructed, looking to the guards who stood on either side of the castle gates. It seemed to take them a moment to recognise the windswept young woman before them.

"Of course, Your Highness." One guard nodded, and then his companions wrenched open the doors to allow Galdinia through a small gap. After she slipped through the narrow space, they quickly bolted the gates once again.

Galdinia made her way up the front steps and through the large doors, which were also heavily guarded. The high security of the castle made her nervous; she couldn't imagine the severity of the attack they were facing.

As she stepped into the entrance hall of the castle, Galdinia found herself overwhelmed by a scene of anxiety and chaos. If the streets of Crysterra were in disorder, then the castle had fallen into utter mayhem.

From all wings, soldiers were marching, patrolling each corridor and corner. The attendants and the nobility that hadn't made it out of the city had retreated to the castle and were rushing across the marble floors, some crying out of fear, others barking orders, attempting to keep some semblance of control. They were all too preoccupied to take notice of the princess who was now standing in their midst.

Across the entrance hall, though, rushing down the stairs of the castle, came a very concerned looking Ryden. As he caught Galdinia's eye, his shoulders relaxed in temporary relief. He disregarded the Syndicate member who had been speaking to him furiously and swept across the floor to Galdinia.

"Princess, you're okay!" The solace in his voice was palpable as he pulled her in to his chest, wrapping his arms tightly around her. "Thank the Gods you're okay."

"I'm fine, Ryden," Galdinia said hurriedly, pulling back from the governor. "What's happening? Who's attacking?"

"Soldiers from Lund in the Starlight Mountains, they have attacked the Northern Gates," Ryden said breathlessly, guiding Galdinia from the entrance hall towards an unoccupied sitting room at the front of the castle. "We don't know what provoked them, but they have nearly breached the gates. We have lost hordes of soldiers up there and I think it's only a matter of time until they are inside the city walls."

"Is there any sign of Draven or Valah?" Galdinia asked, her voice rushed.

"Not at this stage," Ryden replied, shaking his head. "I fear that the army from Lund have colluded with them though."

"To take the throne," Galdinia added, her eyes glazing over as she stared across the room and into a blackened and empty fireplace.

"I'm sure that is their intent, yes," Ryden conceded, coming to stand beside Galdinia. "But we haven't sighted them yet, so we can't be sure."

"I have."

Ryden paused. "What?"

"Up the Shadowed Coast, I saw Valah's ships," she said, her eyes fixed on the ash that was piled in the hearth. "She could be minutes out by now, unless the army is able to sink her ship before it arrives. My aunt and uncle may very well be on the ship with her."

"Of course," Ryden said, more so to himself than to Galdinia. "They must have persuaded those from Lund to attack from the north to distract and harm our forces. We have to send our soldiers down there now!"

"The commanders already are," Galdinia said. "I heard the platoons being instructed to protect the docks. They were departing just as I came through the castle gates."

After a brief pause, Ryden said, "I'm so sorry, Princess."

"What for?" Galdinia asked, now confused herself. This attack wasn't his fault.

"I promised to protect you after your father passed, and now the capital is being attacked from both sides just one week after his death. I am sorry for my dishonesty earlier too. I have not held up my end of the bargain."

Galdinia looked up to her father's most trusted advisor, shaking her head. "I'm sure my father wanted you to throw all other responsibility to the side in order to look after me, but I can assure you that is not what I need right now. I need you to do what is best for the capital —for the country."

"Yes, but you are my priority. I have to help keep you alive, otherwise we won't have a country to protect."

"Who says I need protecting?"

"Princess, forgive me, but with your lack of powers, I am unsure—"

Galdinia snapped her fingers and the fire in her hand travelled to the fireplace, setting the remaining wood ablaze. Its light and heat emanated across the room, hitting them both full force in the face.

"My journey to the Crystal Temple was fruitful," Galdinia said simply, clicking her fingers once again to calm the ravaging fire to a simmer. Using her gift felt both strangely comforting and foreign; she wasn't sure when she'd get used to the feeling.

"Princess!" Ryden exclaimed as he clasped her hands in his. "The Gods have finally answered our prayers!"

"They certainly have." Galdinia smiled back, revelling in a moment of joy in the midst of darkness. "And now I can help protect Elderguard."

"We still need to get you to safety," Ryden said curtly, releasing Galdinia's hands and standing up straight, as though he had suddenly reminded himself that he was the governor. "I will take you to the catacombs below the castle or out to the Endless Sea where we can hold up until the fighting ends."

"Ryden, what are you talking about?" Galdinia asked, all sense of joy being sucked out of the room. "Did you not just see me turn those ashes into a wall of flame? They need me out in battle!"

"Don't be ridiculous, Princess. We can't have you anywhere near oncoming weapons and attack. You are simply too valuable."

"Ryden, didn't we just have this conversation? You don't have to try to protect me; your duty is to our country. If I don't go ward off the enemy, then I will no longer have a throne to sit on!"

Before he could respond, the door of the room was thrust open, and in the doorframe stood a soldier whose silhouette eclipsed the chaos outside. He took a few steps forward into the room before he took his helmet off to reveal his long chestnut hair and ash-covered face. Despite the mess and the echo of her words that still rang in her head, Drystan looked as glorious as ever.

"Princess, Governor, we need to get you both to safety," Drystan said formally, standing at attention across the room from them.

"Drys," Galdinia said, moving towards him. Despite his stoic exterior, Galdinia could see the pain in his eyes. "What's happening out there?"

"An army from Lund have breached the capital walls and are making their way towards the castle," he said in his most official voice. He was trying so hard to be brave. "Please come with me. I have been instructed to accompany you both to the catacombs."

"Very well," Ryden said from behind Galdinia, striding towards the door. Drystan turned to follow him, but Galdinia reached out and caught him in the gap between his armour at his elbow. Beneath the chain mail, she could feel the heat of his skin. Or perhaps it was the residual burning of the fire on her hands. She still wasn't sure how the flames might affect her.

"Drystan, wait," Galdinia said, pulling him back to face her. "I'm so sorry for the things I said to you earlier. I was hurt and emotional."

"It's fine, Princess," Drystan said, half turning his face to look at her. "We need to get you to safety."

"No, wait." Galdinia tried to keep her voice even. He was doing exactly what she asked him to; he was being a soldier in her city, nothing more. How Galdinia wished she could take those words back.

"Princess, I need to make sure you're safe," Drystan said firmly, slipping his arm out from her grasp.

As he did, Galdinia caught his hand with hers, causing his head to whip back in her direction. He stared down at their interlocked fingers as she tried to hold on to him for one more second. He looked at her, and for a moment she saw a glimpse of the boy she fell in love with when she was just a child. They were running through the castle grounds as young teenagers; they were spending hours reading between classes by the fire in the library; they were standing beside the lake in the cool air of the moonlight, lips almost touching, hearts thudding in their chests.

Then his hand was gone, and their gaze was broken.

Galdinia followed him closely as they made their way back into the entrance hall of the castle. While there was still chaos written over the faces of all those that surrounded them, three lines of soldiers now barred the front doors, each of them holding their weapons at attention.

"Princess!" The familiar bell tone of Lord Bentley's voice cut through the noise of the room, and all three of them stopped in their hurried steps.

Bentley had clamoured up the steps of the castle and pushed past the lines of soldiers. In his hand was a broadsword, which still seemed to be clean, unlike his appearance. He had forgone his jacket, and the rest of the forest green ensemble he was wearing earlier that day had been torn and was stained with ash and dirt, his waistcoat flapping open by his sides. His brilliantly blonde hair still stood out against his grimy appearance.

"Lord Bentley!" Galdinia exclaimed as he walked towards them with a limp. "What happened to you?"

"I went up to the Northern Gates to try to assist the Royal Guard, but it was futile. They only managed to just hold back the Lund army before I made it out. I had to come find you and thought it best to start here. Thank the Gods you're alright!"

Galdinia could see his genuine concern for her. She wrapped an arm around his waist, taking his free one over her shoulders, trying to assist him in simply standing.

"What were you thinking?" Galdinia said, her voice halfway between a scold and a laugh. "Did you really think you could fend off an attack without armour or training?"

"Excuse me, Your Highness, but I'll have you know that I did two years of training as part of my studies," he said, eyebrows raised. "I'm actually pretty good with a sword. It's a shame I didn't have a bow and arrow at my disposal."

At that moment, a dreadful crash ripped through the air, causing shrieks to erupt throughout the castle.

"The castle gates," Drystan hissed, coming to stand beside Galdinia and Bentley, Ryden in tow. "Princess, we have to get you to the catacombs now."

"Agreed," Bentley said quickly, putting his weight back on his own leg with a wince, taking his arm off Galdinia's shoulders. She still kept her arm around his waist for support. "They have explosives; that's how they got through the gates. We have to take her to the catacombs immediately."

"If we take her to the catacombs, the entire castle may come down on her," Ryden said, shaking his head. "We can take her through the library and out to the eastern docks."

Galdinia felt Bentley stiffen beneath her hand wrapped around his waist.

"What if they're already at the docks?" he asked, his face hard. "Surely the catacombs are safer."

"We have to take that chance. I can help get as many people on boats at the docks as possible," Galdinia interjected. Bentley still looked unsure.

"The tunnel entrance and gate beneath the castle are concealed, and only Galdinia and I have access. Should the enemy already be at the docks, you'll be able to conceal yourself in the tunnels at the very least," Ryden said fervently, trying to convince Bentley. "It is our best chance to keep Galdinia safe. We can't risk the catacombs."

As the men spoke, Galdinia watched Drystan closely. His mind was obviously whirring. His eyes darted across the hall as he tried to look beyond the lines of soldiers who were now marching down the castle steps towards the fallen gates. He looked back at Galdinia, and she could see his heart being torn in two between his duties: his duty to his country and his duty to his heart. No matter the words they had shared earlier and the way they had both broken each other's trust, she knew he still wanted nothing more than to protect her. He was the person she felt most safe with, and yet she knew that she couldn't go with him now.

She looked at Bentley, who despite his lopsided stance, looked ready to shield her with his own body in an instant.

"Drys, you have to stay here." Galdinia took a step forward and placed a hand on his chest plate. As if he had finally given in, he let his shoulders relax. "Bentley can keep me safe. You know you need to be here."

Was this it? Galdinia considered the boy in front of her, finally allowing herself to let go of her childhood fantasies and dreams of growing old with Drystan. Somewhere deep down, she knew it couldn't happen. She couldn't be queen with a soldier by her side, and he couldn't go back on his pledge to put his country first. She didn't even know if Ryden could sway the Syndicate to change the laws around who the queen could marry. In that moment, they both knew this was a goodbye to the childhood they had once shared.

Drystan pulled Galdinia in quickly to his armoured body, holding her tight. She briefly tucked her face into his neck, breathing in his warm scent that was masked by sweat and smoke. Drystan pressed his lips against the top of her head for one final moment of lack of restraint.

"I'm sorry, Gal," he whispered into her hair so only she could hear. "I love you."

She revelled in the sound of her name on his lips. A moment later, he pulled back from her and she instantly missed the touch of him beneath her hands.

"Get her to safety and protect her with your life," Drystan practically growled at Bentley, his eyes ferocious as he put his helmet back onto his mess of hair. "Consider this your last night if you don't."

"Of course, she is my highest priority," Bentley replied, trying to stand as tall as he could. Galdinia didn't enjoy being spoken about, but she didn't think this was the moment to speak up for her sense of autonomy.

There was another shriek of metal twisting against metal, causing everyone in the entrance hall to duck in terror.

"Go!" Drystan roared before turning his back on them and marching towards the castle doors. He was walking away from Galdinia as a soldier and as a man.

"Princess, I need to go see about anyone that has already gone down to the catacombs," Ryden said as the three of them rushed across the entrance hall towards the corridor that would take them to the western wing. "Keep her safe, Bentley."

"As discussed, Ryden, I am perfectly capable of protecting myself," Galdinia said, her voice firm.

"Of course," Ryden said in an attempted apology. "I will see to it that I find you both as soon as possible. Help others, but you must get on one of those boats."

"Right." Bentley nodded, putting an arm around Galdinia, holding her close.

Galdinia caught one last glance at Ryden before moving with Bentley down the long, winding hallway.

"Are there no other ways out of the castle?" Bentley asked, his injured leg slowing them down as she tried to support him.

"There's another entrance through the attendants' quarters, but that will bring us out near Main Court, which isn't much help," Galdinia explained, trying to pull Bentley quickly down the hallway. She hoped to keep him out of danger just as much as he wanted to protect her; his injury made his chances in battle far less hopeful.

They stopped in front of the doors of the library, and Bentley stood still, halting Galdinia's entrance into the room.

"Maybe I should go back out to the entrance hall and help them fight," Bentley began, turning to Galdinia. "If I can find a bow and arrow, I could—"

"Bentley, no offence, but I don't think you're going to be any help to anyone in your current state. We need to get you onto a boat and patched up. You need protecting just as I do, Pup."

Even at her use of his nickname, Bentley's expression of concern did not shift. Had it only been that morning that they were sitting on the terrace eating a delightful breakfast together, where Bentley had professed his love for her and asked for her hand in marriage? How had they arrived here?

"We need to go," she said decidedly as another bang sounded from the direction of the entrance hall. Every moment they tarried was another moment lost that could have been spent getting citizens to safety on the water.

Galdinia wrenched open the door of the library, stepping into the darkened room. It seemed no one had lit the fires today, so she stood in pitch black as the door thudded closed behind them. At the thought of fire, her body longed for the heat of flames again, but there were none in sight, and she had left her fire from the temple in the sitting room hearth. They would have to make their way to the trapdoor blindly.

"Hello, Princess." Galdinia's heart stopped at the sound of a frighteningly recognisable, velvet-smooth voice that crooned at her from across the room.

The strike of a match sounded from the direction of the voice, and a small yellow light hovered in the air. It danced through the darkness and rested in the bottom of a nearby lantern, which, once lit, shed light on the room around her. The fire called to Galdinia and she had to restrain herself from reaching out to it.

Across the large mahogany table in the centre of the room, surrounded by fallen books, stood Valah, dressed in black from head to toe, as though she were one of the shadows that crept around the walls, flickering in the lamplight. Galdinia's pulse thundered throughout her body as Valah parted her lips to speak again.

"I've been expecting you."

33

"Valah," Galdinia said breathlessly as the dim light from the lantern cast the slender woman's knife-like shadows across the walls of books.

"Hello, Princess." Her voice crawled through the darkness.

"How did you get in here?"

"You don't really think I've forgotten all of the castle's secrets, do you?" Valah asked as she took two long strides along the length of the table. "You weren't the only princess to grow up in these walls." She ran a finger along the spines of the books lined up along a nearby shelf. "This was one of my favourite ways to escape the throes of royal life. You know how it is."

Valah was speaking as though to an old friend, as if they truly had anything in common. This made Galdinia's skin prickle, and she could feel the heat beneath her skin stronger than ever before.

The woman continued to stride around the table towards the princess. She stopped at the corner closest to Galdinia and propped her arm up on a nearby chair. Her casual and comfortable stance forced Galdinia's brows to furrow together.

"You don't seem all that pleased to see me. I thought you would have been longing to talk to someone who truly understands you, someone who has stood in your shoes and felt your pain."

"You have no idea how I feel," Galdinia spat between tight lips.

"Don't I?" Valah was settling in, and Galdinia considered how difficult it would be for her to harness the flame in the lantern as she cursed herself for relinquishing the fire in the sitting room. It was small, but she had hoped that her brewing anger could help her build it into something more. "Well, let's see: I grew up with friends who never truly understood the pressures of being a princess, my parents were ripped from me before I could become queen, and then I was banished so far from the throne that I never got a whiff of my true place in this world until decades later—right now. Do you really think I don't know how you feel?"

"You think you know what my childhood was like? What my loved ones are like?" Galdinia let out a joyless laugh. "You don't know anything about me."

"Is that right? Well, let me ask you, where are they all now? Your father's body is lying in the Crystal Temple ready for burial beside your mother; your only other family, your aunt and uncle, are making their way to the castle now to support me in my victory; that red-headed noble girl is probably out on the seas, far away from the battle, cowering on a boat with her all-too-important parents; your ever-loyal young soldier friend is out there somewhere, likely on his last leg. And —oh no, that's it. There's no one left."

Galdinia was shocked by Valah's knowledge of her friends, but she tried to keep her exasperation masked. Despite wanting to know how the woman came to learn about Neryda and Drystan, she had to maintain her strong facade.

"I'm not alone here, am I?" Galdinia asked, standing her ground as she turned to look at Bentley, who was still standing behind her at the door to the library. His eyes were downcast.

Now Valah was the one to laugh. "Who, Bentley?" Galdinia didn't know how Valah could have possibly known his name. Valah looked at Galdinia with mock concern, her eyes full of pity. "He's a good actor, isn't he? If he really made you think he cared for you, then he's done his job."

Galdinia's heart trembled in her chest, and she felt as though she couldn't breathe.

She turned to look at the blonde boy at the door. He raised his eyebrows and looked at her cautiously, as though Galdinia was hearing news she should have predicted. His childlike smile, charming dimple, and warm expression were but a shadow now. He didn't deny Valah's accusation. He simply stood there, his eyes empty.

As she looked at him, she realised that he wasn't guarding the door for their protection but to ensure she couldn't leave the room.

"Lord Bentley," Galdinia gasped, unable to fathom the truth that stood before her.

"And he's barely a lord at that," Valah said matter-of-factly, evidently pleased with herself. "The Penrose family have been pining after a juicier slice of The Edges since before he was born, and their alliance quietly shifted to the west when your father took everything from them a decade ago in the Battle of the Midlands. The moment word had spread to us that Bartemus was looking for suitors for his darling daughter, Lord and Lady Penrose suggested their delectable plan: send their son to the capital to earn the trust of the princess and pave a way to the throne. It didn't take long to send off a compelling letter to the Syndicate from a long-standing ally, or so they thought. With their status and Bentley's charm, our prospects for success were high."

"You were her pet this whole time," Galdinia rasped, turning to look back at Bentley. "What were you going to do tomorrow when you got to my coronation?"

"Princess, there was never going to be a coronation," Valah said from across the table, leering at Galdinia.

Galdinia took a step back from Bentley. He had been priming her for this moment, earning her trust and drawing her in. He had blind-sided her and led her to this meeting with Valah. Galdinia didn't know how she had let herself be manipulated by this painfully charming man. His eyes held a glimpse of remorse, but she felt she was on the verge of launching herself at him, so she turned her attention back to Valah.

"Why?" Galdinia asked, exasperated. "Why did you go to the trouble of deceiving me with this wretched plan? Why not just come and take the throne from me? Heaven knows you could have if you really wanted to."

"Although that would have been preferable, simply waltzing into the capital and snatching my crown off your pretty little head isn't the simple act you may think it is," Valah patronised Galdinia, staring at her along her paper-thin nose. "Sinking my teeth into you via a wolf in sheep's clothing was so very satisfying. I was able to keep an ear to the ground in Elderguard while establishing an alliance with your wretched aunt and uncle. Knowing that Bentley was here to influence your every move this week and ultimately bring you to me was significantly easier—and arguably cleaner—than coming here blindly on my own."

Galdinia didn't think that the inevitable bloodshed could be considered clean, but she didn't want to imagine what Valah regarded as messy.

Galdinia turned back to Bentley. "You asked me to marry you." Her voice was but a breath, almost pleading. "Why?"

Bentley's eyes shifted between Galdinia and Valah as he considered his words before speaking.

"Like Valah said," Bentley began, his voice lower than she had ever heard it, "my family and the portion of The Edges that they govern have been suffering for too long. We were desperate for change. After everything my parents told me about you and your father, I thought it would be far more feasible to win your heart than stage a coup without leverage." *Ouch.* "You weren't what I was expecting though."

Bentley took a step towards Galdinia, who stepped back from him, glaring daggers in return.

"No," she whispered.

"Oh, Bentley," Valah said with a roll of her eyes, "I think you've committed a little too much to the part. You can drop it now."

Bentley's eyes shifted to Valah, then back to Galdinia. He seemed caught between worlds, unsure what to say next.

Galdinia felt like a child again. She had put her heart on the line and believed in a story that was too good to be true. Of course it was too easy, too simple. She felt so foolish.

"In short," Valah went on, "playing with you before taking the throne, whilst also having someone inside the castle to feed me information about this week's festivities and your emotional instability, made it significantly easier to walk in here today."

"My emotional instability?" Galdinia said quietly.

"Daily crows from Bentley telling me all about your struggles with your lack of powers really brightened my day. It's much easier to take down an heir that is both without their gift *and* hopeless."

My gift.

Galdinia sent a silent word of gratitude to the Gods for keeping her mouth shut in the entrance hall. At this stage, nobody in this room knew that the princess had been given her gift. Valah had come here alone believing that she could take care of Galdinia herself, assuming she hadn't been given her gift.

Galdinia reminded herself of Ilyon's words in the underground bunker of the barracks when she first tried tapping into her gift: *Make a connection with the flame.* She started to lightly—and inconspicuously—rub her fingertips together, seeking the heat from the flickering flame in the lantern behind Valah. She wanted nothing more than to send it flying over Valah's hand still perched on the back of the chair beside her.

"Not to mention the updates about your inability to maintain some semblance of authority in these walls. Today's message about your forbidden puppy love was particularly delicious." As Valah spoke, Galdinia considered Drystan, who was at this moment fighting for his life to protect her and his city, all the while thinking he could trust Bentley to watch over her. "It really sounds like I'm doing you a favour by taking the responsibility of being queen off your hands."

Before Galdinia could respond, there was a banging sound at the back of the library, deep in the shadows of the shelves. She could barely make out the figure stalking through the darkness towards them. As the princess' uncle stepped into the dim light, Valah rolled her eyes. Draven looked more dishevelled than usual and the sight of him made Galdinia's blood boil.

"I told you to stay at the docks," Valah seethed, spitting her words in Draven's direction. "You should be directing the battle."

"It's getting a little too vicious for my liking," Draven said, brushing cobwebs and dust from his shoulders; Galdinia hoped that his trek through the tunnels beneath this room had been arduous for him. "Besides, Edana is using her powers to our betterment; no one can weave water like that woman. Where's your watch dog?"

"Reynard is taking care of securing that asset we discussed." She glanced over her shoulder at Draven, and he nodded briefly. "And you've arrived just in time to say goodbye to your niece."

"You can't do this," Galdinia hissed, her eyes flicking in Bentley's direction and then back to Valah and her uncle. "There will be outrage across the country! My father has loyal followers throughout the kingdom. You won't last two days on the throne."

"My, my, what lies has your father been feeding you, dear girl?" Valah asked. "He was an aristocratic dictator who only cared about his precious little capital city and the rich people within it. There are cities upon cities of civilians who have been forgotten about and thrown into disarray since your father was placed in charge. He has been the cause of one too many battles in the name of 'peace'."

"You're lying!"

"Oh no, Galdinia," Draven said softly, cutting into the argument, "he practically banished me and your aunt to the Shadowed Coast the moment my father's crown was placed on his head. He didn't care about anyone outside of this city's walls. That's how he handled things: out of sight, out of mind. Why do you think the Lund army were so willing to join our cause? They want to see this country reformed as well."

"This country needs a real leader who will lead them to greatness," Valah said, taking slow steps towards Galdinia. "Not a child who stands in the false shadow of her father and pretends to know anything about running a country."

"And which of you two will it be then?" Galdinia asked, taking a step back from Valah, trying to bide herself some time as she felt for the connection with the tiny flame. "If you think you'll get on the throne before him without a knife in the back, you are sorely mistaken."

"Please, Galdinia, don't patronise us," Draven said from across the table. "We have our arrangements, but thank you for your concern."

Galdinia's eyebrows rose as she started to piece together the unspoken messages in the room. She had assumed that Valah would take the throne, yet here she stood with her uncle who appeared so quietly confident. She may have hated her uncle, but she didn't think he was that daft.

"You're trusting Valah to allow you to be crowned?" Galdinia asked in genuine surprise. "You're as good as dead then, Uncle. She has been pining after the throne for years longer than you! For goodness sake, your parents killed hers. She won't let another Elderwin rule this kingdom, and you're a fool if you think she will."

Galdinia enjoyed being the one to speak for others for a change, and to do so in front of her enemies made it all the sweeter. Even if she was minutes from losing her life, she still soaked up the power she felt.

"As your uncle said," Valah hummed, maintaining an even tone. "We have our arrangements."

"Whatever your arrangements," Galdinia went on, beginning to feel the edges of the heat from the flame in her palm, allowing her connection to it to start to simmer, "you will not be working together after today. You're both simply too proud to keep each other around longer than necessary."

Galdinia could see her uncle's eyes ablaze. She knew she had struck a nerve in him. Even if he had planned to kill Valah after their ascension to the throne, she could see the doubt in him as he realised his demise may supersede that.

"You don't know anything about political strategy or ruling a kingdom," Draven said through gritted teeth, now visibly angered by his niece. "Valah and I have agreed that I will take the throne and she will be my governess. We have an equal army here, so should we turn on each other, we would see our own demise soon after. This isn't our first battle, young Galdinia."

The shadows of the small lantern fire flickered across Valah's face and for a brief second, Galdinia saw the expression of tiresome frustration pass over her features.

"Actually, Draven," Valah crooned, not bothering to look at her supposed ally as she addressed him. "My forces make up about two-thirds of this evening's army."

"You think your army and the army from the mountains are that great in number?" Draven scoffed, frowning at Valah.

"No, but with the soldiers from the east, my numbers are stronger."

"The soldiers from the east? They are my allies—"

"You'd like to think that, wouldn't you?" Valah asked smoothly, and Galdinia watched as her uncle's face fell into exasperated shock. "We have had connections to rebel armies in the east for decades. It wasn't difficult for me to ask their captain to agree to your request to be allies when you approached them. They hate Elderwins almost as much as I do, so he was more than happy to oblige, especially when I promised that I'd put an end to your abhorrent family by week's end."

Galdinia watched the two carefully. Valah still faced her, her eyes boring into the princess' as she spoke. Draven stood beside the table, a sickening expression shadowing his face.

"You were going to betray us all along," Draven croaked, angered with himself that he hadn't anticipated this happening sooner.

"Your niece may have overestimated herself, but she is perceptive," Valah said, her eyes still on the princess. "I will not kneel to any other ruler in this kingdom."

With these words, Draven threw out a hand, his powers catching on the lantern, sending it crashing across the table. The small flame erupted into a ball of fire, taking up much of the space above the table. The room filled with heat and the sudden explosion of light had Galdinia shielding her eyes with her forearm. Valah turned to face Draven but stood her ground, now staring at the man beneath the flames with an expression that suggested she was merely inconvenienced by his outburst. Bentley still stood strong at the door, but his eyes were fixed on the flames. Galdinia wondered if he could keep it at bay. Could she take control of the flame in the presence of both Bentley and Draven? She hoped that the Gods' power and Ilyon's training were enough to help her merely survive.

"I will not let the crown slip through my fingers again!" Draven roared over the crackling fire.

Valah simply flicked her wrist and the ball of flame halved in size, its oxygen supply being sucked from it. Galdinia could feel the wind all around them, dancing through her hair. With another flick, Draven's eyes went wide, and his chest stopped moving. His mouth gaped as he gasped for air and his focus on the fire dissolved. Galdinia looked again at Bentley, who was staring into the flames, keeping them steady. Draven fell to his knees as he clutched at his throat, a horrid gasping sound escaping his stunned lips.

Valah wasn't suffocating him, she was sucking the air from his very lungs.

Draven tried to reach out to the flames, but his body buckled, and he was suddenly on all fours, reaching out to Valah from the ground, his eyes becoming bloodshot and his face pale white. Any hope he had of controlling the fire was lost as he tried to beg for air between fruitless gasps, his hands now reaching out towards Valah.

"Draven," Valah said easily, "the crown was never within your reach."

With one more flick of her wrist, the last of the oxygen in Draven's body was ripped free and her uncle stared ahead, his face lifeless. Moments later, his body crashed to the ground. Galdinia let out a short cry; she hated her uncle, but she hadn't prepared herself to watch him die before her very eyes. She turned from Draven's lifeless body and glimpsed at Bentley. He winced and his face was more disgust than dignity as he too turned away from the atrocity. Did he fear he may be close to experiencing a similar demise?

The flaming ball had now diminished in size to that of Galdinia's fist. Bentley didn't bother sending it back to the lantern. He just kept it hanging in the air over the table.

Valah turned from Draven's body and looked back at the princess, as though his death had been a mere disruption to her evening.

Steeling herself, Galdinia again tried to feel for the flame across from her, sensing her power in her fingertips. She knew she didn't have long and needed to act swiftly.

"Apologies you had to see that, Princess," Valah said softly, slowly walking towards Galdinia. "But he was becoming too much of an inconvenience."

"My aunt will be furious," Galdinia said, her voice rough in her dry throat. "She won't rest until she sees an end to you."

"She will be as good as dead the moment I get word to my advisor," Valah replied, taking another slow step towards Galdinia. "Not to worry."

Galdinia knew she was running out of time and needed to focus her powers again. She could feel Bentley's power tugging on the fire as well, and she hoped he wasn't aware of her growing connection to it.

"You will use your power—a gift from the Gods—to take innocent lives tonight," Galdinia spat, glaring into the dark eyes of her enemy. "What kind of queen does that make you?"

"We need a queen with strength and, ultimately, powers. You haven't been ordained by the Gods, so at this point you're not even an option." Valah's words were heated now; she was losing her patience. "No one will remember you this time tomorrow when I'm sitting on that throne."

As Valah came to stand directly in front of the princess, Galdinia could feel the heat building in her fingers, running along her arm and into her chest. She wasn't sure if it was all directly from the flame or the anger that was rising in her, but she could feel the Gods' unrelenting power coursing through her nonetheless.

"You are mistaken, Valah," Galdinia practically whispered, clenching her fists in the darkness, harnessing her new power to her greatest might. "I can assure you that I will be sitting on that throne before you."

With the force of her anger behind her, Galdinia threw her arm out in an arc towards the flame. The power within her pulled it across the room, and the small ball of flame became blade-like as it cut through the room towards Valah's back. Blindsided, Bentley crouched to the ground, shielding himself from the unexpected movement while Valah fell to the floor with a pained shriek. The flame landed in Galdinia's palm, the fire now out of Bentley's control. She closed her hand around it and ran backwards into the shadows of the library shelves.

"Get her!" Valah roared.

As a pair of footsteps echoed behind Galdinia, she hurled herself into the depths of the stacks, trying to maintain a sense of her bearings in the darkness. She considered opening her palm to light her way, but she thought against it; spreading a fire throughout a library full of books wasn't the most logical attack. Instead, she charged forward, dodging shelves and pushing stacks of books to the ground in her wake.

Galdinia weaved through the library, attempting to find her way to the exit tunnels beneath the castle. As she went to turn another corner, a shelf came crashing down before her. Galdinia had to jump to the side to avoid being struck by the avalanche of books. In a second,

Bentley stood over her with his sword in his hand. He reached down towards her, and Galdinia prepared herself to be struck in the face, but instead, Bentley pulled her up by the arm.

"Bentley?" Valah's screech came from across the room, beyond the surrounding shelves.

"I've got her!" he called, holding Galdinia in place against a bookshelf.

"You're a fool too if you think she won't do the same thing to you that she did to my uncle," Galdinia hissed, her voice quiet.

"I can fend for myself."

"Can you? She is ruthless and she will murder you the moment you're of no use to her anymore. It sounds like you've almost reached your expiration."

"Bring her to me!" Valah cried.

Galdinia felt the air in the room become suddenly thinner. While her heart was pounding in her chest, no matter how hard she sucked in a breath, she couldn't quite quench her need for air. Valah was drawing the oxygen from the room, trying to drag Galdinia back into her grasp.

"The only way you will survive her is if you get on a boat and sail out into the sea," Galdinia said breathlessly. "She's not going to let you live if you still exist in the same kingdom."

Bentley held her where she was, his eyes betraying him; he looked remorseful as he looked at her.

"I don't have any other option," he said finally, pulling Galdinia towards the nearby stacks that led back to Valah, his own breath short. "We need what she has promised us. I'm sorry."

"Bentley, don't do this," Galdinia hissed, pulling against his strong grasp. "I can't spare your life if you plan on dragging me back to her."

Galdinia could feel the flame vibrating in her hand, calling on her to be wielded. She still could not fathom the betrayal that she felt because of this man. The night before, he had been caressing her face so convincingly, and now he was dragging her to her death.

Reflexively, Galdinia brought her hands up to his arm and squeezed, allowing the fire in her palms to do the work for her. Bentley let out a cry of pain and fell to his knees, letting go of Galdinia's shoulder. The smell of burning flesh filled her head as she stumbled back from him.

Before Bentley could get to his feet again, Galdinia threw her foot into his chest, sending him sprawling backwards into a nearby shelf, showering him in books. Desperately, she threw the fire across the nearby shelves in order to momentarily barricade herself from Bentley. The books went up in tremendous and instant flames, a bonfire quickly building beside a groaning Bentley. She beckoned a small flame back to herself, and he stared up at her, the flames reflecting off his glassy eyes as he caressed his singed arm. She knew he could have placated the fires. He could have controlled them and sent them towards her. But he didn't. He merely stared at the princess between the burning books and shelves.

"She got away!" he yelled desperately from the ground. His eyes were firm on hers, and he mouthed a single word: *run*.

She turned and by the light of the fire quickly found the trapdoor that she needed. Draven had left it open, so she jumped down, bypassing the ladder, dropping through the eight-foot shaft, and landing with a thud on the paved ground. She ignored the pain in the soles of her feet and raced down the tunnel, keeping her hand tightly grasped around the flame that still rested in her palm.

She followed the dim light that cast through the tunnel from the outside world as she ran. As she got closer to the opening of the tunnel, she could start to hear the cries of the battle out in the city. She wondered how far into the castle the enemy had made it. Were they in the throne room? Had they gone down to the catacombs? She couldn't think on it too long. She needed to get to the heat of the battle and stop their forces.

34

GALDINIA ARRIVED AT THE GATES OF THE TUNNEL, WHERE THE LOCK had been butchered by Valah in order to access the castle. She pushed her way through, ran through the caves, and finally, down to the eastern docks. Here the last of the nobility had boarded their ships and yachts and were fleeing the city to take refuge out on the water. Galdinia could only hope that Neryda and her family were kilometres out to sea by now. She wouldn't be surprised if an enemy ship was on its way around the south bank at this very moment.

Noting that there wasn't anything else to be done at the docks, a dishevelled looking Galdinia made her way around the castle walls and back towards the square.

Galdinia kept her fingers tightly bound around the little flame from the library. Its warmth comforted her as she picked up the pace and ran into the streets of Elderguard. With each step she took, the chaos grew louder and more ferocious. The sounds of screams, the clanging of metal on metal, and the billowing smoke of numerous fires filled the air. She had to get to the battle and help her people.

As she made it deeper into the city, Galdinia passed civilians who were crying, huddled in the streets. Some shrieked in pain while others cried over the bodies of loved ones that lay still in their arms. Wounded soldiers were slumped on street corners as their comrades came charging through alleyways towards the frontline. Galdinia tried not to stop for those who were crying in pain or lying lifeless. She knew that the only way she could help them now was to rid the city of their invaders.

She continued to wind her way through the streets and finally stepped out into the square. From this vantage point, she could see the true brutality and magnitude of the conflict. Galdinia stood frozen in horror.

The square was littered with soldiers and the remnants of the banquet. Upturned tables, ruined plates of food and decorations lay scattered across the ground. The side of the square closest to the castle was flanked by the Royal Guard, while soldiers of the mountains and the west came streaming in from the streets on the other side, fiercely attacking anyone that stood in their way. The smoke that had been billowing in the air beyond the castle was twice as large as it was when she entered the building, now engulfing the sky to the north. The deep hues of the sunset cast an orange glow over the battle, making every swing of a sword look more vicious.

Galdinia watched as a group of soldiers from Lund stretched out their hands before them, and she was blinded by a blazing light. She had to shield her eyes behind her forearm as the stark white light pulsated through the square, blinding her soldiers, providing an opening for Valah's forces to cut through the masses. Her breath caught in her throat as she watched the horror of the scene across the square.

It was true: the Lund soldiers were Light Lenders, and they had sided with Valah to attack the capital.

Although she had read about the people of Lund receiving Lender gifts hundreds of years ago, she was still astonished. Despite their reclusive nature, they had managed to keep this from the crown, but Galdinia knew she couldn't stop now to question it.

As the fighters lowered their hands and stepped forward with their axes, swords, and shields raised, Galdinia's heart broke for her city— for her country. She looked upon both allies and enemies, realising that they were seeking the same thing: safety. *This is no way to achieve that*, she thought, perplexed by the violence of her people. But were they her people? Valah had said that her father's relationship with those outside of Elderguard was strained at best and she couldn't imagine them fighting like this for such a cutthroat woman simply for the fun of it. This was deeper than that. She needed to protect her home and make things right. She sent up a quick prayer, asking for strength and for guidance to help her people.

Without another moment's hesitation, Galdinia threw herself into the battle at full force. She ran beside soldiers who moved in to replace their fallen comrades. They gripped their swords tightly and raised their shields; Galdinia opened her palms by her side and felt the flame warm in her right hand.

Just as she was about to break into the heat of the violence, a deep voice called to her. "Princess!"

Ilyon charged to her side, his face wearier and his armour ash covered. Soldiers raced past them into the conflict, and she looked at her captain, relieved to see him safe.

"Ilyon," Galdinia said with an exhale, silently thanking the Gods for keeping him alive.

"You're okay," he said, his voice rasping as he took her by the arm and pulled her back into the thick of their soldiers, away from the front line of battle.

"I am," Galdinia said, looking over her shoulder at her tired army, "and I really need to be helping our soldiers."

Galdinia watched as Ilyon considered this, looking at her with concern welling in his eyes. She knew that he was questioning whether he should condone sending the princess into battle or not. He had trained her all week for this moment, for her to be able to use her powers and defend against oncoming attacks. They both knew that her training was far outweighed by the soldiers that she would come up against, but it would be futile asking her to protect herself and run. He had watched her use all her strength and might to try and conjure a power that was not yet alive within her without relinquishing until she had been overcome with grief. Asking her to abandon her people would be pointless, and Galdinia hoped he realised that.

The growing sounds of the battle quickened his response.

"The battle here is treacherous, but the enemy has fallen upon the castle."

"Ilyon, they're Lenders!" Galdinia said, breathless, still trying to wrap her mind around this fact.

"I know," he replied, shaking his head. "None of us were prepared for that. The Royal Guard hasn't set its eyes on the Lund army for centuries. We need to protect the castle."

"I was just there," Galdinia said quickly. "I was ambushed by Valah, and Draven is dead."

"What?" Ilyon was outraged.

"She came through the library entrance and attacked me. She killed him in front of me, and I barely made it out," Galdinia said before lifting her chin. "Bentley is a traitor."

"Princess—"

"We don't have time to discuss it now. Valah won't be far away, so we need to get back to the castle to take her out. Where are your forces now?"

"I've sent most of our Wielders and Weavers to the south to try to fight off those incoming from the sea. If you can wipe out as many enemy soldiers here on your way up to the castle, I think we may have a chance of fending them off. Most of our Flourishers are at the Northern Gates trying to tame the fire."

"Right," Galdinia said quickly before considering her current state. On the ground beside her lay a discarded shield that she took up and strapped onto her left arm. "I'll push back the soldiers here and we'll fortify the walls again."

"Princess," Ilyon said quickly, "please be careful. We all need you on the throne at the end of this."

"And I will need my captain," Galdinia assured him. "I'll meet you at the Northern Gates."

Galdinia turned and hurtled her way through the hundreds of royal soldiers in their onyx-black suits of armour. They stood out against the oncoming enemy; the Lund soldiers wore their traditional garb of furs and leathers, while Valah's soldiers were dressed in their dull grey suits of armour. As the first of the enemy approached, Galdinia threw her right hand out, sending an arc of flames across them all, heating their armour and causing them to fall to their feet. Some of her own nearby soldiers stood in awe as their enemies dropped to the ground before them.

Galdinia did not stop. She continued to move across the square, throwing her flames in every direction, watching them dance at her will across the bodies of hundreds of soldiers who charged towards her. She didn't need to kill them, she just needed to make a path for her and her soldiers to get to the castle. She concentrated on the ebb and flow of the flames as they grew and shrunk at her will. She manipulated them into different shapes as they shot through the air. The astonishment of both her own soldiers and their enemies was confirmation enough that they had not seen such a Flourisher like this in battle.

Galdinia ran up Main Court once more and she commanded the fire to sweep up the road before her, sending enemies crashing into nearby walls, dropping their weapons and shattering the windows of the buildings around them. She hastened up the road and helped a group of her own soldiers who were being attacked by six Lund soldiers, some with hands aglow with light, others with frighteningly sharp blades raised, ready to strike. The men from the north fell to the heat of the flames instantly and her soldiers were able to finish them off in her wake.

The faces of the oncoming soldiers who were aiming for the castle turned to the princess, their eyes burning with fury. She drew in a deep breath and aimed her concentration at the flames in her hands. She pressed her palms together and felt the pressure rising, her fingers trembling with the growing power. Galdinia released her breath and sent a pool of fire up the road towards the enemy, the fire sweeping through the street effortlessly. Those that did not feel the burning wrath of her gift ran from the blaze, screaming for a retreat.

Moments later, she heard the deep blast of a horn from the north. She drew the flames back to her hands, shrinking them down to a more manageable size. Galdinia turned to the soldiers of the Royal Guard by her side, their breaths heavy, their bodies tired.

"They're retreating!" one of the soldiers cried, sending up a cheer among his comrades. Galdinia's eyes narrowed on further up Main Court where the plumes of smoke were the thickest.

Had she managed to push the enemy back with her powers already? Had they feared the power of the princess so terribly? Was

Valah afraid of losing more of her soldiers to someone she had called weak and unfit to be queen? Galdinia felt pride settle in her chest.

"Princess!" Another of Galdinia's soldiers drew her attention back to the castle, pointing to the gates that were now lying on the ground in a tangled heap of metal. There were still cries of pain coming from her home.

Galdinia took off over the road and up the path up to the stairs, where dozens of soldiers were trying to fend off their enemy. Without a second thought, Galdinia propelled balls of flames in the direction of her soldiers' competitors, sending them to the ground or running in pain. She was met with faces of astonishment, desperate relief, and fear. Her soldiers were exhausted and couldn't quite believe their weary eyes. She looked out for the sweep of familiar chestnut hair among her army, but she had no luck locating Drystan in her brief moment of reprieve.

Through the conflict of another wave of soldiers, while attempting to ignore the bodies that lined the path, Galdinia hurtled up the stairs to the castle. She caught a glimpse of metal from the corner of her eye and managed to block an oncoming sword with her shield. The princess fell to the ground, landing awkwardly on the stairs of the castle. Her head hit the edge of a step, sending flashes of light and stars in her view.

Above her, with his sword inches from her face, was one of Valah's soldiers, his eyes fierce and hungry, his teeth bared. Galdinia pushed against her shield with all her might, feeling for the flame in her palm as her head swam in pain and her vision became dizzy. She could feel the warmth, but when she tried to corral it, her thoughts shuddered. The soldier bore down on her shield harder, bringing his blade closer to her face, his eyes ravenous. Galdinia used both hands to push up against her shield, her mind unable to focus on her attacker and her flame simultaneously. She watched in horror as the tip of his blade inched towards her cheek, the metal piercing her flesh as she turned her face away.

As his sword should have been driven into the side of her head, the soldier's body went limp, and Galdinia heard his sword clang to the stairs beside her. She turned back to her attacker, who was now lying atop her shield, a sword lodged in his back. Behind him stood a soldier of the Royal Guard, his hand still on the hilt of his sword that was buried in their enemy. His blood ran down the shield and pooled at Galdinia's side.

Her soldier hauled the body off her and helped her to her feet. Her right sleeve was soaked in the blood of the enemy, still warm as it clung to her arm. Now that she was standing, she could feel her senses returning and her head clearing.

"Thank you," Galdinia said breathlessly, holding the flame tightly in her grasp as she looked upon the entrance hall of her home.

Soldiers were in combat, swinging swords and blocking attacks; the bodies of the fallen—both soldiers and those that worked in her castle—were slumped on the ground around them; picture frames had come crashing down from the walls; and there was a long crack in the marble floor stretching the length of the hall. Galdinia felt ill at the sight, still feeling the blood of her opponent on her arm. The reality of death crashed into her all at once.

All of these people were dead or dying because of her, because she wasn't fit to be queen.

No.

The voice was not quite audible, and while she was sure she heard it ringing in her ears, Galdinia knew that no one else heard the rebuttal.

This is not your fault.

Galdinia spun around, positive that the booming voice was coming from behind her. That was when she saw the true nature of this battle.

From the top step of the castle entrance, she was able to look down upon her city burning in the fires of their enemies, the outer wall crumbling into the sea and the black sails of rival ships waving beyond them. The cries and screams of her injured and dying people floated up to her.

This wasn't her doing. She hadn't brought this upon her city; this was the work of something far more evil than she had imagined. She knew that Valah was a lying narcissist, but this went beyond anything she thought possible for that wretched woman. Galdinia wouldn't stand watching her city fall while blaming herself. Finally the Gods had ordained her to be queen, so she was going to behave like it and save her people.

Galdinia threw her shield to the ground and closed her eyes, feeling for the flicker of flame in her palms. The fire licked at her fingers as she imagined just where she needed it to travel in order to bring down her opponents. In a moment, she turned to face the entrance hall and opened her eyes again. She began throwing her arms in arcs across the room, sending small spears of flames into the chests of her enemies. They flew true and without restraint, much like how she felt in that moment. The fire listened to the commands in her mind, following the trails she set before them as they took down each enemy one by one, moving faster than her first victim's sword had fallen to the ground. She moved through the room with her arms outstretched, sending the flames in all directions across the hall, under archways, over the stairs, and into nearby rooms. She could sense their movement, and she sent each flame in the direction of the soldiers that would succumb to them. Her own soldiers stood dumbfounded, watching in awe as their princess disintegrated their enemy in seconds.

When the final enemy came crashing to the ground, the entrance hall fell silent and all eyes were on the princess in the centre of the room, her arms still outstretched as she commanded the flames back to her hands. Galdinia felt the full force of the power of her gift heat in her veins, beneath her skin and in her chest. Where worry and anxiety had sat before, she could now feel the strength of her gift—the strength of the Gods.

"Princess, thank you," a nearby soldier rasped, kneeling to the ground before her. His neighbouring comrades matched his stance and suddenly a wave of soldiers, civilians and castle attendants bowed their heads to their ruler. Across the room, Galdinia saw a very broad man lower to one knee, his mouth open and eyes bulging. She hadn't seen Evarius since the feast and knowing that he had just witnessed her gift in all its glory made her heart swell with pride.

Galdinia had never felt more like a queen. But the fight wasn't over.

"Soldier," Galdinia said, speaking to the man who had bowed first, wiping the dripping blood on her cheek with her still clean sleeve. "Have you seen a young soldier by the name of Drystan Allard?"

"Your Highness, I last saw him leave with his battalion to help fortify the Northern Gates after the siege on the castle."

Galdinia's heart sank. Of course that was where he would be. The Northern Gates were where the billowing smoke was coming from; the Northern Gates were what had fallen first; the Northern Gates were the last place she expected to find Drystan breathing.

"Gentlemen," Galdinia called, addressing the room of still kneeling soldiers. "We must secure the Northern Gates in order to secure a victory. If you are physically able and still consider me to be your princess—your queen—then I ask you to march with me!"

Galdinia's voice boomed through the hall and was followed by the cheers of fifty men who stood to their feet and followed the earnest queen down her castle steps.

35

THE ROAD THAT LED UP TO THE NORTHERN GATES WAS TREACHEROUS, but Galdinia made quick work of the enemy soldiers there. With her growing confidence in her abilities and the adrenaline that coursed through her veins, she was able to clear the path for her soldiers. She appeared to be more phoenix than woman as she almost flew up the road, sending balls of fire in all forward directions, bringing the allied soldiers of Valah, Draven, and Edana to their knees in cries of pain. While she didn't think she'd get used to the sounds of their screams, she found the strength to power on past them. The thought of driving these enemy soldiers from the capital spurred her on; the prospect of finding Drystan kept her fires alight.

Her soldiers behind her took out most of the enemies that attacked from the sides and her company grew as those fighting around the castle joined their ranks after a helping hand from Galdinia's flames. These attacks, though, began to thin as they got closer to the gates; she wondered how many of them had started to retreat at the news of a queen with flames for hands. Was it Valah's fear of Galdinia's powers that had drawn them back?

As they reached the top of the road, Galdinia and her army slowed. The Northern Gates had been entirely ripped from their hinges and appeared to make up much of the kindling that was feeding the fire at the base of the wall where it once stood. The fire had engulfed one of the surrounding towers and was reaching up into the sky beyond the cement walls of the city. Galdinia could feel the pull of the flames as she stood before them. She felt the raw and raging power of the fire rumbling inside of her, the heat beckoning to her.

To her surprise, there were no enemy soldiers left in the vicinity. Soldiers in black armour stood huddled together, protecting each other's backs and looking around wildly for any oncoming attackers. Some enemy soldiers were shackled and lying on the ground, apparently taken prisoner. It looked like most of Elderguard's soldiers from the square had found their way up to the gates, including Ilyon.

"Princess, you made it out!" he said in great relief. He had lost his helmet at some stage and had a deep cut just beneath his left eye, which was weeping blood.

"What's happening here, Captain?"

"We couldn't believe that Valah called for a retreat. We tried to take out as many of the enemy soldiers as possible as they rushed through that opening in the wall"—he pointed to the aftermath of an explosion in the city wall about fifty metres down from the fire—"and many of the soldiers that came from the city centre were running in utter terror, speaking of balls of flames."

Galdinia couldn't suppress a small smile as she pressed her fingers tightly into her hands, concealing her fiery weapons from onlooking soldiers. Ilyon's face softened as he smiled at the princess with quiet pride.

"There's no way Valah would have retreated on her own volition," Galdinia said, looking into the flames that stretched over the walls before them, her smile fading quickly.

"I don't know that she had a choice. They seemed to be losing a lot of men to this new attack. I've had word from the docks that their ships are retreating also."

"We need to start fortifying the walls. We don't know if they will attack again." Galdinia looked around her, desperate to find Drystan now that she had a better lay of the land. "Captain, have you seen Drystan?"

"No, Your Highness, I'm sorry," the captain said, shaking his head.

"The last I saw of him was just before the retreat sounded, and he was putting up a tough fight."

That was exactly what Galdinia was afraid of.

Another horn blast sounded, this time from beyond the gates. It did not sound to be one of retreat but rather a command. A hush fell over the remaining soldiers at the burning gates.

Galdinia turned towards the flames and lifted her hands into the air, aware of the eyes now turning to her. She faced her palms outward and this time, instead of sending out her flames, she began to manipulate the fire that billowed before them. She pushed her hands outwards and watched as they parted at the middle, creating a small opening in the raging blaze. The monstrous size and power of the flame sent a pressure along her arms and into her chest, locking her shoulders up. Galdinia persisted and held her ground, telling her body that she could control this towering fire just as she could the spears she sent flying through the castle.

As she held her arms strong against the flames, she took a few short steps forward, stepping onto the ashen gate that lay before her.

"Captain, if you want to do your duty by protecting me, please stay close," Galdinia called to Ilyon as she felt sweat begin to drip down her temples and neck. The captain was at her heels in an instant and the two of them carefully walked through the walls of fire.

The heat from the surrounding flames was almost unbearable and at this proximity, their skin should have been scorched. However, Galdinia was not only manipulating the size and shape of the fire, but also its heat. She kept her arms firmly outstretched as they walked.

When they cleared the flames, Galdinia released her hands, and the fire came rushing back to meet again in the middle. Galdinia heaved in deep breaths of exhaustion as she looked out along the Eastern Road, the glow of the beginning of dusk lighting what appeared to be the remains of the enemy army standing at the edge of the Bear Jaws Valley. They were framed by the rock formations that gave the valley its name. About fifty metres in front of the army, halfway along the road, stood three figures, bathed in the harsh red tones of the sun: Valah, her right-hand man Reynard, and—

"Drystan." His name was tumbling out of Galdinia's mouth before she could catch herself, her voice echoing across the chasm between them.

He was hunched over, his arms limp by his side, and was being awkwardly held up by Reynard. At the sound of her voice, he lifted his head and looked at her. Even from this distance, Galdinia could see the pain and exhaustion he felt. Every hurtful word she had thrown at him dissipated. No matter how angry she was for the betrayal she felt, she needed him to be safe. She couldn't allow Valah to touch this piece of her heart.

Galdinia began to stalk forward, her hands moving in slow circles, calling the fire from behind. Without looking at the flames, she drew them into great swirling balls, using this fresh surging rage to draw upon her power. She could feel the fire forming in her shadow.

"Not so fast, Princess," came Valah's voice, gliding on a wind that she sent across to Galdinia. "You won't want to be sending your precious fire in our direction."

A shiver raced down Galdinia's spine as Valah's eerily close voice swept into her ears. It sounded as if she were standing right beside her. She watched as Reynard held a glistening knife up to Drystan's throat. Galdinia halted, her hands still, the huge balls of flames suspended in the air behind her.

"Good, Princess," Valah said softly, her voice carrying to Ilyon and Galdinia as easily as Galdinia had sent out her flames in the entrance hall of the castle.

"Let him go," Galdinia hissed, knowing her voice would reach Valah on the breeze she now controlled. She kept her arms stiff by her sides but continued to swirl her fingers, building the pressure behind her in the balls of flames.

"I think we may take this one as a souvenir," Valah crooned, a wicked smirk growing on her lips. "Unless you want to give me the throne now in exchange? I think that may be a fair trade. Bentley did tell me just how special this one is to you."

The crackling of the fire hung in the air.

"Don't do it, Gal—" Drystan's pained voice was cut off as Reynard slammed his fist into Drystan's left jaw, sending him slumping onto his knees, helpless before Valah. A cry escaped Galdinia's lips, and she took another step forward. Reynard's grip on the knife tightened as he pointed it towards Drystan.

"Tut tut, Princess." Valah spoke again, eyeing off Galdinia's weapons of fire.

"Let him go," she growled once again.

"When you're ready to give me back what's mine, I'll consider giving you back what's yours." Valah's voice pierced the air, ricochetting off the capital walls. "I'm not a patient woman, Princess. You'd better hand over my crown soon."

Valah reached her hand up in the air above her and snapped her fingers. The crack reverberated through the chasm and in a moment, the wind flew through from the valley behind her, picking up a wall of dust, sending it in Galdinia and the captain's direction. Galdinia released her hold on the flames as she shielded her eyes with her arms and fell to the ground, the strength of the gale knocking her off her feet. The swirling winds created whips out of her hair, sending dust and debris into every crevice of her face and clothing. It took everything within her not to inhale the dirt.

A minute later, the wind subsided into a light breeze and the dust settled around her body. Galdinia slowly opened her eyes in a squint, her face coated in dirt. She looked across the now empty chasm. They were gone.

"No!" she screamed as she stood to her shaky feet, using what energy she had left to sprint towards the valley opening.

"Princess, no!" Ilyon was on his feet in a moment and chasing after Galdinia. Despite his own tiresome legs, the princess could not outrun the Captain of the Royal Guard. He reached her within a few long strides, and he wrapped his arms around her, pulling her into his armour.

"We can't let her get away! Not now! We are so close!" Galdinia began to cry, her chest heaving. "She can't take him! She can't!"

"Princess, we cannot go after her into unknown territory. Our army is too tired."

"So is hers!" Galdinia continued to struggle against Ilyon. "I can take her on myself, I just need..." She began rubbing her fingers together, feeling for the heat of the fire that she had so quickly become accustomed to, but it didn't come. She struggled to strain her head backwards, and her breath caught in her throat.

The fire of the gate, as well as the flames in her hands, had been extinguished by Valah's whirlwind. The only lights that were now cast over them were the first wisps of dusk, which would slowly turn into night. Her body yearned for the safety she had found in the flames. She reached her senses out, searching for a nearby fire to draw upon, but she couldn't locate one. She felt so defenceless.

Galdinia looked back over the chasm; Drystan, Valah and her army were now lost beyond the curve of the tooth-like rocks.

Galdinia allowed her body to relax and fall back into Ilyon's as she was overcome with wailing tears of heartache and anger.

SEVENTH DAY OF MOURNING

36

GALDINIA KNELT ON THE ALTAR OF THE CRYSTAL TEMPLE, HER KNEES resting on a plush velvet cushion. The semi-sheer skirt of her dress billowed around her and fell in cascading waves. The white fabric, light and airy, was dotted with hand-embroidered gold stars, which shimmered in the late afternoon sun that streamed through the walls of the temple. Her hair fell in luscious curls around her shoulders, not a lock out of place. Although her makeup was set impeccably on her face, a cut on her lip and one across her left cheekbone stood out among her otherwise smooth skin.

Two small flames glowed in her palms, which rested on her lap. The high priestess had offered them to her as part of the ceremony to demonstrate her gift to those that gathered at her coronation. It felt strangely easy to prove herself as queen after the events of the previous day. This was a confidence she had never felt before.

"Princess Galdinia," the high priestess began, her voice echoing throughout the temple, "bloodline of King Bartemus and Queen Anae Elderwin, ordained by the Gods and gifted as a Fire Flourisher. Today you will leave your title of princess at this altar."

The high priestess removed the dainty tiara from Galdinia's head and placed it on a stand to her left. She then picked up Galdinia's mother's crown, whose starlight crystals shone and glistened in the light that filtered through the crystalline walls. The high priestess placed the twisting vines of gold on Galdinia's head. It rested heavily yet comfortably in place.

"And you will rise and go with your palms of fire and your queen's crown."

Galdinia stood and turned to face the temple. The audience was much the same as those in attendance at her father's funeral seven days earlier—full of nobility and flanked on all sides by the Royal Guard. However, half of the remaining soldiers from the previous day's attack were on the isle, while the other half were protecting Elderguard with refurbished weapons on a constant rotation. Galdinia felt a sense of apprehension about being here in the temple after such destruction merely one day before. She told herself to try to ignore that fear until the end of the ceremony, taking comfort in the warmth of the flames in her hands.

To distract herself, she gazed down at the front pews where Ryden, Ilyon and Neryda sat, the former two looking worse for wear. Despite their physical ailments and bruised egos, Galdinia insisted on her coronation still occurring today. After the disgrace that was the unmasking of Bentley, the Syndicate didn't have a leg to stand on and came to the realisation that the princess was ready to take her throne alone. The ferocity with which she spoke to her governing body was lethal and they unanimously agreed to her coronation after seeing her gift. It didn't bother Galdinia that it was not the affair they had hoped for. She simply wanted the title that was owed to her, the title that she had fought so hard to keep out of a traitor's hands.

The other faces in the room were ones of exhaustion, but they looked upon Galdinia with pride and gladness. If anyone was unsure of Galdinia's ability to lead the country before the attack on the capital, those feelings had been swept away as word spread of how she drove the enemy from Elderguard and faced Valah head on.

After Ilyon had carried the princess back within the city's walls, she managed to finally calm herself. She ached to chase after Valah and her army, but she knew prudence would need to avail in her actions moving forward. After another sweep of the city, Ilyon was able to confirm that the few remaining enemy soldiers had been rounded up and put in the prison cells in the barracks, where they would be

MEGAN GILBERT

heavily guarded at all hours. A platoon of soldiers had inspected the castle after Galdinia had wiped out the entrance hall. Deep within the tunnel from the library, they found a wounded Bentley, who, once he had a knife to his throat, did not fight the soldiers as they too locked him in a cell in the barracks.

Once reunited hours after the attack, Galdinia and Neryda cried as they embraced on the shattered steps of the castle. Neryda's family had early warning of the attack due to their proximity to the castle and were some of the first out at sea. Despite her anger in being forced from the attack, Neryda complied and was able to help other vessels leave the docks quickly by drawing them across the sea with her gift. When Galdinia mentioned paying her almost-fiancé a visit in the prison to Neryda, the two of them huddled in her bay window in the early hours of the morning, her best friend insisted against it.

"Let him stew," Neryda spat. Galdinia wondered if Neryda hated Bentley more than she did. After that, Galdinia didn't mention him again.

Now, almost exactly twenty-four hours after Galdinia had been blessed with her gift, she observed the same temple and all those within it, there to pay their respects to the new queen. Yet she couldn't help but notice the gaping void that Drystan left as she looked into the crowd. He was one of the people she had always hoped—and assumed—would see her become queen, given that he was one of the few people who truly believed she would make it to this moment. Her eyes welled at the thought of him somewhere far beyond the capital in the depths of Crysterra.

The high priestess' voice cut through Galdinia's thoughts. "Presenting Queen Galdinia Anae Elderwin of Crysterra, Flourisher of Fire, first of her name," the high priestess announced triumphantly. "Take your place among your people, bring light to the darkness, and may the Gods bless you forever and always. Amen."

The room echoed a chorus of, "Amen."

All in attendance stood and lifted their faces to the young queen. Galdinia's eyes swept across the sprawling room of capital nobles and citizens. With her hands by her sides, she drew her fingers into tight fists, causing the flame of each torch to swell twice in size, the heat of the fire resonating deep in her chest.

334

The kingdom of Crysterra had a Fire Flourisher queen, and the heat of her gift resonated around the room as a witness.

∿

After the ceremony, Galdinia took the royal sailing boat back to the mainland with the Syndicate and Neryda, her best friend's arm wrapped around her own. Ilyon stood atop the stern of the boat behind the wheel, controlling the water around the boat to propel them forward gracefully and efficiently. Galdinia watched as her city slowly became larger as she approached it from the water. There was still evidence of the previous day's attack: crumbling sea wall, abandoned enemy ships, and collapsed buildings. Her heart ached at the sight of the needless destruction.

Upon arriving back on land, Galdinia was escorted back to the castle in a horse-drawn carriage, one that she thought she may become accustomed to riding in now that she was queen. Neryda, Ilyon and Ryden sat silently around their queen as the carriage pulled them up Main Court. The eyes of many citizens could be seen peering into the windows of the carriage as they moved past, some waving excitedly, others smiling hesitantly, and some staring in awe. The princess who had been so easily discredited one week earlier was now the queen, and by all accounts, one of the most powerful Fire Flourishers Crysterra had known in centuries. That morning, Ilyon himself commented on Galdinia's exceptional power, astonished by the spheres of flame she had conjured at the Northern Gates. Ilyon quietly told her that he wondered what kind of damage they would have done had she released them from the invisible binds that she held them with, allowing them to descend upon Valah and her army.

They had not yet spoken at length about the attack though; Galdinia knew that the days ahead would bring lengthy discussions about their enemies and strategies moving forward. Despite this, there was still one topic that Galdinia felt she needed to address with her most trusted advisors, and being alone with them in a coach with Neryda felt like as good as any place to bring it up.

"Ryden, Ilyon," Galdinia began, turning her attention from the windows and looking at the two men who sat across from her. "There

335

was something Valah and my uncle said last night in the library that…
well, it hasn't been sitting right with me, and I need to ask you
about it."

The two men shared a quick glance before Ryden said, "Of
course, Your Highness. Anything."

"They said that my father didn't care for the citizens of Crysterra,
at least not the ones outside of Elderguard." The eyes of Ryden, Ilyon
and Neryda were fixed on the queen as she spoke. "They said he was a
dictator and was the cause of many battles in recent years. I know
there has been unrest across the provinces since the downfall of the
Pyrins, but I thought my father started to tame that."

Again, Ilyon and Ryden looked to each other. Ryden spoke for
them.

"As I'm sure you have already started to learn, in order to be the
ruler of this kingdom, you must make sacrifices." Ryden was even in
his tone, but Galdinia could sense the trepidation in his words. "There
is no perfect way to run a country; in order to please one person, you
may disappoint five others.

"After the Pyrins were removed from the throne, your grandparents were met with equal parts praise and resistance. The few within
Elderguard that loved the Pyrins were loyal. Those outside of the
capital that experienced the hardships that came with their ruling had
high expectations for things to change. Your grandparents made way
for positive change for the kingdom as a whole. When they passed
away, your father was left with a hefty mantle; he not only had to
become the King of Crysterra, he also needed to come good on the
promises your grandparents had laid out.

"Your father's lifestyle prior to being crowned as king wasn't a
secret, so the responsibility that he had to take on was quite a shock to
his system. What may have taken a skilled and prepared leader five
years to accomplish, it took your father ten. He was noble, loyal, and
moral, yes, but he was also young and had a lot to learn. Given the
unstable nature of the kingdom at the time, your father actually did
quite well to step into his parents' very large shoes. However, he was
faced with unrest in the south, famine in the Midlands and silence
from the north. He spent many years trying to salvage Elderguard's
relationships with the provinces.

"While I'm sure Valah and Draven sensationalised the situation, their words are founded in some truth. Your father was working on ending generations worth of agitation, which could have been perceived as slow."

"Your father was a great man," Ilyon interjected, his voice low. "He was a king trying to keep his country afloat, care for his citizens and do what was best for his daughter. It isn't a surprise that his enemies would use his mistakes against you."

Galdinia sat on their words before replying. She could feel Neryda's hand tighten around the crook of her arm where it rested.

"I didn't realise how unstable things were beyond Elderguard," Galdinia concluded, looking between her advisors. "It sounds like there is a lot of work to be done in the provinces."

"Your father started that work, but yes, there is much to do," Ryden said in agreement, nodding to the queen.

"And I will be the one to do it." Although it was a statement, there was still the air of a question in Galdinia's words.

"You were ordained by the Gods, Your Highness," Ilyon replied, his eyes flashing to her crown. "You will be the channel through which they outwork their plans. They want a united kingdom just as much as we do. This does not need to rest on your shoulders alone."

After the week they had had together, Galdinia took the captain's words to heart. He had spurred her on when she felt like giving up; he had given her a reason to hold on to hope. Given her new weighty responsibility as queen, she knew she needed to listen to their wise counsel and not the quiet voice that nudged her towards that all-too-familiar doubt.

"Thank you," Galdinia said, looking to them both. "I'm going to need your continued support to bring our country back together. But first we have to plan our rescue of Drystan."

Ilyon and Ryden shared another glance.

"We can discuss that tomorrow, Your Highness," Ryden said assuredly.

Galdinia frowned. "Drystan is our priority," she pushed on, her expression firm. "The only reason Valah took him was because she knew what he meant to me. I won't rest until he's back on Elderguard soil."

"Of course," Ryden went on. "All I mean is that there's nothing we can do about it tonight. We will discuss it tomorrow when we can properly strategise with our new queen."

"You'll get him back," Neryda said, her tone low and reassuring as she squeezed Galdinia's arm.

"The Royal Guard supports you entirely, Your Majesty," Ilyon assured Galdinia, his eyes intent on hers. "You have my word."

With that, Galdinia let it go. Her heart ached for Drystan, and she wanted nothing more than to saddle up a horse and ride to the Wetlands tonight. But she needed to heed Ryden's advice; she was exhausted, as were her advisors, so a clear mind and a new day would allow for better preparations, particularly now that her mother's crown sat atop her head.

Once back on the castle grounds and away from the scrutinising eyes of her citizens, Galdinia finally let her shoulders relax, her perpetually tensed muscles finally easing.

"You did so well today," Neryda said, taking her friend by the arm once again and walking with her up the stairs to the castle, Ilyon and Ryden walking ahead of them. There were cracks in the stone steps and some debris still remained.

"Thank you, Ner," Galdinia replied, looking away from the signs of destruction around them.

"Your parents would be so proud of you," Neryda said before adding, "I'm so proud of you. It took a lot for you to get here, but you're finally where you're meant to be."

Neryda glanced up at Queen Anae's crown that sat atop Galdinia's head, sparkling in the late afternoon sun.

"It feels right," Galdinia said, stepping into the entrance hall. "It hurts, and I fear that there is still so much to know and learn, but it feels right."

Neryda knew that there was so much more than just her crowning that her best friend was referring to, so she simply nodded.

"And there's still so much to fix," Galdinia added, casting her eyes across the room.

The entrance hall had been cleaned of all remnants of the fight— bodies, blood, and ash—except one: the crack in the marble floor that ran the length of the room. It started at the base of the stairs and ran all the way to the doors of the castle.

At the bottom of the stairs stood three blacksmiths, all staring at a large melting pot on the ground. One of them was using her Flourisher gift to boil the pot, sending a burning hot flame snaking around the cauldron-shaped vessel. Galdinia could feel the heat of the flame from across the room; her body longed for it.

After a few seconds, the two other blacksmiths picked up the melting pot by its handles, each man wearing thick leather gloves to protect their skin from the hot metal. They carefully tipped the molten liquid into the crack of the marble, and a stream of iridescent gold cascaded down and along the crack. It trickled down the crevice, shimmering as it moved with the ease of water. It stopped near the queen's feet and instantly began to harden, filling in the floor's scar.

"There might be a lot to fix," Neryda finally replied, turning to look at her friend. "But that isn't today's concern. You should rest."

Galdinia returned Neryda's smile and wrapped her arms around her, holding her close. "Breakfast tomorrow?" Galdinia asked, her voice muffled by Neryda's hair.

"Raff's cinnamon scrolls on your bed," Neryda confirmed with a short nod, pulling back from her friend. "I'd expect nothing less."

Neryda squeezed Galdinia's hands before she turned to walk down the castle steps, her burning red hair practically glowing in the golden light of the sky. Galdinia turned back to the almost empty castle, the blacksmiths now inspecting their work on the marble floor. Galdinia walked past them, trying not to disturb their work, and silently moved up the stairs, her governor and captain having already moved down to the Syndicate's wing.

Galdinia made her way up the winding stairs and walked to a room she hadn't visited in a week.

Although the smell of sickness had dissipated, the air in her father's chambers felt thick and musty, and she suspected that the doors and windows had not been opened since her father's body was removed. His much-too-large bed was neatly made with fresh sheets, and the usual jug of water and goblet had been removed from his bedside stand. Galdinia walked to the large windows on the western side of his room and pushed back the heavy velvet curtains, allowing the final moments of direct sunlight to stream into the room.

The capital was bathed in the golden light of sunset, and in the distance, the Isle of Crystal shimmered. Although she knew she could only see so far, Galdinia tried to imagine she could see the Shadowed Coast, beyond The Edges and all the way to the Wetlands. She faced directly into the sun, staring towards thousands of kilometres of land, her eyes unable to distinguish any perceivable features beyond the walls of the city.

Somewhere closer to the setting sun sat Drystan in Valah's clutches, being used as bait to lure her in. Galdinia's eyes flashed towards the south. While the life of her innocent friend (did she have the right to call him anything other than that?) sat in the mysterious darkness of distant lands, her would-be-paramour-turned-traitor sat in the cells beneath the city's barracks. She knew that seeing Bentley would be a mistake, just as Neryda had convinced her, but she found herself regularly daydreaming about lighting his cell on fire. No matter how many times Ilyon reassured her that he was secure and could not escape, Galdinia still thought ending his life would be much safer for everyone.

Subconsciously, Galdinia's hands had balled at her sides, and she felt the heat rise in her chest. She needed to learn to control this anger, harness it, perhaps, but control it nonetheless. She didn't need to cause another fire in her home.

Drawing her thoughts away from Bentley, Galdinia looked back to her kingdom. The sun finally slipped beneath the horizon, setting the sky alight in the first fiery moments of dusk. Her kingdom was now cloaked in warm hues of pink and orange. The kingdom that had nearly escaped her, had nearly been ripped from her fingertips, now lay in demanding beauty before her.

Seven days prior, the thought of becoming queen and being coronated with her mother's crown felt unattainable and implausible. Now that she was here, gazing at her kingdom, Galdinia was prepared to fight to the death to keep it.

37

THE THRESHOLD OF ELDERWIN MANOR WAS STREAKED WITH BLOOD, mud, and tears.

The dark interior of the building seemed somehow darker than usual. The few lit candles cast long, thin shadows across the ornate walls and heavy furniture. The trail of blood continued across the foyer, up the stairs, along the corridor, and through the door of the drawing room. The track ended on the black teakwood table at the centre of the room.

At the head of the table, Edana Elderwin sat cocooned in a weighty fur blanket. She was hunched over the end of the table and looked like an enormous marsupial as she heaved and wept. From her mouth came muffled cries.

Before her, lying on the table, was the body of her murdered husband. He was covered in burns and bruises from the fire and falling shelves of the library in Crysterra Castle. Edana's hands were in his hair, which was matted from sweat and arid blood. She shed a sea's worth of tears as she wailed and choked by his side. No interruption from servants with food or drink would placate her; she demanded to be left alone.

Edana sat like this for hours, falling in and out of consciousness, her body aching as she sat bent over his body, having not cleaned the residue of the battle from herself yet despite having been home for hours.

The grandiose clock in the corner of the room awoke her with its resonant midnight chime. She sat up and looked around the room, ready to protect herself from an enemy that was not there. She was alone with Draven's body in the safety of her home. As she stood for the first time that evening, her spine and knees cracked at her movement. Her neck was sore, and her eyes were stinging. She looked down at her hands: her tears, mixed with the constant stroking of Draven's hair, had stained her palms red. Where there was often the shine of the water that she controlled, there were now the remnants of her husband's life.

His life had been unceremoniously ripped from him in a moment of betrayal and rage. When she found him minutes too late, Edana cried over his body in the burning library, using her gift to keep the flames from him. She finally pulled Draven from the wreckage, finding a nearby soldier who didn't recognise them to find a horse and cart to help get her husband to the docks. Valah was long gone by the time Edana made it to their ship, and she managed to set sail with the last of the fleeing soldiers of the south.

Edana stood then in the drawing room, her body crying out in pain. Her hands were discoloured, and her heart shattered somewhere between her lungs.

In a fit of rage and despair, Edana harnessed the water in a nearby pitcher on the mantelpiece and hurled it into the wall. The glass shattered into a thousand fragments.

Her hands searched for more water in the room, seeking to cause more destruction. Instead, she noticed a lamp on the sideboard across the room. She walked to it and picked it up gingerly, examining it with careful eyes. Draven would have been able to control this flame. It was possible that he was the one to last fill this lamp with oil. Just as Edana insisted on a vessel of water being available in every room, there was always a lamp, candle, or piece of flint within the lord's reach in his own home.

Edana moved back to the table and held the lamp over Draven's body as she stared into the small fire at the tip of the lamp. Her fur coverings and tearstained face made her look like a deranged woman in the flickering light of the fire. Perhaps she was. Perhaps this final act of cruelty by Valah had sent her into a place she never thought she would go.

"I will take your life, Valah Pyrin, just as you took my love's," Edana said, still staring into the fire. "Goodnight, my sweet husband, my king."

Edana tilted her hand and let the oil pour from the opening of the lamp, sending a cascading waterfall of oil and flame over her husband's body. She moved her arm as she poured, allowing the flames to encompass his entire being. She then dropped the lamp to the ground and cast her eyes once more over her husband's burning body before turning from the blaze and leaving the room, a trail of seething fury following her.

The end

Queen Galdinia will return in book two of The Crystal Crown Trilogy.

If you enjoyed *Princess of Dawn*, it would be greatly appreciated if you could leave a quick review on Amazon and/or Goodreads.

Visit megangilbert.co, or scan the QR code below, to find links to your favourite reviewing platforms.

ACKNOWLEDGMENTS

It is true that this story is not entirely my own. While much of Galdinia's story is based on personal experience, it is only by the love of Jesus that I was able to put these words on a page and not let imposter syndrome stop me from sharing it with the world. For that, I am eternally grateful.

Thank you to my family and friends who have supported me throughout my creative journey. Your belief in me has fuelled this dream and brought this book into existence. Thank you for always asking for updates, for keeping me accountable to my dreams and for asking if there's a character based on you in these pages. Maybe now you can decipher that for yourself.

To my husband, Jack, I cannot put into words how thankful I am for you. Your unfailing faith in me as a writer spurred me on in (the many) moments of fear, self-doubt, and utter panic. You are my number one cheerleader, and I literally couldn't have done this without you. You are more than I could have asked for in a best friend and husband, and I know this dream wouldn't have come into fruition without you.

To Miranda, my confidant and possibly the biggest fan of Drystan to ever live, you are a gem. How thankful I am for the many nights of brainstorming how to get out of plot holes, planning sequels, and discussing ways you can ensure your favourite characters survive the series. You are the Neryda to my Galdinia, always. Thank you for your constant love, support, and utter excitement.

Thank you to my alpha readers, beta readers and proofreaders for your invaluable feedback and encouragement. In particular, thank you to Tash, Beth, Bree, and Bek; you read this novel early on when it had a different title and was still very much in development. Thank you for your care and love for this story. Thank you Mum, Alysha, Tash & SJ for doing a final check of my words before they entered the world.

I did not work on this final product alone, and I would not have been confident publishing it without the expertise of my editor, Katie Wolf, whose fresh eyes and professionalism made it ready for publication. Additionally, this story is wrapped in a perfectly stunning cover by David Gardias, which I will always be fawning over. Thank you, David!

About two years ago, I told a handful of my students about *Princess of Dawn*, and my book-loving mentor girls have been pestering me about reading it ever since. Here you go, ladies! Your Mother G will always be thankful for your encouragement and constant interest. May you always be the queens you were born to be—make Galdinia proud!

It would be remiss of me not to acknowledge three women who have had a pivotal influence on my writing: Leigh Bardugo, Tomi Adeyemi, and Victoria Aveyard. You have created stories that have inspired me to write my own, and I will always shout your genius from the rooftops. Thank you for the stories you have shared with this world and their significant impact on my life as a writer.

Finally, thank *you*. Without readers, my story would be sitting on a shelf somewhere, untouched, collecting dust. Thank you for your investment in this story and taking the time to read these words. I hope it made you laugh, question the world around you, and instil you with the confidence to chase your dreams. I can't wait to keep journeying with you into the rest of Galdinia's story.

Thank you to the following people who supported me in my pre-order campaign by purchasing one of the VIP bundles; you are the real heroes! You significantly contributed to the publication of the first edition of *Princess of Dawn*, and for that, I am eternally grateful.

Nick & Pam O'Flaherty
Tom & Wendy Gilbert
Emily Smith
Bec Scott
Charlotte Laidlaw
Zoe Sherwin
Tash Gardner
Alysha Magee
Maggie & Craig Henderson
Lucy & Phil Hubbard
Gail Henderson & Nelson Larrosa
Ben & Liv Gilbert
Eva Foster
Concetta McKenzie
Sally Tingley-Walker
Mish Swavley
Esther Cox
Emily Burke
Tanya Kenny
Jess & Jason Henderson
Brian & Channing Lowe
JoAnne Hogan
Rebekah Hammond
Miranda Harry
Jacob & Sarah-Jane Leung
Sue Marks
Maisie Nevin
Georgia Williams
Simone Bullen
Denise Fellows
Harri Gilbert
Kaitlyn Hawkins
Luisa Smith

Frankie McManus
Joseph Hollington
Eddie Croxford
Annalise Forsyth
Michael Dickinson
Bree Wilson
Becca Tweed
Treene Stanmore
Abby Fuller
Ben & Eleanor Reardon
Dan & Caley Korocz
Brigitte Norsa
Emma Watts
Louis Baumann
Virginia Parker
Mahli Hill
The Peterson Family
Sara Tandurella
Dana Chaya
Sophie Renton
Amy Donald
Charlotte & Tim Exton
Angelique Matthews
Alicia Nigro
Gianna Mancini
Sarah Williams
Sheree & Matthew Buchanan
Marg Lancaster
Chloe Dziura
Molly O'Leary
Lauren Kirkpatrick
Brittany Douglas
Emily Fam
Laura Scherrer
Phil & Sharonne Fourie
Erin
Darci Cate-Hay

Bridget Mitchell
Lauren Stevenson
Katelin Plover
Phoebe Ettridge
Ruby & Mitch McDonough
Mya Ramos
JK Hegarty
Purpose Advisory
Tina Taylor
The Drain Family

ABOUT THE AUTHOR

Megan Gilbert is a writer, reader, English teacher and peppermint tea drinker from Sydney, Australia. Through her post-graduate studies in creative writing, she has delved into a variety of genres, text types and mediums. Her first love is speculative fiction, particularly fantasy. She seeks to write stories that inspire young and new adults to read more avidly.

Megan is passionate about writing stories for young people, especially young women, through fantasy stories with strong female leads and challenging plots. Having worked with teenagers for many years, she believes it is imperative to provide young adults with stories that promote positive representations of managing mental health and body inclusivity, in particular.

'Princess of Dawn' is Megan's first foray in the publishing world and looks forward to exploring Galdinia's story further in the remaining books of the Crystal Crown Trilogy.

www.ingramcontent.com/pod-product-compliance
Lightning Source LLC
Chambersburg PA
CBHW030515120726
47904CB00005B/1476